HER FIRST-DATE HONEYMOON

BY
KATRINA CUDMORE

manufacturing processes conform to the legal environmental regulations of
the country of origin.

Printed and bound in Spain
by CPI, Barcelona

MILLS
BOON

First Published in Great Britain 2017
By Mills & Boon, an imprint of HarperCollins*Publishers*
1 London Bridge Street, London, SE1 9GF

© 2017 Katrina Cudmore

ISBN: 978-0-263-92274-5

23-0217

A city-loving book addict, peony obsessive **Katrina Cudmore** lives in Cork, Ireland, with her husband, four active children and a very daft dog. A psychology graduate, with a MSc in Human Resources, Katrina spent many years working in multinational companies and can't believe she is lucky enough now to have a job that involves daydreaming about love and handsome men! You can visit Katrina at www.katrinacudmore.com.

For Ben
See, the middle child isn't always forgotten!
Love Mum

CHAPTER ONE

'I ADMIRE YOUR TENACITY, *cara*, but I meant it when I said no.'

Matteo Vieri lay down and spread his body behind the woman already warming his bed. His hand curled around her slim waist. The only light in the room came from the corridor, and in the dark shadows, with her head tucked low into the pillow, he struggled to see her in detail. But beneath his fingers he felt her body edge towards him.

Irritation bit into his stomach and refused to let go, but he forced his voice to remain a low playful tease. 'The last woman who crept into my bed wasn't seen for days. Leave now, or I swear you won't see daylight for a very long time.'

He wanted nothing but to sleep. Alone.

Earlier, when she had phoned him while he was en route to Venice, she had told him she was leaving tomorrow for her home city of New York, but she had promised him a night to remember. They had dated intermittently in the past, when their paths had crossed. It had been fun. But recently he had realised that beneath her cool sass lay fantasies of a future together, so he had good-humouredly turned down her offer. Again. But she obviously hadn't listened and now she lay in his bed.

He stifled a curse.

It was past midnight. His bones ached for a shower and the oblivion of sleep.

'*Cara*, it's time for you to leave.'

Beneath the silk of her nightgown her ribcage jerked. His hand stilled.

Something was wrong. Her scent was wrong. The dip of her waist was wrong. The endless curls in her hair, brushing his hand, making him itch with the desire to thread it through his fingers and pull her towards him, were wrong.

His breathing, his heart, his thoughts went on hold. The red traffic lights of confusion waited to switch to the green of clarity.

Her head inched upwards until wide eyes met his: perplexed, scared, startled.

His own disbelief left him speechless.

Caspita! Who was this stranger lying in his bed?

And then he wanted to laugh. Could this week get any worse?

His starved lungs sucked in air. He could barely make out her features, but still a lick of attraction barrelled through him. Her scent—the clean low notes of rose— the enticing warmth of her body, the mass of hair tumbling on the bed sheets made him want to draw her into him. To take solace in her softness, her femininity, from the craziness of his life.

Her mouth opened. And closed. She swallowed a cartoon gulp. Her mouth opened again. Her lips were full, the hint of a deep cupid's bow on the upper lip. A dangerous beauty.

Her body stiffened beside him. Seconds passed. Two strangers. In the most intimate of settings.

A tiny sound of disbelief hiccupped from her throat.

Then, in a shower of rising and falling sheets and blankets, she flung off the bedclothes and darted towards the door.

In one smooth movement he followed her and yanked her back.

Long narrow bones crashed into him, along with a tumble of hair, a scent that left him wanting more.

'Who are you? What do you want?'

Her voice was a husky rasp, heavily accented, sexy, English. A voice he had definitely never heard before.

Attraction kicked again. Strong enough to knock him out of his stupor. His earlier frustration lit up inside him. Bright and fierce.

He pulled her towards the wall and flicked on the bedroom chandelier. She winced, but then hazel eyes settled on his, anger mixing with shock.

She attempted to jerk away but he gripped her slim arm tighter.

A flare of defiance grew in her eyes. 'If you don't let me go I'm going to scream until the entire neighbourhood, all of Venice, is awake.'

A growl of fury leapt from his throat. 'Scream away. My neighbours are used to hearing me entertain.'

A blush erupted on her cheeks. She dipped her head.

Satisfaction twitched on his lips. He lowered his mouth towards her ear. 'Now, tell me, do you make a habit of breaking into homes? Sleeping in strangers' beds?'

Emma Fox knew she should be scared. But instead an anger, a rebellion, surged in her. She was *not* going to be pushed around again. Her heart might be doing a full drama queen routine in her chest, but the pit of her stomach was shouting, *Enough!* Enough of false accusations. Enough of people telling her what to do. Enough of the mess that was her life.

She grabbed the hand clinging to her upper arm and tried to prise his fingers away. 'What on earth are you talking about? I haven't broken in. I was invited to stay here by the *palazzo*'s owner.'

Her captor took a step back to stare down at her, but

his grip grew tighter. For the first time she saw his face. Her heart went silent. Why couldn't he be on the wrong side of handsome? A few blemishes here and there, a little cross-eyed, perhaps. Instead she faced a gulp-inducing, knee-knocking magnificence that stole all her composure.

His golden-brown eyes flared with the incredulous impatience of a man used to getting his way. 'Signorina, that is impossible. *I* own Ca' Divina. This is *my* property.'

He let go of her arm and moved to the door. He slammed it shut and stood guard in front of the large ancient door, arms crossed.

'Now, tell me the truth before I call the *carabinieri*.'

The *carabinieri*. He couldn't. Her stomach tumbled. She had spent a nightmare morning in police custody only yesterday. She couldn't go through *that* again. The disbelieving looks. Then the impatient pity when they'd realised she was nothing but a patsy in the whole debacle.

Fear tap-danced down her spine and she began to shiver. She was wearing only a barely there nightdress and longed to cover up. To walk away from this fully clothed man, armoured in an impeccable dark navy suit and maroon tie, and from the way his eyes were travelling down her body critically. Something about him triggered a memory of seeing him before—but where? Why did he seem familiar?

She backed towards the bed, away from him, and spoke in a rush of words. 'I'm telling the truth. But how do I know who you are—perhaps *you're* the one who has broken into the *palazzo*.'

He threw her an *are you being serious?* look. 'And I've woken you up to have an argument? Not the usual behaviour of a thief, I would expect.'

'No, but—'

He rocked on his heels and inhaled an exasperated breath. 'In my bedside table you'll find a tray of cufflinks with my monogram—MV.'

She opened the top drawer of the lacquered and gilt carved bedside table with trembling fingers. Beside a number of priceless-looking Rolex watches sat a platoon of silver, gold and platinum cufflinks, all bearing the letters MV.

A sinking feeling moved through her body, draining her of all energy. 'I don't understand… I was in a café earlier today and a lady… Signora…'

Her mind became a black hole of forgetfulness. Across from her, her prison guard scowled in disbelief. Flustered, she tried to zone him out. She had to concentrate. What had her saviour's name been?

'Her name was Signora… Signora Ve… Vieri… Yes, that was it—Signora Vieri.'

He unfurled his arms and walked towards her across the antique Oriental rug covering the *terrazzo* floor. A treasure perhaps imported when the Venetian Republic had been the exploration and commercial powerhouse of Europe centuries ago.

His mouth was a thin line of frustration, his already narrow lips tight and unyielding. 'What did this Signora Vieri look like?'

His words were spoken in a low, dangerous rumble and she became unaccountably hot, with flames of heat burning up her insides at the menace in his words and the way he was now standing over her, staring down, as if ready to murder the nearest person.

Her vow to toughen up, to refuse to kowtow to anyone ever again was going to be tested sooner than she had anticipated. She squared her shoulders and looked him right in the eye. Which was a bad idea, because immediately she lost herself in those almond-shaped golden-brown eyes and forgot what she was going to say.

The anger in his eyes turned for the briefest moment

into a flare of appreciation. Her heart swooped up her throat like a songbird.

But then the appreciation flicked to exasperation. 'I don't have all night.'

Toughen up. That was her mission in life now. She had to remember that. She clenched her fists and tossed her head back, ready for battle. 'I have no idea what's going on here but, despite what you obviously think, I have not been involved in anything untoward. Signora Vieri offered me a place to stay. I accepted her offer in good faith.'

He loomed over her, tension bouncing off his huge, formidable body. 'Tell me what she looked like…or is this just a convenient story? Perhaps you'll be more co-operative for the *carabinieri*.'

Alarm shot down through her and exited at her toes, leaving a numb, tingling sensation behind. She began to babble. 'She's in her early fifties…animated, kind, concerned…full of energy. Brown bobbed hair. She has the cutest little dog called Elmo.'

He exhaled another loud breath and walked away.

She spun around to find him standing before the bedroom's marble fireplace. The huge gilt mirror on the mantel reflected his powerful tense shoulders, the glossy thickness of his brown hair.

'My grandmother.'

'*Your grandmother!* She mentioned that her grandson sometimes stays here… I was picturing a toddler. Not a grown man.'

For a few long seconds he stopped and glared at her, leaving her in no doubt that she had said something wrong. What, she had no idea, but the temperature in the room had dropped at least ten degrees.

'*Nonnina* is sixty-seven. And she has a soft spot for waifs and strays. Although this is the first time she has actually brought home a human one.'

'I'm not a waif or a stray!'

'Then what are you doing in my bed?'

Memories of his hand burning through the material of her nightdress, of the shaming stream of pleasure that had flowed through her dreams until she had woken fully taunted her, causing her confusion to intensify.

'Who did you think was in your bed when you climbed in beside me?'

Her question earned her a tight-lipped scowl. 'A friend.'

Unease swept over her at the prospect of that huge, frankly scary-looking lion's head brass knocker on the front door sounding at any moment, and having to explain her presence to another person tonight.

'Are you still expecting her?'

His eyes swept over her lazily. 'No.'

Every inch of her skin tingled. For a moment she gazed longingly towards her suitcase, propped open beside an ornately carved walnut dressing table. She hadn't had the energy to unpack earlier, but had fallen into bed after a much needed shower instead.

She moved towards the suitcase, aware he was following her every move. She grabbed the first jumper from the messy jumble spilling from it and pulled on the thick-knit polo neck. A shiver of comfort and relief ran down her spine; she no longer felt so susceptible to his dangerous gaze.

He moved back across the room towards the door. 'I need to speak to my grandmother.'

'She isn't here.'

He pulled up short. 'What do you mean, she isn't here?'

'She said she had to return home to Puglia. That there was an emergency.'

He shook his head in disgust and twisted away. He rolled his shoulders and then his spine in a quick, impatient movement, the fine wool of his suit jacket rippling in a fluid motion. He moved with the ease of the super-rich. Even his hair—a perfect one-inch length, tapering down in a perfect straight line to hug the tanned strength of his neck—looked as though it had been cut with diamond-encrusted scissors by a barber to the nobility of Europe.

This room—this *palazzo*, this stunning city La Serenissima—all so grand and overwhelming, proud and mysterious, suited him. Whereas *she* felt like an alien amongst the wealth and elegance.

Wealth. Elegance. A grandmother with the surname of Vieri…

Her brain buzzed with the white noise of astonishment while her heart jumped to a *thumpety-thumpety-thump* beat. No wonder he looked familiar.

'You're Matteo Vieri, aren't you?'

The owner of one of the world's largest luxury goods conglomerates.

He unbuttoned his suit jacket and popped a hand into his trouser pocket. 'So you know who I am?' His casual stance belied the sharp tone of his response.

Did he think she had engineered her stay here because of who he was? Engineered being in his bed for his arrival? Did he think she had designs on him romantically? That possibility, if it hadn't been so tragic, would have been laughable.

'I used to work at St Paul's Fashion College in London. One of your companies—VMV—sponsors its graduation show.'

'*Used* to work?'

'I left last week to move to Sydney.'

Well, that had been the plan anyway. Until it had all fallen apart. When was life going to start co-operating with her, instead of throwing her endless grenades of disastrous calamity?

Yet more uncomfortable heat threaded along her veins.

She had slept in *Matteo Vieri's* bed. He was one of Europe's most eligible bachelors. She needed to clarify how all this had happened.

'Your grandmother told me I was welcome to use any room I wanted. I didn't realise this room was yours.' She paused and gestured around the room to the walnut four-poster bed, the pale green silk sofa—all so beautiful, but without a trace of him. 'None of your belongings are on display, no clothes… I had no idea it might be someone's bedroom.'

'When this *palazzo* was built in the fifteenth century not much thought was given to adjoining dressing rooms… my clothes are further down the hallway.' He spoke like a bored tour guide, tired of the same inane tourist questions.

'But your bathroom is full of…' She trailed off, not sure how to say it. It was full of delicious but most definitely girly shampoos and conditioners, bath and shower gels, lavish body lotions…

He gave her a *don't push it* frown. 'I do own those companies.' His lips moved for a nanosecond upwards into the smile of a man remembering good times. 'Those products are there for my dates to use.'

She tugged at the collar of her jumper, feeling way too hot. The image of a naked Matteo Vieri applying one of those shower gels was sending her pulse into the stratosphere.

She went to her suitcase and squashed the lid down, fighting the giddiness rampaging through her limbs, praying it would zip up without its usual fight.

'I'll move to another room.'

He stood over her, casting a dark shadow over her where she crouched. 'I'm afraid that's not an option. You'll have to leave.'

She sprang up, her struggle with the suitcase forgotten. 'But I have nowhere to go! I spent all of today searching for a hotel, but with it being Carnival time there are no rooms available. I've tried everywhere within my budget. Meeting your grandmother…her kind offer of a room was like a miracle.'

'I bet it was—an invitation to stay in a *palazzo* on the Grand Canal in Venice!'

Did he *have* to sound so cynical? 'I appreciate this situation is far from ideal, but I have nowhere else to go. I promise I'll stay out of your way.'

He adjusted the cuffs of his shirt beneath his suit jacket with a stiff, annoyed movement. His cufflinks flashed beneath the light of the crystal chandelier. 'I apologise for my grandmother's behaviour. She shouldn't have given you a room without my authorisation. I have a busy week ahead, with clients from China coming to Venice for Carnival. It does not suit me to have a house guest.'

'Are they staying here?'

'No, but—'

'Honestly—I've tried every hotel in Venice.'

He glared at her, and for a moment she was transported back to her *pointe* classes as an eleven-year-old, when she used to shake with fear about getting on the wrong side of the volatile ballet master.

'Why are you in Venice, Signorina…?' His voice trailed off and he waited for her to speak.

'Fox. Emma Fox. I'm here because…' A lump the size of the top tier of her wedding cake formed in her throat. She gritted her teeth against the tears blurring her vision. 'I was supposed to be here on my honeymoon.'

His stomach did a nosedive. *Dio!* She was about to cry.

Something about the way she was fighting her tears reminded him of his childhood, watching his mother battle her tears. Unable to do anything to stop them. To make life okay for her. Not sure why she was crying in the first place when he was a small boy other than having a vague understanding that she was waiting for his father to come back. The father he'd never known.

And then in later years, when she had accepted that his father was never going to return, her tears had been shed over yet another failed relationship. But he hadn't even tried to comfort her in those years. His own pain had been too great—pain for all the men who had walked out of his life without a fight, father figures, many of whom he had hero-worshipped.

People let you down. It was a lesson he had learned early in life. Along with coming to the realisation that he could only ever rely on himself. Not trust in the empty promises of others.

A loud sniffle brought him back to his present problem. To her lowered head he said, 'On your honeymoon?'

She emitted a cry and bolted for his bathroom.

This time his grandmother had gone too far. To the extent that he was tempted to follow her down to Puglia and give her a piece of his mind, this time not falling for her apologies and pledges to behave. Nor, for that matter, being diverted by plates of her legendary *purcedduzzi*— fried gnocchi with honey.

He understood her compulsion to help the poor and homeless—but to invite a stranger into his *home*!

He knocked at the bathroom door. 'Are you okay?'

'Yes…sorry. I'll be out in a few minutes.'

Her voice went from alto to soprano, and several notes in between. A muffled sob followed. He winced and rubbed at his face with both hands.

He leaned in against the door. 'We both need a drink. Join me downstairs in the lounge when you're ready.'

He hurried down the stairs. Memories chased him. Those nights when he was seven…eight years old, when he would crawl into his mother's bed, hoping he could stop her tears.

In the lounge, he threw open the doors onto the terrace. Venice was blanketed in a light misty fog. Sounds were muffled. He saw the intermittent lights of a launch moving on the water, its engine barely audible. Technically it was spring, but tonight winter still shrouded the city, and the cold, damp air intensified its mysterious beauty.

He spent most of his year travelling between his headquarters in Milan and his offices in New York, London and Paris. Always moving. Never belonging. The nomadic lifestyle of his childhood had followed him into adulthood. He had hated it as a child. Now it suited him. It meant that he could keep a distance from others. Even acquaintances and those he considered friends would never have the opportunity to hurt him, to walk away. *He* was the one in control instead. It was *he* who could choose to walk away now.

Venice was his one true escape. It was why he had no regular staff here in Ca' Divina. He liked the calm, the peace of the building, without sound, without people awaiting his instructions. Here was the one place he could be alone, away from the intensity of his normal routine. Away from the constant expectations and responsibilities of his businesses, his family.

But tonight the calm serenity of both Venice and Ca' Divina were doing little to calm his boiling irritation. The maverick, eccentric, brilliant chief designer for his fashion house Ettore had thrown a hissy fit—no doubt fuelled by alcohol—whilst being interviewed by a Chinese news team last night. He had not only insulted the reporter but also implied that the exclusive department store chain that sold his designs in China was not worthy of doing so.

The exclusive department store chain Matteo was delicately negotiating with over contracts for the extensive expansion of product placement for *all* his brands.

The company quite rightly had not taken kindly to the designer's words, and had seen it as a huge public insult to their honour. This loss of face—known as *mianzi* in China—might have damaged their relationship beyond repair.

The chain's president and his team were arriving in Venice tomorrow evening. He had a lot of apologising to do and reassurances to make to ensure they understood how much he valued and respected them as a partner. It was vital the trip went well. Or else several of his lines would be in serious financial trouble.

He twisted around to the sound of footsteps on the *terrazzo* flooring. The last thing he needed was to have to deal with a stranger's problems.

She reminded him of a Federico Zandomeneghi portrait in Ca' Pesaro, the International Gallery of Modern Art located further along the banks of the Grand Canal. Delicate, elegant features, a cupid's bow mouth, a perfect nose, porcelain skin, long thick brown curls almost to her waist, tucked behind her ears.

Below the cream polo-neck jumper she was now wearing a pair of skinny jeans and tan ankle boots. She'd tugged the neck of the jumper up until it reached her ears. The tears were gone, but despite the resolute set of her mouth she looked worn out.

Almost as worn out as *he* felt.

'What can I get you to drink?'

'A whisky, please.'

He poured her whisky and a brandy for himself into tumblers, trying to ignore how physically aware he was of her. Of her refined accent, her words clipped but softly spoken. Of her long limbs. Of the outline of the tantalising body her nightdress had done little to conceal earlier. Of her utter beauty.

He brought their drinks over to the sofas at the centre of the room and placed one on either side of the coffee table in between them. He sat with his back to the canal.

She perched on the side of the sofa and stared out through the terrace windows with an unseeing gaze, the hands on her lap curled like weapons ready to strike out. Eventually her eyes landed on his, and the sudden flare of vulnerability in them delivered a sucker punch to his gut.

Despite every fibre of his being telling him not to—she might start crying again—he found himself asking, 'Do you want to talk about it?'

She took a sip of her whisky. Depositing the glass back on the table, she reached down to her left ankle and gave it a quick squeeze. Sitting up, she inhaled deeply, her chest rising and falling. A flash of heat coloured her cheeks. The result of the whisky or something else?

'Not particularly.' Her clipped tone was accompanied by a haughty rise of her chin.

'In that case I'll go and make some phone calls to arrange a hotel room for you.'

He was at the door before she spoke.

'My fiancé…I mean my *ex*-fiancé…was arrested early yesterday morning—at four o'clock, to be precise—for embezzlement.'

She tugged at the neck of her jumper. He returned to his seat and she darted a quick glance in his direction. Pride in battle with pain.

'He stole funds from the company he worked for; and also persuaded his family and friends to invest in a property scheme with him. There was no scheme. Instead he used the money to play the stock exchange. He lost it all.'

'And you knew nothing about it?'

She stared at him aghast. 'No!' Then she winced, and the heat in her cheeks noticeably paled. 'Although the police wouldn't believe me at first…' She glanced away. 'I was arrested.'

'Arrested?'

She reached for her glass but stopped halfway and instead edged further back into the sofa. 'Yes, arrested. On what was supposed to be my wedding day.' She gave a disbelieving laugh. 'I was let go eventually, when they realised I was his victim rather than his partner in crime.'

Her eyes challenged his; she must be seeing the doubt in his expression.

'By all means call Camden Police Station in London, if you don't believe me; they will verify my story. I have the number of the investigating officer.'

His instinct told him she was telling the truth, but he wasn't going to admit that. 'It's of no consequence to me.'

That earned him a hurt glance. Remorse prickled along his skin. But why was he feeling guilty? None of this was his doing. What on earth was she doing in Venice anyway?

'Do you think it was wise, coming to Venice? Without a hotel booking? Wouldn't you be better off at home?'

She crossed her legs with an exasperated frown that told him he wasn't getting this. 'I *did* have a hotel booking. Or so my ex told me. But he never transferred the funds so the booking fell through. He also cleared out our joint bank account. Anyway, I don't *have* a home. Or a job. I moved out of my apartment and resigned from the college because my ex was being transferred to Sydney with his work and I was joining him.'

'And your family?'

A flicker of pain crossed her face. But then she sat upright and eyed him coolly. 'I don't have one.'

Despite all the hurts and frustrations of the past, and the fact that he had far from perfect relationships with his emotional and unpredictable mother and grandmother, he could never imagine life without them. What must it be like to have no family? Had she no friends who could take their place?

'Your friends…?'

With her legs crossed, she rotated her left ankle in the air. Agitated. Upset.

'I appreciate your concern, but I'm not going back to London. I have no home to go to. I can't go back… I can't face everyone. I need some time away. After I was released from police custody I checked out of the hotel we'd been staying in…' She paused and bit her lip, drank some whisky, grimaced. 'I ran away.'

'You're a runaway bride?'

Her generous full mouth twisted unhappily. She refused to meet his eye.

'I'm not putting my friends out by sleeping on their sofas. My closest friend Rachel has just had a baby; the last thing she needs right now is a lodger. This is my mess—it's up to me to sort it out. My ex might have stolen everything from me, but he isn't going to stop me from living my life. I've always wanted to see Venice during Carnival. And I fully intend doing so.'

Her mouth gave a little wobble.

'We had organised our wedding for this week so that it coincided with Carnival.'

She was putting up one hell of a fight to keep her tears at bay. He felt completely out of his comfort zone.

'I'll pay for your hotel room by way of compensation for any inconvenience my grandmother's actions may have caused.'

'I don't want your money.'

Old memories churned in his stomach at her resolve. He knew only too well that it masked vulnerability.

He remembered throwing guilt money from Stefano, one of his mother's boyfriends, who had just shoved it into his hands, off the balcony of Stefano's apartment. He had got momentary satisfaction seeing Stefano's shame. It had been short-lived, though, when he and his mother had been forced to sleep in a homeless hostel that night.

He had stayed awake all night, unable to sleep, vowing he would never be in that position again. Vowing to drag his mother out of poverty and to protect her. Even if her behaviour *had* led them to sharing a room with eight strangers. He would be a success. Which meant he would no longer be held hostage by poverty, by the lack of choices, the motives of other people.

It was an ambition he was still chasing. He still needed to leave behind the spectre of hunger, the fear of not being in control, still needed to prove himself, still needed to make sure he protected his family…and now the tens of thousands who worked for him.

He looked at his watch and then back at her. She was blinking rapidly. Unexpected emotion gripped his throat. He forced it away with a deep swallow. 'It's late. We can talk about this in the morning.'

'I can stay?'

The relief in her face hit him like a punch. This woman needed compassion and care. His grandmother should be here, finishing the task she'd started. Not dumping it on *him*. He was too busy. In truth, he didn't know how to help her. He didn't get tangled up in this type of situation. He kept others at arm's length. No one got close. Even his mother and grandmother. And that was not going to change.

'You can stay for tonight. Tomorrow I will organise alternative accommodation for you.'

Half an hour later Emma lay on cool sheets in the bed of another bedroom, her mind on fire, wondering if the past few hours had actually happened.

A knock sounded on the door. She sat up and stared at the door dubiously.

'Emma—it's Matteo.'

Her heart flipped in full operatic diva mode. Did he

have to speak in a voice that sounded as if he was caressing her? And what did he *want*? Had he changed his mind about her staying?

She cautiously opened the door and drank in the sight of Matteo, freshly showered, his thick brown hair damp, wearing nothing but pyjama bottoms. The golden expanse of his hard sculptured torso instantly left her tongue-tied. And guilty. And cross. She should be on honeymoon right now. Not staring at a stranger's body, trying to keep lustful thoughts at bay.

She folded her arms. 'Can I help you?'

Her ice-cool tone did little to melt the amusement in his eyes.

An eyebrow—a beautiful, thick eyebrow—rose. Without a word he raised his hand and held out a toy polar bear, barely the size of his palm, grey and threadbare.

'Snowy!' She grabbed the bear and held it to her chest.

'I found it under my pillow.'

'I forgot about him…thank you.'

His head tilted to the side and for a tiny moment he looked at her with almost affection, but then he looked back at Snowy with an exasperated shake of his head. Probably questioning the wisdom of allowing a grown woman who slept with a diseased-looking toy polar bear to stay in his home.

He turned away.

She should close the door, to signal that his appearance was of little consequence, but instead she watched him walk back to his room—and almost swooned when he ran his hand through his hair, the movement of the powerful muscles in his back taunting her pledge to give men a wide berth.

He swung back to her. 'I'm sorry about your wedding.'

A thick wedge of gratitude landed in her chest. She

wanted to say thank you, but her throat was as tight as a twisted rag.

He nodded at her thank-you smile.

Her heart beat slow and hard in her chest.

They stood in silence for far too long.

He seemed as unable to turn away as she was.

Eventually he broke the tension and spoke in a low, rolling tone, *'Buonanotte.'*

Back inside the room, she climbed into bed and tucked Snowy against her. She was fully aware, of course, that the first thing she should do in her bid to toughen up was to banish Snowy from her bed. But when she had been a child, alone and petrified at boarding school, he had brought her comfort. And, rather sadly, over fifteen years on she needed him more than ever before.

So much for Operation Toughen Up. An hour in the company of Matteo Vieri and all her vows and pledges to be resilient and single-minded had melted into a puddle of embarrassing tears and ill-advised attraction.

But tomorrow was going to be different.

It *had* to be.

CHAPTER TWO

THE FOLLOWING DAY, mid-morning sunshine poured into Matteo's office. He stood up from his desk and stretched his back, grimacing at the tightness at the bottom of his spine.

They said bad things came in threes. Well, he had just reached his quota. First, his exasperating but gifted designer had publicly insulted his most valued clients. Then his grandmother had invited a stranger into his home. And now his event co-ordinator for the Chinese clients' trip had gone into early labour.

His designer was already in rehab.

He would have to put in extra hours to ensure the China trip ran perfectly...which meant even less sleep than usual.

And as for Signorina Fox... Well, he had news for her.

He walked down the corridor of the *palazzo*'s first floor, the *piano nobile*, his heels echoing on the heritage *terrazzo* flooring. He hadn't seen or heard from Signorina Fox all morning. He had a sneaking suspicion that she was deliberately staying out of his way in the hope that he might let her stay.

The lounge balcony windows were open. Shouts of laughter and passionate calls tumbled into the room from outside. Stepping into the early springtime sunshine, he came to an abrupt halt.

Crouched over the balcony, her chin resting on her

folded arms Emma was focused on the canal, oblivious to the fact that her short skirt had risen up to give him an uninterrupted view of her legs. Legs encased in thick woollen tights that shouldn't look sexy. But her legs were so long, so toned, that for a brief moment the ludicrous idea of allowing her to stay and act as a distraction from all his worries flitted through his brain.

He coughed noisily.

She popped up and twisted around to look at him. A hand tugged at her red skirt. Over the skirt she was wearing another polo-necked jumper, today in a light-knit navy blue. Her chestnut hair hung over one shoulder in a thick plait.

'I hope you found my note?'

'Thank you—yes…it was a lovely breakfast.'

The exhaustion of last night was gone from beneath her eyes. She gave him a *can we try to act normal?* smile and then gestured to the canal.

'There's the most incredible flotilla sailing up the canal—you must come and see.' Her smile was transformed into a broad beam, matching the excitement in her eyes. She beckoned him over.

He should get back to work. But it seemed churlish to refuse to look. The canal was teeming with boats, and onlookers were crowding the *fondamente*—the canal pathways.

'It's the opening parade of the Carnival,' he explained.

For a few minutes he forgot everything that was wrong in his life as he joined her in watching the parade of gondolas and ceremonial boats sail past. Most of the occupants, in flamboyant seventeenth- and eighteenth-century costume, waved and shouted greetings in response to Emma's enthusiastic waves.

Seeing the contrast between her upbeat mood now and the sobs that had emanated from his bathroom last night twisted his stomach, along with the memory of his grand-mother's words this morning. He had called her with the intention of lambasting her, only to be pulled up short when he'd learned that she had gone home because one of the homeless men she helped had been involved in an accident, and that she had helped Emma because she had found her in a desperate state in a café yesterday.

He pushed away the guilt starting to gnaw a hole in his gut. He had enough problems of his own. Anyway, he didn't do cohabitation. He had never shared his home with anyone. And he wasn't about to start with an emotional runaway bride.

Below them, the regatta started to trail off.

'I have found alternative accommodation for you in the Hotel Leopolda.'

Her smile dropped from her face like a stone sinking in water. 'Hotel Leopolda? The five-star hotel close to St Mark's Square?'

'Yes.'

She stared back at the canal, a small grimace pulling on her mouth. 'I can't afford to stay there.'

'I'll take care of it.'

She stepped away from him before meeting his eye. 'I said it last night—I'm not taking your money.'

'I can appreciate how you feel. If it makes you happier, you can repay me some time in the future.'

'No.' Those hazel eyes sucked him in, dumped a whole load of guilt on his soul and spat him back out again.

'I'll make some calls myself—check the internet again. I'll find somewhere suitable,' she said.

This woman was starting to drive him crazy. He had had to use all his influence to secure her a room. He doubted she would find anywhere by herself.

'I want to resolve this now. My event co-ordinator for the Chinese trip has gone into early labour. I'll be tied up with organising all the final details for the visit for the rest of the day.'

She stepped back towards him, her crossed arms dropping to her sides. Concern flooded her eyes. 'I hope she'll be okay. How many weeks pregnant is she?'

He had no idea. It had been a sizeable bump. Once he had even seen a tiny foot kick hard against the extended bump during a meeting. It had been one of the most incredible things he had ever seen.

That image had haunted him for days afterwards. Catching him unawares in meetings, distracting his concentration. Bringing a hollow sensation to his chest, a tightness to his belly, knowing he would never see the first miraculous stirrings of his own child. Knowing he would never be a father. Knowing he would choose the empty feeling that came with that knowledge over the certain pain of letting someone into his life, of risking his heart in a relationship.

'I'm not sure...eight months?'

Did she *have* to look at him so critically? Suddenly he felt he had to defend himself. 'I asked for flowers to be sent to her.'

'I don't think flowers are allowed in hospitals these days. Anyway, I reckon flowers are the last thing on her mind right now.' She threw him another critical stare before adding, 'I hope she and her baby will be okay.'

Why, all of a sudden, was *he* the villain in all of this? 'Of course I do too. My employees' welfare is of great importance to me. It's why they all receive a comprehensive healthcare package.'

'I'm glad to hear it.' Her tone didn't match her words. Her tone implied he was a close relative of *Wall Street*'s Gordon Gekko.

'About your accommodation...'

'How long are your clients here for?'

Hadn't she heard him? This conversation was supposed to be about her leaving. 'Why do you ask?'

'Have you someone to take over from your event planner?'

A tight dart of pain prodded his lower back. He stretched with a quick movement, but it brought little relief. 'No. My event management team are already stretched, co-ordinating the upcoming spring/summer shows. Most of the team are already in New York, getting ready for the shows there.'

She pulled her lips between her teeth as if in thought. When they popped back out they formed an even fuller pout, had turned a more sensual red than usual. Emphasising their cupid's bow shape. She had a beautiful mouth...

A sudden urge to take her in his arms and taste those lips gripped him. Maybe he was more stressed than he'd realised?

Emma's mind whirled. Could she drum up the courage to suggest *she* take over the event planner's role? Work for Matteo Vieri? Without question it was what every ambitious marketing assistant dreamt of. She should be genuflecting right now in front of this business legend; this marketing genius, instead of deliberately trying to antagonise him. What was *that* about?

A niggling thought told her that not only was she trying in vain to ignore how attracted she was to him—especially when he openly stared at her with interest, as he was doing right now, with particular attention focused on her mouth—but that it would hurt to have another person reject her. Which, rationally, she knew was crazy. They barely knew each other. But even after so many rejections it still hurt when others turned her away.

Working for him would be the kick-start her career needed. Even a week of working with him would open doors for her.

But she was a mess.

She had come to Venice to heal and to get her game plan together. She felt hollow and abused. She was in no position to deliver the best performance of her career.

A mocking voice echoed in her head. *You said you were going to toughen up. Time for action and a lot less talk.*

And having a purpose, being busy, might stop the stream of guilt and sadness that was constantly threatening to break through her defences—defences of shock and numbness, of a determination to tough it out. Being in control, having a structure to her days, was what she needed.

She spoke before she had time to talk herself out of it. '*I'll* do it.'

His gaze moved from her lips to her eyes. Very slowly. So slowly that time seemed to stand still while her cheeks spontaneously combusted.

'*You?*'

Did he *have* to sound so appalled by her proposal?

'In my role at the fashion college I often helped pull events together—from the graduation show to organising the visits of academics and sponsors. Last year I co-ordinated the visit of some members of a faculty from a Chinese fashion college. I'm in need of a place to stay… you need an event co-ordinator.'

'But you're on holiday.'

'My career is more important. I'll be frank: having the Vieri name on my CV will be priceless.'

He seemed to be considering her proposal. For a moment hope danced before her eyes. But then he cut that hope off at the legs with a single determined shake of that movie-star-meets-roman-emperor head.

'It's not a good idea.'

'Why?'

'This trip is of critical importance to my companies. The delegation is coming to negotiate contracts which would see the large-scale expansion of our product placements in China's most prestigious department stores. Nothing can go wrong.'

For a moment she considered backing down, admitting that she was probably the wrong person for the job. But she had to believe in herself.

'You can brief me on it this morning, and then I'll liaise with the travel agents and hotels involved. I'll also double-check that all the protocols involved with hosting Chinese guests are followed. If there are any issues I will notify you immediately.'

He leaned one hip against the balcony and folded his arms. 'It's not a nine-to-five position. You would need to attend all the scheduled events with me.'

'That's no problem.'

Those brown eyes darkened. 'We will be working closely together.'

'That's fine.'

Liar! Why is your belly dancing with giddiness if that is the case?

'Please understand I never mix business with pleasure.'

Why was he telling her that? Was her attraction to him so obvious?

'Of course. Exactly my sentiments.' She took a deep swallow and forced herself to ask, 'So, can I have the job?'

'Tell me why I should give it to you.'

This would be so much easier if he wasn't so gorgeous—if he wasn't so self-assured, so ice-cool.

'I will work myself to the bone for you because I have so much to prove. To you—but especially to myself.'

He stared at her as though she was a discount store garment made of polyester. It looked as if she would be packing soon. A heavy sensation sat on her chest—embarrassment, disappointment.

'As I'm stuck, I'll let you take on the position—but any mishaps and you're gone.'

His scowl told her he wasn't joking. Her ankle and heart began to throb in unison.

He came a little closer. Studied her for far too long for her comfort.

'You will need to stay here…'

For a moment he paused, and a heavy boom of attraction detonated between them. She fell into the brown sultry depths of his eyes. An empty ache coiled through her. Heat licked against her skin. She pulled the neck of her jumper down, suddenly overheating.

Matteo stepped back, tugged at his cuffs and cleared his throat. 'I will require frequent briefings from you, so you will need to stay here. I'm hosting a reception in the ballroom on Thursday night, which I will want you to co-ordinate and host alongside me.' He flicked his hand towards the *palazzo*. 'If you come with me to my office I'll brief you on the event schedule and then pass you the files.'

Emma walked alongside him, her enflamed skin welcoming the shade of the *palazzo*. But her mind continued to race, asking her what on earth she had just done.

Could she keep her promise that nothing would go wrong? What if she slipped up and he saw even a glimpse of how attracted she was to him? An attraction that was embarrassingly wrong. Humiliatingly wrong. Shamefully wrong. She had been about to marry another man yesterday. What was the *matter* with her?

They walked side by side into the deeper shadows of the *palazzo*, and she felt guilt and sadness closing over her heart.

Later that afternoon, his phone to his ear, Matteo walked into the temporary office Emma had set up for herself in the *palazzo*'s dining room.

Sheets of paper were scattered across the table. He tidied the paper into a bundle. A long navy silk crêpe de Chine scarf dotted with bright red gerbera daisy flowers was tossed across the back of a chair, the ends touching against the *terrazzo* flooring. A bright exclamation against the dark wood. He folded it quickly and hid it from view by placing it on the seat of the dining chair.

His call continued to ring unanswered.

Where *was* she?

He had told her to be back at the *palazzo* by four so that he could take her to see his stores on Calle Larga XXII Marzo. She needed to be familiar with his companies and their products before her interactions with the clients.

Before lunch they had spent two hours running through the visit's itinerary. Two hours during which he had questioned his judgement in agreeing to her taking over the event co-ordinator role.

With her every exclamation of delight over the events planned, with every accidental touch as they worked through the files, with every movement that caused her jumper to pull on her breasts he had become more and more fixated with watching her.

And throughout the morning she had progressively impressed and surprised him with her attention to detail. Impressed him because she had picked up on some timing problems he hadn't spotted. Surprised him because, tidiness-wise, the woman was a disaster.

Obviously timekeeping wasn't a strength either.

The Chinese delegation were arriving in Venice this evening. He had to be at Hotel Cipriani at eight to greet them on their arrival. Emma had travelled over there, at her suggestion, after lunch to meet with the hotel co-ordinator and the interpreter employed for the duration of the visit.

He hit the call button again.

After yet more infuriating rings, she eventually answered.

He didn't wait for her to speak, '*Dove sei?* Where are you?'

'I'm not sure.' There was a hint of panic to her voice. 'After my meetings in Hotel Cipriani I decided I would visit the restaurant booked for the clients later this week on Giudecca. I found the restaurant and spoke to the owner and the chef. But when I left I must have gone in the wrong direction, because I'm totally lost. I can't find my way back to the *vaporetto* stop.'

Now he really *was* regretting his decision to employ her. 'Can't you ask someone to help you?'

'I have! But each time I follow their directions I end up even more lost down another narrow alleyway.'

Dio! 'Can you see a street name anywhere?'

'Hold on…yes, I see one! Calle Ca Rizzo.'

'Stay there. I'll come and get you.'

'There's no need. I'll—'

He hung up before she had time to start arguing with him. It was already past four.

Emma placed her phone back into her padded jacket's pocket, her already racing heart now acting as if it was taking part in the international finals of the one hundred metre sprint. The day had been going so well until she had gone and got lost in this warren of laneways or, as they were called locally, *calli* that made up Giudecca, an island suburb of Venice.

Her meetings in the opulent surroundings of Hotel Cipriani had gone smoothly, all the little extras she'd requested had been accommodated, and she had then made her way to Ristorante Beccherie, excited at the stunning views across the water to St Mark's Square, the Basilica di San Marco and the Campanile clearly visible under the clear blue sky.

After her meeting at the restaurant she hadn't minded getting lost at first. She had been enchanted by the three- and four-storey medieval red-brick houses on deserted narrow alleyways, by the washing hanging between the houses like bunting, the endless footbridges crossing over the maze of canals. The lack of the sounds of the twenty-first century because of the absence of cars.

But as she'd grown increasingly disorientated, her uneasiness had increased. She'd ended up in dead-end alleyways, silent and beautiful courtyards with no obvious signage.

Matteo was annoyed with her. No—scratch that. He'd sounded ballistic. Would he fire her on her first day?

She walked over to the canal that ran diagonally to the start of Calle Ca Rizzo and moved down onto the canal steps. The temperature was dropping and the cold stone bit against her skin.

Matteo was like Venice. Utterly beautiful but completely frustrating. All morning she had tried to remain professional, but she had been constantly distracted.

Distracted by his deep, potent musky scent when he moved closer to her to point something out in the file sitting between them.

Distracted by the perfect fit of his grey trousers on his narrow hips when he stood.

Distracted by the sight of his large hand lying on the table beside her: golden skin, wide palm, smooth knuckles, long, strong fingers tapering off into pale pink nails, all perfectly clipped into smooth ovals. Several times she had lost her concentration to those hands, dreaming about them on her skin, removing her clothes…

She had been glad of an excuse to get away from the *palazzo*, needing some space to pull herself together.

She dropped her head into her hands. What was she *doing*? Why was she having these thoughts? She wasn't interested in men. In any form of relationship. She had a job to do. And falling for the boss was not only out of the question it was beyond stupid. Well, she *hoped* she still had a job to do. Maybe not when he arrived...

Fifteen minutes later she saw him stop on a footbridge further down the canal and stare towards her. His hip-length black wool pea coat was topped with a dark grey woollen hat. The pull of attraction tugged on every cell in her body. His mouth was turned downwards in a *you're in big trouble* scowl.

She jumped up and tried to match his stride in her direction, but her legs were too wobbly so she careened her way along the canal bank, probably looking as if she had recently consumed a considerable amount of Chianti.

When they met her words of apology became lost. His hat hugged his skull, emphasising the intensity of his golden-brown eyes framed by thick black eyelashes, the beauty of his honey-coloured skin, the proud straight nose, the no-nonsense mouth softened by the cleft in his chin.

That gorgeous mouth hardened. 'We are late for our appointments.'

Did that mean he wasn't going to fire her?

Without another word he walked away and she followed alongside him, over countless bridges and through a maze of *calli*. They passed few people, and in the tight confines of the laneways he seemed taller and more powerful than she remembered.

She gave a quick summary of her meetings, updating him on any changes. Hoping his mood might improve. He made no comment but gave an occasional nod. At least he was listening.

Eventually they arrived at the broad reach of Canale

della Giudecca and he led her to a sleek, highly polished wooden motor boat moored at a landing stage.

After untying the two mooring ropes he held the stern tight against the wooden stage. He held out his hand to her. 'You need to climb aboard.'

She hesitated for a moment, suddenly wary of touching him. But, with the boat swaying in the choppy waters, she decided she'd risk holding his hand over the chagrin of being crushed against the landing stage.

His hand encased hers, and his powerful strength guided her on board. For a crazy few seconds she was engulfed by the sensation that she would always be safe with him in her life.

With practised ease Matteo pulled the boat away from the stage and was soon heading across the canal towards St Mark's Square.

'I'm sorry I got lost. I didn't mean to inconvenience you.'

He gave that ubiquitous continental shrug that might mean he accepted her apology with some reservations or was so irritated by her that he couldn't speak.

At first she thought he was going back up the Grand Canal to Ca' Divina, but just west of St Mark's Square he turned right and slowly motored up a smaller canal. The canal was busy with gondolas, the majority of their passengers embracing and kissing couples.

She plucked her phone out of her pocket and pressed some buttons mindlessly. She had thought she wouldn't mind seeing couples together, enjoying this city of romance. Boy, had she been wrong.

A heavy pain constricted her chest.

She was supposed to be here with her husband. Not with a man who was clearly irritated with her. Not with a man who in truth she was more attracted to than she had ever been to her fiancé.

That truth was shaming.

That truth was bewildering.

'As I explained this morning, five of my companies have a presence here on Calle Larga.'

Matteo came to a stop outside the type of store Emma would window shop at when walking along Bond Street in London but would never dare to enter, knowing her monthly salary wouldn't even buy her a set of barely there but, oh, so gorgeous underwear.

He pointed along the bustling street. 'Verde for handbags, Marco for shoes, Osare is the label for our younger urban clients... Gioiello stocks daywear, and...' Gesturing to the store behind them, he added, 'And VMV for the discerning.'

Was he aware of the constant looks of appreciation he received from passers-by? How within the VMV store a bevy of model-like assistants were flapping their arms in excitement at his imminent entrance?

'I had hoped to take you into each store so that you could familiarise yourself with our product range.' He threw her a reproachful frown. 'But that will not be possible now. We only have time for your fittings.'

With that he turned, and the door of the store was magically opened by a stealthy doorman Emma hadn't seen lurking behind the glass pane.

Matteo gestured for her to enter first.

She took a step closer to him and in a low voice asked, 'What do you mean, "fittings"?'

'You will need dresses and gowns for the various events you will be accompanying me to during the week.'

'I have my own clothes.'

With a raised critical eyebrow he ran his gaze down over her body. Okay, so her black padded jacket and red skirt mightn't be the most glamorous, but she did own some nice clothes.

'I mean I have suitable dresses back at the *palazzo*.'

He stepped closer, his huge body dwarfing hers. His head dipped down and he glared into her eyes. 'I don't have time for this. Let me be clear. You are representing my companies this week. You have to wear clothing from the lines. It's not negotiable. If you don't like it then I'm happy for you to leave.'

Emma gave a quick nod and, with dread exploding in her stomach like fast-rising dough, stepped inside the store and sank into plush carpet. She opened up her padded jacket and yanked at the collar of her jumper. She was burning up. Not only from the heat of the store but from the unfriendly gazes being thrown in her direction by the models.

Matteo walked through the store, pointing out garments which were immediately whisked away to the rear of the store.

'*Bene.* I've selected the gowns which I think will suit you.' He exchanged some rapid words with the woman who had accompanied him in his selection of dresses. 'Andreina will help you try them on.'

Emma smiled warily at the six foot ash blonde diva standing before her. In return she received a cool blue stare. Boy, was she glad she had been waxed to within an inch of her life in preparation for her wedding.

The fitting room was like nothing she had ever seen. A bottle of Prosecco on ice sat on an antique side table, with velvet grey chairs at either side. The floor was tiled in marble, and giant gilt-edged mirrors filled three walls.

She looked at the row of dresses awaiting her. And then at Andreina, who was staring down at her ankle boots, her forehead pinched in obvious disbelief at the water stains on the suede. Yeah, well, maybe Andreina should try walking from Camden Police Station to Highgate in icy slush.

Her stomach lurched. She felt like a gauche fourteen-year-old again, facing her mother's critical stare. Forced to wear only what her mother approved of.

Time for Operation Toughen Up again.

She propelled Andreina by the elbow towards the door. 'I'll call you if I need any help.' She closed the door on a stream of Italian protest, adrenaline pumping.

She approached the dresses warily. She would get this over and done with as quickly as possible. She stripped off her clothes and grabbed the first dress to hand. Her stomach lurched again. She pulled the silk bodice over her head, felt layer upon layer of fine tulle falling from her waist down to the floor. She twisted her arms around to her back in an attempt to tie the bodice but it was hopeless. She needed help.

She fought against the tears stinging her eyes. She couldn't bear the feel of the material on her skin.

A knock sounded on the door. She ignored it.

'Emma, what are you doing?'

Matteo.

She called out, 'None of them suit. I'll just have to wear my own clothes.'

The door swung open.

'For crying out loud, Matteo, I could have been undressed!'

He crossed the room towards her, his eyes darkening. 'I see near-naked models backstage at fashion shows all the time.'

'Well, I'm *not* a model, am I?'

His mouth pursed, and then he asked with irritation, 'Why are you upset?'

'I'm not.'

He threw her an exasperated look. 'That dress is perfect for you—what do you mean, it doesn't suit? Look in the mirror and see for yourself.'

She turned her back on the mirrors, refusing to look, unable to speak.

He came closer, and she gave a yelp when she felt his fingers on the back of the bodice, tying the tiny fastenings.

'Please don't.'

He ignored her protest and continued to work his way down the bodice. Her spine arched beneath his touch as startling desire mixed with the upset dragging at her throat.

At first his movements were fast, but then he slowed, as though he too was weakened by the tension in the room— the tension of bodies hot and bothered, wanting more, wanting satisfaction.

Finished, he settled one hand on her waist while the other touched the exposed skin of her back above the strapless bodice.

'*Cosa c'e'?* What's the matter?'

She couldn't answer. She longed to pull on her skirt and jumper again. To cover every inch of herself. To not feel so exposed. So vulnerable. So aware of him.

'Look into the mirror, Emma. See how beautiful you are. I wasn't comparing you to models.'

She could not help but laugh. 'God, it's not *that*…it's just.'

His hands twisted her around until she was staring at herself in the mirror.

Sumptuous silk on brittle bones.

She spun back to him, her eyes briefly meeting his before looking away. 'I'm sorry…it's just these dresses remind me of my wedding dress.'

CHAPTER THREE

HOW COULD HE have been so stupid? Stupid to have agreed to let her work for him. Stupid not to have foreseen how these dresses might remind her of her wedding. Stupid to feel a responsibility towards this stranger. It was all so illogical. He barely knew her. He had too many other problems, responsibilities, in his life. But something about this woman had him wanting to protect her.

His hand moved to touch her, to lift her chin so that he could gaze into her eyes. To offer her some comfort. But he stopped himself in time. She was an employee. She was a runaway bride just burnt in love. He had to keep away from her.

'I will ask Andreina to help you undress. You do not need to try on any more.'

'No. It's okay. I'm sorry…this wasn't supposed to happen.'

He needed to get away. Away from the close confines of this dressing room. Away from how stunningly beautiful she looked in the gown, pale skin against ivory and purple silk. Away from the pain in her eyes he didn't know how to cope with, didn't know how to ease.

'I'll get Andreina.'

Her hand shot out and her fingers encased his wrist. She gave it a tug to halt him. 'Not Andreina. Please will *you* help me untie the bodice?'

Why was she so adamant about Andreina?

He untied the clasps of the bodice, saw her shoulder blades contract into a shrug above the bodice.

'All the dresses are stunning. I would be very proud to wear them. I just need to get used to the idea.'

Her voice shook just like her body.

More than ever he needed to get away.

'Let's talk about it outside.'

He walked out of the fitting room, wanting to get away.

Wanting to go back and take her into his arms.

Five minutes later she joined him outside the store.

Instead of guiding her back to his boat, he led her towards Campo di San Moisè. At the footbridge that led to the square and the baroque façade of Chiesa di San Moisè he found what he was looking for—a street vendor selling *frittelle*, the Venetian-style doughnuts only available during Carnival. He ordered a mixed cone.

They stopped at the centre of the footbridge and he offered Emma a *frittella* before biting into a *frittella veneziana*. The raisins and pine nuts mixed into the dough were the sugar hit he badly needed.

Emma bit into her *frittella crema pasticcera*, filled with thick custard cream, and gave a little squeal. The custard escaped from the doughnut and dripped down her chin.

Desire, thick and desperate, powered through his body.

They stood in silence, eating the *frittelle*, and he wanted nothing more than to kiss away the grains of sugar glittering on her lips.

The deep upset in her eyes was easing.

He needed to get this over and done with.

'This isn't going to work. I should never have agreed to it.'

She touched her fingers to her mouth and brushed the granules away, heat turning her pale cheeks a hot pink.

'I'm really embarrassed…about getting lost and about what happened in the store. It was unprofessional of me. I promise it won't happen again.'

'You need time to recover from what you have gone through; you shouldn't be working.'

She drank in his words with consternation in her eyes. 'But I need to work—I want to work.'

Why couldn't she see that he was doing her a favour? That this attraction between them was perilous.

'Why?'

She crumpled the empty *frittella* cone in her hands. 'Because I need the money. Because I want to focus on my career and forget the past year.'

Her jaw arced sideways, as if she were easing a painful tension in her jawline.

'He really hurt you, didn't he?'

Her thick dark eyelashes blinked rapidly, her mouth tensing. She angled away from him to face the canal.

She turned back before she spoke. 'Because of his lies and deception, yes. Because of how he hurt other people.'

How had she not known what he was like? Why had she allowed herself to get hurt like this?

Anger swept through him. Together with the recognition that everything she was going through represented every reason why he would never marry, never give his heart and trust to another person. People always let you down, ultimately.

He had trusted, loved, hero-worshipped Francesco, Marco, Simone, Arnaud, Stefano… All his mother's boyfriends. And they had all walked away from him. Showing just how little significance he'd held in their lives. Blood, family—that was all you could trust in. Nobody else.

'Why were you marrying him?'

She jammed her left heel against the bottom of the bridge rail and rotated her foot. 'You mean why didn't I realise what he was really like? I met him last summer. It was a whirlwind romance. We got engaged after four months. He was charming and outgoing. He seemed to care for me a lot. He worked crazy hours and sometimes he didn't turn up for dates… He always had a plausible excuse and I'd eventually forgive him. When we were together he was kind, if a little distracted…but I never saw the other side to him—the lying, the fraud.'

'Four months isn't a long time to get to know one another.'

Behind them a group of tourists walked by, their guide speaking loudly. Suddenly they all laughed in unison. The guide looked pleased with his joke.

Emma looked at them, taken aback. The tips of her ears were pink from the cold. For a moment he considered giving her his hat. Why did he keep forgetting she was his employee? Was it because they had already lain together in a bed? Even if it had been only for a few crazy minutes of misunderstanding?

She went to speak, but stopped. Her mouth quivered and she looked at him uncertainly. Her chest rose on a deep inhalation. 'I wanted a family of my own…to belong.'

She spoke with such loneliness.

He stamped his feet on the ground. The cold was already stiffening his back. 'Did you love him?'

He had asked the question before he had thought it through. It was none of his business. But he had to know.

Hazel eyes filled with confusion met his for a moment before they fled away. 'Can we not talk about this?'

She was right. But a need to know drove him on to say, 'You must have loved him if you were going to marry him.'

She touched her long slim fingers against her temple and circled them there for a few seconds. The faint impression of a ring recently removed was still there, on the skin of her ring finger. Her eyes scrunched shut. 'I'm not certain of anything any more... Maybe.'

'And what if you had married him but then woke up one morning certain you didn't love him—would you have left?'

She looked at him in horror. 'No. *No.* Absolutely not.'

'Why so certain?'

'I wouldn't just walk away. I take my commitments, my pledges seriously. I don't walk away when things get difficult. Turn my back on someone when things go wrong. I do everything to fix it, to accept where we are.' She threw her head back and looked at him fiercely, her nostrils flaring. 'And, before you say anything, I draw a line at criminality. At months and years of lies and deception. Yes, I walked away from my ex—but I could not stay with a man who had so wilfully hurt so many people.'

She inhaled a breath and her jaw worked. Anger fired in her eyes, and she lobbed a grenade of a question in his direction. 'How about *you*—do you ever want to marry? Have your own family?'

Her grenade exploded in his chest. His stomach clenched at the emotional damage of her question. 'It's not for me— my job, my responsibilities mean I wouldn't be a good husband, a good father. I would be absent too much.'

She considered him for a moment, as though trying to decide if he was a con man too. Slowly she nodded, the anger in her eyes receding. 'That's honourable. Others wouldn't even think to stop and consider whether they would be a good husband and father.'

'There's enough hurt children in this world... I don't want to add to them.'

For a moment he thought he had gone too far. She looked at him questioningly.

But then she stood upright and asked, 'Can I have another chance? I promise no more tears or drama. I would

be honoured to wear those dresses. I'll go back and try
them on now.'

Back to business. He should end it now.

'Emma, the future of tens of thousands of my employees rest on this trip going smoothly.'

She nodded with a dignified grace, her eyes holding a
sombre pride. 'I know. And I respect and understand that.
If you firmly believe I'm not right for this position I will
walk away.'

Dio! She was good at negotiating.

He checked his watch. 'Lucky for you, I don't have time
to argue. I want and need from you complete focus on this
client trip. Nothing else. The dresses will all suit you—
I'm sure of it. I will have them delivered tomorrow. Now,
let's go. I need to get home and change.'

The following evening Emma waited for Matteo out on
the terrace, goosebumps of anticipation breaking on her
skin. She was accompanying Matteo Vieri to the Venetian opera house, La Fenice. To see Verdi's *La Traviata*.
In the opera house in which it had first been performed.

She pulled the belt of her wool-and-angora-blend navy
coat tighter. The VMV store had delivered it that morning, along with all the other clothes Matteo had selected
yesterday.

The past twenty-four hours had passed without inci-
dent. No tears on her part. To the clients she presented
a sunny face. At times she had even fooled herself into
thinking she was coping. But in the quiet moments, when
she hadn't been busy, it had all hit her like a *vaporetto* colliding with a gondola.

She still questioned how she had been so blind to her
ex's deceit. And any thoughts of the future left her with
heart palpitations. And then there was the constant anxiety
that she was going to mess up with the clients, with Matteo.

He seemed to be winning over his Chinese clients with a combination of deep respect and vigilant hosting.

She had accompanied the spouses to Murano Island this morning, to view the world-famous glass manufacturing, along with an interpreter and a tour guide, while Matteo and his clients held business meetings. And in the afternoon the entire group had toured the city by gondola.

As Matteo's designated partner, she had accompanied him in the same gondola as the president of the department store chain, Mr Xue, and his wife. It had been oddly intimate, sitting next to him as they had passed under the Rialto Bridge and later viewed the stunning architecture, mosaics and carvings of Basilica di San Marco and the Doge's Palace. He was professorial in his knowledge and passion about both buildings and the history of Venice in general. No wonder he was so successful, with what appeared to be a photographic memory and a charming persona.

Only with her did the charm fade. When they were alone he was quiet, and she could not help but feel he was keeping his distance from her. Even now she had a strong hunch that he was waiting until the last minute to leave his office for their journey to La Fenice.

She would do anything to take back her behaviour yesterday in the VMV store. She had clearly made him very uncomfortable and it had been totally unprofessional.

Every now and again over the past twenty-four hours she had caught him looking in her direction. He would always look away, but not before a blaze of attraction had surged between them.

'My boat is waiting downstairs for us.'

She turned to find him standing at the terrace doors. 'I'm ready.'

She swallowed the other words that were about to shoot out of her mouth. *You look incredible.* Which was the truth.

His dark grey suit jacket skimmed the wide span of his shoulders, and the tailored trousers emphasised the long length of his legs. He shrugged on a long black wool coat, followed by a black wool hat.

As she neared him he handed her a royal blue hat. 'It's cold tonight. You will need to wear some protection.'

The thin-knit hat, the same colour as the appliqué dashes on her navy cocktail dress, had a crystal flower sewn onto it.

Would her heart *please* stop pounding? It was just a practical gesture—nothing else.

'Let me put it on for you. Otherwise your hair might fall down.'

He had to be joking!

But, alas, no. He took the hat from her and delicately pulled it over her hair, which she had coiled up into a tight bun. It was a style she rarely used, for it brought back too many memories of her life as a ballerina. But tonight it had felt apt—not just because it suited the dress but because she needed its severity against how vulnerable she felt about her wedding imploding, the constant stress of worrying if she was doing her job effectively…and her silly, annoying, futile attraction to her boss.

His fingers stroked briefly against the exposed skin of her neck. Her insides melted. He was standing much too close. His scent, his broad chest were too close. His open coat touching against her…too close.

She stepped back. No weakness. Just toughness and protecting herself. That was all that mattered now.

In the darkened theatre, the lovers Violetta and Alfredo begged each other for forgiveness for all the hurt they had caused each other in the past. Their voices soared, their pain and passion for one another holding the crowd transfixed. Alfredo believed that they had a future together, not realising how ill Violetta was…

Matteo could hardly breathe. In his private box, the president of the board, Mr Xue, and his wife were to his right, closest to the stage. Emma was to his left. Because of the way the boxes were angled towards the stage he couldn't see her without turning around. He wanted to turn. He wanted to see if she was okay.

All evening she had done everything possible to make his clients welcome and comfortable. Had been attentive to them at each of the two intervals. But something was wrong. Her body beneath the stunning pencil-fit dark navy dress with dashes of royal blue was too stiff. Her hair, tied up in an elegant bun that matched the knee-length, cap-sleeved gentle decorum of her dress, exposed the tension in her rigid neck.

Violetta fell to the floor. Lifeless.

Behind Mr Xue somebody sniffled.

He had to check.

Her eyes were on the stage. The endless gilt private boxes of La Fenice cascaded behind her. She swallowed hard but did not look in his direction. She was aware of him. He had no doubt about that. Her refusal to meet his eyes sent hot frustration zipping through his muscles. His hands and feet clenched, he shifted in his seat.

The cast moved forward on the stage to take their bows. The crowd stood and shouted their approval. He needed to focus on his clients. But all he was aware of was the ex-asperatingly beautiful woman next to him.

A woman whose slender waist, small full breasts, high firm bottom and long legs left him with distracted concentration, with a hollow feeling in his stomach, with a desperate compulsion to hold her, kiss her, taste her.

She was an employee. A woman recently heartbroken in love. A runaway bride.

He didn't need any further reasons to stay away from her.
If only his libido would receive that message.

With his clients and their tour guide and interpreter safely
aboard the private launch, Matteo watched their boat turning in the water towards the direction of the Hotel Cipriani.

Beside him, Emma quickly yanked the clips from her
hair. Thick curls tumbled down her back. Memories of
her hair fanned on his pillow the night he'd found her in
his bed sent a shock of desire through him. She pulled
on her woollen hat, giving him a surreptitious look. The
uncomfortable suspicion that she was trying to avoid his
help in putting it on set his teeth on edge. He wasn't used
to women pushing him away.

Deliberately, he moved closer. Emma gazed up. Startled. But she didn't look away. Her cheeks grew flushed
and her eyes darkened, making something explode in his
stomach. He adjusted her hat, pulling it down further over
her head. And as he held her gaze he ran his fingers down
the long length of her hair. He was playing with fire but
he didn't care.

He studied her lips in a slow, deliberate drag of his eyes
across their plump softness.

Her lips parted and she gave a low, shaky exhalation.

His pulse throbbed at the base of his neck, urging him
to taste her, to answer the primitive call aching in his gut,
to possess her. To grab her and end this irrational hold she
had over him—this foolish, reckless attraction that burned
brightly between them.

She stepped back unsteadily. She tugged at the collar
of her coat with nervous fingers.

She cleared her throat. 'How are the meetings going?'

He too stepped back. Shook his head, trying to silence
the heavy insistent beat of his pulse.

The meetings. He shook his head again. Trying to focus.

The meetings. They were going slowly. Which was to be expected. But that did not stop it from being exasperating. All his work over the past few years had been jeopardised by his troubled designer.

The fog of desire slowly lifting, he cleared his own throat. 'Thanks to my designer, I'm having to spend time rebuilding our relationship, re-establishing our respect towards them. They value a long-term relationship rather than a specific deal, and that can't be rushed.'

'What are you going to do about the designer? Will you need to replace him?'

'Trust me, I'm tempted to, and it's what my board would like me to do. But I'm not going to. He has been going through a tough time recently, due to some personal problems. He needs support.'

She gave him a smile that slipped like a pulse of pleasure into his bloodstream. 'Your grandmother isn't the only one with a kind heart.'

'I try to protect my employees, my family…' He paused and swallowed against the sudden kick his heart aimed against his ribs. 'Patrizia—your predecessor—gave birth to a baby boy yesterday afternoon.'

A trace of longing pulled at the corners of her smile. 'That's wonderful news.'

He remembered her words about wanting a family.

Suddenly he wanted to have this night over.

'My boat is waiting for us.'

She gave him a nervous glance before gesturing back towards the city. 'I was thinking of walking back… I haven't seen Venice at night yet.' She took a few steps towards the city. 'I'll see you in the morning.'

She was pushing him away. Annoyance lashed across his skin.

'I'll walk with you.'

His suspicion that she was trying to get away was confirmed by her swift response.

'No! No, I'll walk by myself.'

'Do you know the way?'

'Not really… But I'm sure I'll be fine.'

He threw her an unconvinced look. 'I don't want to have to come and find you in the middle of the night if you get lost, like you did on Giudecca.'

She winced at that. 'I suppose…'

He led her in the direction of Piazza San Marco.

They walked in tense silence.

On the narrow Calle Delle Veste, she darted an uncertain look at him before asking, 'Did you grow up in Venice?'

How he wished he *had* grown up in one single place.

'We lived here for a little while. Originally we were from Puglia, in the South. We moved around during my childhood, here in Italy but also in France and Spain.'

'Because of your parents' work?'

Not so much work as where his mother's latest boyfriend had lived. 'There was only my mother and me. Sometimes my grandmother too.'

'So, like me, you had no brothers or sisters.' She said it with a wistfulness that told him she too had dreamed of having some when she was younger. Some allies in life. Someone to talk to.

But then, would he *really* have wanted another child to endure the constant uncertainty of his childhood? The stomach-crunching walk to the door each day after school, wondering if today was the day they were going to pack and leave. Or to be thrown out. The constant fear in the pit of his stomach that his life was going to change again—a new town, a new school, a new man in their lives, but the same isolation, the same insecurity.

They turned into Calle Larga. He pushed away those

memories. Only then did he notice how she was struggling to walk.

He slowed down. 'You're limping—are you sure you're okay to walk?'

She waved away his concern with a toss of her hand. 'I'm fine. It's just an old injury that flares up every now and again.'

He slowed his pace even more, unconvinced by her answer. He held out his arm. 'Take my arm.'

She glanced at his arm as though he was offering her something illegal. She bit her lip. But then with a shaky smile she placed her hand on his arm, her elbow tucked beneath his, lightly touching his side.

They walked along the empty *calle*, with Emma slowly placing more weight on his arm. Their steps, at first out of sync, quickly matched each other, and his body hummed, firing with protectiveness for the beautiful, guarded, troubling woman at his side.

Her hand relaxing even more on his arm, she asked, 'Did you mind moving around when you were a child?'

'I hated it.'

Her eyes snapped up to consider him. 'Really?'

'I was always the new boy at school. Sometimes the other children reacted well—I was a novelty. Most of the time, though, I was nothing but a new target.'

She grimaced, her quick shudder rippling against the side of his body. 'You sound as if you were as unhappy in school as I was.'

'What do you mean?'

'I was at ballet boarding school from the age of ten. I adored the ballet—most of the time—but I was lonely.'

'You missed your parents?'

'Yes…sometimes. But I eventually got used to it.'

He knew there was more to it than that, but seeing the

closed expression on her face he guessed she didn't want to talk about it.

He decided to change the topic. 'Do you dance now?'

He had hoped to move to neutral territory with his question. But by the crestfallen expression on her face and the way she pulled away from him to walk on her own, without his help, he could see it had obviously backfired.

'No. I haven't danced in years.'

'Why?'

He almost preferred the tears of other times to the stony expression on her face now. Tight, pale lips. The off-kilter edge of upset in her jaw.

He thought she wasn't going to answer, but eventually she said, 'I broke my ankle when I was nineteen. I ended up having to have plates inserted, it was smashed so badly.'

It seemed to have taken a huge effort for her to tell him that much. He should ask no more questions. Leave her be. But he wanted to understand.

'Did it happen whilst you were dancing?'

'Unfortunately not—or maybe fortunately. I was out one night and slipped on wet steps.'

They were once again reaching Campo di San Moisè. The tiny square was empty, and the exuberant exterior of San Moisè church, with its dramatic carved stone, stood like a giant wedding cake awaiting its bride and groom. A lone gondolier floated on the canal below the bridge, his night light briefly flickering over his passengers—a couple entwined. He and Emma stopped at the centre of the bridge and looked down into the water.

Emotion welled in his chest. He wanted to reach out to her. Why, he had no idea. 'Your limping tonight…is that because of the accident?'

Her eyes fixed on the passing boat, she gave a knee-jerk shrug. The shrug of someone who had been pretending for too long. Her hands clasped and tightened the belt of her coat around her narrow waist. She stood on one foot. Flicked the other forward and back.

'Yes, sometimes it acts up. Bad weather or stress seem to particularly aggravate it. The past few days—being questioned by the police, having to call my ex's parents... tell them that the wedding was off—has made it ache like never before.'

She spoke with a hard edge, trying to box off her dismay.

'The past few days have been very difficult for you. I admire how determined you are to move on.'

A sad smile broke on her mouth and her eyes dissolved into soft gratitude. 'Thank you.'

'You were upset tonight.'

Her hand flew to her mouth. 'The clients didn't see, did they? I tried not to...' Her voice trailed off.

'No, they didn't see.'

'But *you* did.'

'I pick up on these things faster than others.'

Which was partially the truth. He had spent his childhood attuned at all times to his mother's mood. Now it was a honed skill that was a powerful tool in the boardroom. But he was especially attuned to Emma. None of his guests tonight would have guessed something was wrong, but he had seen...and felt...the very subtle signs as if they shared a special language all of their own.

Which made no sense. And was deeply, annoyingly, frustratingly unsettling.

'Ballet was my life—'

Her voice cracked and she shut her eyes. When she opened them again they pleaded with him to understand.

'It was everything I'd dreamed of. I was on track to a solo position in the Greater Manchester Metropolitan City Ballet. And suddenly it was all over.'

'You still miss it?'

She gave a hurt laugh, as if she still couldn't believe the awful trick life had played on her.

'Hugely. Tonight…tonight was my first time being inside a theatre since my accident. Over the years I couldn't face being reminded of what I was missing…the thrill as you wait in the wings…the elation at the end of a show. I thought I had come to terms with it, but tonight it was such a beautiful production, such a heartbreaking story… I wished I could have been up there on the stage too.'

'If you miss it so much couldn't you teach, or do something else in the ballet world?'

She touched her hand to her forehead and winced. As if that thought alone caused a headache. 'No, it'd be too hard. I can't go back to it.'

Eyes that knew the pain of loss held his.

Something sharp stabbed his chest.

'Do you dance at *all*?'

She shook her head, looked away. 'I haven't danced since I had my accident, seven years ago.'

'In time you may go back to it—don't totally discount it. From how you describe it, I know it was an important part of your life.'

Her mouth tightened and she blinked hard.

He should suggest they move on.

But he wanted to hold her.

Wanted to see her smile.

Wanted to make things okay for her.

'Will you dance with me now?'

She gazed at him as though he had asked her to scale the outside of the *campanile* in Piazza San Marco. 'Dance with you? Here?'

Okay, so it wasn't something most bosses would suggest to an employee. But then most bosses didn't first encounter an employee by finding them lying in their bed. After that, their relationship was never going to be normal.

'We shared *frittelle* here—why not a dance?'

She looked about her. Taking in where they were properly for the first time. 'I thought the buildings looked familiar.'

He held out his hand to her. 'Well…?'

His hand hung in the air. Long tanned fingers.

Her stomach went into free fall.

She wanted to move towards him.

In that moment his hand seemed like a beacon of escape from reality, if only for a fleeting few minutes.

Boom-boom-boom. Her heart shot up to the base of her throat. Clogging her airways.

But what of her resolution to stay away from men? This attraction was nothing more than a manifestation of her loneliness, her vulnerability. The ultimate rebound fantasy.

But it was all so tempting.

She could lose herself in this intoxicating chemistry between them. Forget about everything that was wrong in her life.

Her hand rose up as though independent of her. Tired of her dithering. Her body was intent on making the decision for her, ignoring all the arguments in her brain.

A sexy, satisfied supernova smile broke on his mouth. He tugged her forward slowly, in no rush. His other hand landed lightly on her waist.

Her hand, her arm, her breast, her neck, her belly and then the entirety of her body was blasted with heat, the surge of something unique.

He began to sway and move them around in circles.

He hummed a low tune.

The tremors in her body lessened.

And then laughter bubbled in her throat and escaped into the chilly night air. She laughed at the craziness of the whole situation. Her. Dancing. With Matteo Vieri. In a deserted square in the most romantic city in the world. And the most surprising, crazy part of it all: he had a deep, beautiful singing voice.

He looked down at her with affectionate amusement.

Their eyes locked. The world slowed down.

They moved closer.

His mouth came close to her ear.

His deep humming moved through her body like a caress.

A hot sensual river seeped through her.

She stepped even closer.

Their bodies met.

She closed her eyes. Light-headed against his scent of powerful musk. At the sensation of being held by him. At their feet moving in unison.

She was *dancing*!

Elation and heartbreak constricted her chest.

Tucked into his side, she felt his hard chest pressed against her breast, his hip against hers.

Want tugged at her core. Leaving her weak-limbed.

She shifted in his arms, her hardened nipples grazing against the press of his chest.

She gave a low gasp.

He moved away from her ear.

She looked up.

His eyes had darkened.

With the same heavy desire she was sure shadowed her own.

His head lowered again. Towards hers. Everything inside her went quiet. His lips hovered over hers. She couldn't keep her eyes open.

His breath, with an intoxicating hint of the brandy he had drunk during the interval, feathered over her skin.

Her lips parted. Felt heavy.

His lips moved against hers softly.

Her mind spun.

With a groan he pulled her closer.

And then she was lost to the warm, masculine sensation of his mouth, to the pressure of his hand on her back, the hardness of his body pushed against hers.

CHAPTER FOUR

WHAT WAS SHE DOING?

Emma pulled away. Breathless. Panic pushing her heart hard. It pounded and crashed in her chest. Physically wounding her.

She was kissing a man. Days after her wedding—her life—had crashed and burned. She was kissing her boss.

For a brief second Matteo looked at her in confusion.

'I'm sorry…that shouldn't have happened,' she said unsteadily.

His eyes hardened and his mouth settled into a tight line of annoyance. He gave a curt nod. 'It's getting late. We should go.'

For a moment she looked at him, at a loss. Wanting more. What, she wasn't sure. But not this awkward, tense, angry, frustrated wall that now stood between them.

They turned and walked through the ancient floating city, the clip of their footsteps mocking the silence between them.

Her body was distracted, acutely aware, on high alert to the power and strength, the primitive masculine draw of the man walking beside her.

Embarrassment and guilt ate up any words that tumbled through her brain.

Two days later Emma stared at the event plan for the reception to be held in Ca' Divina that night and marvelled at the neatness of the spreadsheet cells. All so orderly and straightforward. And nothing like the chaos that had ascended on the *palazzo* since early that morning.

She ticked off the box for reconfirming the private launches that would transport the guests to Ca' Divina.

If only she was able to place a satisfying, tension-releasing tick in all the other empty boxes winking up at her, taunting her with their blankness. The caterers, the audio-visual team, lighting and florists were still setting up. They were supposed to have finished over an hour ago.

In her stomach anxiety popped like popcorn kernels. She pushed her hand sharply against her belly. A warning not to give in to her own self-doubts. She had this under control. The reception *would* be a success. Matteo's clients, his A-list celebrity guests and all the local dignitaries would be suitably impressed. Matteo would be impressed.

And maybe then the awful tension that had sprung up between them since they had danced and kissed in San Moisè Square would ease. It was a tension that had seen them talking to one another uneasily, maintaining a ridiculous physical space at all times when they were in the same room, as if standing too close might be dangerous.

Something huge, awkward and unsaid was dangling between them.

Dancing with him had been wondrous, but his strength and care had made her feel even more vulnerable, more susceptible to him.

Raised voices down on the landing stage had her standing up from where she had been working at the dining table out on the terrace and walking to the balustrade.

Matteo was home.

An hour earlier than she'd expected.

He was exchanging terse words with one of the lighting electricians whilst gesturing furiously at some electrical cables lying along the landing stage.

She grabbed her file and ran through the terrace doors,

out into the huge central room filled with stunning frescos that she had learned from Matteo was called a *portego*, and down the wide marble stairs that led to the water gate.

Head down, Matteo charged up towards her. They met halfway.

Anxiety and attraction mixed explosively in her heart, which was about to *jeté* right out of her chest.

Stern brown eyes flaring with coppery tints flicked over her. '*E'tutto pronto per sta sera?* Is everything ready for tonight?'

Her professional smile wavered. And she wanted to weep. Because she wanted nothing more than to step closer. Lay her hand on his arm. Touch the wool of his coat.

Did *he* suffer any of this intense chemistry that made her feel constantly faint?

Did *he* think of their kiss?

Did *he* want, like she did, to have the world sing and shine and sizzle again?

Did *he* spend hours driving himself crazy, thinking about it…and then spend the rest of the day berating himself for thinking such crazy, impossible, self-destructive thoughts?

Probably not.

She clasped the file even tighter in her hand, her nails—French-polished for the wedding—digging into the soft cardboard. 'Everything is on track to be ready…the set-up is just taking a little longer than planned.'

With an impatient sigh he turned away and climbed the stairs at a jog.

She ran after him, cursing the twinge in her ankle.

He stopped at the first room he came to—the cosy and inviting writing room.

Inside, the staff hired to act as cloakroom attendants were still packing the gift boxes that would be given to each guest on departure. They had set up an impressive production line on top of a matching pair of painted credenzas. Skincare products, perfumes and designer sunglasses—all from Matteo's lines—were being placed into exquisite ballet-slipper-pink boxes printed with hundreds of tiny gold VMV logos.

With a shake of his head Matteo turned away.

In the *portego*, he stopped and looked critically at the florists, who were finishing off a huge globe centrepiece filled with pretty roses the same pink as the gift boxes— the signature colour of VMV.

'Isn't it beautiful?'

He didn't respond, but stared critically at the endless cuttings and the florists' paraphernalia on the floor, needing to be tidied away.

In the ballroom he stalked about the double-height room like a matador awaiting the release of the bull. He glared at the audio-visual technician, still setting up, and then rearranged some of the gilded furniture which had been moved to the corners of the room to allow the guests to circulate easily.

Emma bit back on her impulse to ask him to stop, to inform him that she had arranged the furniture in such a pattern deliberately. Instead she said, 'The catering manager and I will be briefing the waiting staff in five minutes. The head of security will be here soon with his team. I will also have a briefing meeting with him.'

Matteo made no comment, but strode out onto the terrace. Emma guessed she was expected to follow.

When she came alongside him he stabbed a finger down towards the water. 'Why is there no red carpet on the landing stage?'

She flicked open her folder. Nobody had said anything about a red carpet. Had she missed it in the schedule? Frantically she scanned the document.

'I didn't know there was supposed to be one. Shouldn't

it be pink, anyway? To keep it in line with the pink VMV theme of the evening?'

He looked at her with a puzzled frown for a second. Then he said, in a slow *I'm trying to control my temper here* voice, 'Just sort it out.'

He turned and stabbed his finger at the terrace table.

'And sort out that mess on the table.'

'Of course.'

'Do you *always* work in such chaos?'

Okay, so she had left some files and paperwork on the table when she had rushed to meet him. But nothing that warranted such a damning tone. Why was he trying to pick a fight with her?

'Is everything okay?'

For a brief second he looked taken aback by her question, but then that hard Roman emperor jawline tensed. 'Why shouldn't it be?' He didn't wait for her to answer but instead demanded, 'Is the photographer here?'

Why did he have to home in on everything that was going wrong with the plan? 'His flight was delayed. He'll be here in the next hour.'

He walked away from her, but turned at the terrace door. 'I'll be in my office. Send the head of security in to me when he arrives. *I'll* manage his briefing. The same with the photographer.'

Unease prickled at the top of her spine. She rolled her head, but a million tiny pinpricks of pressure persisted. Why was he trying to take over her responsibilities?

'There's no need. I have everything under control.'

He yanked off his outer coat and tossed it under his arm. His light grey suit jacket was open and it flared back to give her a glimpse of his powerful torso, flat stomach, narrow hips. Hips that had crushed against her two nights ago.

Desire spun within her—coiling, whipping, hollowing out her insides.

Her hips, her skin, her mouth suddenly wanted him. Wanted his strength. Wanted the undoing effect of his scent. Wanted the feverish pull of his dazzling fingers trailing across her skin.

His expression hardened. 'But that's the problem. You clearly haven't. The *palazzo* is a mess. Nothing is ready. I'm disappointed. I expected better.'

His words sliced through her.

Through her crazy physical draw to him.

Through her pride.

Through all the promises she had made to herself that she was going to be tough, that she was going to stand up for herself.

'The *palazzo* will be ready. Within the next hour. The guests aren't arriving for another three hours.'

She tilted her head and, despite her mouth feeling like two rigid lines frozen in place, dug out a smile.

'I think you should have belief in me and the rest of the crew.'

Her short-lived smile collapsed, and she didn't care that it was replaced with a scowl.

He tossed his coat onto his other arm and stepped back out onto the terrace. His eyes were dark, dark, dark, as if his every feeling towards her had sucked any light out of them.

'You have to earn my belief first, and so far you're not doing a very good job.'

The corridor down to his office was blocked by two waiters carrying a long wooden table in the direction of the lounge. A lightning glare sent them scurrying away. In his haste, the waiter at the back drove a table leg into the calf of the waiter carrying the table at the front. The waiter grimaced hard, but avoided looking in Matteo's direction. Keen to get away.

A shade of guilt accompanied Matteo into his office.

He flung open his laptop. Impatience clung to him. Did it *always* take so long for the laptop to power up?

His clients were stalling. The contracts should have been signed today. For the first time ever he was unable to read his clients, to assess what their negotiation tactics were. Were they still unsure about the relationship? Unsure about the trust and respect between them? Or were they looking to gain an advantage in the contract negotiations?

It felt as though his negotiation instincts had been knocked off course. Nothing had been the same since Tuesday night. When he had danced with Emma. Had held her slight frame in his arms. Had kissed her soft mouth. When nothing had ever felt so right. When in truth it was all wrong.

She had pulled away.

Rightly so.

But that didn't mean it hadn't stung. She had looked aghast. Even now his ego felt affronted by her horror.

He hated how attracted he was to her. How he constantly thought about her. The eternal distraction of her.

He should have been the one to pull away. She was an employee. Living in his home. A bruised runaway bride, no doubt messed up and confused. He hadn't acted honourably. That was what stung the most.

Finally the email icon popped up on his laptop.

He leaned forward in his chair and clicked on a New York Fashion Week update from the head of PR with VMV.

A hot dart of pain stung the base of his spine. He closed his eyes. *Dio!*

Tonight *had* to go smoothly. Thousands of his employees were depending on him. This business was his life, his everything. What would he be without it?

Tonight he was about to reveal his final bargaining chip to secure the deal with his clients. A promise that the globe's hottest celebrity couple, Hollywood stars Sadie

Banks and Johnny North, would open his collections at the Chinese clients' flagship stores in Hong Kong and Beijing.

Sadie and he had dated years ago, and had kept in contact for business purposes. She and Johnny were both going to attend the reception tonight. Their first appearance since their surprise marriage a fortnight ago, conducted in complete secrecy with only immediate family and friends in attendance. Sadie had worn a VMV gown.

Denied shots of the wedding, the media and public would be clamouring for a photo. Which, of course, would be taken with the president of China's most prestigious department store chain standing in between them.

The reception needed to be relaxed, slick, effortless. Everything it currently wasn't.

A knock sounded on his door. Before he had the opportunity to respond Emma entered and introduced a short, intent-looking man. The head of security.

Matteo gestured for the man to sit. Emma sat next to him, across the desk from Matteo.

Her hair was tied back in a ponytail, and she wore a white blouse with thin aqua-blue strips, a wide bow on the high collar. Beneath: dark navy tailored trousers. Her only obvious make-up was a deep red lipstick on her generous cupid's bow lips. Desire hit him hard. For a moment he could only stare at her. His fingers itching to undo each tiny pearl button running down the front of her blouse.

She was the cause of his negotiating instincts being off course. *She* was to blame. She had asked him earlier to believe in her. He had learned a long time ago not to trust in anyone but himself. That was not going to change any time soon—especially with a woman who had such a disturbingly bewitching effect on him.

Frustration wrapped around his throat. 'Emma, I will handle this.'

Ignoring him, she twisted to face the head of security, flinging her head back defiantly. She delivered a killer smile to the man, whose focused demeanour crumbled into a smitten gaze.

She passed him a file. 'This is an updated list of guests. Prince Henri is no longer able to attend.'

Matteo sat back in his chair as Emma continued to brief the security head. Anger fused with his earlier desire. Tension leached into his muscles. He forced himself to maintain restraint. Until he got her alone.

He couldn't fault her performance. She provided the head of security with every key piece of information he needed and easily answered all his questions.

But he *could* fault her insubordination. Her intrusion into his life. He *could* fault his own absurdity in feeling things for this woman that had him unable to concentrate in meetings. That had him craving the opportunity to spend time with her, to talk with her, to touch her, to taste the exhilarating heat of her mouth again.

Ten minutes later the meeting was wrapped up. The head of security provided Matteo with reassurances that, together with assistance from the local *carabinieri*, his team would be able to handle any potential security issues.

Emma walked to the office door with the security head. She offered Matteo a brief nod. Throughout the meeting she had held his gaze resolutely whenever he'd addressed her. He had deliberately pinned her with a furious stare. Wanting to see contrition in her eyes. Contrition for not obeying his orders. Contrition for turning his life upside down from the moment he'd found her lying in his bed.

'Emma, please wait.'

She stood by the open door as the security head walked away.

Music floated on the air. The string quartet rehearsing in the lounge.

For a moment he couldn't speak—couldn't break away from the powerful beauty of her hazel eyes. The soft, tender, romantic music wrapped around his heart—and then frustration hurled through him again. He gritted his teeth against his own insanity.

'Close the door.'

She did as he asked, but stayed at the now closed door, her shoulder hugging the edge of the door frame.

'I said that *I* would handle the briefing with the security head.'

Her body gave a start at the anger in his voice but then she stood upright, tilting her head back to gaze at him. 'It's okay. I was free and I had the most up-to-date guest list.'

'No. It *isn't* okay. I said that I didn't need you.'

Perspiration was breaking out on Emma's skin.

Her heart was banging a slow booming beat in her chest while the soulful melodies of Shostakovich's 'Romance Theme from The Gadfly' continued to seep under the closed door. Adding to her sense of foreboding.

She had guessed that Matteo wouldn't be happy with her leading the briefing. But she hadn't bargained on the alarming fury in his eyes. The dangerous coiled energy pulsating from his every pore.

Logic and her heart teamed up to beg her not to speak. Not to ask the one question boiling in her stomach.

But her new-found reckless defiance didn't heed them. 'Are you like this with *all* your employees?'

Her heart thundered in disbelief that she said those words out loud. She took small consolation from the fact that she hadn't also asked if it was only with her that he acted so harshly. *Because of their kiss.* Did he regret it so much? Was he determined to push her away?

'When I need to be.'

'Matteo.' Her throat tightened even at saying his name.

Regret punched her gut. But then anger overtook her. Anger that she was so drawn to this man. Anger that all her pledges to toughen up, to protect herself, had been nothing but empty promises.

She stepped away from the door. 'You employed me to do a job. Please let me do it.'

'Are you always this obstinate?'

'No. And unfortunately I have paid dearly as a result.'

'Meaning?'

'I allowed my ex to convince me that a short engagement was the right thing, when in truth I wanted more time. I allowed my mother and father to push me, to control every part of my life.'

She paused, emotion caught in her throat. She wanted to turn around and walk out of his office. Away from the hardness in his eyes. She didn't know where her throat ended and her heart began. Both were aching…a continuous fault line in her chest.

'I should have pushed for what I wanted and maybe then they would have had more respect for me.'

He folded his arms. His jaw tightened.

He looked down at his desk.

He unfolded his arms.

He pressed the metal of one cufflink. And then the other.

He prodded some paperwork.

He looked back up, his gaze trailing over the wall behind her, inhaled deeply.

He looked at her briefly and then gestured to the chair where she had earlier been seated. 'Sit down.' He stopped and exhaled a lungful of irritation. 'Sorry, *please* sit down.'

The second time around his voice was more conciliatory. Less harsh. Almost like the voice of the Matteo who had taken her in his arms the other night.

She sat, but kept her mask of imperturbability firmly on. She held his gaze, refusing to acknowledge the horrible vulnerability stirring in her stomach.

'I do respect you.'

She raised a single eyebrow.

He continued. 'Tonight *has* to go well. The clients are refusing to sign. Tonight I have to persuade them to do so. I expect that when they meet Sadie Banks, who is a brand ambassador for VMV, they will fully appreciate the mutual benefits of our alliance.'

Fresh unease grabbed hold of her stomach at the thought of all the sophisticated guests attending the reception. What on earth was she going to speak to them about?

'What role do you want me to play tonight at the reception?'

He drew a hand across his face, his long fingers brushing against his lips. Tired. Puzzled. Weary. 'You're my co-host, as with all the other events. Why would it be any different?'

The vulnerability chilling her bones, setting her on edge, had her speaking out, needing to understand where she stood with him. 'After Tuesday night I wasn't sure.'

He shifted in his seat. 'That obviously was a mistake.'

A mistake?

She knew it was. But hearing him say it in such a cold, dispassionate tone was like a slap.

'Yes, it was.' She gave him a polite smile, despite the anger propelling through her, making her want to snarl instead. 'I think they call it a rebound kiss.'

His jaw worked. And then a cruel smile crept onto his mouth. '*Cara*, we both know that was a lot more than a rebound kiss.'

His voice, dangerous but laced with sexy appeal had her shooting out of her chair. 'I must go and check if the photographer has arrived.'

* * *

Matteo gave a low curse. He felt as though his stomach had sunk down to the bottom of the canal.

He slammed shut the lid of his laptop. What was the matter with him? Why was he playing mind games with her?

He called to her retreating back. 'Being with anyone is a bad idea for you right now...especially someone like me.'

She twisted around. 'Like you?'

'I date women, Emma, but I'm not interested in anything serious. My longest relationship lasted less than six months. I have never even lived with a woman. I'm not interested in the emotions and demands of a relationship.'

Her mouth pursed indignantly. 'Do you *really* think that I want to be in a relationship? After everything I've gone through? I want to be on my own, to be independent, create my own life. I'm not trusting a man again for as long as I live.'

'But you said the other day you wanted a family.'

'Well, I can't have one now, can I?'

The thought of her with another man stuck in his throat like a bite-size canapé, but he forced himself to say, 'Not all men are like your ex. In time you'll meet someone else.'

She threw her eyes heavenwards, as though he was trying her patience. 'I'm not interested.'

Somewhere deep within him longing stirred. His stomach clenched at the way it grabbed his heart. Without thinking he said, 'Give yourself time. I can see you with lots of *bambini*.'

'I really don't think so.' She spoke with a dispassionate tone but her eyes told the truth of her vulnerability.

A vulnerability that was uncomfortably familiar.

He knew he should shut down this conversation. That he was single-handedly pulling them both into dangerous territory. But something inside him needed to know.

Needed to know if it had hurt her as much as it had him to be rejected.

'On that first night you said you have no family. What did you mean?'

She considered him for a moment and then said starkly, 'When I was no longer able to dance my parents made it clear that they no longer wanted me in their lives.'

'Why?'

'Because they blamed me for ruining everything.'

'Ruining what?'

'Their dreams of having a daughter who was a world-famous ballet star. I told them time and time again that that had never been going to happen, even if I hadn't got injured. I was a good ballet dancer, but I was never going to make it onto the world stage… They persisted in thinking otherwise.'

'And just because you couldn't dance they pushed you away?'

She gave a dispassionate shrug. 'Yes, and it's understandable. They spent years supporting me financially. They both worked two jobs to put me through ballet school. They had no life other than ballet—the endless rehearsals and auditions, travelling to see me perform. Supervising me stretching in the evenings. Repairing my kit. They sacrificed everything. And I let them down.'

'It was an accident.'

'I know. But to them it was the end of the world.'

Defiant hazel eyes held his, but her voice and her lips, too tightly marshalled, told another story. One of pain and bewilderment.

And Matteo realised he had never felt so undone.

In the past he had always effortlessly moved women in and out of his life with words full of charm and regret. But for some reason he wanted to help Emma. Even knowing that to do so would be dangerous, that he should be keeping his distance, not becoming desperate to know her better, to wipe away the fear and anxiety that were now flooding her eyes.

'But your parents, the accident, your wedding…none of what went wrong is your fault. You're so matter-of-fact about it all. Aren't you angry?'

'Matteo, you're my boss. Why are we talking about this? What does it matter?'

'Just because I'm your boss doesn't mean that I can't be human.'

She arched an eyebrow at that.

He touched the platinum of his cufflinks. Cleared his throat and said, 'Life has been pretty unfair to you recently.'

'I can cope on my own.'

Her defiant tone had him demanding, 'So is that why you are staying here?'

She didn't answer—just looked away, her mouth twisting unhappily.

'Can you reconnect with your parents? Is that an option?'

She leaned back against the wall beside the door with a tired exhalation. 'No. After my accident I thought that maybe with time they would adjust. Accept what had happened. I'd send cards for their birthdays, for Christmas, but they would just send them back unopened.'

'Why were they so unforgiving? It was an *accident*.'

Her eyes moved upwards to the eighteenth-century frescoed ceiling, a blush the same colour as her lipstick appearing on her cheeks. 'Because I had had a glass of wine the night I fell down the steps at the nightclub I was in. They chose to believe that I was drunk. When I wasn't. They blamed me for going out. For choosing to spend time with my friends rather than focusing exclusively on my ballet.'

How could they have turned her away? Their own flesh and blood.

'They should have put you first—your happiness. That should be every parent's priority. What about your friends? Were they able to help?'

'My friends back then were supportive at first…' Her hand moved up and drifted across her neck, her fingers tapping against her skin. 'But they were all in the ballet world. I drifted away from them eventually. It was too hard for everyone. I could see their guilt when they spoke about ballet in front of me…'

For the first time since she had entered his office she looked at him with total honesty, no artificial mask of hardness.

'And it tore me apart.'

Her sadness filled the room with the stinging effect of invisible tear gas.

His throat stung…his chest felt heavy.

He suddenly wished he had been there for her. Had known her when she was nineteen. Had known her even earlier. Had been able to protect her from life's unfairness.

She closed her eyes for a few seconds, her face tightening into a wince. 'I just wish I'd stood up to my parents, to my ex.'

'What do you mean?'

Instead of answering she glanced uncertainly towards the chair where she had earlier been seated. She edged back towards it and sat. Her eyes fixed on to a point over his shoulder, she said, 'I had a very intense relationship with my parents. I was an only child. There was a lot of expectation. I always wanted to please them. But even when I was selected at a competition or an audition, and I looked out at them in the audience…I knew that on the way home they would only talk about the next audition, how to get

me to the next level. The extra classes they would organise.
The money they were saving to send me to ballet school.'

'That was a lot of pressure for a child.'

'I guess… I loved dancing so much…but it was lonely.
I was never allowed to spend time with my friends. When
the neighbourhood children knocked on the door for me to
come out and play my mother would refuse to let me go.
I thought ballet boarding school would change all that…
and it did eventually—I made some good friends—but for
the first few years I was homesick.'

She tilted forward in her chair and squeezed both knees
with her hands. Tight. Memories were causing a line of
tension to dissect her forehead.

'At some auditions my mum used to be really nasty about
the girls she saw as my rivals. People would overhear—it
was horrible. I tried to get her to stop but she wouldn't… It
was so embarrassing. And unfair. The other girls thought
that I was the same as her; it took a long time before they
realised I wasn't. I never stood up to my parents because I
was frightened that they would take away what I loved so
much. My ballet lessons. The funding for the ballet school.'

She looked down towards her feet. Not looking up, she
gave a shrug while her body tilted ever so slightly forward
and back, propelled by the movement of her feet.

'Being on stage was magical. In the rehearsals, in ballet
class, I would lose myself to the beauty of the movements.
Even when I was injured and struggling, ballet gave me
life. Happiness.' She looked up suddenly, her eyes sparking
with anger. 'But if I had been brave enough to get past my
fear of upsetting my parents—been tougher and pushed
for what I wanted—told them that I didn't want them con-
trolling every aspect of my life—maybe they would have
backed off, become less obsessed. Not have been so dev-
astated when it all came to a crashing end.'

'You can't blame yourself for their reaction to the accident.'

She gave a *you don't understand* sigh. 'It was the same with my ex. Maybe if I'd said no to him, that I wanted a longer engagement… So many people wouldn't be hurt. Now his poor parents have not only his embezzlement to deal with but also the embarrassment of the wedding being called off on the day of the ceremony. They had invited over a hundred of their friends. They're lovely people… His mum was so happy about us marrying. They were both so proud of him.'

'You're not to blame.'

'But what about my behaviour? I didn't rock the boat, say no, stand up to my parents, because I wanted to stay in ballet. I didn't tell my ex that I didn't want a rushed wedding because I wanted a family of my own so badly. I was so damn *passive* in it all. I refused to listen to my own doubts about marrying him. Was I putting my own happiness in front of what was right for my parents? For my ex? Was I complicit in things going so badly wrong? I should have been stronger, tougher.'

CHAPTER FIVE

MATTEO SPRANG FROM his chair, hating to hear her blame herself. 'You had the right to want those things. A career in ballet and…'

Pain shot from his spine down into his glutes.

He lowered his head and gave a low curse.

'And a family.'

His heart began to pound unaccountably and he found it difficult to speak.

'Nobody would blame you for wanting those things.'

He turned away from her cool shrug to look out of the window.

Soft, decadent Botticelli clouds hung over the red-tiled rooftops and the endless church domes and *campaniles* of Venice, pausing at the will of the unpredictable breeze to dance before the sun.

He had long ago accepted he would never have a family of his own. He never wanted to have his heart ripped in two ever again. Why, then, did it sadden and disturb him so much to talk about family with Emma?

'It doesn't matter anyway. It's all in the past.'

He turned around at her words. The clipped, clear tone was not really her voice.

'Now I just want to focus on my future, on being truly independent. I'm tired of being answerable to others. I want a career I can be proud of. And I'm going to fight for it.'

'By fighting me?'

'Not fighting you. Standing up to you. Because I'm good at my job, Matteo. And I want to be a new me. More independent… I want to be hard-headed and resilient.'

'I'm no pushover.'

'Good.' She stood and walked to the door. 'And now that we understand one another, the first thing I'm going to do is show you some Pilates stretches for your back.'

Puzzled, he said, 'My back?'

She cast a critical gaze over him. 'It's obviously hurting you. What caused it?'

'I was sailing last summer, and after I'd winched in a sail in heavy seas it felt a little tighter…it's been bothering me ever since.'

'What has your doctor said about it?'

'Nothing. I haven't had the time to visit him.'

She shook her head, disappointed in him.

He stood a little straighter. He took care of himself physically. He didn't need Pilates. 'Thanks for the offer, but I have business to take care of.'

She threw him a challenging gaze. 'Now, let's not have a stand-off over this. You've said that tonight is important to you. I know how energy-sapping pain is. Let me show you some exercises that might ease yours. Less pain will allow you to enjoy tonight more and concentrate better.'

She didn't wait for his answer, but spoke as she walked towards the door. 'There isn't enough room in here. Follow me upstairs. The floor space in one of the bedrooms will be perfect.'

A little while later, lying on an antique rug in the *sala azzurra*—the blue bedroom—staring up at the Virgin-blue ceiling, Matteo couldn't decide if he had lost his mind or whether it was rather enjoyable to be lying beside Emma. Pretending to listen to her instructions when in truth his concentration was shot to pieces because she kept touching him.

So much for keeping her at arm's length.

'Now that you have your chin, shoulder blades, arms, pelvis and feet correctly positioned, we will start with a basic move: the leg slide.'

Sitting up beside him, while he remained lying on the floor, with his legs bent, she moved her hands once again onto his hips and applied a gentle pressure. He swallowed a groan.

'Remember to keep a neutral pelvis position.'

Dio! Had she *any* idea what it was like to have her so close? To have her fingers touching him?

'Now, on an inhale slide your right leg out until it's fully extended, and on an exhale pull it back into position.'

He did as she said.

She lay down next to him. 'Good—now do the same with the left leg.'

He followed her count for drawing alternate legs in and out. Next he drew alternate arms back to reach behind him, with Emma all the time telling him to focus, to maintain a neutral position. To breathe.

This was a workout his *nonnina* would enjoy.

'Are you sure that these exercises are of use?'

'Absolutely. They're a major part of any dancer's life and I still practise Pilates every day. It strengthens your core and it's vital in recovery from injury. These exercises are hugely beneficial to people with back pain.'

They finished the arm extensions and Emma sat up. 'The exercises will help, but you need to visit your doctor too.'

'I will after this week.'

'You *could* say it with a little more conviction.'

'I'm busy.'

She tucked her feet underneath her bottom, her crossed legs folding easily into a yoga position. She leaned towards him. 'Being stressed is a major cause of back problems.'

'I'm not stressed.'

She folded her arms and gave him a *who are you trying to kid?* look. 'Stress always aggravates my ankle. Why is the China deal so important to you?'

He shuffled on the ground, suddenly uncomfortable lying in such a vulnerable position. 'Can we just focus on the exercises, please…? The photographer will be here soon.'

She studied him for a moment, but then with a shrug said, 'Fine—let's move on to the bridge exercise.'

She instructed him on the movements needed with her hand touching his stomach. The gentle weight burnt through the cotton of his shirt. Her little finger rested on the silver buckle of his belt.

Dio!

'Remember to keep your pelvis neutral. And *breathe*. You're not breathing!'

What did she expect? He was having to lie there pretending that his body *wasn't* a heat-seeking missile about to launch. Having to fight every instinct that was yelling at him to intercept those torturous touches and pull her down on top of him and kiss her for the next fortnight.

Why hadn't he just said that this wasn't working earlier in his office? That having her live here in Ca' Divina was akin to torture? Knowing that she was lying in her bed at night, only a few doors away… A thought that had kept him awake, pacing the terrace into the early hours every night.

He was even more out of control than Ettore's head designer.

Her hand pressed a little more firmly. 'Now, one verte-bra at a time, sink your spine down to the ground.'

He needed to speak. To distract himself.

'I need the Chinese clients to sign because many of our other major markets are contracting due to recessions and political instability.'

She lay down beside him once again and silently indi-cated that he should follow her lead in pulling his left leg in towards his body and then his right leg. She hugged her own legs with a graceful flexibility.

He gazed back up at the ceiling. She would never dance in a ballet again. How incredible it would have been to see her dance.

Without looking, he knew she was staring directly at him. His heart slowed as beautiful dread moved through him.

Why was she getting to him so much? Why did he feel such a thumping connection with her?

His gaze blended with hers. And despite himself he smiled at her. Wanting to reach out.

Rosy-cheeked, she smiled back. That smile touched something inside him every time she punched him with it. And then her gaze whooshed away. As if she had been caught unawares.

The door to the bedroom was slightly ajar. From down-stairs he could hear the quartet rehearsing. The sound of raised voices. But it felt as though they were alone in a co-coon of connectedness. Of understanding. With the early spring sun warming the room.

Her hands were clasped together on her stomach, as if in prayer. Her lips worked for a while before she spoke. 'What might happen if they don't sign?'

Just like that the peace of a few moments ago was shat-tered. His fear for the business fused with his fear about what was happening between them.

'Worst-case scenario: I'll have to shut down some operations. Consolidate. Which will put people out of work.'

'That upsets you?'

He had been about to stand up. He needed to walk out the tension in his body. Move away from the power she exerted over him. But her question, so quietly asked, so full of softly spoken understanding, had him looking back into eyes that practically swallowed him up with empathy.

'I set up my factories in areas with significant unemployment and poverty. People will struggle to find alternative employment. I put years of training into giving them the skills required. They depend on me.'

'You gave them skills—skills they can bring to other employers.'

'Yes, but there *aren't* employers in those areas.'

'But having so many skilled workers might attract new employers into the area. Maybe some of your staff will go on and set up their own companies. Whatever happens, it doesn't have to be the end. There's always another solution.'

Taken aback by her arguments, by the fact that she was challenging him, he considered them for a moment in silence. And quickly dismissed them. She didn't understand his level of responsibility to so many people. Already irritated, he felt a spark of annoyance as a truth he had been ignoring flamed into life when he thought further about her words.

'Am I the solution to *your* current situation?'

She stared at him, her mouth silently opening and closing. 'Are you asking me if I'm using you?'

'*Are* you?' he shot back, vocalising the hurt and frustration coiling in his body.

She looked away and stared up at the ceiling. 'What have I done to make you think that?'

Her voice was low, resigned. The voice of someone

who wasn't surprised by his unfair question. The voice of someone who was used to being disappointed by others.

Guilt tore through him. 'I'm sorry.'

'Do you want me to leave?'

Above him, the Murano glass of the bedroom chandelier swayed slightly as a breeze blew through the ajar door.

He should say yes.

He shouldn't be lying here with her, distracted from his responsibilities.

He shouldn't be feeling so attracted—*Dio*, so innately connected—to a woman who had been so recently hurt.

But all those shouldn'ts failed to cancel out his desire to spend time with her. 'I want you to stay.'

She nodded to this. And then her entire body gave a shudder.

She was shaking off his earlier words.

Shaking *him* off.

He sat up. Needing to put this right.

She looked at him warily.

'I'm cautious about who I let into my life.'

At first she nodded, but then she sat up too. Her head bent, she ran her fingers over the blue and ivory motifs on the rug. 'I can understand why… I would be too, in your position.'

She looked at him with solemn eyes, filing away another piece of information on him. And then a small smile broke on her mouth.

It grew even wider.

She gave a giggle which danced into his heart.

She toppled sideways, reaching out a hand to the rug to steady herself.

Vibrant. Elegant. Fairy-tale pretty.

'Finding me in your bed must have been a huge shock!'

He found himself grinning alongside her. 'It was a most unusual homecoming present.'

She tilted towards him, amusement lighting up her face. 'I've never seen myself as a *present*.'

Her voice was light, playful, teasing.

'A beautiful, distracting present to keep me sane this week.'

Why was he talking to her like this? Why did he have an unstoppable urge to flirt with her? To see her smile and laugh.

'I'm glad I have my uses.'

They sat and smiled at each other.

Foolishly, light-heartedly, soul-enhancingly.

Life buzzed in his veins.

A door closed downstairs.

His fingers tingled with the urge to reach out, to place his hand on her bent knee, to connect physically with her.

To untie the bow at the neck of her blouse…to curl her hair between his fingers.

To kiss her. To have some fun. To know her better.

Her smile slowly faded. And was eclipsed by eyes full of questions and longing.

The same longing that was banging in his chest.

Longing which filled the cavity of space that separated them.

He needed to get them back on solid ground. To establish the nature of their relationship. To stop flirting with her.

'You know, my back *does* feel better. But we need to go downstairs… You should be supervising.'

It took a few seconds for the giddiness in her belly to dissolve and for reality to take its place. He was her boss. She had to protect herself. Stop allowing her physical attraction to him overrule all logic.

He had taken off his jacket when they had come upstairs and draped it on the back of a chair. He had also reluctantly removed his tie and shoes, at her suggestion. He sat before her, his legs bent and crossed, almost matching her lotus position. She was desperately trying not to stare at the powerful strength of his thighs, the captivating narrowness of his hips, the broadness of his chest beneath his white shirt. He dominated the room.

A question was twisting and twisting in her airway, being driven upwards by the unease flapping in her stomach like a hundred butterflies trying to escape.

'Is this going to work?'

The soft espresso warmth of his gaze moved to the coolness of coffee *gelato*.

'It can work if we are both clear that this is a *business* relationship. Two colleagues working together for another few days.'

She wanted to ask what would happen at the end of the week. Would they ever see each other again?

But how on earth was that going to work? A billionaire retail legend and a marketing assistant…a runaway bride.

He studied her, waiting for her to speak.

And the puzzle in her brain as to how they could possibly be just colleagues was constantly jumbled by her glances at him. Thick dark eyebrows were drawn in, there was an evening shadow on his golden jawline, his wide mouth set in neutral…all waiting, waiting, waiting. Waiting for her to speak. But all she could think of was how much she wanted to run her fingertip across that jawline, down his powerful neck, along the topography of his shoulders.

The chemistry between them was about to burn her up. She had never before met a man who literally took her breath away with his looks alone.

Maybe they *could* be colleagues for this week. And in years to come she would look back on the week she'd spent in Venice with this most beautiful man with hopefully fond memories. And her heart intact.

Being his colleague and having the professional friendship that entailed she could just about handle.

Anything more would be devastating.

So it was time she put her 'colleague' mask on and ignored the way her body was screaming out for him like a truculent toddler in the sweet aisle of a supermarket.

'Colleagues need to be honest with one another—do you agree?'

Cautiously he answered, 'It depends…'

She shot him a challenging look. 'I've told you about my parents, my past…things I have never spoken about before.'

His eyes narrowed suspiciously. 'Okay…what's your point?'

'I have a question. When you've accomplished so much, why are you so tough on yourself? I've seen the light on in your office late into the night. You work so hard. Why are you so driven? So worried about the future?'

He rested a hand behind him on the rug and leaned back, considering her question. His silver belt buckle winked up at her. *Remember me? Remember how it felt to touch the hard muscles of this stomach?* No unengaged abdominal muscles there. Just firm muscles layered below hot skin.

Her eyes darted up to where he had undone his top button. Golden skin called to her. She inhaled a deep breath, her insides collapsing into a puddle of desire.

'Because I have people dependent on me—my employees, my family. I have responsibilities that *demand* that I worry, take nothing for granted. Anticipate the worst.'

His words and his serious tone pulled her out of her visual voyage of discovery. Immediately she felt guilty. What type of colleague was she? To be distracted by the superficial when he was telling her something so important?

'That's a whole load of responsibility for one man to carry.'

His eyes held hers and whipped open her soul. Even before he spoke her heart began to thump in anticipation.

'I grew up in poverty. I know how awful it is.'

His tone was bleak. His eyes held hers for a moment, memories haunting him, punching her in the stomach.

He continued, 'I can't be responsible for putting my employees back into a situation where they are struggling on a daily basis to eat, to pay their bills. To see no future for themselves or their children. Having no choices in life. The shame and feelings of worthlessness.'

'You have strong memories of those days…of your childhood?'

'Yes.'

Things were starting to make sense now…his grand-mother's kindness. 'Your grandmother taking me in…she feels responsible too?'

He nodded grimly. 'She's involved with a number of organisations for the homeless.'

Her heart tumbled to see the way he was trying to act detached, his stoic expression, the matter-of-fact way he spoke. When the tight lines at the corner of his eyes told another story.

'Were *you* homeless?'

He studied the rug for a few seconds, his arms folded in front of his chest. His head rose and he stared at her, with his jaw set in *don't pity me* tightness.

'For a few days, yes. My mother, grandmother and I had all moved from Puglia to Milan. We were staying with my mother's then boyfriend. They had a row. He threw us out. We had no money and nowhere to go.'

'How old were you?'

'Fourteen.'

What must it have been like to be a young teenage boy, facing living on the streets?

'Were you scared?'

'We slept for four nights in a doorway in a back alley. It was daunting…but the worst thing was the humiliation. I swore then that I would never allow it to happen again—that I would always protect my family from such embarrassment.'

'That's what drives you? The reason you put such pressure on yourself?'

'Yes.'

'But you need to accept what you have accomplished too, Matteo. Believe that if you did it once you can do it again. What's the point of everything you've achieved if you can get no happiness, no sense of reward from it?'

'That isn't of importance.'

'That you are happy? Satisfied? Why not?'

'If I'm satisfied I'll stop being so driven. And that's dangerous.'

'But you need both—to have drive and also to be happy.'

He shook his head vehemently, not prepared even to consider her arguments. 'I can't be complacent. Not in this industry.'

'Of course—I accept that. But maybe you need to accept what you've achieved—and most importantly believe that you *will* deal with whatever the future brings. Don't let the fear of poverty, of homelessness control you. They are only fears, thoughts… They're not a reality now. You've proved yourself, Matteo. By everything you have achieved. You need to believe that you can do the same again if necessary.'

His eyes narrowed, their coffee *gelato* now frozen rock-hard. 'Do *you* believe in yourself?'

She hated the way he had turned this back on her. But

maybe, if she was honest with him, he might see that there was some merit in what she was saying.

'Probably not enough.'

She paused and realised that the burden of guilt she had been carrying around—about her parents, her accident, her wedding—felt a little lighter now that she had spoken about them and Matteo's insistence that she wasn't to blame.

'But you know what? Each time I've been knocked down I've come back… When my career in ballet was snapped away from me… My wedding. Other paths have opened up to me.'

He looked so burdened by the responsibilities he was carrying, she wanted to ease his tension, to see him smile again.

So with a cheeky grin she added, 'I even got to meet *you*—which has to be some consolation.'

The hard lines of his face dissolved into a charismatic smile—shining eyes and gorgeous white teeth. 'Whoa! Careful or I might get a big head.'

Trying not to swoon, she tried to adopt a cool-girl pose of easy nonchalance. 'Of all the men I have met, you are the one person who deserves to have a massive ego. But you don't.'

His head dipped. Was it her imagination or did his cheeks colour ever so slightly? Crikey, this guy *really* knew how to get to a girl.

When he looked back up he cleared his throat, his expression telling her little of what he was thinking.

'I take nothing for granted.'

'Which is good…but maybe you should start enjoying what you have—even a little bit.'

He leaned towards her and those brown eyes were alight with mischief. 'I'm lying here on the floor with you when I have an important reception to host in less than two hours. Is that a good enough start for you?'

That expression about cutting off a limb in order to get something… Well, right now she understood it perfectly. Because every atom in her body was crying out to lean in towards him, to touch the smooth golden skin of his cheek, to touch her lips to his.

The friendship of a colleague.

She had to remember that was all she could—should— hope for.

With a man who set her alight with a single look.

A man who through his power, strength and empathy made her feel like a real-life Odette from *Swan Lake*.

CHAPTER SIX

EMMA STABBED THE 'send' button on her text message, clasped her phone tight in her fist and went and stood by her open bedroom door. She peeked down the frescoed corridor. It was empty. She stepped back into her room, quickly patting the loose curls of her pinned up hair, testing its stability.

Please, please let him read my message. And soon.

The first guests were due to arrive any moment now. She dashed across the room to the windows overlooking the Grand Canal.

A powerful motor boat was already approaching Ca' Divina's landing stage. The lights of other intimidatingly expensive boats were following in its wake.

She stepped a little closer to the window, the better to peer through the ripples of the antique glass. The scene below was illuminated by the discreet low lights on the landing stage. And just then the person waiting to disembark looked up at her.

Sebastian King! The world-famous composer.

She had seen his name on the guest list. But seeing him in reality was a whole different matter.

And now he was staring up at her, clearly amused.

She leapt away from the window. Her pounding heart was sending flames of heat onto her cheeks.

'Guests are already arriving. Why aren't you ready?'

She spun around, her heart slipping into a wild allegro beat.

Dressed in a dark midnight-blue suit, a light blue shirt and a navy and silver tie, Matteo did a pretty good job of filling the extrawide doorway.

She swung away from him and reached behind her to point a finger at the cause of her delay. 'I can't fasten the back of my dress. That's why I texted you. I need your help.'

She turned back in time to see his mouth tighten as he moved towards her and then she looked away. Back out to the lights shining from the delicately carved windows of the Gothic *palazzo* across the canal.

His scent wrapped around her. Musk with a hint of vanilla.

She dragged in a deep breath against the quiver in her belly.

He worked in silence, his fingers tracing against the top of her spine. She held herself rigid, determined not to let the threatening shivers escape. But as his fingers moved across her bare skin she instinctively arched her back. Feeling totally exposed.

Her full-length gown had a wide cut-out section at the back, all the way down to her waist, exposing most of her spine. A gold chain was sewn into one border of the barely there side panels, and she needed Matteo to secure it to the gold clasp sewn onto the other side panel. With the gold chain unsecured she was in danger of the whole dress slipping off. Which, considering she was unable to wear a bra with this dress, was definitely not a good idea. Especially with a papal representative attending tonight.

'I expected you downstairs ten minutes ago.'

His voice, a sensual caress even when he was admonishing her, was so suggestive of carnal pleasures it left her rubber-boned.

She swallowed against the shimmers of desire skipping along her skin.

'The mixologist didn't arrive. I had to organise a replacement.'

Those strong hands twisted her around. A flicker of amusement sent golden sparkles radiating through his brown eyes.

'I like a martini with lemon peel.' Then the amusement in his eyes died and he inhaled a deep breath that spoke of hidden unease beneath his cool exterior. '*Andiamo*. Let's go.'

'I have to do my make-up.'

'You don't have time.'

He had to be kidding!

'I can't meet your guests with no make-up on.'

'Yes, you can.' His eyes travelled over her face, quietly devouring her. '*Sei bellissima*. You look beautiful.'

There was a low, seductive note to his voice and she suddenly felt light-headed.

'You don't need make-up. Your skin is perfect.'

His hand moved to take her elbow, and although her bones now felt like melting rubber she jumped out of his way and wobbled over to the dressing table. There she grabbed her favourite scarlet lipstick and quickly applied it, a swirling vortex of panic and desire spinning inside her as she tried to ignore Matteo's dark and dangerous reflection in the mirror glass.

She twisted back and ran to the stairs.

On the first step Matteo joined her and held his hand to her elbow, steadying her progress as she tottered down on much too high gold sandals that she would never have dared buy herself.

He pulled her to a stop halfway down and pointed at her feet unhappily. 'Those sandals are much too high for you. I asked for them to be delivered before I knew about your ankle.'

She took her arm from his continuing grip and placed her hand on his elbow instead. With a little push she urged him forward. 'They're fine, honestly. Let's go.'

She couldn't let him see how nervous she was about co-hosting the reception with him. How, now that it was an imminent reality, her self-confidence had fallen through the floor. She was a runaway bride, duped by her ex, rejected by her parents. A failed ballerina. How on earth was she supposed to entertain some of the world's highest achievers? She was about to let Matteo down. Let herself down.

They made it to the *portego* just as Sebastian King climbed the final steps of the stairs leading up from the landing stage.

Matteo and he embraced, with a lot of clapping each other on the back.

'Sebastian, let me introduce you to Emma Fox.'

Sebastian King was a big bear of a man, with a ruddy complexion, an easy smile and a tight crew cut that left only a light covering of grey stubble on his head. He took her hand, and then yanked her in for a hug.

'Was it you I saw staring out at me from the window?'

She gave him a non-committal smile and dared a quick look in Matteo's direction. He gave her a *what were you doing?* frown.

Time to move the conversation on.

'I'm so excited to meet you. I saw you perform at The Lowry in Salford with my school. I was only twelve but I have such wonderful memories. I'm a huge fan.'

Sebastian gave a loud chuckle. 'Delighted to hear it, my dear. Been to see any of my recent work?'

She could feel herself pale. 'I'm afraid not. But I hope to.'

It was Sebastian's turn to look unimpressed. He twisted

away. 'What direction is the bar?' His tone said that he needed a drink. *Now.* And some decent company.

She was about to apologise to Matteo for her less than auspicious start, but pulled back her words. Apologising would only add to her humiliation and her sense of not belonging here. Of being out of her depth. So instead she smiled warmly at a group of glittering guests coming towards them, her insides filling with dread.

She had nothing in common with any of these people. What was she going to say to them all? And what if something went wrong with the reception? Would she cope? Would Matteo forgive her?

The next half an hour passed in a whirl. She shook hands and smiled. Nodded as Matteo spoke to his guests, more often than not in rapid Italian, only understanding the occasional word. So much for the *Beginners' Italian* podcast she had listened to religiously every morning on the way to work, daydreaming of effortlessly ordering a *bellini* in Harry's Bar.

It had been arranged that the Chinese delegation would be the last guests to arrive—a silent signal of their importance and status. But as they began to ascend the stairs, stopping to point and gaze at the frescos and gilt-adorned walls and high ceilings, Matteo lowered his head and said in a low, urgent voice, 'Sadie and Johnny haven't arrived yet. I need to call her. Take the delegation through to the ballroom once I have greeted them. Introduce them to the other guests.'

Her stomach thumped to the floor. And her heart followed soon after. Apart from the famous faces, she wouldn't remember who was who.

She leaned closer to him, panic pumping through her body. Totally out of her depth. '*I'll* call Sadie. You go with Mr Xue and the rest of the delegation.'

He pulled back and gave her a curious look. 'But I have

her private number—you don't. Is everything okay? You seem—'

She jumped in, not wanting to hear any more. She needed to pretend she was fine. She had asked for this job. She owed it to Matteo to deliver. 'Everything's fine. I just thought you would prefer to accompany Mr Xue into the ballroom, but I would be delighted to.'

He threw her another curious look. He obviously wasn't buying her breezy tone.

She led the delegation away and entered the ballroom with her heart doing a Viennese waltz. Her mind went blank when she was confronted by a sea of faces.

What did the President of the Region of Veneto and his wife look like again?

She needed to think. Get her act together. She was the one who'd promised Matteo that she was more than able for this role.

She called the translator to her side. 'Elena, I would like to introduce the group to the President of Veneto. Can you direct us towards him? And then will you please stay and translate? I will bring other guests over and introduce them to the delegation.'

For the next ten minutes she moved through the room with a coolness she definitely wasn't feeling, approaching other guests and inviting them to meet with the Chinese delegation. Each time she brought them forward she prayed she had got their names and titles right.

After what felt like several lifetimes of tight, terrified smiles and introductions, Emma gave a massive sigh of relief when she turned to find Matteo entering the room with Sadie Banks and Johnny North at his side. A shiver of recognition and excitement ran through the room.

Johnny North—her teenage crush.

Even more handsome and laid-back sexy in real life. Taller than she'd thought.

She stared at him, and second by second felt her teen-age dreams fizzle away.

She gave a huff of disbelief.

Just like that her teenage crush had disappeared in a puff of smoke.

All thanks to Matteo.

He was her secret crush now.

A crush who was staring at her with a dark scowl.

She tried to wipe the starstruck expression off her face and gave him a quick, professional *I have everything under control* smile.

His shoulder twitched, but he turned away to speak to Sadie and then Johnny. Together they moved through the room. They spoke to the other guests with smiles and laughs as they walked but did not stop until they'd reached the Chinese delegation.

No longer needed, Emma slipped away to check on the rest of the *palazzo*. Glad to escape. Glad to be busy and to put a lid on how vulnerable she felt tonight.

First she checked in with the head of security. Then, in the lounge, she paused to watch the replacement mixologist tossing bottles of spirits and assorted fruit in the air, egged on by the crowd surrounding him, who were dancing to the beat of the music being played by the DJ in the corner.

Waiters were discreetly mingling amongst the guests with trays of Prosecco and the exquisite canapés she had tasted with the chef earlier, when she had given her approval for them to be served. Langoustine tails, gnocchi *fritti*, parmesan and poppyseed lollipops.

A magician dressed in eighteenth-century costume passed through the crowd performing tricks, adding to the carnival atmosphere.

Coming out from the lounge into the *portego*, she gave a brief smile to Matteo. He and Mr Xue were having their photo taken with Sadie and Johnny in front of a fresco showing Odysseus's ship in turbulent waters.

She walked away, but her spine tingled with the uncomfortable certainty that a set of unhappy, much too observant brown eyes were boring into her back.

She worked her way through the ballroom, checking that everything was going to plan. The string quartet were playing beautifully, at the perfect volume, the lighting was subtle, and the guests all had food and drink at hand.

Heading in the direction of the kitchen, to check in with the chef, she gave a small yelp when Matteo came up beside her and with a hand to her bare back silently guided her in the direction of his office.

Inside, he did not turn on the light.

He stepped close to her. 'Is everything okay?'

In the dark room he seemed even bigger than usual, his body acting like a magnet, drawing her in towards him against her will. She longed to place her hand on his waist, beneath his open jacket, against the cotton of his shirt, to feel the reassurance of his strength, of the tight muscles she had felt earlier when showing him the Pilates stretches.

She stepped away from him towards the faint outline of his desk. 'Yes, of course.'

'I want you to circulate amongst the guests and try to look like you are *enjoying* yourself.' He said the second half of the sentence in a tone of mild exasperation.

'I need to check that everything is running smoothly.'

'Yes, but as my co-host you need to relax… *Dio*, Emma, I don't want to have to worry about you tonight.'

Embarrassed heat licked against her skin. She gave silent praise that they were standing in the near dark. Her throat thick with disappointment that she was failing, she asked, in a much too high-pitched voice, 'What do you mean, worry about me?'

'You should be having fun—not looking as though this is hard work.'

'But it *is* work. I want to do it properly.' On the cusp of blurting out how overwhelmed she felt, she drew back from it and said in a self-mocking tone, 'I just don't know what to chat to the guests about… I can hardly speak to a Nobel Laureate about the weather, can I?'

'No, but you can enquire if he's enjoying Venice. Introduce him to some other guests. I need you to host alongside me.'

He spoke in a gentle voice, as if he was willing her to relax. To enjoy the night. He should be cross with her—angry, even. He didn't have the time to be taking her aside and encouraging her like a naïve intern.

Tears welled at the back of her eyes.

She swallowed hard. Pushed them away.

'Okay, I'll relax… It's just that I don't want to let you down tonight. I know how important this reception is to you.'

He stepped closer. He held her gaze.

'You're not letting me down.'

His voice was low, deep, sincere. Her heart did a *grand jeté* across her chest.

She opened her mouth to speak but no words came.

His hand moved up as though to touch her, but then dropped back to his side. 'I have to go.'

She nodded and he turned and left the room.

For a few minutes she leaned against the office wall, trying to compose herself.

Inhaling deep breaths.

Cracking her knuckles. That was something she hadn't done since she was a teenager. Hadn't done since the ballet master had rapped her on them for doing so.

Despite every logical warning her brain was yelling down to her heart, she had to face up to a certain fact: she was falling for Matteo. Physically…and perhaps emotionally. A psychologist would have a field day with her. No doubt the words 'rebound' and 'poor decision-making' would feature. These feelings were pointless. She did not *want* another relationship. Not that she supposed Matteo had any interest in her anyway, beyond physical attraction.

Her conversation with him earlier in the day came back to her…his insistence that she wasn't to blame for her past…his belief in her.

She pushed away from the wall. She had to stop her negative thoughts. Stop feeling so self-conscious and unsure. She was here to do a job.

She walked into the ballroom, full of great intentions. And straight into Johnny North. He gave her the smile that had stared back at her from her bedside locker throughout her boarding school years. That *come and rebel with me* smile. That had been her teenage desire. To rebel against the restrictions of boarding school, her parents' expectations.

A rush of excitement fizzed through her. It wasn't too late. She could still rebel, walk away from all her insecurities. Be tough and carefree. Forget the past and move with confidence into the future.

She held out her hand to him. 'Emma Fox.'

He shook her hand and asked in his American drawl, 'So, what brings you to Venice, Emma Fox?'

'I'm on the run.'

He gave her a grin of approval. 'You're my type of girl.'

Matteo tried to pay attention to the conversation between Mr Xue and Sebastian King about a concert Sebastian had conducted at the Beijing National Centre for the Performing Arts last year. But his attention was continually diverted across the room, to where Johnny North was holding court with a rapt audience of one. Emma. Pink-cheeked and dazzlingly radiant. Her porcelain skin glowing against the poppy-red colour of her dress.

Porcelain skin that was so soft it had sent juggernauts of lust powering through him earlier, when he had touched her bare back whilst fastening her dress.

He had longed to touch his lips against that skin…from the top of her long, elegant ballerina neck all the way down her spine.

Stopping to inhale her delicate rose scent.

Despite the saga of Sadie being late and needing to focus on the final subtle negotiations with Mr Xue, he had been seconds away from pulling her into his arms and kissing her soft mouth in the darkness and the seductive silence of his office.

Irritation twisted in his chest and he clenched his teeth. Okay, so she was mingling with the guests now, as he had asked, instead of dashing about the *palazzo*, clearly uncomfortable. But did she *have* to pick the most handsome guy in the room to chat to? And did she *have* to look so enthralled with him? And why wasn't she moving on? Talking to other guests? Talking to *him* instead of Johnny North.

He excused himself from his present company and made his way over to Emma and Johnny. Johnny had one shoulder touching against the frescoed wall of the ballroom. Matteo gave him a lethal stare and without batting an eyelid Johnny moved away from the wall. Matteo stood next to Emma and placed a hand on her lower back. Sometimes men didn't need any words.

Nearby, Sadie left the company of a group of national politicians, cross-party differences forgotten in their collective star-struck veneration as Sadie flashed them her trademark traffic-stopping smile, and swept towards them to plant a kiss on Johnny's cheek. He pulled her tighter towards him and whispered something into her ear. Sadie giggled and gave him a playful push.

As one they looked up, love and happiness radiating from their every pore.

Beside him, Emma tensed.

Sadie moved forward and extended her hand. 'Hi, I'm Sadie… Sadie North.' She laughed and gestured helplessly. 'I'm still getting used to saying my married name.'

Emma smiled, but lines of tension pulled at the corners of her eyes.

'Are you from Venice, Emma, or are you visiting too?'

'She's running away, apparently,' Johnny said, with a wink in Emma's direction.

Sadie clapped her hands in delight. 'Really? How exciting! I couldn't think of anywhere more awesome to run to. Right? Isn't Venice seriously incredible? Gosh, so many times in the past I was tempted to run away. Especially from some of the directors I have had to work with! Not to mention some of the disastrous relationships I've had.'

Sadie paused and, looking in Matteo's direction, gave a light laugh.

'Not counting *you*, Matteo, you were one of the good ones.'

Beside him he could feel Emma stiffen even more. Sadie had no filter. Maybe that was what made her such an acclaimed actor. She was open and candid and most of the time she got away with it, because people found her directness and fun personality refreshing. But tonight, on the high of new love, she was oblivious to the signals Emma was giving that this conversation was making her uncomfortable.

But perhaps it was just he who could read Emma? Maybe others wouldn't see the subtle signals. It was a thought way too disturbing to spend time pondering on.

Sadie's hand moved onto Johnny's chest. 'But now I no longer want to run.'

The honeymooning couple shared an intense and private look.

Emma flinched.

His stomach dipped with sharp regret.

For Emma. For himself.

What Sadie and Johnny shared they would never have.

Sadie twisted back to them, her eyes shining with the wonder only those newly in love and small children could conjure. 'Isn't Venice so cool? The buildings, the food, the canals, the Carnival…it's all so beautiful. It's just perfect for a honeymoon.' She turned to Johnny, who was looking down at her with fond amusement. 'I want to come back here for each of our anniversaries.'

Emma's body gave up a hard tremor that vibrated against his hand. She was staring at Sadie and Johnny with a haunted expression. Shame and guilt ripped through him.

He needed to get her away from here. He should have anticipated this.

But before he could speak Sadie said, 'Matteo, you never told me about Emma. How long have you been together?'

He forced himself to give a casual shrug. 'We're just colleagues.'

'Ah. That's a shame. You're cute together.'

He gave a tight smile. 'We had better circulate.'

Then, to his horror, he realised that there were tears in Emma's eyes.

He was about to suggest that they step out onto the terrace for a moment when Elena the interpreter approached.

'I'm sorry to interrupt, Signor Vieri, but Mr Xue has asked to meet with you in private.'

It could only mean one thing. Mr Xue was ready to sign the contracts. His instinct that the deal would be finalised on the news that Sadie and Johnny would open the collection had been right.

He should get those contracts signed now. He had copies ready and waiting in his office.

But what about Emma? Could he leave her in this vulnerable state?

Should he talk to her, reassure her, and let Mr Xue wait? It should be no contest.

His business, or this woman he had only known for a matter of days.

He leaned down towards Emma and said, 'I'll be back in a little while.'

He gave a swift nod to Sadie and Johnny before walking towards Mr Xue, Elena following.

Alone with Sadie and Johnny, Emma looked at the honeymooning couple, who were now playfully teasing each other, oblivious to her. Oblivious to the entire room.

For the first time since the police had knocked at her door in the middle of the night she felt her heart shatter. The shock and disbelief were finally giving way to the reality of everything she had lost. All those fantasies she'd had of a beautiful wedding day. A romantic honeymoon. Of finding her own family.

Her heart shattered because she and her ex had never had the love, the fun, the chemistry that was between Sadie and Johnny.

Her heart shattered out of happiness for the couple before her. Touched by the magic playing between them. Touched by the glow lighting up their eyes. Touched by the heartbreaking happiness pulsating from them both.

Her heart shattered because Matteo hadn't realised just how hard it was for her to witness a couple on honeymoon, to hear Sadie talk so exuberantly about her time in Venice.

Or maybe he had realised and had still opted to go and speak to Mr Xue.

And who could blame him with so much at stake?

He'd made the right decision.

But that didn't stop the hurt. Didn't stop the loneliness creeping along her veins. The reality that she was alone in this world. The horrible hollowness in her soul.

We're just colleagues.

His words to Sadie gathered around her shattered heart like barbed wire.

She shouldn't want anything else but the friendship of a colleague. But the chemistry between them was so intense, so personal, it was hard to keep it at bay.

And now everything was mixed up. People thought she was here as Matteo's partner. Nobody had realised she was the event co-ordinator. Had she compromised her professional standing?

She distractedly said goodbye in Sadie and Johnny's direction, but they were so taken up in each other she wasn't sure if they even noticed her walk away.

She moved about the *palazzo*, trying to focus on managing the reception. She forced herself to stop and talk briefly to some of the guests, but she felt too vulnerable. Too confused.

Was her attraction to Matteo just a way of not facing the pain of her wedding imploding? A distraction from guilt and sadness and her fears for the future? Was she hoping he'd save her instead of saving herself?

Back inside the ballroom, the quartet had been replaced by a jazz band with a soulful lead singer who reminded Emma of Ella Fitzgerald. Couples were out on the dance floor, dancing to a slow number.

'*Vuoi ballare?* Do you want to dance?'

She arched her neck away, a long shiver of awareness darting down her spine at Matteo's question, breathed against her ear from behind…a slow, sensual caress on her exposed neck.

He didn't wait for her to answer. Instead he took her hand and led her out onto the dance floor.

He held her close to him and they moved to the slow rhythm of the music.

She tried to resist him, her body rigid as she stared at the fine navy wool of his jacket.

He pulled her closer, whispered in a teasing, sexy tone, 'Relax, I don't bite…unless provoked.'

Immediately she felt undone.

His hand resting on her hip sent waves of desire to the centre of her body. She yearned for his thumb to stroke the delicate skin around her hip bone.

Standing so close to him, surrounded by his raw potency, one hand resting on his broad shoulder, her other hand lost in his grasp, she felt her heart double over, craving intimacy and closeness with him.

She stared at the broad silver and navy diagonal lines of his tie. Wanting to move even closer to him. Knowing she should move away. Protect herself. Be nothing more than his employee. Be a strong and independent woman who thought of nothing but her career. Who didn't fall for false fantasies.

She dared a quick glance up into those golden-brown eyes which stared back at her with open concern.

That concern could either undo her or reinforce her resolve to be distant from him. She chose the latter. 'I thought you had a meeting with Mr Xue?'

'I've organised for us to meet tomorrow morning instead.'

Confused, she asked, 'I assumed he wanted to meet about signing the contracts—are they still holding out?'

'No, just now Mr Xue confirmed that he wants to sign. There are some small outstanding issues that still need to be resolved, but they won't be a problem. I decided that we should wait until tomorrow to address those.'

Why hadn't he wanted to sign tonight? She knew how important those contracts were to him. A horrible thought occurred to her.

'Were you worried about leaving the party…? If you'd had another co-host would you have taken the time to sign the contracts tonight?'

He held her gaze, his expression sombre. 'I should have realised meeting Sadie and Johnny would be difficult for you.'

'No… Yes… But that was no reason to put off the signing.'

'It can wait.'

'But why, when it's so important to you?'

His mouth thinned. 'You're an employee and I put you in a difficult situation. I take the welfare of all my employees seriously. I could see that you needed my support.'

This wasn't what she wanted. She didn't want to need him. Or anyone else. She wanted, *needed* to stand on her own two feet. To be independent.

'I can manage by myself. I don't need you.'

Those brown eyes held hers with an assured certainty. His mouth was a serious line.

'Yes, you do.'

CHAPTER SEVEN

STANDING BESIDE MATTEO on Ca' Divina's landing stage, Emma waved goodbye to the last of the guests before curling her arms tight against her waist. Warming herself. Fending off the pinpricks of awareness that she was alone once again with Matteo. Not quite certain how she felt about that.

It was gone one in the morning. Most of the other guests had left two hours ago. But the remaining group—associates of Matteo—had stayed and chatted around the outside terrace table, wrapped up in coats and blankets, warmed by outside heaters and *grappa*, snug against the cold February air, while the staff had tidied up inside.

Matteo had insisted that everyone speak in English, so that Emma was included in the conversation. He had kept her by his side all evening, his hand resting on her back, guiding her as they moved amongst the guests. It was a hand that was way too comforting. A hand that had at times fooled her into feeling that she had found someone who would care for her; protect her—before her brain kicked in and told her that she was a fool.

It was all nothing more than a rebound fantasy. She was projecting onto Matteo her need for security. Her fears for the future. All the uncertainties facing her. Where would she live? How long before she got a job? Before her meagre savings ran out?

And that wasn't fair on him. Or herself.

He was her boss—a colleague.

Nothing else.

He didn't want a relationship.

The lights and the noise of the engine on the launch taking the guests away faded across the water. The only sound that remained was the lap of water against the walls of the *palazzo* and the landing stage.

'I'm sorry about Sadie; I should have realised that meeting someone on honeymoon would be upsetting for you.'

He spoke slowly, as though needing her to understand the sincerity of his words.

She bunched her hands in the pockets of her wool coat, felt the soft material grating against the tension in her fists. She needed to keep this conversation professional. Keep her guard up against his employer's concern. Against how physically aware she was of him.

'I didn't need you to cancel the meeting with Mr Xue.'

He pointed towards the *palazzo*, gesturing for them to head back inside. 'You were upset. I couldn't leave you... especially when I could have prevented it.'

The red carpet, hastily organised via a business contact of the caterers, still remained on the wooden landing stage, soaking up the sound of their footsteps.

'But why delay signing the contract?'

Matteo held open one of the heavy wood-panelled double front doors for her, and then busied himself shutting and securing it once they were both inside. When finished he turned and regarded her with a look she couldn't quite decipher.

The hired staff had left prior to the departure of the last of the guests. Matteo now locking the two of them into the *palazzo*, all alone, suddenly felt very intimate. Very personal.

He took off his coat, dipping his head down. When he

looked up his jaw worked for a few seconds, as if he were fighting something inside himself.

'You said today that I need to believe I can deal with whatever life throws at me. You're right.'

He paused for a short breath, but then continued on at a fast pace. Sounding as though he needed to say all this now or never.

'I need to stop worrying about the future; it's too draining. For as long as I can remember I've felt a huge burden of responsibility. It's still there, but I need to get things into perspective and know what my priorities should be.'

'You didn't need to delay the meeting because of me… or insist I stay with you all night. I'm an employee… I don't expect any of that from you.'

Her voice echoed off the high ceilings of the entrance hall. Sharp and petulant.

He walked to the stairs and waited on the bottom step for her to follow. A new tension pulled on his mouth. When she'd joined him he pointed down at her sandals.

'Take them off.'

Taken aback, she stared down at her feet blankly. And then, not quite knowing why, she set her mouth into a fierce scowl. 'No.'

He glared at her, his eyes dark with anger…and passion.

A current of desire whooshed through the air.

He flung his coat onto the balustrade. It slid for a second before coming to a stop beside one of the carved figures of a young woman holding a light aloft that topped both of the stairs' newel posts.

He placed his hands on his hips.

She gave him a *don't you dare* stare.

Which only seemed to embolden him.

In one quick movement he was beside her. Then he was walking up the stairs with her in his arms.

She wanted to demand to know what he thought he was

playing at. But she wouldn't give him the satisfaction of showing she cared enough to ask.

Crushed against the hard heat of his chest, the muscles of his forearm tense beneath her back, she felt long fingers clasp around her outer thigh. She refused to look up at him. Flames of desire burned in her belly.

He dropped her at the top of the stairs and gave her a stare of utter exasperation. 'I could see that you needed support tonight. Why are you blaming me for wanting to be there for you?'

Her confusion boiled and simmered inside her, along with frustration. Because she damn well wanted him to kiss her right now. To feel his body pushed against hers.

'You're my boss!'

He threw his hands upwards at her shouted words, but something in his eyes—a tiny hesitation before he spoke— told her that he too had his doubts about what was happening between them.

'So? Can't a boss care?'

No. Not when there's fire between you.

She rubbed her hand against the tightness in her temple 'It's all getting too confusing.'

He didn't speak, and in the unsettling silence she pretended a sudden fascination with Odysseus's ship on the wall behind his shoulder.

'I'm fond of you, Emma. I want to help.'

His low-spoken words curled around her. Like a tight fist around her heart.

She wanted to tell him that she was afraid. Afraid of falling for him. Afraid of how intensely she liked him already. Afraid of how attracted she was to him.

With a helpless questioning show of her palms, she gave him a truth she could hide behind. 'Why help…when I'm more of a burden to you than anything else?'

'No.'

He moved closer. His eyes dared her to look away, to deny what he was saying.

'I like spending time with you. I like how you stand up to me. Your sense of humour. Your enthusiasm.'

She couldn't listen to this. She had to ignore his words and how badly her heart wanted to believe him.

She shook her head and gave him a teasing frown. Pretended that it was all rather amusing. 'Really? I spend more time in tears than anything else.'

'You found out on your wedding day that the man you were about to marry was corrupt—of *course* you're in tears.'

Hearing his blunt words killed the pretence. And in the face of his soft, searching eyes which refused to look away, the truth bubbled out of her.

'I don't know what I want any longer.'

Embarrassed by her admission, she moved away and walked over to the window overlooking the canal on the opposite side of the room.

So much for being tough.

How did Matteo manage to get to her every time they spoke?

How did he manage to cut through every pretence?

Why did she feel protected yet in deep danger whenever she was with him?

When Matteo eventually joined her they both stared out of the floor-to-ceiling picture window to the lights of Venice. In a low, matter-of-fact voice, he said, 'I have to leave on Sunday for New York Fashion Week. We have two more days together.'

His eyes swept over her face, waiting for a response. She looked at him blankly, feeling numb at his words. Two days. That was all.

His chest rose heavily as he inhaled a deep breath. 'Mr Xue and his team are travelling to Verona tomorrow after our early-morning meeting. I would like to spend the rest of the day with you—show you Venice.' His mouth curled downwards and he shrugged. 'But it's up to you.'

She needed to understand why he was being so kind to her. What did he want? What could she possibly give him?

'Why are you doing this?'

His eyes narrowed, impatience flaring. 'Why did you spend time showing me those Pilates moves today?'

She didn't have to think about her answer.

'Because I wanted to help you.'

But she stopped herself before she could add, *And I wanted to spend time with you, connect with you. Touch you.*

A reluctant smile grew on his mouth. But his eyes stayed startlingly sober. 'Just as I want to help *you.*'

She closed her eyes for a moment. What was she going to do?

She was still unsure when she opened them again. But seeing him silhouetted against the backdrop of Venice, his face set hard with pride, his eyes burning bright with the strength of his commanding but compassionate personality, she knew he would only ask once. If she said no, the next two days would be nothing more than a business formality.

'I would like to see Venice with you.'

She had tried to speak in a dispassionate voice, but it came out in a rushed whisper.

He nodded, not giving any other reaction, and she spun away, gabbling, 'I'll see you in the morning...'

She was almost at the stairs when he called out, 'You'll need help undoing your dress.'

Her heart and stomach collided midway in her body, and then sickeningly ricocheted back to where they belonged.

She rolled her shoulders before walking towards him,

telling herself just to get it over and done with. He was a colleague. Undoing her dress. Nothing more.

She slipped off her coat and turned her back to him.

His hand touched against her skin.

She jerked away.

Desire—strong, excruciating, wonderful—streamed through her, pooling in her core. Exquisite pressure.

He made no comment, but stepped closer.

His fingertips grazed her skin again. She dipped her head against the fresh wave of need which engulfed her, leaving her afraid to breathe.

The unclasped chain fell downwards, its heavy cool weight swinging like a pendulum against her bare skin.

She should move away. But she stood there and wrapped her hands around her waist. Vulnerable. Exposed. Electrified.

His hand touched the top of her spine. And then, inch by inch, ran down her back to her waist. A definite, deliberate movement. The movement of a man wanting to possess.

Her body gave another intense shiver.

His lips briefly skimmed the top of her shoulder blade.

For a moment she stood there, hoping he would go further. But then she understood. There would be nothing more. Tonight.

She walked away from him, each step an effort. Walked away from the one place where she belonged.

The following morning Matteo left the Hotel Cipriani with a burning sense of having been robbed.

The Chinese deal had been signed.

He felt relieved. But nothing else.

None of the sense of accomplishment that usually came with such a major deal. None of the pleasure that he'd taken yet another step up on the ladder of life, away from the lower rungs that led to the crypts of poverty.

He should be happier.

He manoeuvred his boat around the busy traffic on the Grand Canal, irritation and tiredness destroying any hope of him revelling in his success in the beauty of the Old Lady of the Lagoon on a blue-sky spring morning.

He had woken early, doubts whispering in his ear.

What had he done? Why the hell hadn't he signed the deal last night, when Mr Xue had been ready to do so? What if Mr Xue had changed his mind overnight? Just what had he sacrificed for a woman he'd only known for a handful of days?

Last night at the reception it had felt so right to want to be with her. To want to protect her. To actually *do* something about her resonating words earlier, telling him that he must believe, trust that he could handle whatever life threw at him. That he couldn't allow his fear of poverty, of failing others, to control him.

But in the darkness none of that had seemed so obvious, so right.

He couldn't go back to Ca' Divina yet. Even though he wanted to see her. Wanted to hear her voice. Wanted the calm that formed in his stomach every time he was with her.

The unfathomable sense of belonging that settled on his heart when he was with her.

He needed to clear his head.

At Ca' Foscari he swung the boat towards Campo Santa Margherita in the *sestiere* of Dorsoduro.

As ever, the picturesque square was a serene refuge. Locals were enjoying an early coffee at the cafés lining the square, buying bread at the bakery reputed to be the best in Venice, others were buying fish and vegetables at the market stalls.

Usually he would order an espresso at the bar and drink

it quickly. Always pressed for time. Today he sat out at one of the pavement tables with his espresso.

Dog walkers, grandparents holding the hands of unsteady toddlers, students from the local university—all ambled through the square. Happy to enjoy the start of another Carnival day.

When had he last sat and watched others go by?

Had he ever?

Emma.

She was changing everything.

With her he felt a connection, a bond that was familiar, comforting, yet exhilarating. A physical attraction that was tearing him apart. But there was also her intelligence, her sense of fun. Her vulnerability.

Her pride, her resilience, her strength.

She had lost her career, her family, and had battled to rebuild her life. And now she was determined to rebuild it once again, in the face of yet another abysmal setback.

Yesterday, when she had shown him the Pilates moves, she had done so with such serious intent that he'd known it was important to her to see him better. She cared for him. He could see it in her eyes. In the way her body rocked towards him.

He drained his cup and stared up at the fifteenth-century carving set high up in the building. Santa Margherita and the dragon who had tried to consume her.

His heart suddenly lurched and began to free-fall.

His mind buzzed.

He fought the realisation forming there. Tried to put a stake in the heart of that thought. But it fought back. Ready to consume him.

He was falling in love with Emma.

Was that possible?

The dragon was open-mouthed. Ready to attack again.

This wasn't what he wanted.

This was his worst nightmare.

To fall in love.

He had seen how love had destroyed his mother. Had destroyed his childhood.

This was the last thing he'd ever wanted.

To fall in love with a woman who couldn't, *wouldn't* love him back.

How many times had she said she didn't want to be in love?

She reminded him of himself. Of how definite he'd been about not wanting love.

Until she'd came along.

He was falling in love with the one woman he couldn't have.

This couldn't be happening.

This was why he had always sworn he would never love.

He had stopped believing in love when he was a teenager. Knowing that ultimately it would destroy you.

He felt sick.

He had to pull back.

He had to detach himself from her.

But he couldn't walk away. Not yet.

He wanted the next few days. He wanted to be with her. Two days. No more.

The scheming crocodile loitered behind the little boy who was happily fishing, oblivious to the danger he was in. The children standing in a corner of Campo San Polo, enraptured by the puppet show, shouted and screamed for the little boy to run away.

Their shouts were deafening, and Emma playfully grimaced in the direction of Matteo. But he didn't notice her. In fact for the past half an hour, since they had left Ca' Divina, he had been distant. Distracted.

A vine of anxiety wrapped itself around her left ankle—

not quite hurting, but tight enough to warn her what was to come if she didn't shake off her uneasiness.

What was the matter?

Was he already regretting his decision to spend the day with her?

The sun slanted off his face, highlighting his golden skin. His thick dark eyelashes only occasionally flickered, as though he was in a trance. His mouth was a constant thin line.

Nervous attraction zinged through her veins. She clenched her hand against the temptation to reach out. To touch his cheek. To whisper, *Is everything okay?* To have him smile again.

This morning she had lain in bed, her body twisted towards the bedroom window and the majestic pale pastel buildings and faded red-tiled rooftops beyond. Knowing she had two choices.

Give in to her fear that she would be hurt and walk away now. Away from this too intense, too soon, too confusing relationship.

Or embrace these two remaining days. Two days that could give her a lifetime of happy memories.

But for that to happen she *had* to remember their relationship was boss and employee—colleagues at best. Nothing more.

She moved closer to him and rested her hand on his arm. He looked down at her with a frown, as if he was unsure of everything about her. For a moment awkwardness, suspicion, doubt passed between them.

The twisting sack in her chest tightened. He had changed his mind.

His eyes held hers but then flew away. As if he didn't want to look there.

She was about to make a joke—anything to lighten the tension between them—when she stopped herself. She was doing it again. Being passive. Afraid to rock the boat. Afraid that Matteo might reject her. Afraid that if she spoke her mind he might be angry, dismissive, provoked. Everything she had spent her childhood trying to prevent.

Her stomach lurched and her throat suddenly felt like nothing more than a thin straw through which she had to speak.

It would be so much easier to smile. To jolly him along. Not to have to face the reason why he now didn't want to be here with her.

The spacious square reverberated to the sound of voices. Friends chatting loudly outside pavement cafés. Children chasing around the fountain. Others giggling and whooping on the temporary ice rink. The sounds echoed off the surrounding tall historic buildings.

Sounds which made the silence between them as they walked through the square even more pronounced.

She cleared her throat. 'We can go home if you like.' Her trepidation was hidden behind her sharp, snappy, defensive tone.

He looked at her impassively, as if quietly contemplating her offer. No quick denial, as she had secretly hoped.

'Do you want to?'

No! He wasn't turning this back on her.

She was about to tell him so when her phone began to ring. She flung open her handbag, leaving the two handles hanging from her forearm, and began to rummage through it. Where was it? She could hear it, but for the life of her she couldn't find it.

With a huff, she moved to the window of a nearby antique shop, dominated by the huge gilt frame of a dark religious artwork, and balanced her bag on the stone window ledge as she continued her search. Eventually she found it—under a pile of paperwork.

It was the tour guide, calling from Verona to give her an update on how the Chinese delegation was faring.

She spoke to the guide with her back deliberately towards Matteo, but in the window's reflection she could see that he was staring at her, his arms folded impatiently.

Dressed in a grey wool overcoat, open at the collar to reveal a light blue shirt and a navy pullover, his broad frame loomed large in the window reflection. Dark and menacing. And unfairly gorgeous.

Her anger, her defensiveness, was sinking as fast as it had risen.

When she turned back to him she had reverted to her professional mode. 'That was the tour guide. The group have booked in to their hotel and are about to tour the city. I've confirmed that they need to be back in Venice at five tomorrow, as the ball is starting at eight.'

Tomorrow evening Matteo was hosting the delegation at one of the Carnival's masked balls. She would be Matteo's partner again.

It would be their last event together.

The morning after he would be leaving for New York.

They might never see each other again.

That thought had her inhaling a deep breath against the loneliness that sideswiped her.

The vine clinging to her ankle tightened.

She opened her handbag and threw her phone back into its depths.

Matteo stared in after it. 'I'm surprised that you were able to find your phone in the first place…' He paused and grimaced, as if he was looking into the bowels of hell. 'In *there*.'

Did he have to sound so appalled?

'A woman's handbag is her business. Nobody else's.'

He tucked his arms into a tighter fold across his chest. And shot her an unimpressed eyebrow-raise.

She was about to ignore him. But then the new Emma stepped forward. The Emma who had got on the plane at Heathrow, determined to have her week in Venice. The Emma who'd sworn she would be tough and take no non-sense from anyone again.

Well, she was going straight to the top in giving some-one a piece of her mind: Matteo Vieri, the Italian god of fashion.

Her jaw jutted out.

Her shoulder blades were so rigid she reckoned they would easily slice someone in two.

'I had a childhood of not being able to have a hair out of place, in a sterile home that smelt of bleach. That's to blame for my preference for messiness. What about you…? What's made *you* so proper…so strait-laced?'

So the legendary Matteo Vieri *could* do astonishment.

His mouth dropped open for a couple of seconds. And then it slammed shut.

His hands landed on his hips 'Strait-laced?'

'Yes…nothing is ever out of place in Ca' Divina. You are always immaculately groomed. Cufflinks always per-fectly aligned, your hair always looking like you're on a fashion shoot. Do you *ever* look messy?'

His expression shifted from narked to nonchalant, as did his tone. 'I own several luxury goods companies. It's my duty to look good. I'm representing my businesses.'

True. But that didn't mean he didn't have down time. Time when he relaxed.

'Do you even *own* a pair of jeans? A tee shirt?'

He gestured to a street that ran beside the church of San Polo, indicating that they start walking again.

The street quickly narrowed to a laneway that could barely accommodate them both walking side by side. She tucked her handbag closer. Worried that in the tight confines she would bump into him. Worried that she might not be able to move away if she did.

'I own…a pair of jeans.'

His deadpan voice held a poorly disguised hint of humour.

A smile broke on her mouth. 'One! Most men I know own at least a dozen.'

His mouth twisted but his eyes were alight with humour. 'Well, I'm *not* most men, am I?'

Despite the shadows of the narrow alleyway, the day suddenly felt bright. Hopeful.

She gave him a cheeky smile. 'No. You're certainly not.'

He smiled back. The doubts, the unease of earlier erased.

They crossed over a canal and he led her down another side alleyway. 'We need to buy you a mask for the ball tomorrow night. There's an atelier down here, close to Campo San Rocco.'

Along the alleyway they passed two boys kicking a soccer ball against a wall, the dull thud in competition with their lively lyrical chatter.

'I liked your friends last night.'

Mischief sparked in his eyes. 'You sound surprised.'

Her mouth twitched. She cleared her throat. 'They're different to you—more laid-back.'

He slowed down as they approached a shop window adorned with masks. Some were stark and frightening, with long, exaggerated pointed noses—the masks of death and plague. Others were ornate and elegant, wisps of beauty and intrigue.

He caught her teasing tone and threw it back to her with an amused shrug. 'I guess…'

He rolled his shoulders and his eyes grew serious.

'Last night I remembered what you said yesterday about trying to enjoy life more, not worrying about the future.'

He gave her a small smile. 'I think you might be right, so I've decided I want to spend time with my friends. In the past I wouldn't have asked them to stay, wanting to catch up with work instead.' He paused and a brief storm of doubt passed over his expression. Quickly it cleared to calm certainty. 'I also wanted them to meet you.'

Not even trying to pretend that she wasn't shocked by what he'd said, she asked, 'Why?'

'You mean a lot to me.'

What did he mean by that?

She opened her mouth to ask, but clamped it shut again. She didn't want to hear his answer.

She wasn't ready for any of this.

So she laughed and said, 'You could have fooled me! All morning you've been acting as though you don't want to be here.'

For a moment he looked as if he was going to argue. His eyes swept over her. Her heart pleaded with him not to. Something even deeper within her pleaded with him to tell her that he felt what she did too.

He tugged at the bottom of his coat sleeves, a rueful grin transforming his expression to one of playful teasing. 'I didn't get enough sleep last night, and I woke early. Can we start again?'

'Do I hear the hint of an apology in there?'

'Yes. I'm sorry.' His smile grew even wider, a sexy challenge now sparkling in his eyes. 'Now, I think it's about time you and I had a little fun.'

CHAPTER EIGHT

An hour later, close to Campo San Giacomo dell'Orio, in the *sestiere* of Santa Croce, they paused for lunch at one of Matteo's favourite restaurants in Venice—Alloro. The tiny restaurant, located on the banks of a narrow canal, had a dark wooden interior infused with over a century's worth of cooking aromas: garlic and rosemary, the earthiness of truffle, the hit-you-at-the-back-of-the-throat power of Asiago d'Allevo cheese.

Emma, bright-cheeked from the sharp February air, handed the blue and purple striped box containing her mask for tomorrow night's ball and her navy woollen coat to the maître d', who then showed them to their table overlooking the canal.

Their knees clashed as they settled into the small table, and for a few brief seconds a blast of heat fired between them. Deep longing. Two souls in need.

Emma was the first to look away. Her hands moved quickly to tuck a loose curl behind her ear before she straightened first her knife and then her fork on the starched white linen tablecloth.

He poured them both some water, his gut twisting.

So much for staying detached, unaffected by the realisation that he was falling for her. He had spent most of the morning quarrelsome and argumentative, frustrated with every feeling he had for her.

But the truth of his attraction to her had been determined to leak out. His willpower had proved useless against the continual adrenaline rush of physical chemistry and the emotional connection of being with her. Hope and pleasure were strong-arming fear and resistance.

In the designer's studio she had tried on various styles of masks, at first carefully watching for his reaction.

But then something dark and sensual had whipped between them.

Her eyes had toyed with him from behind the masks. Dancing hazel eyes that could be his undoing.

They had grown bolder and bolder in their teasing and flirting.

Casual touches had skittered across his skin, jolts of pure pleasure.

Smiles had spoken of heart-pounding delicious desire.

For the first time ever he wasn't listening to his own cool logic. The logic that was telling him to walk away. That this was uncharted territory he shouldn't be meddling in. That to have had his heart broken as a child was one thing. To have it broken as an adult would be a whole different matter.

Opposite him, Emma stared at the lunch menu with a frown, her lips silently shaping the words she was reading.

'Would you like some help deciding?'

She shook her head without looking up, her expression fierce. 'No, thank you.'

He smiled to himself. Another piece of his heart was falling for this determined woman.

The waiter returned with a glass of Prosecco for Emma and white wine for him, as he had ordered.

On a deep breath Emma placed her food order in faltering Italian.

The waiter advised her, also in Italian, that her risotto

would take thirty minutes to prepare. She blushed and looked at the waiter clearly confused.

Matteo translated for her, trying not to smile.

She nodded that it was okay, giving the waiter a faint smile.

When the waiter left, he lifted his glass. 'To new friends.'

Emma touched her glass to his and then gave a quick shoulder-roll. She drew in a deep breath. *'Ai nuovi amici.'*

'I'm impressed.'

'No, my pronunciation is terrible. I tried to learn some Italian before the wed—'

Her eyes swept away from his.

At first she grimaced. Then a haunting sadness settled over her features. Remembering the past was physically hurting her.

He shifted in his seat, his heels digging into the parquet floor.

Top notes of disgust and anger filled his nostrils to think of her ex, but deep in his belly the only note was one of jealousy.

She had almost married another man.

What if he had seen her out on the streets of Venice with her new husband?

Would the rage of attraction he had felt for her the first time they'd met still have been the same even though she was in the arms of another man?

Would he have walked away with a sense of loss?

With feelings he couldn't process for a woman he had merely passed in the street?

But would he have been better off if he *had* only seen her from a distance?

Would he have been better off never even setting eyes on her?

He lanced those uncomfortable, troubling thoughts with

a question that drew him back to the reality of their situation.

'What are your plans for the future?'

Emma tugged at the neck of her cream polo-neck jumper. The same jumper she had worn the first night they had met.

'I'm going back to London.'

'To your old job?'

Her hand rubbed against her neck and then patted upwards to the base of her ponytail, her fingers attempting to smooth down the renegade curls that insisted on breaking free from the confines of her elastic band.

'No. I want to start afresh. I've enjoyed this week, so I've decided that I want to work in event management full-time.'

'You've done an excellent job for me. I'm sure you'll be very successful.'

She rested an arm on the table, a shoulder and an eyebrow rising simultaneously in challenge. 'I wouldn't go so far as saying *excellent*.'

'You're intelligent, flexible, personable and warm…and most of the time you're organised. You have all the traits needed to be a successful event manager.'

A deep blush erupted from the depths of her jumper, spewing upwards. She angled herself away from him, a hand hiding the lower half of her face. Pride and embarrassment vied for dominance in her gaze.

Ultimately neither won. Instead she batted away his words with a smile that was too fleeting, too nervous, too forced.

'And what's in the future for Matteo Vieri? World domination?'

She didn't trust him.

She didn't trust what he said.

He gritted his teeth and tried to ignore the sharp tap of

her distrust that was prodding against his heart like the tip of a sword.

Threatening to stab him.

He slowly twisted the circular base of his wine glass on the linen cloth. Disquiet rolled in his stomach. *He needed to protect himself.*

'It's going to be a busy year. I have all the upcoming Fashion Weeks, I'm looking to expand aggressively into South America and I'm in the midst of a major renovation of my villa on Lake Garda.'

She nodded. And nodded again.

She yanked once more at the neck of her jumper. Beneath it her throat worked. Her pale toffee-mixed-with-peppermint eyes held his, but with a hesitancy, a sadness that sent that emotional sword she wielded straight through his raging heart.

'We're both going to be busy.'

Yes. Living separate lives.

The waiter arrived with their antipasti: asparagus and quail eggs for Emma, *carpaccio* for him.

He lifted his knife and fork, tasted his food and lowered his cutlery again.

Too distracted to eat.

The urge to connect with her, to reach out, detonated within him.

Without any thought he heard himself blurt out, 'When I was a child I lived close to here for a few years.'

Why had he told her that?

She too lowered her cutlery, her antipasto barely touched. 'What do you remember?'

Tension pinged like electric shocks in the small of his back. He moved forward in his chair and rested both arms on the table, stretching his spine. 'The apartment was on the third floor. I could see the Frari Campanile clearly from my bedroom window. At night, I used to pretend that...'

The words that had been spilling out of him dried up in an instant.

He had never spoken to anyone about his childhood before now.

He needed to stop.

'Pretend what?'

He didn't answer her question. Instead he stared down at the brilliant whiteness of the tablecloth, the loneliness of those years engulfing him.

Itchy, suffocating heat blasted his insides.

Her knees bumped against his. Her hands landed on his. Long, slim, pale hands that sat lightly against his skin.

Not cloying or overpowering.

Just there.

His heart decelerated.

He closed his eyes.

Eventually he spoke. Needing to tell her. 'I used to pretend that my father watched me from the Frari Campanile. That he had come...that he had found me.'

'Found you...what do you mean?'

Her voice was gentle. Her eyes, when he looked up, were calm and accepting, inviting him to tell her all about himself. Inviting him into her life. Inviting him to trust in her.

Maybe if he showed that he trusted her she would learn to trust in him.

But at what cost?

Time slowed down. Around them people chatted. A gondola with no passengers on board passed outside their window. Was the gondolier going home to his family? To his wife and children?

'I never knew...' He paused, unable to finish the sentence, unable to say the words *my father*.

'But you wanted to?'

'Up until I was nine years old I believed he would one day come and live with us. My mother said that he would.'

'But he didn't?'

'No. My mother told me when I was nine that she had met a man and we moved into his apartment in Rome. I kept asking her… What about my father? How would he find us now that we had moved? She told me that he would never come. That he didn't even know that I existed…and she had no way of letting him know.'

'Who *is* your father?'

A tight cord wrapped around his throat. He struggled to swallow. 'Apart from his name…Paul…I don't know.'

Her fingers curled a fraction more tightly on his hands.

Her cool skin was a balm to the heat burning in his stomach.

'My mother was eighteen when they met. He was an American student, travelling through Europe. He and my mother met at a music festival in Rome. They spent the weekend together. It was only after he had left that my mother realised that she was pregnant.'

'Did she try to find him?'

'She knew his first name—Paul—but couldn't remember his last name. She hadn't thought it was important. They were teenagers having fun.'

'It must have been tough for your mum, bringing you up alone.'

'We didn't have a lot of money. Her work was precarious. She worked as a model; but never got the big-earning jobs. My grandmother lived with us too, on and off.'

Memories collided in his stomach. He sucked in some air at the punches they delivered. The constant worry of not having money. His mother's mood swings. The sobs coming from behind the bathroom door at night. Her red-rimmed eyes clashing with her cheery smile when she walked from the bathroom in a cloud of steam. Pretending, burying, denying.

Those memories pushed upwards, heavy in his chest, spewing from his throat.

'When I was younger she never dated. Now I know she was hoping that my father would return. That by some miracle he would find her. On the tenth anniversary of them meeting she even went to the concert venue. Hoping he'd be there. She told me all this when I was older. All night she stood outside. Hoping. But he never came. After that she gave up hoping and started dating other men. She ping-ponged from one relationship to another. Within weeks of her meeting a new boyfriend we would move in with him. We even moved countries so that she could be with them. Invariably she would either end the relationship or behave so appallingly that her boyfriend would end it.'

He took a gulp of his wine.

'When I was sixteen she broke it off with a man who was perfect for her, who loved her. She would have had a good life with him. I knew she was fond of him so I was angry, frustrated. We had a massive argument which ended in her admitting that she had never got over losing my father. She claims that she fell in love with him the moment she first saw him, queuing ahead of her at the entrance to the concert, but didn't realise it until after he had left. She says that she's still in love with him.'

The waiter came once again and glanced at their table, clearly confused as to why their plates were still practically untouched.

Matteo asked him to take them away.

When the waiter had gone, Emma gave him a wide-eyed look of disbelief. 'She's still in love with him? Even though they only spent a weekend together?'

He couldn't blame her for her incredulous tone. 'I know. I told her she was living a fantasy. She disagreed. But ever since that night when we argued she hasn't dated again. She says that she now realises she was always trying to replicate her love for my father with other men. And that it will never work because her heart is still with my father.'

'That's so sad. For her and you.' Her tone was sombre, sincere.

He shrugged. 'These things happen. She was a good mother in most respects… She looked so young that when I was a boy people assumed she was my older sister. That my grandmother was my mother.'

'Did you mind that people thought that?'

He *had* minded. A lot. Not only had he not known his father but people had constantly assumed the wrong person was his mother.

'It didn't help that we constantly moved, and my mother stood out compared to the other mothers. She was so much younger. She never managed to become part of a community. It always felt like we were on the outside.'

'I'm sorry.'

'I'm not. It taught me that I needed to be self-reliant. It gave me a determination to succeed.'

'And you *have* succeeded.'

Had he? Until this week he had thought he had. But now all those certainties about what he wanted in life were crumbling.

'Perhaps.'

'I'm sorry you never got to know your dad, Matteo. For your mum to love him so much still he must be a special person. And I'm sorry your childhood was so disruptive as a result…it's all really sad.'

He drew back into his own chair.

It *was* sad.

He had never thought of it like that before.

Instead he had shut himself down. He had lived only for protecting himself against poverty, against allowing others to hurt him again. Had he been living in an emotional vacuum all that time?

Emma was waiting for him to respond. He could not meet her eye.

He tugged at his shirt-cuffs. 'I got used to it. Lots of children grow up in one-parent homes.'

'Yes…but it sounds like your mum was always searching for happiness. That must have had an impact on you.'

He closed his eyes for a moment. But the darkness did nothing to assail the memories of the summer when he'd turned twelve.

Francesco.

In the corridor outside his Turin apartment. Begging his mother not to leave. Clinging to him. Feeling Francesco's arms so tight around his torso that he couldn't breathe.

Francesco begging his mother not to take him away. Not the boy he considered his own son.

Panic had gripped him.

He'd been terrified that she would take him away. Equally terrified that she might leave without him.

Now his throat felt raw with emotion. A separate entity from the rest of his body. As if all his emotions were concentrated there.

He wanted this conversation to end.

Now.

It had gone too far.

He didn't want to talk about his past any longer.

'I guess.'

The only indication that Emma wasn't convinced by his answer was an almost imperceptible narrowing of her eyes before she asked, 'Are you close to your mum now?'

Their argument when he was sixteen had left them both raw and bruised, but in the years since they had formed a truce. A truce based on burying the past. Ignoring past hurts. It had worked for them. Hadn't it?

'Yes. And with *Nonnina*—my grandmother…'

Glad of a way to break the heavy emotion bouncing between them, he smiled and added, 'Even if she *does* bring home waifs and strays.'

Her eyes duelled with his for a few seconds. A smile of tenderness lightly lifted her full lips. But then it faded. 'You're lucky to have them.'

Her words were spoken with a gentle wistfulness.

It pulled him up short.

Despite all their faults—his mother's tempestuous nature, his grandmother's anger on behalf of the poor that so often got her into trouble with the authorities—he *was* lucky to have them in his life. He had never stopped to appreciate just how much before now.

'Yes, I guess I *am* lucky,' he said.

He had family.

Emma had none.

A wave of protectiveness towards her swept through him. What was the future going to bring her? Who would look out for her? Who was going to be in her corner, fighting for her, supporting her, cheering her on?

Who was going to ask the hard questions? Challenge her?

'Will you go back to ballet?'

Emma's fingers trailed lightly against the rosemary growing in a small green metal pot to the side of their table. She prodded the pot with a finger until it tilted.

Why on earth was he asking her about ballet? Hearing him speak about his childhood had brought a feeling of closeness and understanding between them. She didn't want it to end. Talking about ballet was the last thing she wanted to do.

'Where does your mum live now?'

'In Puglia. What about you going back to ballet?'

He wasn't going to let it go. The challenge in his eyes told her so. Why was it so difficult to answer his question?

Was it because of the intimacy that had been growing all morning? Their earlier argument? Their laughter in the mask studio? Matteo opening up just now about his past? The connection, closeness, *confidence* of his admissions? The fact that he trusted her enough to share his past?

It was thrilling, yet terrifying. Could she ever again trust a man enough to reveal what was in her heart?

For a few seconds she hesitated on the brink of telling him everything—how she was terrified of dreaming again. Scared to dare risking her heart to ballet, to a man. Her fear of it all going wrong yet again.

'Go back to ballet? Why should I? It's in my past.'

Much too intelligent soft brown eyes held hers. 'It doesn't have to be.'

Her gaze shifted to the elegant middle-aged couple at the next table, who were leaving amidst much chatter and laughter. The woman was searching under the table for forgotten items. The man was patting his pockets. Mentally checking his belongings.

'I want it to be in my past.'

'Why?'

His quietly spoken question crept through the cage of fear engulfing her heart, and the tender expression in his eyes released—just a little—the burden of failure clogging her throat.

'Because it hurts too much to think about what I lost.'

'But you could create a new future in ballet through teaching, Pilates instruction, choreography... Maybe you can find something even better than you had ever hoped for.'

'And what if I don't? What if it only brings up bad memories or I fail again?'

'You have to take risks in life, otherwise it will be a life half lived.'

He was wrong. Risks...daring to dream...led to bitter

disappointment, despair. She would prefer to live a life of caution, knowing just how cruel life could be, rather than have every hope wiped out again in the blink of an eye— in the seconds it took to fall down some stairs, the seconds it took for a policeman to rap at your door.

'I want to focus on my career.'

'You can have more than your career.'

'Seriously? *You*, Mr Workaholic, are telling *me* that?'

'Nobody said I was perfect.'

From where she was sitting he seemed pretty perfect to her. His open-necked blue shirt hinted at the golden-skinned muscular chest beneath, and long, elegant fingers were toying with his glass...toying with her heart.

'So are you saying that *you* might open up your life to other things?'

Matteo rocked back in his chair, answering her question with a brief shrug.

Irked by his nonchalance, feeling a desire to provoke him, she asked, 'How about a relationship?'

He leaned forward in his chair, his hand once again twisting and twisting the stem of his glass. 'Maybe, if... *Dio*, I don't know.'

He threw himself back into his chair. Raised a hand in the air in exasperation.

Outside, the sun disappeared behind a white puffball cloud. The shaft of light that had been highlighting the chestnut depths of his hair, the golden tone of his skin, disappeared.

The chatter of the other diners dimmed in her ears. Her heartbeat drummed against her chest.

'She'll be a lucky person.'

His eyes searched hers. 'Will she?'

She bit down on her impulse to laugh, to tease him. To ask him glibly why *any* woman wouldn't feel lucky to be the partner of a gorgeous, intelligent, kind man.

But to do so would be a disservice.

He deserved more from her. He deserved the truth. Not some superficial answer.

She shuffled forward in her chair, leaned towards him.

Her eyes locked with his and her heart was now in her throat, her tummy coiling tighter and tighter.

'Only if you open your heart to her.'

Her answer came out in a whisper.

He blinked as he took in her words. And then his gaze became one of tender intensity.

He was looking at her in a way that no man had ever stared at her. As though she was the only person alive, ever to have existed.

Her heart sank back down into her chest and exploded into a million droplets of pleasure, of wistfulness, of emotional desire for the man sitting opposite her.

The waiter appeared at her side, a large white circular porcelain plate in each hand. She jumped in alarm. For a moment she had forgotten where she was.

When the waiter had left, she dubiously prodded her risotto with her fork. It was ink-black in colour.

Not what she had expected.

She glanced over to Matteo.

'Your first time having black cuttlefish risotto?' he asked with a teasing grin.

'It's so strange-looking—not exactly appetising.'

'Try it—it's delicious.'

'It looks like something spewed up by a volcano.'

He shook his head, laughing. 'Trust me...try it.'

She picked up some grains with her fork. Stared at it for a while and then tentatively popped it in her mouth. Salt. The taste of the sea. Garlic. She tried another forkful. And then another. She lowered her fork with a sigh.

'Oh, wow. That's *so* good. I'll have to add it to my list of favourite Italian food.'

'You like Italian food?'

She took another forkful and answered his grin with her own smile. 'I *adore* Italian food.'

He spiralled some of the spaghetti from his soft-shelled crab, langoustines and tomato sauce dish before saying, 'You'll have to come back and visit again some time.'

He spoke as though his invitation was sincere. As though he actually believed it would be possible.

She hid her confusion behind a teasing smile. 'Maybe. Although it's much more likely that the next time we meet I'll be at the end of a walkie-talkie while you are swanning around some glitzy event in London.'

His eyes twinkled. 'I'll make sure to wave to you.'

She gave a sigh and shook her head. 'We're really from different worlds.'

'No. Same world. Same problems and doubts.'

Hardly. He was rich and successful. She was a runaway bride without a job or a home. But now was not the time to point those facts out. Now was about forgetting about the past *and* the future.

'If I'm in a good mood I'll make sure to send you over a martini with lemon peel instead of champagne.'

He paused in twirling his pasta. 'You remembered?'

Her heart danced with pleasure at being the focus of his smile. 'Of course.'

He reached over and stole some of her risotto. 'And I'll tell the host just how incredible his event co-coordinator is.'

She playfully pulled her plate out of his reach. 'Make sure to add that I'm deserving of a bonus.'

As they ate the rest of their meal they spoke about food. Matteo grew increasingly appalled on hearing Emma's description of her boarding school fare.

As the waiter cleared away their main course Matteo said, 'Tinned sausages, gravy and potatoes…? It sounds horrible.'

Emma gave a shudder. 'Trust me, it tasted even worse.'

Matteo frowned hard, as though her boarding school's food was an affront to all humanity. When the waiter had left, he said, 'I will cook for you some day…to make up for all that terrible food.'

At first they smiled, both enjoying the teasing. But then their smiles faded. And Emma felt her cheeks grow hot. Her entire body, in fact.

His eyes darkened.

Silence pulsated between them.

He leaned towards her.

Her heart wobbled and quivered and pinched in her chest.

Serious, intent, masculine eyes devoured her, travelling down over her mouth, her throat, lingering on the pull of her jumper over her breasts.

'I have a surprise I want to show you.'

Her stomach tumbled at the low, sensual timbre of his voice.

She nodded.

Followed him on giddy legs when he stood.

Outside, she didn't object when he reached for her hand. His touch sent her heart careening around her body. The ever-growing ache in her body was physically hurting now.

Ten minutes later she found herself at the rear street entrance to Ca' Divina.

Puzzled, she asked, 'What about my surprise?'

Opening the door, Matteo unbuttoned his coat and gave her a mischievous smile. 'A little patience, please.'

Emma paused at the door, thrown by how much she wanted to be here. In Ca' Divina. Alone with him.

Inside, she followed him up to the second floor. At the end of the corridor, past all the bedrooms, Matteo pressed firmly against the pale-blue-painted wall. A hidden door popped open. Emma gave a gasp of surprise.

Behind the door was a staircase, a skylight high above it filling the wood-panelled stairway with warm light. Dense, peaceful air filled the enclosed space.

At the top of the stairs he opened a dark wood-panelled door and led her out onto a flat red-brick roof terrace. Large bay trees in pots were dotted around the vast space; all-weather outdoor furniture stood at the centre.

She moved about the terrace, her hand lifting silently, a huge beam of excitement on her face. Pointing to St Mark's Basilica, Campanile San Giorgio Maggiore in the south, the Rialto Bridge to the east, the utter beauty of the Grand Canal below.

She left out a happy, thrilled laugh. 'This is so *incredible*.'

Matteo leaned against the stone balustrade overlooking the canal. Watching her. Amused. 'I told you to trust me.'

She was feeling decidedly giddy. Especially with the way he was looking at her. Interested. More than interested. With a definite spark.

She gave him a cheeky smile. 'So you did.'

He gestured to her to come over to where he was standing. A quick, flirting curl of his index finger. There was a lazy, sexy smile on his lips. Something dark and dangerous sparking in his eyes.

Adrenaline zipped through her.

She went and stood beside him. Convinced he must be able to sense the buzz vibrating through her body.

He turned and pointed to the south. 'Do you see the red-brick *campanile* to the east?' She nodded and he continued, 'The *palazzo* next to it is where, according to legend, Casanova once lived.'

His voice was low, knee-wobblingly sexy. He was flirting with her.

Her heart thrashed against her breastbone. A light, swirling ache went through her. She inhaled deeply, her lungs fighting her juddering heart.

'Casanova…the gambler…' she paused and looked him in the eye, trying to ignore the heat firing in her cheeks '…the famous lover.'

He edged a little closer to her. Inches separated them as they stood against the balustrade. A light breeze fanned her burning cheeks.

'Apparently he once held a lover imprisoned there when he didn't want her to leave.'

Her entire body tingled. In a croaky voice she said, 'He was a renowned lover…maybe she didn't mind.'

She stared into heated, dangerous, intent eyes.

His hand reached out and grabbed the belt of her coat. He pulled her towards him.

A dangerous smile broke on his mouth. 'I wonder how many nights he kept her there, imprisoned in his bed?'

Every bone in her body melted. 'I suppose until he was satisfied…'

His head moved down towards hers.

Musk and vanilla…his heat grew stronger. Set her heart to a different beat.

His mouth hovered over hers.

He breathed out, his warm breath playing on her skin.

For a lifetime they remained inches apart, their bodies pulsating, time suspended.

He pulled her in even closer to the hardness of his body. 'I can't stand this any longer.'

His deep voice, impassioned with need, spun like magic thread around her, pulling her closer and closer.

In a sigh, she breathed, 'Me too.'

His hand captured her cheek. A thumb stroked the sensitive skin beneath her ear. *'Voglio fare l'amore con te.* I want to make love with you.' His grip tightened. 'I want to take you to my bed. *Now*.'

She closed her eyes, moved her head so that her lips grazed against his palm 'I want that too.'

He drew back an inch, blinked hard. 'What about the future?'

She shook her head an inch to the right. To the left. Desire had left her too weak to move with any more effort. 'We don't have one…but we *do* have now.'

'And that's enough?'

She hesitated. Her physical need for him was making her dizzy. The core of her body was shouting out for him. Silencing her heart, which wanted to know what she was playing at.

He opened her coat, pushed up her jumper.

On a gasp she breathed out. 'It has to be.'

CHAPTER NINE

AT LUNCHTIME THE following day Emma paused at Matteo's office door. Her mouth dried as she drank in the broad width of his shoulders beneath his dark blue shirt, the fact that his hair was still dishevelled from when she had run her hands through it earlier.

But in the pit of her stomach unease stirred.

She pushed it away. Disquiet, doubts, disbelief—they could come tomorrow.

When he was gone.

Sadness and regrets were for the future.

Not now.

She knocked lightly on the office door. 'Hi, I'm back.'

Matteo leaned away from his desk, a hand running through his hair, smoothing it down. A sexy smile grew on his gorgeous mouth, competing for her attention with the fondness shining in his eyes.

He nodded towards the shopping bags she was carrying. 'You found what you needed?'

She walked further into the room and dropped the bags to the floor. Her hand touched against the soft brown leather of the tub chair in front of his desk.

'Eventually. Thanks to a lot of pointing and hand gestures. Although at one point it looked a distinct possibility that we were about to have a fish that resembled a deflated soccer ball rather than mussels for lunch.'

His laughter tripped along her veins. Her fingers squeezed the soft leather of the chair. For a moment it felt as if gravity didn't apply to her. Dizzying memories came of their heads colliding in bed last night and Matteo pretending to be concussed. She had tested that pretence by slowly kissing him, until he had groaned in capitulation and tossed her onto her back.

She should go and make lunch. Her forfeit for being the first to beg in a game this morning.

His laughter died. And now his intense gaze wrapped her in a bubble of glorious hope.

'I missed you.'

She looked away. Unable to cope with the sincerity in his eyes. 'I doubt that—you were engrossed in your work just now.'

With a playful grin Matteo stood and walked towards her.

Anticipation tickled her insides. She was not going to blush. Or think about what he had done to her body last night. How she had moaned as his mouth had travelled down her body, staying far too long at her breasts.

He stood over her, his grin now plain sexy, thanks to the heat in his eyes. His scent rocketed through her senses, leaving her temporarily stunned and having to fight the temptation to close her eyes, sigh, lean into him.

'You're determined not to believe a word I say, aren't you?'

She had to brazen it out. Not give any hint that last night had changed anything. Pretend that it *hadn't* left her wanting to crawl right into his skin and know him better than anyone else in this world.

'As I've told you already, it's the new me...tough, independent.'

He sat on the corner of his desk, his long legs in exquisite navy wool trousers spread out before her. Earlier, before she had left for the market, he had kissed her in the kitchen as they'd tidied up after a late breakfast. His hips had moulded against hers, which had been pushed against a kitchen cabinet, and her fingers had marvelled at the smooth texture of the fabric of his trousers and the strength of the muscle and hardness beneath.

'How about we put that alleged toughness to the test?' There was a dangerous glint in his eye.

She pointed to the grocery bags on the floor. 'What about lunch?'

He gave her a *you're not so tough now, are you?* grin and beckoned her forward with the curl of a finger. 'Come here.'

His command was spoken in a low, husky voice. His smile had disappeared. His eyes devoured her. Her heart thumped and pounded and ricocheted around her chest. Desire left her faint with the craving to be in his arms again.

She stopped two paces away.

When he didn't react, she edged a little closer.

And then a little closer again.

No reaction.

He was torturing her.

She edged forward. Need driving her on.

She came to a stop less than six inches away.

Other than devouring her with his eyes, he didn't respond.

Inside, she yelled for him to touch her, to kiss her again. To reach out for her. To complete her.

On the outside she didn't move a muscle. Determined not to be the first to move. Determined to prove—to herself as much as him—that she was tough. Determined to believe that she could walk away from him whenever it suited her.

He reached forward and slowly drew down the zip of

her padded jacket. Need pooled in her core. She wriggled a little, trying to ease its beautiful pressure.

'*Mi piace come baci.*'

Oh, Lord, she was going to lose her mind. Did he *have* to speak in such a low, sexy whisper? She swallowed hard, her throat's tightness an alarming contrast to the loose panic of her heart.

'What does that mean?'

'*Mi piace come baci*—I love how you kiss me.'

'Oh.'

His hand snaked beneath her jacket. Then a finger curled around the belt loop of her jeans and yanked her between his legs. He leaned in towards her, only inches separating them.

The heat of his body encircled her, sending her hazy thoughts off into recess.

'*Adoro come mi fai sentire.*'

He really wasn't playing fair. 'What does *that* mean?'

'I love the way you make me feel.'

Oh, crikey, she was going down. And fast.

Despite herself, she closed the gap between them. Her hip inched towards his lap. Her mouth was almost touching his.

'*Ho bisogno di te.*'

His breath smelt of mint, of toothpaste. His fingers were slowly untucking her tee shirt from her jeans. Slow, unrushed movements, sensual in their laziness. Sensual in the knowing confidence that she wouldn't object. That this was exactly what she wanted.

'And that?'

His head angled perfectly to align with her mouth. 'I need you.'

With a groan she landed her lips on his. She wanted to cry out when he didn't respond at first. But quickly she realised he was happy for her to be in control now. For her to lead the way. She captured his head in her hands and deepened the kiss. Then her hands moved down to his, and silently she urged him to touch her.

Within minutes she was standing before him, her jacket and tee shirt gone, only her jeans and red satin bra remaining.

They made love on the floor.

Hot, desperate, addictive love.

Knowing their time was running out.

Outside his bedroom window darkness had settled on the city. The ball was in less than two hours. He should wake Emma. But she was lying beside him, her arms sprawled over her head on the pillow, the blankets at her waist, and he wanted more time to watch her. Watch the rise and fall of her ribcage, the perfect globes of her breasts. Watch the invitingly open lush cupid's bow shape of her mouth, the flush on her porcelain skin.

She was staggeringly beautiful.

And sleeping with her had been the most heart-wrenching, honest and tender experience of his life.

She was a gentle lover. Almost shy. And she responded to his every touch with wonder shining brilliantly from her eyes.

They had spent the past twenty-four hours in each other's arms. Ravenous for one another.

He was in love with her.

And he was lost as to what to do.

She said she didn't want a relationship, to love again. But with time would she change her mind?

And, even if she did, what if she said she did love him only to walk away one day? After he had given her his heart.

He was in love with her.

But he would never tell her.

Because to do so would mean that she would have the power to leave him.

And that he could never cope with.

Emma stabbed her brush into the almond-coloured eye-shadow. The fine powder crumbled beneath the force. She swept the brush along one closed lid. When she was done she stared at the reflection of the bedroom in the dressing table mirror. Why did she feel she no longer belonged there?

She closed both eyes and grimaced as her heart floated downwards into her stomach, where it rocked to the nervous tension already there.

She had to stop thinking.

Get through the next few hours.

Now should only be about appreciating her remaining precious hours with Matteo.

She opened her eyes in time to catch the already ajar bedroom door opening more fully in the mirror's reflection.

Matteo, dressed in a tuxedo, stepped into the room.

Goosebumps ran along her skin.

She pulled the edges of her dressing gown closer together.

Her heart, her body, her mind were all alert to him. Silently calling out to him.

Unspoken words stole into the room and beat in the air between them.

Matteo walked towards her. Her pulse raced faster with each step. He came to a stop directly behind her, a hand touching against her loose hair.

'I'll help you dress.'

She yearned to lean back, to have his fingers once again bury themselves in her hair, to have his fingertips caress her skull, her neck, her back.

Start pretending, Emma. Come on. Start acting tough. Don't you dare start believing in dreams again.

'Thanks, but it has a side zip. I'll manage by myself.'

His eyes narrowed before he turned and walked to the antique tapestry-covered chair beside her bed. 'I'll wait while you get ready.'

She wanted to say no. That to have him watch would be too intimate. That it was what somebody in a relationship would do. That it wasn't what they were about.

But she couldn't find the right words of protest.

Her dress was lying on the bed. A pink strapless floor-length silk gown, shot through with threads of peach and gold.

'Turn away.'

Engulfing the small chair he was sitting in, Matteo flashed a hand through his still damp hair. '*Per carità!* You cannot be serious. After the past twenty-four hours?'

'This is different.'

'Why?'

Because I couldn't bear to have you watch me...couldn't bear the vulnerability I would feel.

'I don't know, but it is.'

Throwing both hands up in the air, Matteo stood and walked to the bedroom window.

Emma quickly peeled off her dressing gown and stepped into the dress.

'You have a beautiful body.'

Her head shot up. Matteo still had his back to her. She pulled up the bodice to cover her bare breasts.

She gave a huff of disbelief. 'Hardly—in comparison to the naked models you see all the time.'

He twisted his head around—not enough to watch her, but enough to mark his presence, his control of the mood in the room. 'I don't care about other women, what they look like. I'm telling you that your body is mesmerising.'

There was more than a hint of annoyance to his voice.

She gave a laugh, needing to keep this conversation light and teasing. 'I believe you.'

He turned fully, his jaw set hard, a warning look flashing in his eyes. 'I never lie.'

She looked down and fiddled with her zip, wishing she *could* believe him. Wishing life hadn't taught her not to trust what anyone said.

She'd intended not to react, not to say anything, but when she looked up and into his eyes she heard herself say in a low voice, 'Is that a promise?'

Silence fell on the room. Matteo did not move a muscle. Dark and brooding, with the sharp contours of his athletic body clearly defined by the bespoke slim-cut tailoring of his tuxedo, he stared at her with an intensity that had her heart pounding in her ears, goosebumps serrating her skin.

He lifted his head in a gesture she had thought was one of arrogance when they'd first met, but now she knew it was one of intense pride and honour. 'Of course.'

She wanted to believe him. Not to be so scarred by her past. She wanted to walk to him and kiss him tenderly. She wanted to find adequate words to express the emotion pirouetting in her heart. She wanted to cancel the ball and spend these last hours alone with him, in his arms.

But to do so would mean allowing herself to hope, believe, trust, dream again.

Things she could never do.

So instead she fluttered her hands through the heavy silk of the gown's skirt and gave a single pirouette. 'Well, Prince Charming, am I okay to go to the ball?'

Matteo walked towards her, the seriousness in his eyes fading to amusement. A smile appeared on his mouth. '*Sei bellissima.* You are beautiful.'

* * *

The orchestra played 'The Blue Danube' and hundreds of masked faces twirled and spun around Matteo in the gilt and frescoed ballroom.

But he only searched for one: the delicate golden wired half-mask Emma had chosen in the atelier yesterday morning.

He smiled as Mrs Xue spoke excitedly of her trip to Verona from behind her full-faced *volto* mask, stark white with gilding around the eyes. The beauty of the Basilica… The pictures she'd taken of Juliet's Balcony… All the while he was searching, searching, searching. Needing to see Emma. Suddenly wondering how he was going to let her go.

And then he saw her. Moving towards him in the arms of Mr Xue.

She danced as though she was walking on air—fluidly, elegantly, joyfully. Her long hair lifted and bounced behind her. Those she passed turned around and stared in her direction. Captivated. Her dress sparkled beneath the lights of the Murano glass chandeliers running down the centre of the ballroom, her mask spun with gold adding to the pull of her beauty.

The music came to a stop and he led Mrs Xue towards them. He bowed to Mrs Xue and held out his hand to Emma. Silently inviting her to dance.

Below her mask her mouth gave a polite smile, but there was unrest in her eyes.

They danced slowly, but then the tempo quickened.

They danced on, to the uplifting music, but second by second her body grew stiffer in his arms. Her back arched. Her hand in his was tense.

Inside, a part of him was dying. All of a sudden he was incapable of speaking to her—even as her boss, never mind her lover. He wanted to hear her laughter. To feel that world-altering connection again. But no words came. He struggled even to look at her. It hurt too much. To know what he was about to lose. All he could do was stare blindly into the distance. Focus on the warmth and softness of her hand in his. How perfect it felt in his grasp. A perfect fit. Enticing. Nourishing. *Home.*

He heard himself ask, 'Is everything okay?'

Her response was equally polite. Impersonal. Strained. 'Yes, of course.'

He glanced down quickly and then away. Felt a dragging pain in his heart. As though it was bound by two gondolas travelling in opposite directions on a dark foggy night.

'What time do you have to leave tomorrow?'

She spoke with an edge. Was she dreading tomorrow as much as he was?

'I need to be at the airport for nine.'

She tucked her head down so that he couldn't see her eyes, but her fingers curled even tighter around his hand.

'So early?'

He grimaced at the regret in her voice. 'Unfortunately.'

Another couple moved too close to them and the woman collided hard against Emma. She gave a gasp of surprise.

The woman began to apologise, the heat in her cheeks below her half-mask showing her distress.

Emma held out her hand and touched the woman's bare arm. 'I'm fine, don't worry.'

The warmth and kindness of Emma's reassurance shifted something inside him. The way she'd touched the woman—empathetic, dignified—the gentleness of her tone. *This* was the type of woman he wanted to spend his life with. Centred. Compassionate. Caring.

He couldn't let her go.

The couple moved away.

Emma's eyes met his. Sad. Determined.

'I'll leave at the same time as you tomorrow.'

Confused, he pulled back from her. 'Why?'

Her gaze moved to the centre of his throat. He swallowed hard. Remembered her lips and tongue swirling over that tender skin at sunrise this morning.

'I've booked a hotel for my final days here in Venice.'

Not understanding, he said, 'I had assumed that you would stay in Ca' Divina.'

The hand resting on his arm tightened for a moment before her touch grew slack. 'That wouldn't be right.'

'Why?'

She shrugged. 'You've done enough for me.'

Her voice was impatient.

What was going on? Why was she springing this on him now?

Something hot and angry stirred in his stomach. She was walking out on him. He had fallen in love with her and she was walking away. He had thought she would stay. That he would leave for New York knowing that she was still in Ca' Divina. While Emma had remained there they would have had a connection. He would have had a legitimate reason to call her and see how she was doing. He had even envisaged her sleeping in his bed.

But instead she was walking away. Walking away from his home. From his hospitality. Walking away from their week together and the memories contained within the walls of Ca' Divina. Walking away from *him*.

And it didn't seem to be of any significance to her.

Anger leached from his stomach. Poisoned the rest of his body. His jaw locked. Every muscle tensed.

'Why didn't you tell me that you would be leaving?'

Her head snapped up. 'Why should I have?'

'Because it would have been polite.'

Those beautiful slender shoulders rose again. In a casual throwaway gesture that cut him in two.

'What does it matter when I leave? I thought you'd be relieved.'

The poison was in his throat. In his mind. He wanted to yell. But he forced his voice to remain cool, detached. 'Relieved?'

Emma couldn't read Matteo. There was anger in his eyes. But his voice was businesslike. Remote.

'It's time we both move on.'

She could hear herself speak…in the voice of another person. A person who was relaxed about moving on. Happy and accepting. While in truth, inside, her ribs felt as if they were going to snap under the pressure of sadness building in her chest.

Matteo gave an impatient sigh. And then fiercely, begrudgingly, he said, 'Come and work for me in Milan.'

She laughed out of confusion. A short, bitter noise.

'Work for you?'

She heard Matteo curse under his breath and then he yanked off his black half-mask.

The tips of his cheeks were red, agitated. 'I need a replacement for my event co-ordinator whilst she's on maternity leave.'

She wanted to cry. But instead she said dismissively, 'I can't work for you, Matteo.'

The redness in his cheeks spread. He lowered his head and eyeballed her. 'Why not?'

Because I will only fall in love with you even more.

She looked away, irritation layering on top of her sadness and confusion. How dared he speak to her in such a demanding tone?

She gritted her teeth, yanked off her own mask and said in an ice-cold tone, 'Because it would be too awkward—we've slept together, for heaven's sake. Anyway, I need to get back to London. Sort out accommodation, a job… I need to focus on my career. I want to go home.'

Those brown eyes were no longer soft, but as hard as rain-parched earth. 'And London is your home?'

A lifetime of hurt bubbled inside her. For the first time ever she felt a true, raw need to be tough erupting.

She inched closer to him and looked him steadily in the eye. 'Yes. London is my home. It's where my career will be.'

He nodded, but she could tell from the hard determination in his eyes that he wasn't going to leave it without a fight.

'I want you to stay. Give it six months. You don't have to commit to anything permanent. Think about what great experience you will gain. How it will look on your CV.'

Incredulously, she asked, 'You want me to give up my life in London?'

Those eyes, parched of emotion, held hers. 'I don't want you to go… I like what we have. You don't have an apartment or a job in London. Why not move to Milan? I have an apartment in Porta Venezia you can use.'

She was *so* sick of being used. First her parents. Then her ex. Now Matteo wanted to use her for his own ends. In the workplace and no doubt in the bedroom.

She planted her feet firmly on the ground. She was sick of dancing with him. Sick with herself for thinking he might be different.

She snatched her hand out of his. Jerked her other hand away from his arm. 'Because it's *my* life. I'm not some… bit on the side. I'm not interested in having a relationship with you for a few months. I can't function like that. And, frankly, I'm insulted that you would think that I would be happy being your…your kept mistress.'

He stepped closer to her and lowered his head. 'I'm asking you to *work* for me—nothing else. Why are you making such a big deal about it?' he demanded in a furious voice.

She jerked away.

What was he saying?

If he didn't want to sleep with her, was he saying that he had no interest in her? No desire for her? How could that be when attraction sizzled between them?

Or was she mistaken?

Was this all one-sided?

Pride called for her not to speak. But her pain, her hurt, her confusion were too great. 'Are you saying that you don't *want* to sleep with me again? That it would be a business arrangement only?'

He shook his head. Lifted his arms in exasperation. Confusion drifted across his features before he asked furiously, 'What do *you* want, Emma?'

Tears were forming at the back of her throat. With a cry she whispered, 'I don't know. I don't *know*, Matteo. But I certainly don't want this.'

CHAPTER TEN

EMMA RAN FROM the ball, the music and lights fading with every step, and tugged on her coat. The freezing night air was an affront to her hot anger.

She darted down the nearest side street.

Move to Milan? Work for him? Be his paid lover?

Hurt, fury, and a feeling of utter naïvety all twisted wildly in her stomach, moving upwards like a tornado until they gripped her throat. She could barely breathe.

Her ankle throbbed.

Blindly she hobbled along the maze of *calli*, cursing her exquisite pale pink Marco sandals, not made for cobbled streets. She had the vague hope that she'd finally stumble upon a recognisable landmark. But she didn't care that she was lost. Or that there were few people out at this time of night.

She wanted to be alone.

She wanted to try to understand why his proposal had stung so deeply.

She wanted to understand why it felt as though the past week had been nothing but a lie.

The connection she had thought they'd shared had been nothing more than a delusion on her part.

Their relationship was nothing more than a physical attraction for him.

Not an emotional connection.

Not the deep understanding of another person—the ability to read their needs and respond to them.

After everything she had said, how could he think that she'd be happy to uproot her life, turn it upside down for a man? A man who said he never wanted a permanent relationship.

How on earth would she manage to walk away from him after six months, a year, when it already felt so gut-wrenchingly awful to face the thought of him leaving tomorrow?

And the most infuriating, feet-stamping, tantrum-inducing part of all of this was that she didn't *want* to be in love.

But she was.

She loved him.

How could she be so stupid?

How could she be so foolish to fall in love with a man who had always said he didn't want to be in a relationship?

How could she be so reckless to allow herself to get hurt again?

On a humpback bridge she came to a stop at the apex and stared along the silent flowing water of the dark canal below.

It was snowing. How hadn't she noticed before now? Slowly swirling fat flakes dropped onto her outstretched palm. The flakes melted instantly against the heat of her skin. Just as the connection, the trust, the respect, the feeling deep in her bones that she had met her soulmate had melted tonight.

Pain radiated from her ankle. Cramping her calf muscle. She curled her toes and lifted her leg to rotate her ankle. Balanced on one leg, she wobbled and almost fell over.

She wanted to scream at life to give her a break.

She needed to get home.

Out of the cold.

But it wasn't home.

When had she even started to consider it as such?

Emptiness swept over her. She twisted away from the canal and tottered down the steep slope of the bridge on numb feet. Overwhelmed at the thought of a future without Matteo.

Before, she had clung to the hope that she would have memories to sustain her. Memories of a kind, generous, empathetic man.

Now she was no longer certain if that was who he really was.

Had he just been playing her? To get her into his bed?

She slipped and lurched along a narrow *calle*. The tall buildings either side seemed to be bearing down on her. Echoing the thin, stiletto fall of her footsteps.

The snow continued to fall.

A church bell rang out nearby.

She followed its sound.

And gasped when she walked into San Marco Square, blanketed in a thin layer of snow. Only a few solo, silent mysterious figures traversed the square, disappearing and appearing again from the arcades of the *procuratie*.

A sharp pain gripped her ribs. Forcing the air from her lungs.

She wanted Matteo to be here.

To witness the beauty of the square with her.

To hold her hand. To pull her tight against his body. To warm her. To hold her safe. To hold her for ever.

She turned her back on the square.

She knew her way back to Ca' Divina from here.

She would sleep and leave early tomorrow. And start her life afresh.

Her tears were pointless. She swiped at them, every muscle in her body hardening. She was furious with herself. For every single decision she had taken this past week.

* * *

She woke to feel her heart pounding a slow, heavy beat. Without opening her eyes she knew he was there. The adrenaline swamping her muscles, the tingle on her skin, the alertness in her brain—all told her that he was in the room.

Should she open her eyes? Confront him? Perhaps even manage to say goodbye in a civilised manner.

But would she run the risk of falling prey to his chemistry? To her weakness when she was around him?

She ground her teeth together. Annoyed with herself.

She snapped her eyes open.

He was sitting in the blue floral tapestry chair beside her bed, his bow tie undone, a dark shadow on his jawline and shadows below his eyes. Eyes that were studying her as if he was trying to stare into her soul.

She wanted to pull the covers over her head. To turn away from the awful compulsion invading every cell in her body to fold back the covers and silently ask him into her bed. To lose herself in him again.

Instead she pulled herself upright and hugged her knees against her.

They sat in silence. He held her gaze but she looked away. Her lips clamped shut. Her teeth aching. She was determined not to say anything.

'Why did you run out of the ball?'

His voice was low, gruff, tired.

She drew her knees tighter into her chest. Disappointment grabbed at her heart and then an even stronger, more breath-stealing sadness yanked at her chest. Her jaw ached with the pressure of trying not to let out a cry.

She swallowed time and time again, but her upset was still clear when she asked, 'Do you know me so little that you have to ask that question?'

He leaned back in his chair and folded one leg over the

other. The cold, hard expression of a CEO going in for the kill was on his face. 'You embarrassed me in front of my clients.'

She jerked back against the pillows of the bed, shock and anger erupting from her. 'Are you *serious*? Is that all that you care about?'

He leapt from his chair. Tense and dark. Prowled beside her bed. His shoulders bunched tight. A hand tore through his hair in disbelief. 'I needed you there. As my partner. And you left me.'

There was raw pain in his voice. Distressed pride in his eyes.

Speechless, she stared at him. Her mouth opening and closing. She had hurt him. How, she had no idea. But she had. And her heart ached. Ached for him. Ached for the mess they both were in.

'What's going on, Matteo?'

He glanced briefly at her. Flinging exasperation and anger at her. 'I can't stay here. Let's go for a walk. I'll meet you downstairs in twenty minutes.'

She moved forward. Trying to reach him. 'Why?'

Matteo, already at the bedroom door, twisted around to her, the ache inside him shooting out in furious words. 'Because we need to talk and I'm not doing it here.'

He gestured impatiently to the bed and then stared at her. Defying her not to understand how it was too painful a reminder of their hours spent together making slow, passionate love time and time again.

Too painful a reminder of how it was the way they had first met. In the intimacy of a bed. Inches apart. Staring into the eyes of a stranger. Who wasn't a stranger at all.

Anger flowing through his veins, Matteo stormed into his bedroom. After a rushed shower he dressed in charcoal wool trousers and a light grey shirt, both suitable for the long journey ahead in his private plane to New York.

He should have packed yesterday evening. But instead he had spent that time in bed with Emma.

He slammed some clothes into his suitcase with a carelessness that made him wonder if he was losing his mind.

Hurt convulsed through him. He steadied himself by locking his knees against the side of the bed. Doubled over above the open suitcase. Pain ripping through the centre of him.

She had walked out on him.

He had tried to reach out to her. He had given her a solution that would keep them together for a while. A solution that gave him some hope of a possible future together.

And she had thrown it back in his face.

Walked out on him.

Just like every other person he had ever been foolish enough to allow into his life, to have loved, had done in the past.

They walked in silence through alleyways and squares, over the Rialto Bridge into the *sestiere* of San Marco. The city of bridges, the city of romance, had never looked so beautiful and serene in the early-morning light, with a thin blanket of snow covering the city.

With few people about, they almost had the city to themselves.

In the pink-tinged dawn light, a blue sky was beginning to unfurl.

Words tumbled in Matteo's brain. He wanted to lash out. Pain was burning in his gut. In his heart. In his mind. He pulled his woollen hat down further over his ears, lifted the collar of his coat. The fire inside him intensified the bitter pull of the outside temperature.

'I wasn't trying to insult you last night with my job offer.'

Emma upped her pace, putting distance between them.

Her arms were folded tight across her padded jacket, her suede boots tramping the snow.

'I've upended my life for a man before. I'm not doing it again.'

He caught up with her as she entered Campo della Fava and pulled her to a stop. '*Per carità!* Are you serious, Emma? Are you comparing me to a man who *lied* to you? A *criminal*?'

Her blue-hatted head shook furiously. 'No… I'm not comparing you. But—'

He grabbed her by the arms and pulled her closer. Desperate for her to understand. 'I was trying to find a way for us to see each other for a while. I *like* you, Emma. I don't want us to lose contact.'

An incredulous expression grew on her face. 'You like me.'

It was not a question. More a statement of disgust.

With an angry huff she continued, 'And what happens in six months' time? In a year? Don't you think we're just going to hurt each other?'

He swallowed hard. Thrown by her fury. Her passion. Thrown by how much he longed to cup her pink-tinged cheeks and lower his lips to her mouth. To pull off her hat and lose his fingers in the soft weight of her hair. To inhale her rose scent once again. To know that she was his.

All that desire and want collided with the fear rampaging in his chest, in his heart. He grappled for words. The right words. *Any* words. He was about to put his heart on the line. Could he go through with it?

He swung away from the sight of her peppermint-toffee eyes searching his. Looking…waiting for an answer.

He marched towards the red-brick edifice of Chiesa di Santa Maria della Fava before twisting back again. 'In six months' time, a year, you might be ready for a relationship…a proper relationship.'

Her hands twisted more tightly about her waist. She lifted her chin defiantly. 'A relationship… What do you mean?'

His heart swivelled in his chest.

He felt sick.

He was about to put everything on the line.

His pride. His trust. His sworn promise to himself that he would never show any vulnerability, any need to another person.

What if she said no? Rejected him?

'I've always believed that I would never fall in love.'

He couldn't stand still. He paced up and down before her. Snow crunched under his feet.

He came to a stop. 'But I have.'

He gestured heavenwards, his head falling back. Looking for strength. His heart throbbing.

'I've fallen in love with you.'

Emotion caught in his throat. Suddenly he felt deflated. Empty.

His hands fell to his sides. 'With a woman who doesn't want to be in love.'

Paling, her expression aghast, she said incredulously, 'You've fallen in love with *me*?'

Was his admission so terrible? So unwanted? So wide of the mark from where she was at, what she wanted from this relationship?

Pain and pride slammed together in his chest. He needed to back off. Withdraw. Play it cool.

In a slow, indifferent drawl he asked, 'Is it really that horrific?'

She took a step closer to him. Her icy breath floated on the air towards him. 'Of course not. I'm not horrified. I'm just confused.'

Her hand reached out towards him. He jerked away.

For a moment she looked startled, wounded. But then she asked, 'Why didn't you want to fall in love?'

He closed his eyes. The ache in his chest was worse than the time when his mother had taken him away from Francesco. A thousand times worse. What was the point in answering her question? Did she really care?

He opened his eyes. Hazel eyes laced with tears held his gaze. In a low whisper she said, 'Matteo, please...*please*.'

He was so in love with her.

'When I was growing up my mother dated many men. Some for only weeks, others for longer...twelve, eighteen months. We would move into their homes. We would get to know their families, often their parents, brothers and sisters. I would pretend that I had a family of my own...a home. I would pretend that I had a father. But then my mother would sabotage the relationship. And it would end in one of two ways. Either the man I'd considered a father, and his parents who had treated me like a grandchild, would give in to her insistence that we move on with our lives and let us go, not fighting in any way to keep me a part of their lives. Or, if the break-up was particularly bitter, the man would throw us out onto the street.'

She moved forward and placed her hand on his chest. Just below his heart.

She looked at him and said gently, 'I'm sorry.' And then, 'There's no excusing the men who threw you out, but perhaps it was hard for those other men. Maybe they thought it would be easier for *you* if they let you go.'

Memories of Francesco clinging to him came back. If he'd been in Francesco's position, what would he have done? His throat tightened.

Her hand moved upwards. Now it was over his heart.

Her voice was hoarse. 'You think I'm doing the same thing? That I'm walking away from you?'

He was tired of pretending. Maybe if he had shown her just how upset he was when he was a child his mother would have changed. Those worthwhile father figures would have fought to stay in contact.

'Yes.'

Panic surged through Emma. 'It's not like that… I really like you. I really, *really* like you.'

She paused for breath. Her hand moved up from his heart and for a moment lingered on his jawline. She had an overwhelming need to lay her lips on his. To take the pain from his eyes.

'I can't imagine leaving you.'

She dropped her hand and took a step back. She looked down at the snow, tarnished now by their careless foot-steps.

'But I'm scared. I've messed up so much in the past. My judgement has been so wrong. I'm scared that I'll jump into a relationship for all the wrong reasons.'

Matteo's eyes narrowed. She took some strength from the way he looked as though knowing and understanding all this was the most important thing in the world.

'I'm scared that I've fallen for you because I'm vulnerable. Because I'm confused.'

She tugged off her hat, suddenly too hot. Her brain felt as if it was sizzling. 'I came to Venice swearing that I was going to be tough and practical. Focused on my career. Determined that I was never going to dream again. And then I went and met you. And I *want* to dream. But what if it all falls apart again? I couldn't take it. I'm scared I'll lose you. That one day this dream that I'm living will fall apart.'

For the longest while Matteo stood still, drinking in what she had said. And then he moved towards her. His hand reached for her hair. Tucked some of it behind her ear.

His thumb ran down her cheek and gently he said, 'You're not ready for love. For this relationship.'

She didn't know how to answer. Tears flooded her eyes.

Tears of confusion and frustration. Tears of fear. Tears of love for this man.

'Are you?'

His hand cupped her cheek. He gave a sigh. Regret and sadness deepened his eyes to soft molten toffee. 'I'm not sure,' Emma said.

She stepped back. Away from his touch. Needing to step away from telling him how much she loved him.

'Are we just fooling ourselves? Is this just about the insane chemistry we seem to share?'

He nodded, but then stopped suddenly. 'I've never felt like this with another woman.'

His gaze was now hard, direct. Deeply honest.

She sucked in a breath. 'Nor me with another man.'

His jaw worked. He ran a hand over his hat. Repositioned it. 'We need some time apart to think.'

Her stomach flipped at his words. She couldn't bear the thought of being without him. But she continued on with her sensible routine, refusing to allow her heart to have anything to say in what *had* to be a logical conversation.

'Yes.'

'I'm returning from New York on Wednesday. If we decide individually that we want to try to make this work, let's meet. I'll be at Ca' Divina at five.'

Her head spun. An army of *what if*s marched through her brain. What if this was the last time they would meet? What if he decided he didn't want to be with her? She couldn't meet him in Ca' Divina. There were too many memories there. What if she turned up, wanting a future with him, and he didn't?

A wave of grief, rejection, embarrassment at that thought almost knocked her sideways. 'No, not there.'

'At the church in San Moisè square instead?'

She nodded. 'Okay.'

Their eyes locked. Intense, stomach-flipping, heart-faltering unhappiness, longing and uncertainty bound them together.

Matteo broke his gaze first. He quickly stretched his back in a jerking movement, muttering a curse. 'Stay in Ca' Divina while I'm gone.'

'I can't.'

He shook his head. There was a tense displeasure in the corners of his eyes. 'I need to go back there now, to collect my luggage. My plane is waiting at the airport. Come back with me. You're cold.'

Her throat frozen solid with emotion, she struggled to speak, 'I don't want to say goodbye. Please just walk away.'

For a moment he hesitated. But then he gave a brief nod.

He walked towards her. Her heart fluttered and swooped about her chest. At first she thought he was going to hold her. But his hand touched against hers only briefly before he moved away.

She longed to call out to his retreating back. To halt his long, determined, angry stride.

And then she heard him curse.

He turned around and made straight for her.

He grabbed her.

And kissed her hard.

His mouth, his tongue were demanding. In an instant she was falling against him. Kissing him back just as hard. Needing to feel his strength, his warmth, every single essence of his being.

Her head whirled.

She was losing herself to his taste. To his scent of musk. To the feel of his cashmere wool coat.

She couldn't let go.

And then he was gone.

Pulling himself away. Cursing lowly. Walking away without a backward glance.

But not before she saw the tears in his eyes.

CHAPTER ELEVEN

Wednesday. Four thirty.

MATTEO STOOD AT the entrance to what had been Emma's bedroom. Now it was an empty shell. Just like the rest of the *palazzo*.

He entered the room and walked around it. Restless. Searching. Just as he had searched the rest of the *palazzo*. Searching for some sign of her.

He had hoped that she would have left a note. Some indication of her thoughts before she had walked out.

In the wardrobe he'd found all the clothes he had selected for her. She hadn't even taken the blue hat; he'd found it poking out of the pocket of her navy coat. As if waiting, hoping for her to return.

He propped his head against the carved walnut of the wardrobe door. Weak with weariness and disappointment. She had wanted no reminder of their time together.

Four forty-five.

Across from her bedroom window, on the roof terrace of the house opposite her hotel, an elderly lady tended to her patio garden. She was planting bulbs in flower boxes. Her hands unsteady, she moved slowly but with care. A contented smile on her face.

Had her neighbour ever struggled with a decision? Had she ever been so scared that she felt paralysed with fear?

Emma's fingers stroked the threadbare pelt of Snowy, her toy polar bear, sitting in the palm of her hand. He was staring out of the window too. Looking as bewildered and lost as she felt.

She had rung her best friend Rachel earlier, but hadn't been able to speak to her about Matteo, too upset, her fears too deep inside her to expose them.

What if she went to San Moisè Church and he wasn't there?

What if she went and he *was* there? Waiting. And he said things she didn't want to hear?

Five o'clock.

Emma stopped at one side of the main entrance to San Moisè Church, indecision dancing and colliding with anxiety in her stomach. She steadied herself against a square plinth, the cold stone electrifying her fingertips. The dark green outer double doors were slashed with peeling paint, pushed back to reveal glass-panelled inner doors.

She pulled one of the inner doors open, the fear in her stomach exploding into the rest of her body, leaving her trembling and uncertain if she would have the strength to carry on.

What if he hadn't come? What if he had decided in their time apart that it wasn't love he felt for her after all?

Dusk was settling on the city and the empty church was lit by pale wall lights and hundreds of votive candles, placed in racks and trays in front of bye-altars.

She went and stood by the first pew, her hand touching the grain of the wood. Her heart slowed. She closed her eyes and drank in the calming, distinct and yet light scent of the church: incense, flowers, melting wax.

Centuries of prayer hung in the silent atmosphere. The prayers of the hopeful. The desperate. The fearful.

Her footsteps echoed on the marble aisle. The sound of her aloneness.

She stopped and winced.

Unable to go any further.

Unable to bear the sound of her footsteps.

Knowing he wasn't there to hear them.

She dropped down onto a wooden pew and bent her head.

She had lost him.

What had she done?

And then she heard them.

Other footsteps.

Her head snapped up.

A figure moved behind one of the two thick stone columns that sat before the main altar.

Matteo?

His steps faltered as he approached her where she sat, halfway down the aisle.

Bruised eyes met hers.

His expression was as sombre, as arresting as the knee-length black wool coat, the black cashmere jumper and stark white shirt he wore. He was freshly shaven, and his hair was shorter than it had been before. She wanted to touch him. To feel his smooth skin, hard muscle. She wanted his arms around her. His hands in her hair. The pressure of his body.

Her heart moved beyond her throat to lodge between her ears. Where it pounded to a deafening beat.

His head dropped in a barely discernible nod.

She gave a wan smile in response.

Her bones, her every muscle, her mind all felt weak—powerless onlookers in this event. Her heart had drained every ounce of energy from the rest of her body in a bid to keep working.

She slid along the seat.

Please sit with me. Please let me have a few moments with you.

She didn't look up. Too vulnerable. Too scared he wouldn't sit.

He moved forward, reached her pew. But then stopped.

From the corner of her eye she saw his black trousers, the high polish of his black leather shoes. The neat bows in his laces.

Not moving. Not joining her. A sign of what was to come?

A jolt of pain shuddered through her lungs. A silent wound.

But then he sat. His long legs, muscular thighs grazing against hers.

They swung away from each other at the same time.

He bunched his hands together.

She dared a quick glance.

He was staring towards the altar at an elaborate sculpture showing Moses receiving the Ten Commandments.

She bit down on her bottom lip and closed her eyes. Searing hot pain torched her stomach. She *hated* this distance. This isolation.

And then her breathing slammed to a stop.

His hand was over hers. Holding it. Lifting it up to rest on his leg. His warm, protective, solid hand was holding hers. And not letting go.

Tears filmed her eyes. But she couldn't open them. Not even when the tears ran down her cheeks.

She couldn't stop herself.

His arm went around her shoulder. He drew her in closer. She bent her head and sobbed against his chest.

She couldn't stop herself.

* * *

Emma's shuddering body shook against his. He held her closer. Wishing her tremors and tears away.

She had looked at him with distress, sadness, unease as he had walked down the aisle towards her.

Why?

He tugged her closer. Closed his eyes to the slightness of her body. To the jumble of memories that came.

The first time they had made love. The beauty of her porcelain skin in the pale afternoon sunshine. How they had made love later that night in the shower, with a fast and furious need. Urgent, hungry, teeth-nipping lovemaking. As though they were both desperate to leave a mark on the other. Both afraid of how soon they would have to leave one another.

He buried his head into the softness of her thick curls. Inhaled her rose scent.

Her tears stopped. But still he sat there, Emma in his arms. Reluctant to leave the sanctuary of the church.

With slow movements Emma pulled away. She inhaled a deep breath. The breath of emotional exhaustion.

Pink rimmed her eyes, and the tip of her nose was a deeper hue.

She gave an embarrassed smile, her gaze barely touching his. 'I'm sorry—that wasn't supposed to happen.'

'How have you been?'

Her mouth fell downwards before she attempted a smile. 'Honestly? Not great. It's been difficult, these past few days.'

'Me too.'

She blinked hard. Her throat worked even harder. 'I thought you hadn't come… I thought… I thought…'

Her upset slammed into him. Adrenaline and regret mixed nauseatingly in his stomach. He held her hand for a few seconds longer, reluctant to break away, before he stood. They needed to end this agony.

'Let's go and talk.'

At a small boutique hotel, in a tiny courtyard nearby, he ordered a brandy for them both in the cocktail bar to the rear of the property.

They sat in an alcove, away from the few other customers there.

When their drinks arrived he took a slug of his brandy.

Emma stared at her drink absently before she unzipped and removed her black padded jacket to reveal a cream blouse, with a matching camisole beneath the translucent silk. On her neck hung the fine gold necklace she often wore, scattered with five tiny pendants in the shape of the moon, stars and flowers.

He shuffled in his seat, pushing away the temptation to reach forward and trace a finger along the delicate chain, to feel the pulse at the base of her neck. To be close enough to hear nothing but her breath. To hear her whisper his name. To hear her cries that had wrenched open his heart.

She grasped her glass and drew it in a slow arc across the black lacquered surface of the table. 'Why did you come, Matteo?'

He wanted to turn the question back on her. Have her explain first why *she* came. Still he was uncomfortable at letting his guard down after so many years of building a fortress around his heart.

But he could see the panic, the apprehension, the fear in her eyes. See how she had paled since they had sat down opposite one another.

Her body was curved towards him. Begging him to speak. To explain.

'I thought asking you to come and work with me would be enough. I told you that I was in love with you. I thought that would be enough. But in our time apart I realised that both of those things would never be enough.'

Her head tilted to the side, as though the weight of her questions was too great.

He answered her by adding, 'I'm guessing that you heard from your ex, from your parents, that they loved you. But that they never proved it.'

Regret tingled at the tips of his fingers and toes.

'There's so much more that I should have told you. I should have found the right words to prove my love. I should have proved it by being courageous enough to say those words. To really open my heart to you. To show you what was deep inside me. But I didn't because I was scared. Scared that by talking I would have to fully face up to just how deeply I love you. And how much it would hurt when you walked away.'

He paused for a moment and looked at her. Tried to garner the energy from her to continue on. A small encouraging nod was all it took.

'All those times the men I'd considered to be a father to me walked away, they took a part of me with them. The innocent, optimistic kid who trusted others was pulled apart bit by bit, until I had nothing left but cynicism and a determination never to be hurt again. I closed down. Refused to love. Refused to ever allow myself to feel that pain again.

'But last night, before my flight, I attended a dinner at a friend's apartment. There was a couple there who reminded me of us. They laughed and chatted together constantly. They were so in tune with one another, so happy. And, watching them, I realised that I wanted what they had. A partner in life. A family of my own. Emma, I want *you*.'

A hand dashed up to cover her mouth, which was dropping open. Her eyes were narrowed with caution and doubt.

'But is it me you want or the *idea* of a partner, a family?'

That was the easiest question he'd ever had to answer.

He moved his hands across the smooth table. He opened his palms to her. 'You. Most definitely you.'

She stared down at his hands. And then into his eyes. Still about-to-bolt cautious.

'Why?'

Was this going to work? How had he messed up so spectacularly that she was asking him why he wanted to be with her?

'I wish you didn't have to ask me that question. I wish I'd had the courage to tell you before now. I want you in my life. I love you. I fell in love with you the moment I lay down beside you in my bed. I'm deeply attracted to you, but it's much more than that.'

His heart was throbbing in his chest. Pleading with him—with her—not to let what they had together go. He jerked his hands off the table and curled one fist. He banged it against his throbbing heart. Needing to connect with it. Needing to acknowledge the feelings he had denied for so long.

'It's in *here*—in my heart. A recognition, a familiarity, a sense of belonging together—I don't know what it is, but I know that when I'm with you I'm *me*. There's no pretence. There's no pressure to be something I'm not. I love your elegance, your voice. I love how you mutter in your sleep. I love how you stand with your feet angled, as though you are about to dance at any moment. I love your humour, your touch. I love how you try to act tough when really you're as soft as a marshmallow. You are kind, intuitive…yet strong. I *know* you would fight for those you love.'

He paused. The emotion pouring from his heart was overwhelming his throat. About to drown him in all those words that had been building, building, building in him.

'I love you. I know that might not be enough, but I can't

let you go without telling you all this. You need to know that I will always love you, whatever your decision.'

Emma nodded, and nodded again. As if the forward and back momentum would give her the energy to speak. His words were magical. Beautiful. But she was still scared.

Across from her Matteo, pale, drawn, waited for her to speak.

Deep inside her the truth began to unfurl. She had to open her heart to him. Ask for his support. Trust in him.

But what if he thought she was weak, stupid, needy? What if he didn't like her when she spoke about every deep fear in her heart?

But wasn't that what a true relationship was about?

Hadn't he just been honest with her? And instead of thinking him weak it had made her love him all the more.

On a deep breath she said, 'I came to Venice to heal. To build a wall around myself that nobody would ever penetrate again. I was so tired of being let down. Of my dreams falling apart. And on my first day I met you. Protective, sexy you. A man who didn't want love either. And I immediately fell for you.'

She could not help but smile as a brief, satisfied smile broke on Matteo's mouth.

Then with a shaky exhalation she admitted, 'But it scared the life out of me. I didn't *want* to be in love. So I tried to bury it. Ignore it. But deep within me I knew I was in love from the moment we first kissed. I did everything in my power to tune out the voice telling me that. I told myself that you weren't interested. That *I* wasn't interested. That it was all a rebound fantasy. I looked and looked for a way to find you out, to prove to myself that you would hurt me as much as my ex and parents had.'

She breathed out a guilty sigh. A sigh full of regret.

'When you proposed that I go to Milan and work for you it was the perfect excuse for me to hang on to and justify my fears. Justify walking away when in truth I was in love with you.'

His arm resting on the table, Matteo opened his hand to her, silently asking her to take it. Her fingers curled around his. Her whole body vibrated to a low beat. *Home*.

His voice was low, thick with emotion, when he spoke. 'That's the first time you've said that you love me.'

Was it really? What had she been *thinking*? Had she been so terrified of saying those words out loud?

'I should have told you before but I was scared…scared of dreaming again. I'm petrified something will go wrong. That I'll end up losing you. That something will happen to destroy what we have.'

His fingers tightened on hers, pulled her forward in her seat. He leaned across the table, those brown eyes boring into hers. 'I won't let anything destroy what we have.'

'Do you mean it?'

'Emma, I love you. I want you in my life. Beside me. My mother has spent her life wishing she had done something different. That she hadn't let the love of her life get away. Wondering if he feels the same. Wondering where he is now…what he is doing. If he is happy. I won't live with that regret. I won't let *you* live with that regret.'

'Where do we go from here?'

'I don't want to be without you. Since you came into my life I've realised just how lonely and empty I was before. I'm a happier, better person because of you. I *need* you. I want us to be together. I want us to get married. To be a family. To have children together. Curly-haired, hazel-eyed *bambini*.'

She couldn't help but smile at that image: soft-eyed babies with his golden skin and sucker-punch smiles that would leave her faint with love.

'Are you serious?'

His expression grew stern, as though she had affronted him.

'Do you think I would say those words unless I meant them?'

Her heart skipped a beat at the low, formidable tone of his question, the thin line of his mouth. 'I'm sorry...of course you mean what you say.'

Pain, tenderness, aloneness...all flickered in his eyes.

A bubble of love floated from her heart to her throat, where it popped when she swallowed hard in a bid to concentrate.

Was this really happening?

She had thought they might agree to date, at best.

This was everything she had ever dreamed of. *More* than she had ever dreamed of.

But would she have the courage to say yes?

The courage to believe in such a spectacular, staggering, mind-blowing dream?

To spend her life with the sexiest, kindest, most honourable man alive?

She had come to Venice hoping to harden her heart. But wouldn't doing so—hardening herself, closing herself off to others—mean that her ex, her parents had won? All the people who had hurt her would win?

And *she* would be the loser in all this. She would lose the love of an incredible man. Lose a future full of love. A future of being the mother of Matteo's children.

She would lose the love of her life.

She looked across at him.

He was watching her. Believing in her.

She smiled.

He raised a single eyebrow. Silently asking, *Well...?*

Her smile grew wider. As wide and spectacular as a

Dolomites' snow-covered valley. And then she gave a definite nod.

A tentative smile broke on Matteo's mouth, but happiness was carved into the landscape of his face.

He raised his hand and beckoned her to slip along the seat, to sit beside him.

Which she did.

His brown eyes raked over her face, waiting for her to speak.

'I came to Venice to heal, and I did because of *you*. Dancing with you, being held in your arms healed me. Laughing, kissing, making love with you, every tender touch, every eternal gaze healed me. Your compassion, your wisdom healed me. I would be honoured and proud to be your wife. I love you. With you I feel protected, safe, exhilarated. I want to care for you. Love you. I want to spend my life proving to you how much I love you. How deserving you are of love. I promise I will never hurt you. I want to make up for each time your heart was broken as a boy. I want to complete you.'

His hand touched her hair. Then gently he pulled her mouth closer and closer, his eyes packed with love, desire, joy.

In a low whisper, he breathed against her mouth, '*Voglio stare con te per sempre*. I want to be with you for ever.'

Reluctantly, wanting to stare into those magnificent eyes until the end of eternity, Emma closed her eyes. And lost herself to him.

EPILOGUE

THE HOTEL CIPRIANI'S motor boat sliced through the water and Emma giggled and held firmly on to her veil. Rachel, her bridesmaid today, tried to capture it as it flew behind the boat—a fine net sail, catching the attention of the summertime tourists seeking shade from the late-afternoon August sunshine under the awnings of the cafés lining the Grand Canal.

Beads of nervousness exploded in her stomach when the boat slowed to motor up a side canal. They had both wanted to marry in Venice. And what better place than San Moisè Square and Church? The place where they had first kissed. Where they had both found the courage to dream.

With a nervous hand Emma smoothed down the lace skirt of her gown. Tears blinded her vision. What if she hadn't had the courage that day to believe in her love for Matteo? How empty her life would be now.

In the bare six months she had been with him she had gathered a lifetime of memories. Weekends spent here in Venice, in Paris, on Lake Garda, sometimes alone, sometimes with his friends...*her* friends now too. The nights he would arrive in her office, a floor beneath his executive offices, and kiss her neck and earlobes, kiss her into submission so that she would leave early with him—much to the amusement of her new colleagues, who were captivated by the sight of their boss head over heels in love.

What would Matteo think of her dress? Created by the head designer at VMV, the strapless gown had a full voluminous skirt overlaid with fine lace.

At the landing stage, Matteo's grandmother Isabella was waiting for her, shouting instructions to the driver of the boat, who was pretending not to hear her.

Beside Emma, Aurora, her five-year-old flower girl—daughter of Matteo's Marketing Director and her first pupil in the small ballet school she was opening after the summer—hopped up and down with excitement until the driver lifted her with many giggles to deposit her on the landing stage.

When Emma disembarked, Isabella pulled her into a tight embrace, loudly proclaiming, *'Sei bellissima!'* countless times.

Isabella—the woman who had rescued her. The woman who had brought Matteo into her life. She would walk her down the aisle today. Emotion caught in her throat.

Isabella drew her towards the church, her hand at her elbow, saying quietly, *'Lui ti adora.* He adores you, Emma. Thank you for making him truly happy.'

And then Emma was giggling, because a long pink carpet led the way into the church. Not red. But pink. A gift, she suspected, from Matteo. The same ballet-slipper-pink VMV shade as the thousands of roses lining the aisle of the church. The still air sweetened by their heavy scent.

She smiled at the familiar faces beaming back at her from the packed pews. She deliberately sought out Matteo's mum, at the top of the church, knowing how emotional she would be feeling. Knowing that today she was thinking of Matteo's father. They shared a look of understanding, of fondness, of friendship.

And then, inhaling a deep breath, she moved her gaze across the aisle. To Matteo. Who was standing, turned in her direction.

Waiting.

Her steps faltered for a moment.

She felt overwhelmed by how imposing, how handsome he looked in his tuxedo.

He watched her intently. As though this was the most important moment of his life.

When she reached him he didn't move.

For a moment she wondered if he was having second thoughts. But then, his eyes sombre, he leant towards her and whispered, '*Voglio sognare insieme a te per sempre.* Let's dream together for ever.'

She smiled her answer.

And a dazzling smile—a smile that had her heart floating in her chest, that said, *you are the one*—broke on his mouth.

Emma turned to the priest, impatient to become his wife. His best friend. His partner in dreams.

* * * * *

*If you enjoyed this book by Katrina Cudmore,
look out for*

SWEPT INTO THE RICH MAN'S WORLD
THE BEST MAN'S GUARDED HEART

*Or if you'd love to read about another
wedding-themed story, look out for*

THE SHEIKH'S CONVENIENT PRINCESS
By Liz Fielding

"I'm your man."

She laughed. "Actually, I'm your woman. I'm here if you need someone to talk to. In the past few weeks you've let me be me more than anyone else ever has. Only fair to return the favor." She leaned back on the picnic table, stretching the fabric across her breasts. "And the best part? Once we go back to our lives, we'll probably never see each other again. But even a momentary connection is better than nothing."

He had a feeling there was an underlying meaning to that last part. "Are we still talking about… talking?"

Emily turned to him, giving him a glimpse of gorgeous leg.

"This is me going with the flow." She drew in a deep breath. "Seizing the moment."

"Being reckless."

"That, too. But the great thing about knowing what the possibilities are—or aren't—from the get-go is that there are no expectations. So you can relax and enjoy the moment."

His blood pumped so hard he could hardly hear her. He didn't need to; he knew what she meant. Still… "Emily, I can't take advantage of you."

"I'm not asking you to. But hey, if you don't want to—"

"*Want* has nothing to do with it."

She leaned in close to him. "Actually, it has everything to do with it."

* * *

Wed in the West:
New Mexico's the perfect place to finally find true love!

FALLING FOR THE
REBOUND BRIDE

BY
KAREN TEMPLETON

First Published in Great Britain 2017
By Mills & Boon, an imprint of HarperCollins*Publishers*
1 London Bridge Street, London, SE1 9GF

© 2017 Karen Templeton-Berger

ISBN: 978-0-263-92274-5

23-0217

Karen Templeton is an inductee into the Romance Writers of America Hall of Fame. A three-time RITA® Award–winning author, she has written more than thirty novels for Mills & Boon. She lives in New Mexico with two hideously spoiled cats. She has raised five sons and lived to tell the tale, and she could not live without dark chocolate, mascara and Netflix.

To my five guys
Who made our home more than
we could have ever imagined.
Love you.

Chapter One

The young woman had been eyeing him from the other side of the luggage carousel for several minutes, her pale forehead slightly crimped. Far too wiped out to be paranoid—or return her interest, if that's what it was—Colin instead focused on his phone as he reflexively massaged an unyielding knot in the back of his neck. Although truthfully his entire body was one giant screaming ache after nearly two days either on a plane or waiting for one—

"Um… Colin? Colin Talbot?"

Instinctively clutching his camera bag, he frowned into a pair of sweet, wary blue eyes he was pretty sure he'd never seen in his life. Clearly he was even more tired than he'd realized, letting her sneak up on him like that.

With a squeaky groan, the carousel lurched into action, the contents of the plane's belly tumbling down the chute, bags and boxes jostling each other like a bunch of sleepy drunks. The other passengers closed in, ready to pounce, many sporting the standard assortment of cowboy hats and beat-up boots you'd expect to see in New Mexico. Colin squinted toward the business end, keeping one grit-scraped eye out for his beat-up duffel, then faced the young woman again. Crap, his backpack felt like it weighed a hundred pounds. Not to mention his head.

"Have we met? Because I don't—"

"I was a kid, the last time I saw you," she said, a smile flicking across a mouth as glossy as her long, wavy hair, some undefined color between blond and brown. "When I visited the ranch." She tucked some of that shiny hair behind one ear, the move revealing a simple gold hoop, as well as lifting the hem of her creamy blouse just enough to hint at the shapely hips her fitted jeans weren't really hiding. Hell. Next to this perfect specimen of refinement, Colin felt like week-old roadkill. Probably smelled like it, too, judging from the way the dude next to him on that last leg from Dallas kept leaning away.

The smile flickered again, although he now saw it didn't quite connect with her eyes. She pressed a slender, perfectly manicured hand to her chest. "Emily Weber? Deanna's cousin?"

Deanna. His younger brother Josh's new wife. And their dad's old boss's daughter. Now, vaguely, Colin remembered the gangly little middle schooler who'd spent a few weeks on the Vista Encantada that summer more than ten years ago. Vaguely, because not only had he already been in college, but she was right, they hadn't talked much. If at all. Mostly because of the age difference thing. That she even recognized him now...

"Oh. Right." Colin dredged up a smile of sorts, before his forehead cramped again. "You don't look much like I remember."

Humor briefly flickered in her eyes. "Neither do you."

He shifted, easing the weight of the backpack. "Then how'd you know it was me?"

A faint blush swept over her cheeks. "I didn't, at first. Especially with the beard. But it's hard to ignore the tallest man in the room. Then I noticed the camera bag, and I remembered the photo I spotted at your folks' house, when I was there a few months ago for the wedding. Josh's wedding, I mean." She grinned. "There's been a few of those in your family of late."

Seriously, his brothers had been getting hitched like there'd been a "buy one, get two free" sale on marriage licenses. First Levi, then Josh—his twin younger brothers—and soon Zach, the oldest, would be marrying for the second time—

"In any case," she said, "enough pieces started fitting together that I decided to take a chance, see if it was you. Although you probably wondered who the creeper chick trying to pick you up was."

Colin glanced back toward the carousel. "Thought never crossed my mind."

Out of the corner of his eye, he caught her gaze lower to her glittery flat shoes. "Crazy, huh?" she said, looking up again. But not at him. "After all this time, both of us being on the same plane to Albuquerque."

"Yeah."

This time the sound that pushed from her chest held a definite note of exasperation. "I'm sorry, I didn't mean to intrude on your privacy or whatever. I just thought, since I did recognize you, it'd be weird not to say anything. Especially since we're probably both headed up to the ranch. Unless..." Another flush streaked across her cheeks. "You're not?"

Colin shut his eyes, as if that'd stop her words' pummeling. True, he was exhausted and starving and not at all in the mood for conversation, especially with some classy, chatty chick he barely remembered. A chatty chick who clearly didn't know from *awkward*. Or didn't care. But she was right, he was being an ass. For no other reason than he could. Cripes, his father would knock him clear into next week for that. Not to mention his mother.

"No. I am," he said, daring to meet her gaze. And the you've-gone-too-far-buster set to her mouth under it. A mouth that under other circumstances—although what those might be, God alone knew—might have even provoked a glimmer of sexual interest. Okay, more than a glimmer. But those days were long gone, stuffed in some bottom drawer of his brain where they couldn't get him in trouble anymore. "And I apologize. It was a rough flight. Part of it, anyway."

Although not nearly as rough as the weeks, months, preceding it.

Emily's gaze softened. Along with that damn mouth. Yeah, sympathy was the last thing he needed right now.

"From?"

Since his name was plastered all over the magazine spread along with the photos, it wasn't exactly a secret. "Serbia."

A moment of silence preceded, "And why do I get the feeling I should leave it there?"

His mouth tugged up on one side. "Because you're good at reading minds?"

She almost snorted, even as something like pain flashed across her features. "As if. Then again…" Her gaze slid to his, so impossible to read he wondered if he'd imagined the pain in it. "Perhaps some minds are easier to read than others?"

Nope, not taking the bait. Even if he'd had a clue what the bait was. His arms folded across a layer of denim more disreputable than his yet-to-appear duffel, he said, "You get on in DC? Or Dallas?"

"DC."

"And nobody's picking you up?"

Her mouth twisted. "It was kind of last-minute. So I told Dee I'd rent a car, save her or Josh the five-hour round trip. They've got their hands full enough with the kids and the ranch stuff this time of year, and I can find my own way." Her eyes swung to his again. "What about you?"

"They don't know I'm here."

That got a speculative look before she snapped to attention like a bird dog. "Oh, there's one of my bags—"

"Which one?"

"The charcoal metallic with the rose trim. And there's the two others. But you don't have to—"

"No problem," Colin said, lugging the three hard-sided bags off the belt. Gray with pink stripes. Fancy. And no doubt expensive. His gaze once more flicked over her outfit, her hair and nails, even as his nostrils flared at her light, floral perfume.

Rich girl whispered through his brain, as another memory or two shuffled along for the ride, that his new sister-in-law's mother had hailed from a socially prominent East Coast family, that there'd been murmurings about how Deanna's aunt hadn't been exactly thrilled when her only sister took up with a cowboy and moved to the New Mexico hinterlands. Something about her throwing her life away. A life that had ended far too soon, when Deanna had only been a teenager.

Not that any of this had anything to do with him. Didn't then, sure as hell didn't now. Never mind the knee-to-the-groin reaction to the charmed life this young woman had undoubtedly led. The sort of life that tended to leave its participants with high expectations and not a whole lot of understanding for those whose lives weren't nearly so privileged—

"Hey. You okay?"

Colin gave his head a sharp shake, refusing to believe he saw genuine concern in those blue eyes. Apparently the long trip had chewed up more than a few brain cells.

"I'm fine. Or will be," he said as he grabbed his bag off the belt, dumping its sorry, chewed-up self on the airport's floor beside the shiny trio. "Nothing a shower, some food and a real bed won't fix." Not to mention some sorely needed alone time. "And the sooner we get—" *home*, he'd started to say, startling himself "—back to the Vista, the sooner I can make that happen." Slinging the duffel over his shoulder with the camera bag and commandeering the smaller two of Emily's bags, he nodded toward the rental car desk across the floor. "So let's go get our cars and get out of here."

Jerking up the handle of the larger bag, Emily frowned. "Um…why rent two cars? Wouldn't it make more sense to share one? Besides, don't take this the wrong way, but you do not look like someone up for driving through a couple hundred miles of nothing. In the dark, especially. So I'll drive, how's that?"

That got a momentary sneer from the old male ego— because Old Skool Dude here, the man was supposed to drive—until weariness slammed into him like a twenty-foot tidal wave. And along with it *logic*, because the woman had a point. Didn't make a whole lot of sense to rent two separate vehicles when they were going to the same place.

Not to mention the fact that passing out and careening into a ravine somewhere wasn't high on his to-do list. However…

"You might not want to be confined with me in a closed

space for two-and-a-half hours." Her brows lifted. "I think I smell."

She laughed. "Not that I've noticed. But it's warm enough we can leave the windows open."

"Once we get up past Santa Fe? Doubtful. Spring doesn't really get going good until May, at least."

A shrug preceded, "So I'll put on another layer—"

"But what'll you do for a car once you're there?"

"Dee said there's a truck I can use, if I want. So I was gonna turn in the rental tomorrow in Taos, anyway…"

First off, that shrug? Made her hair shimmer around her shoulders, begging to be touched. So wrong. Second, the image of Emily's perfectly polished person collided in Colin's worn-to-nubs brain with whatever undoubtedly mud-caked 4x4 her cousin was referring to. The ranch vehicles weren't known for being pretty.

Unlike the woman with the shimmery hair who'd be driving one of them.

So wrong.

Then he dragged his head out of his butt long enough to catch the amused smile playing around her mouth. "You really have a problem sharing a ride with me?"

Colin's cheeks heated. "It's not you."

"Actually, I got that. No, really. But I'm beginning to understand what Josh said about you being a loner—"

"I'm not—"

"Even I know you haven't been home in years," she said gently. "That you've barely been in touch with anyone since you left. And then you don't even tell your family you're coming back? Dude. However," she said, heading toward the rental desk, her hair swishing against her back. Glimmering. Taunting. "My only goal right now is to get to the ranch." She glanced back over her shoulder at him, and once again he saw a flicker of something decidedly sharp edged. "Expediency, you know? Your issues are none of my business. Nor are mine yours. In fact, we don't even have to talk, if you don't want to. I won't be offended, I promise. So. Deal?"

With the devil, apparently.

"Deal," Colin grumbled, hauling the rest of the bags to the desk, wondering why her reasonableness was pissing him the hell off.

An hour later, Emily had to admit Colin had been right about two things: the farther north they went, the colder it got; and he was definitely a little on the gamey side. Meaning she'd had no choice but to keep the windows at least partly down, or risk suffocation.

Also, it was *dark*. As in, the headlight beams piercing the pitch blackness were creepy as all get-out. To her, *night* meant when the street lamps came on, not that moment when the sun dived behind the horizon and yanked every last vestige of daylight with it. Her heart punched against her ribs—so much for her oh-I'll-drive bravado back there in the airport, when for whatever reason it hadn't occurred to her she'd never actually driven the route before. Somebody had always ferried her to and from Albuquerque. Sure, she would've made the trek herself in any case, but being responsible for another human being in the car with her…

"Jeez, get a grip," she muttered, turning up the Sirius radio in the SUV, hoping the pulsing beat would pound her wayward thoughts into oblivion. Not to mention her regrets, crammed inside her head like the jumbled mess of old sweaters and jeans and tops she'd stuffed willy-nilly inside her pretty new luggage. Clothes that predated Michael, that she'd rarely worn around him because he'd said they made her look dumpy.

Emily's nostrils flared as her fingers tightened around the leather-padded wheel. Someday, she might even cry.

Someday. When she was over the hurling and cursing stage.

Beside her, a six-feet-and-change Colin snorted and shifted, his arms folded over his chest as he slept. They'd barely made it out of Albuquerque before he'd crashed, his obvious exhaustion rolling off him in waves even more than the funk. If it hadn't been for that picture Dee had shown Emily—a very serious publicity shot of Colin the photojournalist—she would've never recognized him. As it was, between the five days' beard growth and shaggy hair, the rumpled clothes and saddlebags under his eyes, she still wasn't sure how she had. It must've been the eyes, a weird pale green against his sun-weathered face—

Emily released another breath, aggravation swamping her once more. Although with herself more than Colin, she supposed, for not having the good sense to leave well enough alone. Gah, it was as though she'd been totally incapable of stanching the words spewing from her mouth. Apparently heart-slicing betrayal had that effect on her. But seriously—after a lifetime of making nice, *now* she couldn't resist poking the bear? And a grumpy, malodorous one at that?

From her purse, her phone warbled. Her mother's ringtone. Good thing she was currently driving, because… No.

The man shifted again, muttering in his sleep, the words unintelligible. She imagined a frown—since that seemed to be his face's default setting, anyway—

"Crap!"

At the laser-like flash of the animal's eyes, Emily swerved the car to the right, hard, the wheels jittering over rocks and weeds before jerking to a spine-rattling stop. Colin's palm slammed against the dash as he bellowed awake, a particularly choice swearword hanging in the cold air between them for what felt like an hour.

"What the hell?"

"S-something darted out in front of the c-car," Emily finally got out, over the sudden—and horrifying—realization of exactly how close she was to losing it.

"You okay?"

How a gruff voice could be so gentle, Emily had no idea. How she was going to keep it together in the face of that gentleness, she had even less of one. But she would. If it killed her.

Her neck hurt a little when she nodded. "I'm fine."

"You don't sound fine."

On a half-assed laugh, she leaned her head back. Or would have if the headrest had let her. "I almost took out Bambi. What do you think?" She dared to cut her eyes to his, only to realize she couldn't see them anyway. Thank goodness. "Sorry about the sudden stop. Is everything… Are you…?"

"I'm good. Or will be when my heart climbs back down out of my throat." Which he now cleared. "Good save, by the way."

"How would you know?" she said, even as pleasure flushed her cheeks. "Since you slept through it."

"We're still upright. And alive. So I count that as a win."

"Funny, you don't strike me as a look-on-the-bright-side type."

"You'd be surprised."

"I already am. Well." And her heart could stop break-dancing anytime now, she thought as she gripped the wheel. "I guess we should get going—"

"You're shaking."

"Only a little… What are you doing?"

This asked as he got out of the car and walked around

to her side, motioning for her to open the door. "Taking over the driving, what does it look like?"

"You don't have to—"

"Actually, I think I do."

Emily felt her face go grumpy. "I thought you said that was a good save."

"It was. And I mean that. But I'm awake now—"

"Sorry about that."

"—and I'm probably a little better at recovering from stress than you are."

"Heh. You ever driven on the DC beltway?"

"Many times. Although trust me, it doesn't even begin to compare with Mumbai. Besides, once we hit town, do you have any idea where we're going?"

There was that. Because, again, she hadn't driven when she'd been out before. Of course her plan had been to either rely on the car's GPS or—probably better—on Dee or Josh. Which she could still do. But by now she realized she was beginning to slip across that fine line between independent and mule-headed. And she was whacked, too.

"Emily?"

Again with the gentleness. Jerk.

"Fine," she said, climbing down from behind the wheel and marching around to the passenger side, huddling deeper into her sweater coat before strapping herself in. Rocks crunched and rattled as Colin pulled back onto the highway, and Emily felt her jangled nerves relax. A little.

Because for some reason this guy seemed a lot bigger awake than he had asleep. And she wasn't exactly tiny. A fact that had apparently induced no small amount of angst in her petite mother—

"So where are we, exactly?" Colin asked.

"Just past Taos."

He nodded. "You mind if I turn down the…music?"

"Turn it off, if you want. I don't care."

"You sure?"

"I'm sure."

Except the silence that followed made her brain hurt. Strange how she didn't mind the quiet when she was actually by herself. But when there was actually someone else in the space—

"So how come you didn't tell anyone you were coming?"

He hesitated, then said, "Because I didn't want to."

"None of my business, in other words."

His gaze veered to hers, then away.

"And you don't think they might find it weird when we show up together?"

A single-note chuckle pushed through his nose. "Dog with a bone, aren't cha?"

Her mouth pulled flat, Emily shoved her hair behind her ear. But after years of being the peacemaker, the One Most Likely to Back Down... "Guess I don't have a whole lot of patience these days for secrets."

"Even though this has nothing to do with you."

"Me, no. My cousin, yes. And her husband. And his family. So..."

"And you're nothing if not loyal."

She waited out the stab to her heart before saying, "Out of fashion though that might be."

That got a look. Probably accompanied by a frown, though she wasn't about to check.

Another couple miles passed before he said, "And I'm guessing I've been the topic of conversation recently."

"Your name does come up a lot," she said quietly, then glanced over. "Since, you know, you're the brother who's not there. And hasn't *been* there for years."

Seconds passed. "I've been...on assignment."

Exactly what Josh had said, after his and Dee's wedding, his that's-life shrug at complete odds with the disappointment in his eyes. And between the leftover shakiness from nearly taking out that deer back there and feeling like hornets had set up shop inside her brain, whatever filters Emily might have once had were blown to hell.

"From everything I can tell, Colin, your family's great. In fact, most people would be grateful..." Tears biting at her eyes, she gave her head a sharp shake, rattling the hornets. "So what exactly did they do to tick you off so much?"

And to think, Colin mused, if he hadn't agreed to this crazy woman's suggestion to share the car, the worst that might've happened would have been his ending up in a ditch somewhere.

Of course, he didn't owe her, or anyone, an explanation. Although she seemed like a nice enough kid—if pushy— and surprisingly playing the total bastard card wasn't part of his skill set. Besides, in a half hour they'd be there, and he'd hole up in one of the cabins, and she'd stay with her cousin in the main house, and they probably wouldn't even see each other again for the duration of her visit. Right?

Except right now she was watching him, waiting for an answer, those great, big, sad eyes pinned to the side of his face. Yeah, there was a story there, no doubt. Not that he was about to get sucked in. Because he'd come home to get his head on straight again, not get all snarled in someone else's.

"They didn't *do* anything, okay?" he finally mumbled. "Like you said, they're great people. It's just we don't see a lot of things through the same lens."

He sensed more than saw her frown before she leaned into the corner between the seat and the door—at least as much as the seat belt would let her—her arms folded over her stomach. Thinking, no doubt.

"So what's different now?"

"Do you even consider what's about to pop out of your mouth before it does?"

"Probably about as much as you've considered their re-action when you show up out of the blue. And with your dad's heart condition—"

"First off, people keeling over from shock only hap-pens in the movies—"

"Not only in the movies."

"Mostly, then. And second, Dad's not at death's door. He never was, as far as I can tell—"

"And how would you know that if you haven't been there?"

"Because that's what he said, okay? For crying out loud, I did talk to him, or Mom, or both, every day at the time. I'm not totally out of the loop—"

"Even if you prefer to hover at its edge?"

If it hadn't been for the gentle humor in her voice—and something more, something he couldn't quite put his finger on—he would've been a lot more pissed than he was. "They told me not to come home, that it wasn't nec-essary. And my reasons for returning now…" He briefly faced her, then looked away. "Are mine."

"As are your reasons for not giving them a heads-up that you are. Got it."

"You're really aggravating, you know that?"

Her laugh startled him. "Then my work here is done," she said, clearly pleased with herself. Because the chick was downright bonkers. Story of his life, apparently.

"Look," he said, giving in or up or whatever. "If you've been around my family for more than thirty seconds you know they can be a mite…overwhelming en masse."

Another laugh. "I noticed."

"So if I'd called my brother and told him I was coming, you can bet your life the whole gang would be at the Vista to welcome me home." His jaw clenched. "Maybe even the whole town. I know what I'm about to face, believe me. But I'd at least prefer to ease back into the bosom of the clan on my own terms. At least as much as possible."

"I can understand that."

"Really?"

"Like you're the only person in the world who has issues with their family?" she said quietly, not looking at him. "Please."

The sign for Whispering Pines flashed in the headlights, and Colin turned off the highway onto the smaller road leading to the tiny town. Emily shrugged more deeply into her coat; the higher they climbed, the colder the night got. But the air was sweet and clear and clean. And, Colin had to admit, welcoming.

"It's the space, isn't it?" she said, shattering his thoughts.

"Excuse me?"

"Why you've come home. Same reason I'm here now, I suppose. To stop the—" She waved her hands at her head, then folded her arms again. "The noise. The crowding."

The impulse to probe nudged more insistently. He'd assumed she was only there to visit, like people did. Normal people, anyway. Or to attend Zach's wedding, although that wasn't for weeks yet. Now, though, questions niggled. Maybe there was more…?

And whatever that might be had nothing to do with him.

"Hadn't really thought about it," he muttered, ignoring what had to be a doubtful look in response. Shaking her head, Emily dug her phone out of her purse, only to heave a sigh and slug it back inside.

"No signal. Jeez, how do people even survive out here?"

"Same way they have for hundreds of years, I imagine."

A soft grunt was her only reply. Thank God. Although Colin had to admit, as wearying as her poking and prying had been, the silence was far worse, providing a far-too-fertile breeding ground for his own twisted-up thoughts. Because despite the universe's insistence that this is where he needed to be right now, he'd be lying to himself if he didn't admit this felt an awful lot like starting over.

Or worse, failure.

A dog's barking as they pulled into the Vista's circular driveway shattered the silence, although Colin barely heard it over his pounding heart, the rush of blood between his ears. Beside him, Emily gathered her giant purse, then gave him what he suspected was a pitying look before grabbing the door's handle.

"I don't envy you right now," she murmured, then shoved open the door and got out. By now her cousin and his brother were out on the oversize veranda. Even in the screwy light he could see confusion shudder across both their faces.

"You'll never guess who I ran into in the airport," she said, and Colin realized he had two choices: show himself, or turn right around and pretend this had all been a mistake. Except the flaw with plan B was that, for one thing, Emily's luggage was still in the SUV. And for another, she'd rat on him.

So, on a weighty sigh, Colin pried himself from behind the wheel and faced his little brother, who immediately spit out a cussword that would've gotten a good smack upside the head from their mother. Two seconds later, Josh was pounding the hell out of Colin's back, then grinning up at him like a damn fool.

"Holy hell, Col," he said, his eyes wet, and Colin did his best to grin back.

"I know, right?" he said, feeling heat flood his cheeks before he glanced over to see Emily wrapped tightly in his new sister-in-law's arms, bawling her eyes out.

....

Chapter Two

"So how come you didn't say anything?"

Standing at the sink in the ranch's ginormous,
Southwest-kitsch kitchen, Emily set the now-clean Dutch
oven in the drainer, pushing out a sigh for Colin's question. Not that she'd been able to eat much of the amazing
pot roast, especially after embarrassing the hell out of
herself earlier. But her cousin's keeping dinner warm for
her—well, *them*, as it happened—had been a very sweet
gesture. Because that was Dee.

Wiping her damp hands across her butt, Emily turned,
now unable to avoid the scowl she'd ignored—more or
less—all through the late dinner. Even from six or so
feet away, Colin's size was impressive. At least he no longer looked—or smelled—as though he'd recently escaped
from the jungle. And he'd shaved, which took the edge
off the mountain man aura. Somewhat. But with his arms
crossed over that impressive chest, not even his slightly

curling, still-damp hair detracted from the massive mouth-drying solidity that was Colin Talbot. For sure, none of the brothers were exactly puny, but Colin was next door to intimidating. Toss in the glower, and…

Yeah.

"Your brother let you out of his clutches?"

The corner of Colin's mouth twitched. "For the moment. The dog was acting like something was going on outside he thought Josh needed to check out."

And Dee had gone to nurse her infant daughter—after Emily shooed her off, insisting on cleaning up after dinner. No buffers, in other words. And judging from that penetrating gaze, Colin was not-so-patiently waiting for her answer.

She shrugged, a lame attempt at playing it cool. "Maybe because your doing the prodigal son routine seemed like a far bigger deal than—"

"Your wedding getting called off?"

Weirdly, he sounded almost angry. Although whether it was because she hadn't told him, or on her behalf, she had no idea. Not that either of those made any sense. Then again, maybe he was ticked off because of a dozen other things she wasn't privy to. Nor was she likely to be. So Big Guy didn't exactly have a lot of room to talk, did he?

And before those weird, light eyes melted her brain, Emily turned back around to wipe down the sink. "In the interest of journalistic integrity," she said, scrubbing far harder than the stainless sink needed. "I was the one who called it off."

"Because your fiancé cheated on you. Josh filled me in."

The wrung-out sponge shoved behind the faucet, Emily faced him again, her arms tightly crossed over her ribs. "Seriously? You reconnect with your brother for the first time in a million years and you guys talk about *me*?"

"Hey. You were the one who totally lost it the minute we got here. Not me. Although for what it's worth, I didn't ask. Josh volunteered the information. And it was like a five-, six-second part of the conversation. Okay, ten at the most. But I thought you'd probably appreciate knowing that I know." He paused. "Not that I plan on being in your way much. In fact, I'm heading over to the foreman's cabin in a few."

Their gazes tangled for a long moment before Josh and the dog suddenly reappeared, the panting, grinning Aussie shepherd mix trotting over to his bowl to noisily slosh water all over the tiled floor.

"Have no idea what Thor heard," Josh said, striding to the sink to fill a glass of his own. Colin had a good three or four inches on his little brother, who still wasn't "little" by anyone's standards. The Talbots grew 'em solid, for sure. Josh's mossy eyes darted from her to Colin, a quizzical frown briefly biting into his forehead. But whatever he was thinking he kept to himself, thank goodness. Instead he flicked the empty glass toward the sink, then set it back in the drain board before clapping Josh's arm. "Well, come on—let's get you set up. Haven't been out there in weeks, have no idea what condition it's in—"

"Considering some of the places I've slept?" Colin said with a tight smile. "I'm sure it's fine. And I'm about to collapse. We can talk more tomorrow," he said gently at his brother's slightly let-down expression. "Although don't be surprised if I sleep until dinnertime. But promise me you won't tell Mom and Dad I'm here."

"I won't."

"Swear."

Chuckling, Josh pressed a hand to his heart. "To God. Good enough?"

With a nod, Colin walked to the back door where

he'd dumped his stuff; a moment later, he was gone, and Emily turned to her cousin-in-law. Squinting. Josh actually winced.

"Sorry, it kinda slipped out. Then again…" He leaned back against the counter, his palms curled over the edge. "It's not exactly a secret, is it?"

"No, but…" Emily glanced toward the door, where she could have sworn Colin's presence still shimmered. Which only proved he hadn't been the only wiped-out person in the house. "No," she repeated, giving Josh a little smile, which she transferred to the dog when he came over to nudge her hand with his sopping-wet snout. Then she sniffed, blinking back another round of tears.

"You know you can stay as long as you want," Josh said, adding, "I mean that," when Emily lifted watery eyes to his. "You probably have no idea how much Dee talked about you, when she came back after her dad died. About how you saved her sanity after that business with her ex. How you stood by her when your folks…well…"

At that, Emily pushed out a tiny laugh. "Yeah, propriety's kind of a biggie with them. Mom especially." Meaning a knocked-up niece hadn't been part of Margaret Weber's game plan. Although that was small potatoes compared with her daughter's society wedding getting the ax weeks before it was supposed to happen. Never mind that it would have been a total sham.

"In any case," Josh continued, "after everything you did for Dee, anything we can do to return the favor—"

"Thanks. But…"

Her cousin's husband grinned. "What?"

Emily sighed. In the rush of adrenaline that had followed in the wake of discovering Michael's secret, her fight-or-flight impulse had kicked in, big-time. And since fighting had felt like an exercise in futility, she'd chosen flight…as far from Michael and her mother and all those gasps and clacking tongues in McLean, Virginia, as she could get. And where else but to the place that had been a balm to her soul the few times she'd been here as a kid? And where the only person who could effortlessly toggle between being a nonjudgmental sounding board and understanding when Emily needed space lived?

However, now that the adrenaline was subsiding, it occurred to her that this was a newly married couple…a newly married couple with two young children between them, who probably cherished their alone time when said children were asleep. So the last thing they probably wanted, or needed, was some emotionally volatile chick invading their space.

"You guys have to promise me," she said to Josh's bemused expression, "you'll let me know the minute you feel I'm cramping your style."

At that, Josh laughed out loud. "We live with a four-year-old and an infant. Cramped *is* our style. As it will be for many years to come, I expect. Although at least *you* can get your own glass of water if you wake up in the middle of the night. You can, right?"

Emily chuckled. "Not only that, I can even make my own breakfast."

"Then there ya go." Josh leaned over to give her shoulder a quick squeeze. "In case you missed it, we're kinda big on family around here. So not another word, you hear?"

Her eyes burning again, Emily nodded. And this time, not because she was worn-out. Not even because of her own foolishness, letting herself get caught up in a fairy tale that now lay shattered in a million pieces at the bottom of her soul. That had been just plain stupid. Even so, she had no doubt she'd eventually recover. And be stronger for the experience, if not a whole lot wiser. So out of the ashes and all that.

But what yanked at her heart now was the sudden and profound realization of what had been missing from her life to this point, or at least not nearly as much in evidence as it should have been:

The good old Golden Rule, treating others the way you'd want to be treated. At least, as far as being on the receiving end of it went. All her life, it now occurred to her, she'd tried so hard to do what was expected of her, to not make waves. A lot in life she'd been fine with, for the most part. So sue her, she liked making people happy. But how often had anyone else ever done that for her? Other than Dee, that was, who'd come to live with Emily and her parents shortly after her mother died, when they were teenagers.

Now Emily looked at the kind, wonderful man her cousin had married, feeling overwhelmingly grateful for Deanna's happiness…and even more acutely aware of how badly she'd been screwed. And as her cousin joined them in the kitchen, one arm slipping around her husband's waist, resolve flooded Emily, that the next time—if there even was a next time—either the dude would look at her the way Josh looked at Dee or *fuggedaboutit*. Because God knew Michael had never looked at her like that, had he? And look how that had turned out.

"She asleep?" Josh asked Dee, who spiked a hand through her short dark hair. Almost chin length now, grown out from the edgier style she'd worn when she worked at that art gallery in DC. Roots were showing, too, a burnished glimmer against the black ends.

"Out like a light," Dee said, yawning as she leaned into Josh. Again, envy spiked through Emily, at how comfortable they were with each other. How much in love. Which was what came, Emily supposed, from their having been friends first, when they'd been kids and Josh's father had worked for Dee's. But between that and the trip and the events leading to the trip and the weirdness with Colin, Emily suddenly felt used up.

"If you guys don't mind," she said, "I think I'm going to turn in. It's been a long day."

"I'm sure," Dee said, slipping out of the shelter of her husband's embrace to wrap her arms around Emily, hold her close for a long moment. "We'll talk tomorrow. If you want."

"I'm sure I will," Emily said, then left the kitchen, letting the silence in the long, clay-tiled hall leading to the bedroom wing enfold her. Even with the updates to the house from when Dee and Josh thought they'd sell it after Uncle Granville's death, the place hadn't changed much from what she remembered from childhood. But the century-old hacienda, with its troweled walls and beamed ceilings, seemed good with that, like an old woman who saw no need to adopt the latest fashion craze simply because it was the latest thing.

A giant gray cat, curled on the folded-up quilt on the foot of the guest room's double bed, blinked sleepily at her when she turned on the nightstand's lamp. No one seemed to know how old Smoky was, or how he'd even come to live here—like a ghost whose presence was simply accepted.

"Hey, guy," she said, plopping her smaller bag onto the mattress, chuckling at his glower because she'd disturbed his nap. Not to mention his space, since he'd clearly staked a claim on the room in her absence. "We gonna be roomies for the next little while?"

The cat yawned, then meowed before hauling himself to his feet and plodding across the bed to bump her hand as she tugged a pair of pajamas from the case and zipped it back up. Unpacking would come later, a thought that hurt her chest. Not because she was here, but because of *why* she was here—

Dee's quiet knock on her open bedroom door made Emily start. Her cousin had changed into a loose camisole top, a pair of don't-give-a-damn drawstring bottoms and a baggy plaid robe that definitely gave off a masculine vibe.

"Need anything?"

"A new life?"

With a snort, her cousin came over to sit on the edge of the bed, which the cat took as an invitation to commandeer her lap. "I know I said tomorrow," she said as Emily unceremoniously disrobed, tugged on the pajamas. Unlike her relationships with nearly everybody else in her life, she and Dee had no secrets between them. "But… I'm so sorry, Em."

Emily crawled up onto the bed, sitting cross-legged to face Dee like she used to when they were kids. The cat immediately changed loyalties, flicking his poofy tail across Emily's chin before settling in, rumbling like a dishwasher. Smiling, she stroked his staticky fur.

"Better now than later, right?"

Her cousin blew a half laugh through her nose. "At least you're not pregnant," she muttered, then frowned. "You're not, are you?"

It was everything Emily could do not to laugh herself at the absurdity of her cousin's perfectly reasonable question. Especially since the sweet baby girl down the hall wasn't Josh's, but the result of Dee's affair—well before she moved back to New Mexico and reconnected with Josh, whom she hadn't seen since she was a teenager— with a man who'd neglected to mention he already had three children. And a wife. A thought that immediately displaced Emily's inappropriate spike of amusement with anger, at how both she and her cousin had been played for fools by a pair of scumbags who mistook agreeableness for weakness.

Or stupidity.

"What do you think?" she said, and her cousin's mouth twisted.

"Oh. Right. Although sometimes—"

"Not in this case. Although I suppose I should see about having the IUD removed now. Since…" She shrugged, and Dee's eyes went soft.

"Since it's completely over between you and Michael?"

"Yeah," Emily said on a sigh.

"Well…" Dee grinned. "Before you do, who's to say you couldn't have some good old-fashioned revenge sex?"

Now Emily did laugh. Ridiculous though the suggestion was. Towns this small weren't exactly rife with prospects. Which right now was a major selling point, actually, what with her recent self-diagnosis of acute testosterone intolerance. "With…?"

Her cousin's eyes twinkled. "I'm sure we can scrounge up someone who isn't toothless and/or on Social Security."

"Meaning Colin," Emily deadpanned, and Dee's eyebrows nearly flew off her head.

"The thought never even entered my head."

"Right."

"You've gotta admit, he does clean up nice." Emily glared. For many reasons. Then her cousin leaned forward to wrap her hand around hers. "You do know I'm kidding, right?"

"I'm never sure with you."

"Good point," Dee said, the twinkle once again flashing. "But while I do find it serendipitous—"

"Ooh, big word."

"—that the two of you showed up together, and he is a hunk—because clearly the Talbots don't know how to make 'em any other way—it's also pretty obvious he's no more in the market for fun and games than you are."

"Yeah, I kind of got that impression, too. But what did he say? To Josh?"

"It's more what he didn't say, I think. Obviously the man is all about keeping to himself. Even more than most men are," she said, and Emily thought, *Tell me about it*. "But he indicated to Josh he just needed a break. And that it'd been too long since he'd been home. Especially since so much has happened since then. Weddings and whatnot."

"You think he'll stick around for Zach and Mallory's?"

"Who knows? I get the feeling Colin's not big on plans. Or commitments." Dee cocked her head. "And what's with that look?"

Emily punched out a sound that was equal parts laugh and sigh. "That would be me overthinking things I have no business thinking about at all. Especially since I clearly have no talent whatsoever when it comes to guessing what's going on inside someone's head. I mean, really—I knew Michael for *how* many years? And still…" She shook her head. "So presuming anything about some man I've known for a few hours—and half of that he's either been comatose or not around…"

"Em." Dee looked almost exasperated. "First off, there's a huge difference between some dirtwad who's deliberately trying to keep you in the dark and a guy who's simply not big on sharing. With anybody, apparently. Even his brothers barely know him, for reasons known only to Colin. So if you think Colin's got some serious issues—believe me, you're not alone. In fact, Josh said the same thing. Only *I* think—" she squeezed Emily's hand "—that you've got enough junk of your own to work through right now without worrying about someone you don't even know. Because secondly, you're too damn kindhearted. Always have been. Which is probably…" She bit her lip, and Emily rolled her eyes.

"Go on, spit it out. Which is why I'm in this mess, right?"

"Seeing the best in people is what you do," Dee said gently. "Who you are. And I wouldn't change that, or you, for the world. So don't even go there, you hear me? But it does have its downside."

"In other words I need to toughen up."

"Says the woman who teaches kindergartners," Dee said on a short laugh. "You're plenty tough, babycakes. But I think…" Her cousin paused, her eyes narrowed slightly. "What's the longest you've ever gone without a boyfriend? A month? Two?"

Emily started. "I…I don't know. I never really thought about it—"

"Because you've never been alone long enough *to* think about it. And then you reconnected with Michael at that thing at the club, and everyone—his parents, your parents—were all *ooh, perfect*, and…"

"And I fell right into everyone's expectations."

Her cousin's smile was kind. "Especially Aunt Margaret's."

Considering her mother's apoplectic fit when the wedding was called off? Truth. But…

"You never really liked Michael, did you?"

Dee reached over to stroke the cat. "I never really *trusted* him. Gut reaction, sorry. But at first I figured it would probably peter out, so why say anything? Especially since nobody made me God. Then you guys got engaged, and… I don't know. Something felt off. Except then *I* got involved with Phillippe, and, well. Considering how that turned out, I didn't exactly have room to talk, did I? And by then you were deep into wedding-planning fever…" She shrugged, then gave her cousin a little smile.

"You could've still said something."

Her cousin snorted. "And would you have listened? Or taken my 'feelings' as sour grapes because my own relationship had ended so badly? In fact," she said before Emily could answer, "I wasn't all that sure myself I could be objective. Because at that point I pretty much hated anything with a penis."

Clapping a hand to her mouth, Emily unsuccessfully smothered her guffaw. Then she lowered it, still chuckling, only to release another breath. "I can relate, believe me."

"Seriously."

Emily's eyes burned. "You know what's really sad? At this point I don't even know if I was really happy—before the truth came out—or just thought I was."

"Sing it, honey," Dee sighed. "But the good news is, at least we grow. Our hearts get shattered and then we get mad and then we get to work. Which doesn't in the least absolve the creeps of their creepiness. But we gain so much more from the experience than we lose."

"How…adult of you."

"I know, right?" Grinning, Dee levered herself off the bed, tugging her robe closed in the desert chill. "You're gonna be fine, Em. You *are* fine. And you know what else?"

"What?"

Her cousin's gaze softened again. "You're free," she said, bending over to kiss Emily's hair before padding out of the room.

For several seconds after, Emily sat on the bed, stroking the cat who'd returned to smash himself up beside her, his purr comforting and warm.

You're free...

Her eyes watered as the words played over and over in her head. Because for the first time that she could remember...she was, wasn't she? Free from anyone else's *expectations*, like Dee said. Or judgment, or censure. Free *to* finally figure out who she was, what *she* wanted.

More to the point, what she didn't.

True, she'd come for the space. Absolutely. But not to escape. Instead, for the space to claim for herself everything that was rightfully hers.

Including, she realized, the luxury of being herself.

Of being able to do exactly as she pleased without worrying, or even caring, about what anybody else thought.

The headiness almost made her dizzy.

The next morning, Colin sat outside his parents' little house in town, trying to get his bearings before facing them. It didn't help that, despite his exhaustion—or maybe because of it—he hadn't slept worth spit the night before. Didn't help that Emily kept popping into his head, although he assumed that was because she reminded him a touch of Sarah. A touch. The long hair, maybe. Her... freshness. That guileless, direct gaze that revealed more than she probably realized.

More than he could possibly handle. Especially after Sarah.

Especially now.

Releasing a breath, Colin got out of the rental and headed toward the house, shrugging into a denim jacket older than God as he sidestepped the same dinged pickup his mom had been driving for years. The impossibly blue sky framed the small brown house, squat and unassuming behind the huge lilac bushes beginning to leaf out beside the front door, the half dozen whiskey barrels choked with mounds of shivering pansies.

Despite the chill, Colin stopped for a moment, taking in the view. The house sat on the apex of a shallow cul-de-sac in a chorus line of a dozen others similar in size, if not in shape or color. There'd been no plan to Whispering Pines, it'd just sort of happened, lot by lot, house by house. But scraping the outskirts of town the way it was, this lot at least had a decent view of the mountains, which probably made Dad happy. It'd been damn good of Granville to give them the house, after the doctors *strongly* suggested Dad retire. There'd been other provisions, as well. His parents would never starve or be homeless. Still, three generations of Talbots had grown up in the ranch foreman's house, and it'd felt strange sleeping there—or trying to—last night by himself.

It felt strange, period, being here. Even though—

He jolted when the front door opened, although not nearly as much as his mother when she realized who was standing in her driveway. Her hair was more silver than he remembered, the ends of her long ponytail teasing her sweatered upper arms poking out from a puffy, bright purple vest. But her unlined face still glowed, her jeans still hugged a figure as toned as ever and the joy in those deep brown eyes both warmed him and made him feel like a giant turd. It wasn't that he didn't love his family, but—

"Holy crap," she breathed, appropriately enough, and Colin felt a sheepish grin steal across his cheeks.

"Hey, Mom," he said, and a moment later she'd thrown her arms around him—as much as she could, anyway, he had a good eight or nine inches on her—and was hugging and rocking him like he was three or something, the whole time keening in his ear. Then Billie Talbot held him apart and bellowed, "Sam! Get your butt out here, now!" and a minute later his father appeared, his smile even bigger than his wife's. Then Dad practically shoved Mom aside to yank Colin into a hug that almost hurt.

"Don't know why you're here," Dad mumbled, "don't care. Just glad you are."

Feeling his chest ease—because honestly, he'd had no idea how this was going to go down—Colin pulled away, shoving his hands in his back pockets. He'd always thought of his father as this giant of a man, towering over most everybody. Especially his sons. Now Colin realized he was actually a little taller than Sam, which somehow didn't feel right.

"Me, too." He paused. "It's been too long."

"Won't argue with you there," Dad said. Although despite that whole it-doesn't-matter spiel, Dad was no one's fool. Especially when it came to his sons, all of whom had pulled their fair share of crap growing up. And now it was obvious from the slight tilt of his father's heavy gray brows that he knew damn well there was more to Colin's return than a simple "it was time."

"So, where are you staying?" Mom asked. Colin faced her, now noticing she had her equipment bag with her, meaning she was headed out either to a birth or at least an appointment.

"In your old digs," he said with a slight smile.

"So you've seen Josh and them?"

He nodded. "But they didn't know I was coming, either. Neither did anyone else. Zach or Levi, I mean. I'm…easing back into things."

His mother got a better grip on the bag, then dug her car keys out of her vest's pocket. "And unfortunately it's my day at the clinic, so I can't hang around. But dinner later, yes?"

Colin smiled. "You bet."

Mom squeezed his arm, then said, "Oh, to hell with it," before pulling him in for another hug. This time, when she let go, he saw tears. "You have just made my day, honey. Shoot, year. I can't wait until tonight."

"Me, too," Colin said, then watched as she strode out to her truck with the same purposeful gait as always. Nothing scared that woman, he thought. Nothing that he was aware of, anyway.

"She's busier than ever," Dad said behind him, making him turn. "Happier, too."

His twin brothers had been in middle school when Mom announced it was time she lived her own life, that she'd decided to become a midwife. And if for a while they'd all been like a pile of puppies whose mama had decided they needed weaning, right then and there, they'd all gotten over it, hadn't they?

"Um…want something to drink?" Dad said, scrubbing his palm over the backside of his baggy jeans—an uncharacteristically nervous gesture, Colin thought. Mom'd said his father had lost weight after that scare with his heart, even if only because the doctors had put the fear of God in him. Apparently, however, it hadn't yet occurred to him to buy clothes to fit his new body. "It's probably too early for a beer, and I only have that 'lite' crap, anyway…"

Colin chuckled, even as he realized his own heart was stuttering a bit, too. True, he'd never butted heads with his father like his brother Levi had, but neither was there any denying that the day he'd left Whispering Pines for college he'd felt like a caged bird finally being set free. Nor had he ever expected any desire to come home to roost.

"That's okay, I'm good."

Nodding, his dad tugged open the door, standing aside so Colin could enter. The place was tiny, but as colorful and warm as the old cabin had been. Plants crowded windowsills with wild exuberance, while hand-quilted pillows and throws in a riot of colors fought for space on otherwise drab, utilitarian furniture. Interior design had never been part of Mom's skill set—and certainly not Dad's, whose only criteria for furnishings had been a chair big enough to hold him and a table to eat at—but there was love in every item in the room, from the lushness of her plants to how deliberately she displayed every item ever gifted to her from grateful clients.

Love that now embraced him, welcoming him home… even as it chastised him for staying away so long. But…

Colin frowned. "I would've thought if Granville was going to leave the ranch to a Talbot, it would've been to you."

His father snorted. "First off, I wouldn't've wanted it. Not at this point in my life. Which Gran knew. Second…" Dad's mouth twitched. "He also knew exactly what he was doing, leaving it to your brother and his daughter equally."

"Ah."

"Exactly. Because sometimes fate needs a little kick in the butt." Dad squinted. "So. What's going on, son?"

Underneath his father's obvious—and understandable—concern, Colin could still hear hints of the my-way-or-the-highway gruffness that'd raised his hackles a million times ever since he was old enough to realize there was a whole world outside of this tiny speck of it wedged beside a northern New Mexican mountain range. A world that needed him maybe, even if it'd be years before Colin figured out how, exactly. That hadn't changed, even if…

And the problem with voluntarily reinserting yourself

into the circle of the people who—for good or ill—loved you most was that there would be questions.

How truthfully Colin could answer those questions was something else again.

Chapter Three

Sucking in a slow, steady breath, Colin managed a smile. "Why am I back, you mean?"

Dad crossed his arms over what was left of his belly. But the fire in those fierce gray eyes hadn't diminished one bit. "Seems as good a place as any to start. Especially since your mother and me, we'd pretty much given up on that ever happening, to be truthful."

"I stayed in touch," Colin said, realizing how pitiful that sounded even before the words were out of his mouth.

"When it suited you, sure."

Even after all this time he still couldn't put into words what exactly had driven him away. Which was nuts. But all he'd known was that if he'd stayed he would've gone mad.

"I had things to do I couldn't do here," he said simply.

After a moment, his father started toward the nondescript but reasonably updated kitchen to pour himself a cup of coffee from the old-school Mr. Coffee on the counter. "Decaf," Dad groused, holding up the cup before taking a swallow and making a face. Then, leaning one roughened hand against the counter, he sighed. "Not gonna lie, for a long time it hurt like hell, after you left. That, on top of the crap Levi pulled…"

This said with an indulgent smile. Most likely because from everything Josh had said last night, his twin, Levi—who after a stint in the army was now back and married to the local girl he'd been secretly sweet on in school—and Dad had worked out their differences.

His father's gaze met his again. "Although I honestly don't know why I ever thought the four of you would stick around. That you'd naturally be as tied to the place as I was, and my daddy and granddaddy before me. No, let me finish, I've been waiting a long time to say this." Frowning, he glanced toward the window over the sink, then back at Colin. "Then this happened—" he gestured with the cup toward his chest "—and I guess when they put that stent in my artery more blood went to my brain and opened that up, too. And I realized if you expect your kids to be clones of you, you're not raising 'em right. You all have to follow your own paths, not mine. And I'm good with that." One side of his mouth lifted. "Mostly, anyway. But you can't blame me for being curious about what's prompted the surprise visit."

With that, it occurred to Colin his father hadn't seemed all that *surprised*, really. So much for swearing to God. "Josh told you I was here."

"He felt a heads-up wouldn't be a bad idea. I didn't tell your mother, though." His father chuckled. "After all these years—and raising you boys—it takes a lot to pull one over on her. Couldn't resist the opportunity to see the look on her face when you showed up. Although she will *kill* me if she ever found out I knew before she did."

Somehow, Colin doubted that. Sure, his folks bickered from time to time, same as any couple who'd been married a million years. They were human, after all. But there'd never been any doubt that Sam Talbot still, after those million years, knew he'd struck gold with Billie, who'd known a good thing—or so the story went—the instant she'd clapped eyes on the tall, lanky cowboy when she'd been barely out of school herself, and wouldn't do anything to jeopardize what they had. Even if she didn't let him get away with bubkes. It was all about balance with his mother, for sure.

Something Colin would do well to figure out for himself. And *by* himself.

Leaning against a pantry cupboard, he crossed his arms. "I got offered a book contract from a big publisher, for a collection of my photo-essays over the past several years."

His father's brows shot up. "Really?"

Colin nodded. "But I want to add some new material, too. So I need…" His mouth set, he glanced away, then back at his father. "I need someplace quiet to work. To sift through my thoughts about the subject matter."

"Which is?"

He felt his chest knot. "The plight of kids around the world."

Something flashed in his father's eyes. Colin couldn't tell—and didn't want to know, frankly—what. "Refugees, you mean?"

"Among others. Children living in poverty, in war-torn countries, whatever. I want…" He swallowed. "The whole reason I take pictures is so other people can see what I've seen."

"Sounds like quite an honor. That offer, I mean."

"I don't… That's not how it feels to me. It's more that—"

"It's your calling."

"I guess. A calling that came to me, though. I didn't go looking for it."

A smile barely curved his father's mouth. "That's how callings work, boy. They tend to clobber a person over the head. But your own place wouldn't work?"

"College kids in the next unit," Colin said, hoping his face didn't give him away. Although he wasn't lying. Exactly. "One thing they're not, is quiet."

His father's eyes narrowed, as though not quite buying the story. Hardly a surprise, considering he'd survived four teenage boys. Then his lips tilted again.

"And you know what? I'm not about to look a gift horse in the mouth. Or question its motives. I'm just glad you're here. For however long that turns out to be. And I cannot tell you how proud I am of you."

Holy hell—he couldn't remember his father ever saying that to him. About anything. Oh, Dad would occasionally nod appreciatively over something one or the other of them had done when they were kids, but actually giving voice to whatever he'd been thinking? Nope.

Old man hadn't been kidding about the blood flow thing.

"Thank you," Colin said.

And there was the nod. Because clearly Sam Talbot was as surprised as his son. Then he took another sip of his coffee, his brows drawn. "Josh also said Deanna's cousin Emily showed up with you."

Colin smiled. "I think it's more that I showed up with her. We were on the same flight coming in from Dallas."

"Pretty little thing."

"She is." Although not so little, actually. And of course now that Dad had brought her up, those mad, sad, conflicted eyes flashed in his mind's eye. No wonder, now that he knew the reason behind the ambivalence. In some ways it was probably worse for her, since she was younger. Fewer life experiences and all that—

"Well. Just wanted to touch base," Colin said, pushing away from the counter. For a moment disappointment flickered in his father's eyes—a previously unseen glimpse of a soft spot that rattled Colin more than he'd expected. Or was about to let on. "I need to get in some supplies before I can start work," he said gently. "But I'll be back for dinner, remember? Or we can go out, if you'd rather. My treat."

The right thing to say, apparently, judging from the way Dad perked right up. "That'd be real nice, either way. Depends on what your mother wants to do, of course."

"Of course. I'll call around five, see what's up."

They were back outside by now, where that chilly spring breeze grabbed at Colin's hair, slapped at his clean-shaven face. Patches of old snow littered the parts of the yard that didn't get direct sunlight, reminders that up this far, winter wasn't over until it said so…images that at one time would've been nothing more than benign reminders of his childhood. Now, not even the bright sunlight could mitigate other reminders, other images, of how cruel—for too many people—winter could be when *home* had been ripped out from under you.

"Sounds good," Dad said, palming the spot between Colin's shoulder blades. "When you planning on seeing your other brothers? Zach, especially—you two were so close as kids."

Colin supposed they had been, although age and isolation—and being roommates—had probably had more to do with that than temperament. Zach had been the quiet one, the steady one…the obedient one. The one Colin could count on to not judge when he'd go off about not being able to *wait* to get out of Whispering Pines.

"Maybe tomorrow," he said. "After I get settled." Although he supposed the sooner he got the reunion stuff out of the way, the sooner he could retreat into his work.

In theory, anyway.

Back in the rental car, Colin waved to his father as he pulled out of the driveway, then headed toward the only decent grocery store in town. He wished he could say he was looking forward to dinner that night. Except the problem with being around people who knew you—or thought they did, anyway—was the way things you didn't want leaked tended to leak out. He'd put his parents though enough as it was, even if he honestly couldn't say what he could've done differently while still being true to who he was. But for sure he wasn't about to dump on them now, or give them any reason to doubt he'd made the right choices. If nothing else, he owed them at least a little peace of mind, assurances that he was okay.

And if he wasn't…well, he'd figure it out. You know, like a grown man.

The store—all three aisles of it, more like some dinky Manhattan bodega than one of those mega suburban monstrosities—was mercifully empty on this weekday morning. And surprisingly well stocked with a bunch of chichi crap Colin had little use for. He could cook, after a fashion—at least, he'd moved beyond opening cans of soup and microwaving frozen burritos—but he was definitely about whatever took twenty minutes or less from package to stomach. Give him a cast-iron pan, a couple of pots, he was good.

He was about to toss a couple of decent-looking steaks into his cart when he heard, from the next aisle over, the women's laughter…the same laughter he'd heard at the dinner table the night before. Same as then, it wasn't so much the pitch of the laughs that set Deanna and her cousin apart as it was…the genuineness of them, he supposed. As in, one was actually happy, and the other was pretty much faking it. Although whether for her own sake or her cousin's, Colin had no idea.

Nor was it any of his concern.

They were talking about nothing of any real importance that he could tell. Not that he should be listening, but if they'd wanted privacy, yakking in a small store wasn't the best way to go about that. He plunked the steaks in the cart, worked his way over to the pork chops. Yep, he could still hear the two of them. Because again, small store. What he found interesting, though—from a purely analytic standpoint—was how different the cousins' voices were. Deanna's voice was lighter, sparklier, whereas Emily's was...

With a package of chicken legs suspended in his hand over the case, Colin paused, frowning as he caught another whiff of Emily's voice, and every nerve cell, from the top of his head to places that really needed to shut the hell up already, whispered, *Oh, yeah...*

Then he blinked, the fog dispersed and there she was. "Oh. Hi."

One thing about grocery store lights, they weren't known for being flattering. Meaning he probably looked like a neglected cadaver right now. And yet even without makeup—none that he could see, anyway—in a plain old black sweater and pair of jeans, her hair pulled back in a don't-give-a-damn ponytail, Emily was...okay, not *beautiful*. But definitely appealing.

Especially to a guy who hadn't had any in a while. And who, up to this very moment, had been perfectly fine with that. Or at least reconciled to it. Not liking at all where his thoughts—let alone his blood—were headed, Colin looked back at the chicken in his hand. "Hey," he said, realizing he looked about as dumb as a person could look. He finally tossed the chicken in the cart, then looked back at Emily.

Because what else was he supposed to do? Unfortunately, she still looked good. Especially with that amused smile.

"I'm, uh…" He waved at the half-filled cart. "Stocking up."

"Us, too. I promised I'd cook while I was here. In exchange for…" She flushed slightly. "It just seemed fair, that's all. Especially since Josh has his hands full with ranch stuff this time of year, and Dee's getting her gallery set up in town."

"Her gallery?"

"That's what she did, before she moved back. Worked at a gallery. Doing acquisitions and such. But this one will be all hers, showcasing local artists, she said. I figured I could at least help out while I was here. Instead of playing the guest."

Colin nodded. "You know how long you're gonna be here?"

"I'm…playing it by ear."

"You don't have a job or something to get back to?"

"No, actually. Not at the moment. I mean, I did, until…" Looking away, she rubbed her nose, then poked through the packages of ribs. "These are really good done in the Crock-Pot."

"That so?"

"You should look online, there are tons of recipes." By now not even the sucky florescent lighting could wipe out her blush, which started at her neckline and spread to her eyes, making him think of other kinds of flushes, which in turn made him seriously consider sticking his head in the nearest freezer case. "Well. I'll leave you to it. See you around?"

"Sure." *Oh, hell, no.*

Clutching her package of ribs, she walked away, her very pretty butt twitching underneath a layer of clingy denim, her hair all shiny and bouncy underneath the lights.

Colin would've groaned, but that would've been pathetic and juvenile.

But far worse than the kick to the groin was the tug at something a bit farther north, where empathy had staked a claim all those years ago. Because he could—and would—ignore the butt and the hair and, okay, the breasts pushing against the sweater. But those eyes…

Damn it. A blessing and a curse, both, being able to sense another's pain.

Especially when combined with the helplessness of knowing there wasn't a single damn thing you could do to alleviate it.

So. New goal, he thought as he pushed the cart up to the cashier, relieved to see the two women had apparently already checked out. Stay out of Emily Weber's way as much as possible while she was still here.

Which, with any luck, wouldn't be very long.

Limbo.

That was the only way to describe her current state of mind. Or current state, period, Emily thought as, breathing hard, she completed the loop around the ranch she'd been running every day for the past week. Oh, she'd been keeping busy for sure, cooking and cleaning and playing with little Austin and baby Katie, who was teething and drooly and fussy and absolutely adorable when she wasn't screaming her head off. And at least—she rounded the training corral between the main house and the old foreman's cabin—the stress and heartache were easing up… some. Although why she'd thought a week or two away would heal her, let alone really fix anything, she had no idea. At some point she'd have to return to real life, face her parents and her friends and everything she couldn't face before. As it was, she was ignoring her mother's calls, which had become more frequent *because* Emily was ignoring them. Although unfortunately she hadn't yet found the cojones to delete Mom's messages without listening to them.

Then again, maybe listening to them was proof she had more balls than she was giving herself credit for—

"Oh!"

Her cry wasn't enough to scare off the coyote, although the thing did glance her way, as if to ascertain whether Emily was worth its consideration. The critters weren't really much of a threat to the horses, apparently—at least, Josh only shrugged when she'd told him she'd also spotted one on her last run—but City Girl Emily still felt it wise to steer clear.

Until she noticed something fuzzy and small in the dirt about ten feet from the coyote. A possum? Squirrel? She couldn't tell. But the gray varmint, who'd clearly decided to ignore Emily, was closing in, and—

"Get out of here!" she yelled, flapping her arms like a madwoman and running toward the whatever-it-was, startling a bunch of birds from the top of the nearest piñon and spooking a trio of horses in the nearby pasture. "Go on! Get!"

The coyote hesitated, giving her a what-the-hell? look.

"I said—" Emily snatched a fair-sized stone off the ground and hurled it with all her might at the animal, where it pinged harmlessly in the dirt three feet in front of it, raising a cloud of dust. *"Get!"*

And damned if a spurt of pride didn't zing through her when the thing actually took off, loping up the road without looking back. Her heart hammering in her chest, Emily approached the small, now whimpering animal, her chest fisting when she realized it was a puppy. What kind and how old, she had no idea. And what to do next, she had even less. But she had to do something. Unfortunately, Dee and Josh were running errands separately with the kids, and while she knew Josh's brother Zach had his veterinary practice in town, she had no idea whether he was there or not. Besides which, her cousin and her husband had taken both trucks—

The puppy released the most heart-wrenching, plaintive cry ever, and Emily sank cross-legged onto the dirt to pull him into her lap, which was when she noticed dried blood on one of his paws. She carefully touched the spot and the poor little thing cried out in obvious pain. Damn. Hauling in a breath, Emily glanced over at the foreman's cabin a hundred or so yards away. The rental car was there, meaning Colin was probably home, but...

She gingerly hugged the mewling baby dog to her chest, stroking his soft fur and making soothing, if probably unhelpful noises. Despite Colin's living within spitting distance of the main house, they hadn't seen each other since that silly encounter in the grocery store. Dude had serious hermit tendencies, apparently. Although truth be told, given her reaction to him back there in the meat department Emily had been just as glad. Not because of the silly, awkward part, but definitely because of the dry-mouthed, wanting-to-plaster-herself-against-him part. Which flew in the face of everything she was. Or thought she was, anyway. As in, logical. Levelheaded. Not given to fits of insanity.

Never mind that simply sitting here thinking about Colin's mouth and jaw and eyes, *ohmigod*, and that little hollow at the base of his neck was making her feel as though molten ore was flowing through her veins.

"Jeez, girl," she muttered. "Get over it."

As if it was that easy. Because despite keeping busy, and running her butt off every day, and her determination to not think about her shattered heart and the bozo who'd shattered it, her heart had other ideas. In fact, the longer she was away, the more hurt and angry she got that she'd been played for a fool. That she'd let herself be played for a fool, taking the path of least resistance because…why? Because everyone else had been happy?

Clearly, she needed to majorly overhaul her definition of that word. Not to mention her expectations, she thought as her mouth twisted. Meaning she knew full well all this fizzing and bubbling was nothing more than a knee-jerk reaction to Michael's betrayal, a primitive—and completely ludicrous—urge to get even.

The pup whimpered again, nuzzling her collarbone…

Telling her wayward loins to shut the hell up, Emily heaved herself to her feet, the puppy cradled against her chest, and marched toward the cabin.

She thought maybe this was called taking back the reins.

Colin nearly jumped out of his skin when he caught Emily standing outside the front window with something furry clutched in one hand, waving like crazy at him with the other. And apparently yelling. Ripping out his earbuds, he set aside his laptop and reluctantly pushed himself off the leather couch, not even bothering to adjust his expression before opening the door. It'd taken two days before the right words had finally started to settle in his brain to accompany this particular photo. And now they were gone. So, yeah. Pissed.

Emily's flinch—and blush—should've given him more satisfaction than it did. Instead he felt like a jackass. For about two seconds, anyway, before all the reasons he'd gone out of his way to avoid her this past week came sailing back into his befogged brain. Because of that blush, for one thing. That her running togs left little to the imagination, for another. Toss in exercise glow and whatever the hell that scent was that she wore, the one that marched right in and rendered him an insentient blob of randy hormones, and—

His eyes dipped to the puppy, looking about as blissful as Colin imagined he would be cuddled against those breasts.

"Some coyote was trying to get him, or at least that's what it looked like, and I think he might be hurt but I don't have any way of getting him to the vet. If your brother's even at the clinic."

Colin dragged his gaze away from the pup—and her breasts—and to her eyes, a move which jarred loose his libido's stranglehold long enough for *Oh, hell,* to play through his brain.

"Let me see," he said, his knuckles grazing those breasts—damn—before he took the dog from her and carried him into the house. Emily followed, shutting the door behind her and sitting across from Colin when he sat back on the couch.

"Heaven knows how he got here—"

"Dumped, probably. It happens," he said to her stunned expression, then tenderly examined the bloodied paw. The pup whimpered again.

"Don't think it's broken, but I'm not the vet." He paused, gaze fixed on the dog and not on those worried blue eyes. Clearly his afternoon was shot. Not to mention his resolve. "I had dinner with Zach and them the other night, he said he's in the office every afternoon, all day on Saturdays, so…" Still holding the pup, he got to his feet. "So let's go get this little guy fixed up."

"Oh! Um…" Emily stood as well, rubbing her hands across her dusty bottom. Colin looked away. "If you'd lend me the car, I could take him, you don't have to come. I mean—" There went the pink cheeks again. "It's pretty obvious I interrupted you. I'm sure you want to get back to work."

She had. And he did. However…

"You know where the clinic is?"

"In…town?"

Pushing out a sound that was half laugh, half resigned sigh, Colin walked over to the door, snagging the keys off the hook that'd been there probably from long before he was born. "Somebody needs to hold the dog. And it'll be quicker since I actually know where the clinic is. So come on. Unless…" Against his better judgment he gave her outfit a cursory glance. Okay, maybe not so cursory. "You want to change?"

She *pff*'d. "I think as long as I'm not naked, I'm good." And, yep, she blushed again. "What I mean is…"

"I know what you mean," Colin said, swinging open the door and handing back the pup as she walked through it, and her scent walloped his senses, making all those hormones laugh their little hormoney butts off.

Clinging to the bandaged-up pup wearing his Cone of Shame, Emily climbed back in the car, waiting while Colin chatted with his brother, who'd followed him out of the clinic. Hard to believe they were related, frankly, Zach's slender build and straight dark hair making him look nothing like big, solid, curly-headed Colin, a beard-hazed cherub on steroids. It was good, though, to see Colin actually laughing as he talked with his brother, and the genuine guy hug they exchanged before Colin got back behind the wheel.

"You shouldn't have done that," she said, earning her a frown as he rammed the key in the ignition.

"Hugged my brother?"

She rolled her eyes. "No. Paid the bill. Especially since I suckered you into going to the vet with me."

"Is that what you did? Suckered me?"

The humor in his voice made her feel better than it should have. "Whatever," she muttered, and he actually laughed. He backed out of the space in front of the office, then turned toward the center of town, glancing over at the dog. Who, clearly worn-out from his ordeal, had passed out in her lap.

"How's he doing?"

"How do you think?" she said, and Colin chuckled again. But other than a sprain and a fairly minor wound, probably caused when the poor dog got dumped, he was fine. Or would be, once he got fattened up a bit. Although who was going to be doing the fattening hadn't been decided yet. Male, about eight weeks, unchipped—no surprise there—indeterminate breed. Wasn't going to be small, though, Zach had guessed. Emily frowned. "Who'd get rid of a dog they'd already had for a couple of months? And why at the ranch?"

Beside her, big shoulders shrugged. "Maybe it wasn't the original owner. Maybe whoever'd been given the dog decided they didn't want him, figured the ranch was as good a place as any to leave him."

"I can't even imagine." Lowering her stinging eyes to the pup, she toyed with one silky, floppy ear. "At least when I had to give up my dog," she said through a constricted throat, "I made sure he went to a great home. I didn't simply dump him somewhere and leave it to fate."

A moment's silence preceded, "You had to give up your dog?"

"Yeah," she breathed out, facing out the windshield again. The puppy whooped in his sleep, making her smile.

"This little mutt I'd rescued after I first moved into my own place. Barnaby. But Michael was allergic."

"Ah."

Amazing, how much meaning the man could cram into a single syllable. Despite the tightness in her chest, Emily smiled. "It made sense at the time. And it was an open adoption. I get pictures. Updates. He seems happy enough. Especially since now he has kids to play with. But my point is, if I had any idea who tossed this one like he was a piece of trash, I'd rip 'em a new one—"

Colin's stomach rumbled so loudly the pup lifted his head.

"Sorry," Colin muttered. "I hadn't bothered with break-fast, and then you showed up with fuzzy-butt there, and…" He shrugged. His stomach growled again, making the puppy yip and growl back. Sort of.

"Okay, that's settled," she said. "You know where An-nie's is?"

"Of course I know where Annie's is—"

"Good. Then let's go. Since the least I can do is feed you, after everything you've done. Unless you really need to get back right away?"

"No, that's… I mean…" His hand tightened around the wheel. "Now that you mention it, I could eat my weight in tamales right about now. And it's not as if I'm on a time clock or anything. I can stay up all night to catch up if I want. So…sure. Why not?"

Then he tossed a brief grin in her direction and she thought, *And you've gone and done it now, girl, haven't you?* Although what, exactly, she'd gone and done, she wasn't entirely sure. But whatever it was, her own stom-ach was fussing up a storm, too. And not from hunger. Not that kind of hunger, anyway. And yet his accepting her offer pleased her beyond all reason.

Not to mention that smile.

Honestly. The man was the world's suckiest curmudgeon.

"So you know Annie's?" he said.

"Since one of your sisters-in-law works there, I most certainly do," Emily said as they pulled into an empty space in front of the diner, across from the town square. But even after cutting the engine, Colin stayed behind the wheel, one hand resting on the top as he stared out at the nondescript whitewashed building. Shadows from the trees in the square, however, flickered across the giant plate glass window, as well as the trio of small tables and chairs set up to take advantage of the warmer weather, lending, if not exactly *charm*, at least a certain comfortable unpretentiousness that was very appealing. Especially considering the slew of fancier restaurants in town that catered more to the ritzy ski resort patrons than locals. But that was just it: while the pricier places might make their clients feel indulged, Annie's Diner made a person feel like family. As though you'd come home. Emily liked that.

Unbuckling her seat belt, she cast a sidelong glance at Colin and asked, "When was the last time you were here?"

"Too long," he said on a telltale sigh.

Emily shifted the puppy, who'd conked out again. "We certainly don't have to eat here, if you don't want to. I hear that new Asian fusion place is pretty good. Although we'd probably have to leave the dog in the car—"

"What? No, this is fine. And I somehow doubt I can get tamales at the Asian place." Finally, he unbuckled his own seat belt. "But we should probably eat outside. Because of the dog. If it's warm enough, I mean."

In the sun it was. Emily set the sleeping dog on one of the unused chairs, swiveling it around to make a nest between the building's wall and her purse, which she'd grabbed before they'd headed into town. Not ten seconds later, however, they heard a muffled shriek from inside the restaurant, followed by one very excited Annie barreling outside, arms outstretched and babblings of joy tumbling like a waterfall from her mouth. Whatever Colin's reason for leaving Whispering Pines, it sure wasn't because nobody liked him.

The small woman yanked him into her arms, held him back, cackled out, "Holy hell, it's really you!" then yanked him back down again, wisps of her salt-and-pepper hair escaping her messy bun. And Colin, bless his heart, hugged the woman back. She released him again, smacked his arm, then folded her arms across her flat chest, shaking her head. "I'd about given up on ever seeing you again. What brings you back now, after all this time?"

Almost grateful for her apparent invisibility, Emily wondered if Annie noticed the change in Colin's expression, like a lightbulb not firmly seated in its socket. Huh. "Working on a book," he said, his hands stuffed in his back pockets. "Figured this was as good a place as any."

She also caught a flicker of skepticism—as though she didn't quite believe him—in the older woman's expression before she lit up again. "You may not know this, but your mama and daddy are real good about keeping everybody in the loop, showing off your work to anyone who'll stand still long enough for them to shove it in their face. Whole town's proud of you, boy."

Adorable blush, Emily thought a moment before Annie seemed to realize Colin wasn't alone. "Oh, my word, Emily—I didn't even see you sitting there! I'm so sorry! Didn't know you were back in town. But…wait." Confusion blossomed in her eyes for a moment as she looked back and forth between Colin and her. "Did you two come together?"

Emily laughed. "Long story. And solely because of this guy," she said, pointing to the puppy.

"What on earth…?" Her arms still crossed, Annie came closer. "Where did this little thing come from?"

"The ranch. Somebody abandoned him there, we think. So we brought him to Zach to get checked out." Emily bent at the waist to cup the little guy's head inside the cone. "Now we have to figure out what to do with him. I do, anyway. Since I found him."

Annie shot her a look that said her "answer" had only provoked five times more questions. About what, Emily could only guess. But all Annie said was "Meaning you don't want to keep him."

"It's not that I don't want to, it's just…that would be tricky. Since, well, my life's kind of all knotted up right now."

"What with you getting married, you mean."

"Um, actually…" Emily said, and Annie let out a soft groan. Because women understood these things before they were said out loud.

"Oh, honey…no."

"Yep."

"I'm so sorry." The older woman leaned over to pull Emily into a hug before looking back up at Colin. "And I'm guessing you can't take the dog, either."

His brow furrowed, he glanced over at the puppy. "Since I'm rarely in one spot longer than a few weeks… no. I can't. But maybe Josh and Deanna will take him."

"They might at that. If not, I'll be happy to put the word out, see what comes of it." Annie looked back down at the dog, chuckling as he twitched in his sleep. "Sweet little guy. Somebody's gonna love you, for sure. And for goodness' sake, y'all don't have to stay out here if you don't want to! Charley Maestas brings his dog in here nearly every day, nobody cares. Least of all AJ and me."

Colin chuckled. "Isn't there some kind of ordinance against that, unless it's a service dog?"

Annie swatted away his objection. "I won't tell if you won't. Unless you two would prefer to dine alfresco?"

"Actually..." Emily lifted her face to the sun, enjoying its sweet caress, a welcome reprieve from the bitterly cold spring winds that had assaulted the landscape every day since she'd come. "I wouldn't mind. But it's up to you," she said to Colin.

Whatever was going through his head, she had no idea. Although she was guessing quite a bit, judging from the look in those weirdly light eyes.

"Out here's fine," he said, a sudden breeze ruffling his curls.

Which oddly made *Emily* shiver.

Chapter Four

"**Y**ou sure?" Emily said, and Colin tamped down the sigh a nanosecond before it escaped. Because hell no, he wasn't sure. Of anything, to be honest. On the one hand, there'd be other people inside. Other conversations, other noise, other distractions. Out here, it'd just be the two of them. And a comatose dog in a cone. Not much of a chaperone.

"Positive. Since now that I'm out…" He glanced toward the park across the street, where a host of dripping cottonwoods, their branches laden with the beginnings of their electric green summer attire, seemed to worship the clear blue sky. *Innocence*, he thought, wondering where the hell that had come from, before returning his gaze to Emily's and seeing much the same thing there. Or…not? "It occurs to me I've been cooped up too long."

"All righty, then," Annie said—hell, he'd nearly forgotten she was there—then she took their orders: tamales and refried beans for Colin, a BLT for Emily. Colin waited to sit until after Annie went back inside, where they heard her bark their orders to her husband, AJ. Emily grinned, then leaned over to soothe the tiny beast, quivering in his sleep, and something clenched in his chest.

"I still can't believe your fiancé made you get rid of your dog."

Not that it was any of his business what'd gone on between this woman he barely knew and some dude he didn't know at all. But Colin couldn't help it, he had real issues with one member of a couple dictating what the other could and couldn't do. Or at least making them feel bad about it. Meaning from the moment she'd told him about her dog, annoyance had latched on to his brain worse than a goathead sticker.

Emily's brows lifted, disappearing underneath those wispy, goldish bangs as Annie swept out, plunked down two glasses of iced tea and straws, and disappeared again. After a moment Emily pinched three fake sugar packets from the container on the table, ripped off the tops and dumped the crystals into her tea. "I told you," she said as she stirred, "he was allergic."

"There's stuff you can take for that, you know."

Her spoon clanked when she set it on the saucer. "He tried, actually. It made him too sleepy to function. And I think that's called compromise." She took a sip of the tea. "Or don't you believe in that?"

"Compromise is working out an agreement where nobody loses. In my book, anyway."

The pup twitched in his sleep; Emily picked him up, tucking him under her chin. Not easy with that damn plastic thing around his neck. Colin could have sworn the dog grinned. "Is that even possible?" she said, her gaze touching his. "I mean, aren't there inevitably going to be times when somebody has to capitulate? Besides, it was only a dog."

Except, judging from her voice's slight quaver, it was a pretty good guess her words weren't exactly lining up with whatever was going on in her head. Not that he didn't know—all too well—where she was coming from. A thought that was clearly hell-bent on resurrecting old regrets of his own.

Like his agreeing to this meal, for one thing. Colin lifted his own tea to his mouth, took a long swallow. "Like hell," he said softly, setting down the glass, "that it was *only* a dog. And in any case…"

"You don't have to say it," she said with a short, harsh laugh. "But at the time, the dog was the only issue—" Clamping her mouth shut, she shook her head. "I can't believe I was such an idiot." Then she shoved out a short, dry laugh. "Or that you'd be even remotely interested in the soap opera that's been my life lately."

A waitress—young, pretty, perky—appeared with their food, setting down the piled-high plates with a flourish before bouncing back inside. Colin picked up his fork and attacked the tamales. As in he ripped them to shreds. As much as part of him wouldn't mind doing that to Emily's ex. Ignoring the last part of her comment—because as long as they talked about her, they weren't talking about him— he said, "And I'm gonna stick my neck out here and say it wasn't you who was the idiot." At least that got a little laugh. "Hell, Emily—everybody makes mistakes," he said quietly. "Bad choices. Don't beat yourself up."

His face heated. And not only because of the hot-as-hell tamales. And what with them sitting out here in the sun…he was pretty sure she noticed.

But all she did was set the puppy back on the chair and pick up her overstuffed sandwich to take a huge chomp, sending mayonnaise squirting down her chin. Unfazed, she wiped up the mess with her napkin, then sat back in the chair, her arms folded across her ribs as she chewed. Thinking, no doubt. As one did when they had a brain. Which this gal obviously did.

"Yeah, well," she finally said after she swallowed, "giving up the *dog* was the least of it."

Colin frowned. "What else?"

"Teaching." She picked up the sandwich again and took another, neater, bite. "Kindergarten. Because Michael didn't think I should work."

"And what century is this again?"

Her mouth twisted. "His family is ridiculously traditional. Even more than mine, which is saying something." She stared at her plate for a long moment before saying, "It's funny how people assume if you grow up privileged, for lack of a better term, that you're spoiled." Her eyes lifted to his, the space between her brows pleated. "Especially if you're an only child. Not that it's not true, at least on the surface. Certainly I always had whatever I needed. And got a lot of what I wanted. To pretend otherwise would be disingenuous. But weirdly what made me happiest wasn't the stuff, it was making sure everybody *else* was happy."

"Even if that meant giving up something that was so important to you?"

Yep, he might've sounded a little pissed there. If Emily noticed, however, she didn't let on.

"Apparently so," she sighed out. "So naturally it made sense to carry that mind-set into my marriage. Although to give myself some credit, I figured I could talk him into letting me go back into teaching after we got married. So dumb." Her mouth screwed up again. "Sorry."

"S'okay," Colin said, shoveling in another bite of his

lunch. Breakfast. Whatever. "Like I said, you're hardly the first person to…"

"Screw up?"

A dry chuckle pushed from his chest. "Funny how it's a lot easier to tell someone else not to beat themselves up than it is to take your own advice."

"Truth," she said, lifting her tea in a mock toast. Then she frowned. "Nobody's perfect, you know? And Michael and I were attuned to each other's quirks, I suppose. We…" Her eyes met his. "Things were okay between us. Okay enough, anyway."

"Aside from the dog. And his making you give up your career. And his screwing around on you."

Another short laugh pushed through her nose. "When you put it like that…" She finally took a swallow of her tea. "I guess I figured the pluses outweighed the minuses. Well, until the final bombshell, which pretty much cleared the scoreboard. But in the beginning…oh, my gosh, our parents were *thrilled*. In fact, I think they were more caught up in the fairy tale than I was. The socialite's daughter marrying a US senator's son…cue the happy Disney critters flinging sparkly confetti, right?"

Colin almost smiled, but only because Emily did. "When did you find out?"

"About the cheating?" She took another bite of her sandwich. "A few weeks ago. By accident. He'd left his phone out, and I caught part of a text I doubt he'd expected me to see." Colin's brows slammed together. "Not the brightest move in the world. On his part, I mean. Although considering how relieved he looked when I confronted him, frankly I think he let things slip on purpose. Especially when he said that, actually, things would be easier now that I knew."

"Easier? For whom?"

"Exactly," she said. Only this time, he heard—saw—the

scarring behind the innocence. Not to mention a worldliness he wasn't sure how he'd missed. Recently acquired though it may have been.

"And how long were you two together?"

"Three years. I know. Although he *swore* they 'only' reconnected in the last year or so." Her mouth twisted. She looked back at the dog. "In every meaning of the word *reconnected.*" She met his gaze again. "He actually promised it was over," she said, then *pff*'d a little laugh. "As if I'd actually believe him? Not hardly. Oh, and it gets better. It's someone *else* he's apparently known since college. An old girlfriend. Or something."

Shrugging, Emily picked up her sandwich again, poking a bit of bacon back inside the bread before taking another bite.

"You seem amazingly calm about the whole thing."

She *pff*'d again. "I'm nothing if not a product of my upbringing. Never let 'em see you sweat and all that. Inside, though, trust me—it feels like a nest of pissed-off rattlesnakes. Especially since…"

This time, her blush was so furious Colin briefly wondered if she was okay.

"Emily?"

But she shook her head. "Never mind."

And Colin thought he'd wanted to smack the guy senseless *before*. Yes, despite having no clue what lay behind that *never mind.* Because her red cheeks said it all, didn't they? At least, enough. Worse, though, was the realization that his impulse to inflict bodily harm stemmed from something way deeper than simple protective instinct.

And far, far more scary.

"What I don't get is why?"

Her forehead crimped. "I didn't see the signs?"

"Signs? What *signs*?" Colin reached for her hand, having to take care not to crush it, he was so damned mad. "For God's sake, you're not supposed to be looking for *signs* from somebody you *trust*, okay? No, what I meant was…" He let go to cross his arms over his chest. "Why on earth would this dipwad think he could get away with it?"

At least that got her to smile. "I guess because he knew rocking the boat wasn't my style, that…" Her mouth pulled flat. "That I'd do almost anything to not embarrass myself. Or the people I felt I owed."

Owed. What an odd word choice. "Except they all overestimated how far you could be pushed."

She gave him a funny look, a tiny smile poking at the corners of her mouth. "Apparently so. *Especially* once I had all the facts. I might be a people pleaser, but I'm not a masochist, for crying out loud. So strangely I'm actually very grateful for how things played out. Because if I hadn't found out when I did…" Another breath left her lungs. "I can't even imagine the hell that would have been. For any of us, frankly. And I am here to tell you, this chick's doormat days are over. And they probably wouldn't be if none of this had happened."

Only the fierce determination in her eyes was clearly wrestling with what Colin could clearly see was raw heartbreak, that somebody she'd loved—or in any case believed she had—had been lying to her for at least a year, probably longer. Maybe his situation hadn't been exactly the same, but he knew, too, what it felt like, that breath-stealing sensation of having been catapulted into an alternate dimension when you suddenly realized you were in a relationship based on dust—

And seeing the tangle of emotions on Emily's face provoked another spurt of protectiveness. Which was the last thing she probably wanted, and *definitely* the last thing he could afford to feel right now. If ever. But a weird…pride, he guessed it was, flickered in there somewhere, too, that despite her obvious mortification, no way was she going to be, or even play, the victim. Not now, or ever again.

Because this was no child, not by a long shot, but a woman…one whose newfound inner strength was a force to be reckoned with.

A realization that only shined a big bright light on why Colin needed to ignore the physical tug more than ever. Because she'd been used before. And he'd been had. So no way was he even going near that road again, for both of their sakes. But especially hers, he thought, as a family with two young kids passed their table on their way into the diner, and the little girl—four or five, maybe—went nuts over the puppy.

"You can pet him if you like," Emily said, heaving the sleepy little thing up so the kids could get to him, her chuckle warm at the little girl's giggles when the pup nibbled her fingers.

"What's his name?"

"He doesn't have one yet—"

"Why's he wearing that thing around his neck?" the child asked, her face scrunched into a combination of curious and concerned.

"So he won't mess with the bandage around his boo-boo. It's only for a week or so, though. Otherwise he's fine. And we're actually looking for a home for him," Emily said to the kids' parents, grinning. "You interested?"

The mother laughed. "Oh, gosh, sorry—we've already got as many animals as we can handle. But as cute as he is, I doubt you'll have any trouble placing him. Come on, guys," she said to the kids, steering them inside before her resolve crumbled, Colin was guessing. But she smiled back at Emily. "Good luck!"

"So what's the plan?" he asked Emily as she settled the pup into her lap again. "For you, I mean. Not the dog."

"No earthly idea. Although I suppose go back to DC, start the job search. I can probably get another teaching position, if I want it."

"Do you?"

"More than anything. I'm crazy about little kids."

Colin thought of how her voice had gentled as she talked to the little girl, and his own gut cramped. "I kinda got that impression. Private school?"

Her eyebrows shot up. "No. Public. Why would you assume private? Never mind," she said when he flushed, realizing his gaffe. "Don't answer that." Then she snorted. "As close to rebellion as I ever got, first wanting to go into early childhood education, then wanting to work with kids who wouldn't necessarily be 'easy.' Who maybe hadn't had many of the advantages I'd had."

Colin linked his arms high on his chest. "Kind of a sweeping indictment of the public school system, isn't it?"

"More true in the areas I asked to teach than you might think."

"Why?"

A small smile touched her lips, as though she completely understood his question. "Because I saw it as some small way to make a real difference. And yes, I realize a lot of people would call it rich person guilt. Or worse. It's not, though. At least, I hope it's not. God knows my idealism got taken down a peg or ten my first year, but…" Her brows pushed together. "But it got replaced by something much more solid. Much more real. I honestly loved teaching, even on those days when I wondered what the hell I'd gotten myself into. Seriously, if it was just ego stroking I was after, I can think of a lot easier ways to earn a living. Not to mention more lucrative ones."

Smiling, Colin thought of his own work, how he'd gravitated toward chronicling the struggles of those whose lives were defined by them. The more he worked on his book, the more he itched to get back to what his father had rightly identified as his calling. His purpose.

Even as that collided with another, long neglected—and even longer denied—pull he could no longer ignore toward the very place he once couldn't leave fast enough. And which made it even more imperative he ignore the equally magnetic pull from the direct blue gaze across from him. A pull he doubted Emily even realized she was exerting. Especially given her situation.

"So you'll go back home?"

The question seemed to startle her, even though she'd said virtually the same thing seconds before. Emily looked down, chuckling at the blob of tomato that had landed on her chest. She plucked it off, dropped it back on her plate. "*Home* is very important to me. I'm a definite nester. And not gonna lie, one of the things I was most looking forward to was making that nest with Michael, having a couple of kids of my own..." She tossed one hand in the air. "Turning people's heads with my remarkable ability to effortlessly balance motherhood and career, being the gracious hostess as well as..." Another blush stole across her cheeks. "The perfect wife," she finished softly, then snorted again. "A total crock, but there you are. And now..."

The waitress reappeared to clear their places; Emily asked for the check, then gathered her purse off the sidewalk to dig out her wallet. Colin couldn't help but notice her pretty hands, the gleaming polish on each perfect nail, the flawlessness marred only by a slight indentation where her engagement ring had been. He wondered if she'd returned it, only to immediately decide of course she had.

"And now I have to totally reassess what that word means. Where home really is. *What* it is."

"But you just said—"

The pup looked up when the waitress returned with the charge slip for Emily to sign. Tucking her copy of the receipt into her purse, she met Colin's gaze again. "I know what I just said. But I guess you could say things are kind of…fluid right now." She chuckled. "For the first time in my life, I have no one and nothing to answer to. I can do whatever I damn well please. For a while, anyway, until my savings run out." Then, frowning, she looked over at the dog. "And what are we going to do about you, little guy?"

Her genuine concern for the dog, the light shining in her eyes for the little girl a few minutes ago… What kind of creep stomps on a heart that big?

Or worse, takes advantage of it?

Colin got to his feet, plucking the pup off the chair. "Between my three brothers and my parents, I don't imagine we'll have any problem finding a home for him."

The chair squawked against the rough pavement when Emily pushed it back, then stood. "I suppose you're right," she said, even though the look on her face said she wasn't nearly as down with that idea as he would've expected. Despite her trying to pawn the dog off on perfect strangers not five minutes before.

But what he really hadn't expected was how bad that made him feel. Mainly because he was in no position to do anything for anyone to make them happy. Or even feel better. Especially some sweet young thing who'd been not only dumped, but dumped on. And it'd only taken a single lunch to come to the conclusion that Emily Weber's goodness ran soul deep, like some pure, unquenchable river of life.

A river he didn't dare even think of drinking from.

No matter how thirsty he was.

* * *

Chuckling, Emily sat cross-legged on the tiled floor in the ranch house's giant, beamed great room, watching the wriggling, growling little dog play tug-of-war with Josh's almost-five-year-old son, the cone no impediment whatsoever to puppy shenanigans. A breath of fragrant, sunshine-warmed air swept across her face, making her turn toward the open French doors. Soon the high desert evening would suck all the warmth out of the glorious day, but for now she was simply grateful for a sweet, peaceful moment. As was her cousin, Emily guessed when she glanced over to see Dee curled up in the corner of one of the room's leather sofas, her lips curved in a blissful smile as she watched the pup and boy tussle. Josh was out doing chores and baby Katie napped, clearly oblivious to both the pup's yapping and Austin's nonstop, high-pitched giggling.

"I'm really sorry we can't keep him," Dee said for what felt like the hundredth time since Emily showed up with the dog three days before. "But between the baby and getting the gallery set up—"

"It's okay, Dee, really. You don't have to keep apologizing."

"Not that he's not adorable, but training a puppy takes so much time and energy—"

"Dee!" Despite the knot in her stomach Emily strongly suspected had less to do with finding a home for this dog than…other things, she smiled. "I get it." And she really did. Being awakened by a teething baby several times a night was clearly wreaking havoc on the whole family, whether Dee would actually admit that or not. "Sheesh."

But Deanna still looked all verklempt. Probably because, between imminently arriving new babies and wedding planning and the like, none of the other likely candidates could take him, either. Of course, Annie had put up a sign in the diner, as had Zach at the clinic, so Emily felt pretty confident the little hound wouldn't be homeless for long. And Dee did say that as long as Emily was around to take care of him, he could stay there until a more permanent solution was worked out. Although of course the problem with that was she'd only become more attached, wouldn't she?

Seeming to realize she was *right there*, the baby dog swung around and came bounding over in a burst of un-coordinated canine joy to clamber into her lap, where he planted his oversize paws on her chest to give her chin a thorough wash.

Austin folded up onto the floor to smush up beside her, smelling of dirt and sunshine and tangy little boy, and Emily's heart twisted with missing being around "her" kids. "He really loves you, huh?" he said, pressing closer so he could pet the dog, who of course immediately decided the boy's face needed washing, too.

Emily laughed. Then sighed.

Because reassessed goals or no, she was getting real tired of falling in love with things she had to eventually give up—or give up on. A realization that didn't keep her from gathering the pup closer, laughing again when he then started nibbling at the ends of her loose hair.

"I think it's safe to say he loves everybody," she said, planting a kiss on the little boy's messy curls. Life here was loud and crazy and frequently dirty, and the chaos wrapped around Emily's wounded heart like one of baby Katie's soft little blankets. *Perfect*, she decided, was not only unachievable, it was boring—

She laughed when, as she gently tugged on the puppy's velvety ears, Dumbo-style, he swung his head from side to side in a futile attempt to bite her fingers.

"Josh said Thor's old crate is in the tack room," Dee

said. "That might help. Temporarily, I mean." Emily looked up to see apology in her cousin's eyes. "Because between a squealing baby—" as if on cue, Katie's feed-me wail floated out from the baby monitor on the coffee table "—and an overenthusiastic little boy," Dee said with a pretend glower at her stepson, who grinned, "he probably needs his sanctuary."

And despite what Josh had said to her that first night, her bringing in a dog hadn't been part of the game plan.

"Sorry—"

"It's okay, honey, we'll work it out." The wailing became more frantic. "Really."

Yawning, Dee shoved off the sofa, wobbling a bit as she tugged down her long-sleeved T-shirt. Then she held out her hand to Austin. "Wanna come help me change her diaper?"

The little boy made a face, but took Dee's hand anyway, and followed her to the baby's room. Emily let her head fall back against the sofa cushion, shutting her eyes as, with a huge doggy sigh, the puppy promptly passed out.

Sanctuary.

Like the ranch, the town, was to Emily. Had been, anyway, until that lunch with Colin. She wasn't used to men directly meeting her gaze, she'd realized. Not her father, certainly. Or any of her other boyfriends, pre-Michael. And then not Michael, either, at the end, when he must've been suffocating under the weight of all those lies. Hell, yeah, she was still angry with him. But that would wear off, eventually, leaving in its wake an ocean of pity. Because in the long run, it'd be the dirtbag who suffered. Not her.

And either of those were preferable to whatever the heck feelings these were, provoked by that mountain of steely calmness she'd shared lunch with the other day.

A mountain in which were buried all manner of secrets, she suspected. Not national-security-threatening secrets, no—or at least, she didn't imagine—but the kinds of secrets men like that would take to their graves rather than getting all touchy-feely-sharey.

And she'd had enough secrets to last a lifetime, hadn't she?

Her phone dinged—the alarm she'd set to tell her when her brownies were done, since the kitchen was too far away to hear the buzzer. Setting the pup back on the floor, she heaved to her feet and plodded barefoot down the hall, the sweet, heady scent of warm chocolate intensifying as she got closer to the kitchen. It was the fifth batch of brownies she'd made since her arrival, but tough. It wasn't as if she had a wedding gown to fit into anymore, was it?

Although she might want to still fit into her jeans.

Granted, the kitschy kitchen wasn't her style—the hand-painted Mexican tiles were too busy for her taste, the cabinets and floor too dark—but it practically vibrated with Josh and Deanna's contentment. With...*promise.* Deanna's father leaving the ranch to her and Josh equally had been a shock, Emily knew. But for all her uncle's faults, not to mention the mistakes he'd made with his only child—more from cluelessness than malice, it turned out—Granville Blake had definitely gotten one thing right: bringing Dee and Josh together again, even though he'd deliberately separated them as teenagers.

An outcome that gave Emily hope, even as she had to battle hair-singeing envy every time she saw the happy, but exhausted, couple together.

"You do realize you're seriously sabotaging my attempts to get rid of the baby weight, right?" Dee said when she came in with the kids, the drooly, grinning baby slung on her hip like a sack of flour.

"Hey. I'm good with eating them all if that makes you feel better—"

"The hell you say," Dee muttered so Austin couldn't hear, settling into a chair at the huge kitchen table and yanking up her shirt to feed her child before thrusting out her hand. "Hand over the goods now and nobody gets hurt."

Chuckling, Emily cut a huge, gooey chunk of still-hot brownie from the pan, placing it on a napkin before setting it on the table beside Dee, then gave one to Austin, standing beside her with his nose practically in the brownie pan. "Don't let the puppy have any," she said. "Chocolate's not good for dogs."

Not that this was an issue, since after blowing on the brownie for maybe a second the kid basically inhaled the whole thing in two bites, crumbs dripping down his front. Which he caught and shoved in his already full mouth. "C'n I take the dog outside?"

"I suppose," Dee said. "But only out back. And stay by the back steps!"

"'Kay," the boy said, slapping his hands on his thighs to call the dog. "C'mon, boy! C'mon!"

And they were gone, although closing the back door behind them was apparently optional. Probably just as well, Emily thought, smiling again for her cousin. "You want milk with that? Or tea?"

Dee yawned, then nodded. "Milk. Please." Then, her forehead pleated, she lowered her gaze to her noisily feeding daughter. "I suppose we should think about what to feed your daddy for dinner, huh?"

Emily plucked a pecan off the brownies, stuffing it into her mouth. "Why don't you guys go out to eat?"

That got a weary chuckle. "Clearly you've never tried

taking a six-month-old to a restaurant. And Austin eats, like, a single nibble and he's done. It's kind of a waste."

Emily rolled her eyes. "Obviously I meant by your-selves, doofus. When was the last time you and Josh had date night?"

Dee looked at her as though she'd suggested they fly to the moon. "Um…never?"

Not that Josh's parents or brothers wouldn't be willing to take the kids. But hauling the kids to any of their houses, none of which were particularly close to the ranch, was a hassle. Same as it was for any of the brothers to bring their kids out to the ranch at night. And what with Josh's mom never knowing when she might be called out on a delivery, it was hard to rely on his parents, too. Heaven knew this family was joined at the hip, at least in theory. In practice, however, the more babies that got added to the mix, the more logistics weren't in their favor.

Add to that the fact that Josh and Deanna had never "dated" in the traditional sense before they got married, coming into it as they had with two kids already, and…

"Well, now's your chance," Emily said, scooping out a sizable brownie for herself. "No, I mean it—go into Taos, have dinner someplace other than Annie's, see a movie, stay out past your bedtime. My treat, even. And I'll watch the kids. We'll have brownies for dinner—" she stuffed a huge, melty glob of goodness into her mouth "—and watch the Cartoon Network until our eyeballs fall out." Then she laughed at her cousin's horrified expression. "I can follow directions, goose. And I know you've got breast milk in the freezer, so…" She shrugged.

Still, Deanna looked doubtful. Hopeful, but doubtful. "You sure?"

"If I can handle a whole class of five-year-olds, I think I can handle one and his baby sister. Or at least keep them alive until you get back. Besides, it's the least I can do to say thank you for letting me hang out here, all mopey and stuff."

Dee snuffled a little laugh. "You've hardly been mopey."

Not that she'd let them see, maybe. But there'd been more than one night when she hadn't been even remotely able to fend off the pity demons, nights when she'd cried herself to sleep, wanting so badly to be smart and strong and sure, wondering if she ever would. Never letting 'em *see* you sweat—or fall apart—didn't mean you didn't.

"Let me do this," she said. "Please. Let me feel…useful."

Tears glittered in her cousin's eyes as she extended one arm to Emily, pulling her into a hug that smelled of baby and breast milk and Dee's shampoo.

"I take it that's a yes?" Emily mumbled into her cousin's hair, and Dee nodded.

"Good," Emily said, letting go to finish cutting up the brownies, trying to ignore the beginnings of what felt an awful lot like panic.

Chapter Five

Colin heard Austin's shrieks before he rounded the last curve to the house, a sound that sent his heart into his throat and chilled his blood. Of course, then he felt like an idiot when he spotted the boy chasing the puppy and Thor in the front yard, the trio dodging the quivering shadows cast by a half dozen lush cottonwoods, shimmering gold in the setting sun. Then he caught Emily's laughter, as well, and his heart whomped inside his chest a second time. Only harder.

As in, like he'd been sucker punched.

Sitting on a blanket on the patchy grass with the baby, she shielded her eyes from the sun when she spotted him, then waved, grinning. Although even from this distance he didn't think he'd imagined the hesitancy in her smile. The caution. Only then she waved more insistently, beckoning him to join them. That surprised him, actually, considering there'd been no communication between them since that trip into town. Not that there should have been. Because reasons.

And if he'd had a lick of sense he could've waved back and pointed toward the cabin, indicating he had things to do. Only Austin started to wave, too, like he was flagging down a plane, and...well, it didn't feel right, ignoring his nephew. Especially since wasn't this a huge part of why he was here? To at least act like he had a family?

To figure out a few things?

So he hung a right and pulled into the house's driveway, trying like hell not to stare at Emily's flowing, sun-glazed hair, making her look like some damn Botticelli painting, *Venus on the Half Shell* or whatever. Except Venus was naked in the painting and Emily was wearing jeans and a loose sweater. Not sexy at all, let alone naked.

An image he maybe shouldn't dwell on too hard. Although the closer he got and the more her bangs looked like tiny sunbeams dancing across her forehead, the more that became a lost cause. Fortunately Austin came running up, plowing into Colin's legs with a big old grin splitting a face that reminded Colin so much of his daddy's at that age it was ridiculous. Ignoring the bittersweet ache permanently lodged, it seemed, in the center of his chest, Colin swung the little boy up into his arms, almost unable to process the child's immediate, uncomplicated acceptance of someone he'd never seen before a couple of weeks ago.

Although considering his other experiences, why should that surprise him?

"Daddy said you're living in our old house, huh?"

Colin smiled. "I am. For the moment."

"And he said that used to be his old house, too. When he was a kid?"

"Yep. Mine, too. And your uncles'. In fact, I shared a

room with your uncle Zach. The one at the back of the house."

The kid grinned. "That usedta be my room!"

"Get out!" He hoisted the solid little boy up higher in his arms. "In the bunk bed?"

"Uh-huh."

"Top or bottom?"

"Bottom. So all my friends could live on top. They liked it better up there, so I let 'em. Now they all live in a funny net in a corner of my room here. Except Monkey. Monkey lives on my bed."

Behind him, Colin heard Emily chuckle. He grinned for the little boy, even as his heart fisted so hard he wasn't sure how he was breathing. "The bottom was my bed, didja know that?" Austin shook his head. "And *now*—" he poked the boy's tummy, getting a squirmy giggle in response "—you and your daddy live in your stepmama's old house, from when she was a kid."

"I know, they said." The child linked his arms around the back of Colin's neck and gave him a very serious look. "Deedee said I can call her Mom, if I want. But I like Deedee. It's more special." He grinned again. "Like her!"

Thor kowtowed in front of them, tail wagging, barker barking...around the ball clamped in his mouth.

"Gotta go," Austin said, wriggling out of Colin's arms. "Thor wants me to play..."

And he was off, a blur of little boy limbs in the molten sunshine.

"You were actually out in the world again?" Emily teased from the blanket behind him, forcing him to face her. To face...stuff he didn't particularly want to. Because frankly he hadn't yet figured out how—let alone why—she was getting to him in ways he didn't want to be gotten to. And it wasn't only because she was pretty—he wasn't fourteen, for pity's sake—or even because he was lonely, even though that particular demon did occasionally sneak up on him, if he wasn't watching. But it still poked at him, how she told her story the other day, without even once playing the victim card.

"It does happen," he said, allowing at least enough of a smile to keep him from looking like he had a rod up his butt. "Sometimes I need to get out, get away from what I'm working on, take a walk. Go for a drive." No need to tell her why, that he'd been working on a series of photos that focused on one particular little boy he'd met in a refugee camp in Jordan, about a year ago. Right after Sarah. "Helps clear my head so I can be more objective when I go back to work. Josh and Deanna in the house?"

After a moment's speculative look, Emily smiled. "Nope. I kicked them out to give 'em some alone time with each other." The baby, sitting on the blanket in front of Emily, squinted up at Zach, giving him a drooly grin before jabbing her arms over her head, laughing at who-knew-what. Her own laugh even prettier than a nearby robin's trill, Emily grabbed Katie's chubby little hands, clapping them together. "I only hope they don't fall asleep in their food."

Colin felt a more genuine smile push at his mouth before looking out toward the mountains, the tops ablaze in the setting sun—a view he'd seen thousands of time growing up, that now provoked those old restless yearnings. Not for the same things, though, he didn't think. He let his gaze rest again on Emily, curled forward to touch her forehead to Katie's.

No, not for the same things at all.

Still holding his niece's hands, Emily straightened, a teasing grin on her lips. "Um…you could sit, if you want," she said gently. As though she knew what was going on in his head. Which was ridiculous for many reasons, not the least of which was that Colin himself wasn't sure what was going on in there. Just a lot of question marks, all tangled up like the fishhooks in his old tacklebox from when he was a kid. Another thought wedged itself in there, his father's "you are hopeless, boy" headshake when it'd take Colin twenty minutes to pry one free…

"You know," Emily said, letting go of the baby to wrap her arms around her knees. The breeze plucked at her hair; she shoved it back over her shoulder. "Enjoy the sunset. The moment?"

He nodded, mentally laughing at himself. Damn. For somebody who was supposed to be all about going with the flow, he felt about as fluid as cold molasses these days.

What the hell are you so afraid of?

His own voice, this time, prodding him to go places he wasn't ready to go. Not yet. Hell, maybe not ever. Still, right now, he was here. Meaning he could either accept the woman's simple invitation, or retreat to his hidey-hole for no real reason and let her think he had a screw loose. Not that he didn't, but no reason to let her think that.

So he lowered himself to the blanket, his heart turning over in his chest when a gurgling, jabbering Katie launched forward onto her belly and, with much grunting, tried her damnedest to army-crawl toward him.

"She crawls?"

"Not exactly," Emily said, chuckling when Colin leaned in to hook his hands under the baby's arms and lift her toward him. Squealing with delight, the kid slapped a slobbery palm against his cheek, then twisted to plop in his lap, where she released a victorious sigh before grabbing his hand and cramming it into her slimy mouth.

"Here," Emily said, tossing him a little blanket decorated in tiny teddy bears. "She does a great imitation of Niagara Falls these days."

"Thanks."

As he wiped drool off both him and the baby—ignoring her cries of protest—he caught Emily's smile.

"You're good at that."

"I've had practice," he said quietly, not looking at her. The rapidly chilling breeze swept across the yard, cooling the baby spit he'd missed on his hand.

Emily pulled up her knees again, linking her arms around them as she watched Austin and the dogs. "But obviously not with your own kids." Her gaze veered to his. "Or your brothers'."

"No."

Katie clapped her hands, chortling with glee at her brother's and the dogs' antics, and all the old instincts kicked in whether Colin wanted them to or not. Laughing himself, he turned the tiny girl around to let her push herself to her feet, her louder squeals apparently catching his nephew's attention. Austin and the dogs made a bee-line for Colin, the boy barreling into his side like a line-backer, nearly knocking him and the baby over.

"Austin!" Emily yelled, lurching for him. "Watch out, sweetie—"

"It's okay, I've got him," Colin said, snaking one arm around the skinny little waist to halt the inertia while still hanging on to the babbling, oblivious baby. "But you need to be careful, buddy. You could've hurt yourself there. Or your baby sister."

His face instantly flaming, the little boy's gaze swung to the baby, as though suddenly realizing she was there. "Sorry, Katie!" He dropped to his knees, resting a grimy hand on the baby's back. "You okay?"

The tiny girl twisted toward him, bursting into a huge

grin when she saw her brother, then jutting one hand toward him.

"Yes, is the answer," Colin said, then met eyes the same color as his younger brother's. And yep, that was something almost like regret zinging through him, that he'd more or less missed out on the kid's life to this point. And not only his, but Zach's two, as well. Except being around these kids, who had families and *homes* and reasonably stable lives, only made him remember the bigger picture that had kept him away for so long. "Just don't want you to bump your noggin," he said, gently rapping his knuckles against the little boy's skull. The little boy giggled, making Colin's chest ache and his head hurt. Logically enough, considering all those twisted-up fishhooks in there.

Then the boy threw his arms around Colin's neck and gave him a hug, making him ache even more, before dashing off to play fetch with the big dog. The puppy, however, had stumbled over to collapse against Emily's knee, too pooped to pop. Or pup.

Colin set the baby back on her butt on the blanket and handed her a nearby toy, which she promptly crammed into her mouth. Then he nodded toward the passed-out puppy. "You name him yet?"

"Me?" She sounded startled. Looked it, too, wide eyes and all. Then she shook her head. "No. I'll leave that to whoever gives him his forever home."

"So why *can't* that be you? Nothing says you couldn't take him back to DC with you."

"Because my life is one big question mark right now? Or did you forget that part? As it is I'm probably going to have to turn him over to a shelter."

"What? Why?"

Playing with the puppy's ears, she gave a sad let's-be-a-grown-up-about-this shrug. "Because he keeps waking up at night, crying. And poor Dee and Josh get little enough sleep as it is, with babypie over there teething. I came out here to get away from my own problems, not to make more for Dee. Or your brother, who's a saint for letting me stay to begin with—"

"Then leave him with me," Colin heard himself say. At Emily's pushed-together brows, he added, "I don't sleep particularly well at night, anyway. And I'm sure we can find him a home long before…before I leave."

She looked back down at the pup, her mouth set.

"What?"

Her gaze glanced off his again before, with another shrug, she lowered it again to the pup. "I can't figure you out."

"That would make you a member of a very large club, then," he said, and she softly laughed. "So is that a yes?"

"To your taking the dog?" Another shoulder bump preceded, "Sure. In fact, it's an excellent solution. Since I'm in real danger of getting too attached."

"I can see that. Although…" Because if it was one thing he was good at, it was getting himself in deeper. "Feel free to come play with him anytime—"

"It's getting dark," Emily said, shivering as the streaks of red-gold light suddenly faded, instantly leaching the warmth from the air. She called Austin, then got to her feet and reached for the baby, chuckling as the child pumped her chubby little legs for all she was worth when Colin lifted her up. "Well." Settling the baby against her ribs, she nuzzled the downy head before meeting Colin's gaze again, yearning—as well as anger for what'd been snatched from her—leaking from her own. Although he doubted she realized how much. "If you're really serious about taking the dog—"

"Wouldn't've offered if I wasn't," Colin said, pushing himself to his feet, as well.

She nodded, shouldering a strand of hair away from her jaw. "Then you might as well come get his stuff. Food and bowls and…" She flushed. "Toys. Um, I might've bought a few. And Dee said there's a crate in the tack room that Josh used for Thor when he first got him. You might want that, too—"

"Hey, Uncle Colin," Austin said when he reached them, breathing hard as he scooped up the wriggling, licking puppy. "You wanna stay for dinner? There's lots!"

"Uh…thanks, but I don't think that's your invitation to give, dude—"

Shifting the baby higher into her arms, Emily laughed. "It's okay, he just beat me to it. It's what I call a 'whatever casserole.' It should be ready to come out of the oven about now, anyway. It might have identity issues, but it's good, I promise."

"An' there's brownies, too!"

"And there's brownies, too," Emily said, smiling. A little too hard, Colin thought.

"Emily made those." Austin grinned, giggling as he did his best to hang on to the pup. "They're like the best brownies, ever!"

At that, Emily laughed full-out. "Why, thank you, sweetie!"

Then she lifted those sweet blue eyes to Colin's again, sparkling over that smile, defying the sadness underneath, and between that and the promise of dinner he hadn't cooked himself *and* brownies, he might've lost his breath there, for a moment. Or his sanity. Hard to tell. But between those eyes and his nephew's hopeful expression… how could he say no?

"Sounds great," he said, swiping the blanket off the ground and shaking it out.

"You sure?"

"Absolutely."

But only that he was about to dive headfirst into shark-infested waters.

There was nothing sexier, Emily thought later when she walked back into the kitchen after putting the kids to bed, than a big man washing dishes. Especially one holding a spirited conversation with the tiny puppy gnawing his sneaker's shoelace at the same time. Choking back the laugh that wanted so badly to erupt, she stood in the doorway where he couldn't see her, simply watching. Absorbing. Smacking down the latest in an apparent series of wayward thoughts that seriously needed smacking.

Like, for instance, how watching Colin with the kids, his gentleness and humor, had stirred the cinders of three years' worth of hopes and expectations. Oh, she imagined—or at least hoped—she'd meet someone else one day, someone whose hopes and goals meshed with hers. Someone honest and true. Someone worthy of her, damn it. But that day, if it ever came, was way off in the future, after she'd had time to heal. To grow. To make sense of what had happened and make damn sure it didn't happen again.

So for *double*-damn sure she wasn't about to see Colin Talbot as anything except an exercise in proving her newfound strength. So let temptation flaunt itself in her face—no way in hell was she gonna bite.

He turned, startling her, his smile as careful as she imagined hers was. And despite her resolve, despite everything in her that said, "Uh-uh, honey," she wanted to know what his story was. What had put such caution in those pale eyes.

"There's coffee," he said, nodding toward the coffee-maker.

Meaning he was staying awhile? Interesting.

"Thanks." She crossed the tile floor, reached for a pair of mugs from the nearby cupboard. Somehow she didn't think it was her imagination, his gaze on her back. The questions floating in the air between them. Wanting to know more, knowing the folly of going there.

Coffee poured, she cradled the steaming mug to her chest and turned, chuckling at the pup's ferocious growl as he tried to kill the shoelace.

"You've made a friend." She lifted her eyes to his a moment before he squatted to pick up the dog. Thor had plopped in the dog bed by the pot-bellied stove near the oversize dining table, even though it hadn't been lit in days. Now the cat—who generally kept to himself when the kids were awake—plodded over to wedge herself beside the dog, who didn't seem to care one whit when her fluffy tail settled over his snout. "More than one, actually. The kids clearly adore their uncle."

Colin smiled—if you could call it that—as he cocooned the pup in his huge hands. But they weren't all chewed up and scarred, like his brothers'. "The feeling's mutual. Then again, it's not all that hard to make friends with most kids. Some, sure, have a real reason to be leery, but for the most part…" Shifting his gaze away from hers, he shrugged. "It's like their default setting is to be open. Loving." He set the pup back on the floor, shoving his hands in his pockets. "Before life hardens them, anyway."

Curiouser and curiouser. "I know what you mean," Emily said. "I think that's one reason I love teaching kindergarten. Getting them before their innocence gets scrubbed away."

Colin reached for one of the last brownies, stuffing half the thing in his mouth before adding, "These are terrific."

The thing was, after three years with Michael, if it was

one thing Emily was good at, it was spotting a prevarica-
tor…a skill more finely honed by hindsight, it turned out.
Unfortunately. But whatever Colin's reasons for switch-
ing the subject, they were none of her concern. So all she
did was shrug and say, "Can't take much credit, really,
they're from a mix. And I'm good at following directions.
But thanks anyway—"

A breeze shunted through the house when the front door
opened, bringing with it her cousin's laugh. A minute later,
Dee and Josh appeared in the doorway, hand in hand and
grinning like loons. Except then surprise swept across
both their faces when they realized Emily wasn't alone.

"I take it the date was a success?" Emily asked as Josh
crossed to his brother to clap him on his upper arm.

"Honey, just getting out of the house by ourselves was
a success," Dee said, slipping off her denim jacket and
hugging it to her middle. "But yeah…" She grinned over
at her husband. "It was good."

"Although I had this momentary panic," Josh said, "that
we'd discover we really had nothing to say to each other."

Emily laughed. "I take it your fears were groundless?"

"Hell," Josh said, grabbing the last brownie, then waving it toward his wife. "This one didn't shut up the entire
time."

"It's true," Deanna said with a *whatever* shrug. "Like
the dam broke, and all the stuff I either kept forgetting
to say or would fall asleep before saying came roaring
out. We probably won't have to talk again for at least two
months."

Another chuckle bubbled up from Emily's chest, this
time at how effortlessly the Westernized cadences her
cousin had worked so hard to eradicate from her speech
after she moved to DC had reasserted themselves. Gone,
too, was most of the chichi edginess Dee had appropriated

like a costume, leaving behind the Deanna Emily remembered from when they were kids. Only—she caught the wink her cousin gave her husband—much, much happier. Then Dee glanced behind her before giving Emily wide eyes.

"Both kids are asleep?"

"Wasn't that the plan?"

That got an exaggerated sigh. "For you, they both go to sleep. For us…" Her mouth twisted. Emily laughed.

"Beginner's luck, I assure you."

Dusting brownie crumbs off his fingers, which the puppy quickly scarfed up, Josh poked his brother. "So, what? You get roped into sharing the babysitting detail?"

Colin's chuckle sounded almost…relaxed. "Not exactly. They were all outside when I drove by, and long story short…your kid invited me to dinner."

"And you actually accepted?"

"I guess I did."

Dee huffed. "*How* many times over the past two weeks have I asked you to come eat with us and you'd come up with one sorry excuse after another about why you couldn't? I'm thinking maybe I should be offended. Especially since I know you had dinner with Zach and them." Except the light dancing in her eyes said she wasn't, really.

Although the flush sweeping over Colin's beard-hazed cheeks said…something. What, Emily wasn't sure. But then the exchanged glance between the newlyweds made her cheeks warm, too. Which was nuts.

"So Colin said he'd take babydog until we found a home for him," she said, probably too quickly. "And I told him you have Thor's carrier somewhere?"

That got another exchanged glance—these two were about as subtle as an explosion, yeesh—before Josh nodded, then turned to his brother. "I do. We can get it right now if you want."

"Uh…sure. Well…" Colin plucked the puppy, who was attacking his shoelace again, off the floor, as Josh gathered up bowls and dog food and such. "Thanks again. I'll…see you around, I guess."

Then they were gone. And, yep, Deanna turned narrowed eyes on Emily. "And would you like to fill me in before my imagination goes down untold murky paths?"

Emily snorted. "You don't honestly think his being here has anything to do with me?"

"Doesn't it? Only I'm sure I don't have to remind you—"

"That five minutes ago I was engaged to someone else. No, you don't. Although who was the one making all those untoward suggestions about taking advantage of still being, um, *prepared*?"

"And what part of 'I'm kidding' did you not get?"

Shaking her head, Emily snatched the brownie plate off the counter, swiping the crumbs into the trash before cramming it into the dishwasher. "Then before you and your imagination ride off into the sunset…" Buttons pushed, she shut the door, then turned, arms folded over her stomach, which was churning even more than the dishwasher. "It was like Colin said—Austin invited him to dinner, the man said yes. I was surprised, too, but I wouldn't read anything more into it if I were you."

"Because clearly you have no idea how huge this is."

"Dee. I doubt anything more's going on here than Colin's being lonely. Whether he'll admit it or not."

"Which would be my point?"

"Oh, for Pete's sake…" Emily blew out a breath. "Give me some credit, okay? I'm not about to…" Her eyes burning, she shoved her hair behind her ear. "I came out here to get my head on straight. That hasn't changed. Do I find Colin attractive? Sure—"

"At least you admit it."

"I'm burned, not dead. Look, I agree with you, that it was a big deal, his agreeing to have dinner with the kids and me. For reasons I'm not sure even he understands, let alone any of the rest of us. But if you think this has more to do with me than it did…that's nuts."

Her mouth pulled into the thinnest line possible without disappearing entirely, Deanna stared at Emily for a long moment before releasing a rough sigh. "It's just—"

"I know. And while I appreciate your concern…" Emily's eyes burned again. "I'd appreciate it more if you'd trust me enough to let me figure a few things out on my own. Damn it, Dee—the main reason I came out here was so I wouldn't have to listen to my *mother's* incessant harangue, to get away from her constant attempts to manipulate my life into some ideal that only existed in her imagination. Not that she didn't mean well, in her own obsessive-compulsive way, but even though I'd thought I'd broken away from her gravitational pull enough to live my own life, by moving out, by becoming a teacher…"

Emily gave her head another shake. "Clearly I hadn't nearly as much as I'd thought. I'm not an idiot, Dee. I know hooking up with Colin—or, frankly, anyone right now—would be insane and pointless. But how on earth am I ever going to learn how to navigate my own life without actually doing it? Without making my own decisions?" She pulled a face. "My own mistakes, if it comes to that. Which I'm sure it will. What with being human and all. But at least they'll be *my* mistakes. *My* choices. Not somebody else's. For once."

Her cousin crossed her arms. "So what you're saying is, you want the freedom to screw up?"

"Yes! Exactly! Because how else am I going to learn? To *grow*?" Her mouth twisted again. "To grow *up*."

After a moment, Dee crossed the space between them to tug Emily into her arms. "I'm sorry," she mumbled, then pulled away. "You're right."

A raw breath left Emily's lungs. "So no more fretting?"

Dee pushed a laugh through her nose. "Can't guarantee that, but…" One side of her mouth pushed up. "I'll keep my yap shut, how's that?"

"Thank you," Emily said, pulling her cousin into another hug. As victories went, it was a pretty small one. But she'd take it.

Even if she sounded a helluva lot braver than she felt.

Chapter Six

Cradling the little dog to his chest with one hand, Colin followed his brother into the "new" barn. And in an instant the familiar tang of hay and horse, the occasional soft whinny piercing a chorus of equine huffing, provoked feelings and emotions that were becoming increasingly difficult to parse the longer he was home.

Didn't help, either, that the damn dog smelled like Emily, which in turn brought to mind the look on her face when he'd taken the pup. Like a little kid trying so hard to be brave.

Except for the little kid part of that.

"I shoved the kennel in here somewhere," Josh said, his boots clomping against the concrete floor as he passed the stalls on the way to the tack room. There were actually three barns on the property—the original twenties-era structure, closer to the house and rarely used to house livestock these days; and another one like this, all metal and cement and modern amenities.

Colin counted a dozen or so horses in here, most of which ignored them as they passed, although a couple poked their heads over the stall doors, ears flicking in mild curiosity at the wriggling creature in Colin's hand. A particularly stunning roan mare gave a vigorous nod, inviting them closer. Colin obliged, feeling something ease inside him when she stretched her neck to first investigate the pup, then cuff Colin's shoulder. The puppy yipped, thrilled; the mare whinnied in response, then nodded again. Chuckling, Colin stroked her satiny neck for a moment before catching up to Josh, letting the puppy down. The dog promptly scampered off, nose to ground, trying to follow eighteen trails at once.

"Looks like you've got a full house," Colin said from the doorway to the tack room. It was pristine, save for one corner clearly used for storing all the junk not currently in use but too good to pitch. Including a collapsible wire kennel clearly intended for a much larger dog. Not something that weighed ten pounds. On a full stomach.

Josh tossed a grin over his shoulder as he jerked the kennel free of the detritus pile it'd been wedged in. "Gettin' there. Although about half of 'em are boarders. A couple rescues, too…"

He banged off the light and hauled the contraption from the tack room, clattering it onto the dusty floor in front of Colin before smacking his palms across his butt. The pup cautiously approached the kennel, stretching out as far as his little body would allow to sniff at it, only to jump back when the sole of Josh's boot scraped the floor. Laughing, Josh squatted to call the little guy over, reaching inside the cone to scratch one ear until he collapsed beside Josh's boot, tummy bared, to grin upside down up at Colin.

"And a couple of the horses are Mallory's, for her and

Zach's therapy facility. They hope to be good to go by June, did I tell you?"

"Zach did, when I was over there the other night." An evening filled with warmth and laughter…and silliness, he thought on a smile. Because three boys under the age of twelve, that's why. And dogs. And a redheaded spitfire who wasn't about to let a wheelchair clip her wings. Nor the events from her past that had put her in it. "It's good to see him so happy, after…everything."

His brother nodded, but not before Colin caught the squint. Not judgmental, maybe, but definitely questioning. Never mind that the minute he'd heard about the accident more than three years before that had taken his older brother's first wife, Colin had called Zach, saying he'd be on the first plane home if that's what Zach wanted. Except Zach had said no, there was nothing Colin could do anyway. A pretty typical Talbot response, actually, which Josh would realize if he thought about it for two seconds.

Colin was glad, though, that he'd be here for the wedding. He was glad he was here period, he realized as Josh stood and grabbed the crate again, making the puppy clumsily scramble to his feet. And if Emily Weber's presence had something to do with that… Shoot, if he could figure that one out, tackling world peace would be a piece of cake.

He took the crate from his brother to haul it out of the barn, even though they stopped along the way to chat with this or that mare, admire a colt, the pride radiating from his brother warmer than the sun in July. He knew Josh was thrilled to own, along with his wife, the ranch that had been the cornerstone of this part of New Mexico for more than a hundred years. But ranches of this size tended to be more of a financial drain than moneymakers these days, especially since Deanna's father had downsized the cattle end of things years ago.

"Which is why we're more grateful than we can say for Mallory's coming on board with her therapy facility," Josh said in answer to Colin's out-loud musings. Now outside, Josh slugged his hands in his back pockets. A weightless evening breeze nudged at them, the air chilled and somehow fruity, like a crisp white wine. The pup toddled ahead, only to plop his butt in the dirt and lift his snout, sniffing. "Between that and renting out the cabins down by the river during the hunting season, and the occasional rodeo winnings…" Josh shrugged. "We make do. And now that Dee's got her art gallery in town…" He grinned. "It's all about possibilities. Options."

"Or an awful lot of plates up in the air."

His brother chuckled. "Not gonna lie, we're talking risk with a capital *R*. But at least it's our risk to take, to try…" He huffed a sigh. "I know you never felt the connection to the place I did. It was the same with Dee, at least up until a few months ago. But for us, this is home. Simple as that."

As if anything was ever simple. Especially when it came to home and connections and who a person was. Where they were supposed to be.

"And if—"

"We're giving it two years," his brother said, lifting his gaze to a never-ending sky so choked with stars they bled into each other. Then his eyes lowered to Colin's again, shining with a determination that made him realize the goofy kid he remembered had long since left the building. Mostly, anyway. "Between us, we've got enough squirreled away to tide us over for that long while we figure out how to make this all work. Worst-case scenario? We'll sell it, find a smaller place, start over. The world won't end if it comes to that, believe me. But you better believe we're gonna do everything in our power to make sure it doesn't."

Now it was Colin's turn to look away, wondering, as he often did, what had tied most of his family to this place. Why his parents, his three brothers, had taken such firm root in this little corner of New Mexico, even if it'd taken Levi longer than the others, when Colin had wanted nothing more than to break free from it.

What was pulling him back now—

"You okay?" Josh asked, his brother's voice piercing Colin's thoughts.

"Just thinking about how all the stuff that seemed so black-and-white when you were a kid gets a lot more muddied as you get older."

"And I don't even want to know what you're talking about, do I?"

Colin pushed a laugh through his nose. "Probably not." Then he squinted back at the barn. "You doing all the work yourself?"

"Right now, it's still pretty manageable. It's nothing like when we were working cows, thank goodness. That was rough."

"I remember." He snorted. "There was a reason I left."

Actually, there'd been several. But 4:00 a.m. wake-up calls for most of the summer had definitely ranked right up there.

Josh chuckled. "Although I've got a couple high school kids who come after school and on weekends to help out. And Mallory's boy," he said with a grin. "Can't keep the kid away. Already got him training for barrels. Like his mama used to."

"He's, what? Eleven?"

"Nearly twelve. Perfect age. Mallory's probably gonna

need someone to help out with the facility, though, eventually. Especially somebody who's good with kids."

"The way everything else seems to be falling into place," Colin said quietly, "I'm sure that will, too."

His brother grinned over at him. "I'm sure you're right."

The dog trundled over, asking to be picked up. Colin obliged. Only now, of course, Emily's perfume mingled with the night's, poking at all those *feelings* again. At the yearning he'd refused to acknowledge for so long. Then he blew out a half laugh. "This family's positively exploding."

"Isn't it?" his brother said, sounding totally good with that. "Seriously doubt it's anywhere near done yet, either."

Colin frowned at his brother. "Is Deanna…?"

"What? Oh. No. Not that I know of, anyway. Sure, we'd like more kids down the line, but right now we've got our hands full with the two we've got. And the ranch and her gallery and everything. When the time's right. Speaking of whom, I should probably get back—"

"Right. Of course. Except…" The dog clutched in one hand, the kennel in the other, Colin said, "I already made sure Emily knows she can come see this guy—" he hefted the pup, who gave his chin a little lick "—anytime she likes. But it might not be a bad idea, her coming over tonight to help him get settled in."

Briefly raised brows gave way to a lopsided smile as his brother started back to the house, tossing a "Sure thing" over his shoulder as he strode off, his unasked question shimmering in the air between them.

Why?

Not that Colin could've answered, anyway, so thank goodness Josh hadn't asked. Except…a taste of her company had left him wanting more, was all. And considering her own situation, he sincerely doubted there was any danger of her reading anything more into the invitation than there was. Emily Weber was *safe*, in other words.

Whether he was, was something else entirely.

Emily was about to knock on the door when she realized Colin had left it ajar. Although because he was expecting her or he simply wasn't good at closing doors behind him, she had no idea. God knew Michael never had been, so maybe it was a guy thing. Who knew? So she knocked, anyway, telling herself the shiver that snaked up her spine at his deep "Come on in!" was due to the nippy night. Not her brain's having taken a hike to parts unknown.

Although since she was here—instead of, you know, acting like the big girl she was supposed to be and seeing the pup tomorrow or the next day—she supposed the brain-hiking thing was moot.

Still. She had to admit it was nice, being around a man who clearly had no agenda. Despite how he looked at her, as though he could see through to parts of her soul she hadn't discovered yet herself. Which by rights should be scary—

The puppy bounded up to her, a blur of bliss. And cone-free. Laughing, Emily picked him up, then looked across the room into that direct, greeny-gold gaze and lost her breath for a second.

—but oddly wasn't. Instead, she felt…safe. Why, she had no idea, since she barely knew the man. But damned if he didn't absolutely radiate integrity. Goodness. And something else she couldn't quite put a finger on, but that made her think, *Oh, okay. You'll do.*

For now, anyway. For this moment, when her brain was still muddled and her heart was shredded and she knew it would be a long, *long* time before trust and she resolved their differences. Right now, she needed *safe* and *good* and *integrity.*

And a puppy to cuddle, she thought, sinking cross-legged on the worn braided rug covering most of the living room floor to let the thing give her jaw a thorough washing. Dodging the little tongue, she looked around, taking in what looked like a leftover set from a Western movie, circa 1975—scuffed leather and dinged wood, faded geometric-design pillows, the small kitchen a study in murky greens and browns. She'd never been inside when she'd visited as a kid—no reason for her to have been, really—and now she found herself seeing it through Colin's eyes.

Apparently noticing her scrutiny, he chuckled. "It looks better in the daylight."

"I didn't—"

"You didn't have to. Want something to drink? Coffee? Tea?"

"No more coffee. I'll never sleep." She lowered her gaze to the dog. "You took off the cone?"

"The wound's as good as healed. I checked with Zach. He said it was okay. So, tea?"

"Sure. Although somehow you don't strike me as a tea person."

"Not usually, no. But I found some tea bags when I was cleaning out the cupboards. My mother's maybe? Have no idea how good they are, but—"

"Why'd you ask me to come over? Really?"

Halfway to the open kitchen, Colin turned, a frown etched between his brows. But instead of answering, he yanked an ancient kettle off the equally ancient gas stove, then said over the sound of water thrumming into it, "You want honesty?"

"If you wouldn't mind."

He clunked the kettle onto the burner and twisted on

the flame before facing her again, one hand curled on the edge of the counter behind him.

"I didn't invite you here because of the dog. He was just...convenient."

"I see."

His laugh, if one could call it that, matched his expression. "I doubt it. Since I sure as hell don't. But it's not about..." He blew out another breath. "I'm not trying to get into your pants, if that's what you're thinking."

"Actually," she grumbled, "considering my recent past, that would be refreshing." Then, at his puzzled look, she realized he had no idea what she was talking about. "As it happens, Michael became a lot less...attentive, shall we say, the last year or so we were together. He said it was because of his workload. Yeah, well, it was a *load*, all right."

Colin softly cursed, then crossed his arms over that nice, solid chest. "I'm sorry."

"So was I. Then. Now? Not so much."

"Even so, I take it you don't really mean that. That you'd—"

"Find it refreshing to be wanted? You bet. Even though it's equally refreshing that you don't. So figure that one out."

The kettle squealed. Colin snatched it off the stove and poured water into two mugs, tea bag strings dangling down their sides. "It's not that hard, really. You were not only rejected—" he crossed to where she was sitting, setting both mugs on the coffee table next to her before returning to the kitchen "—you were betrayed." He gathered spoons, a sugar bowl, a carton of half-and-half from the fridge. "So right now—"

The stuff now set on the table beside the mugs, he lowered himself to the floor in front of her, looking like the world's largest kindergartner. And he smelled like the wind, damn it. Michael, if she remembered correctly, had never smelled like the wind. Or anything else even remotely…earthy.

And he still hadn't answered her question, had he? About why he'd invited her over. Probably wouldn't, either. Then again, maybe he didn't really have an answer—

"So right now," Mr. Earthy was saying, "part of you wants nothing to do with men. And the other part of you probably wants nothing more than to get even."

Now it was her turn to laugh. Only to see her own pain reflected in his eyes.

"Speaking from experience?"

Nodding, he dumped two teaspoons of sugar into his tea.

"Recent?"

"Enough." He stirred the tea, setting the wet spoon on a napkin before slurping his tea. The dog abandoned her lap for his, only to disappear into the void made by his legs. A second later his little bewhiskered nose appeared over Colin's calves, then vanished again. "Although," Colin said, hoisting the pup back onto the floor between them, "the situation wasn't the same. The dishonesty, however, was."

With that, the light dawned that he *was* answering her question, in his own I'll-get-there-eventually way. Whether he realized it or not. But the upshot was the guy simply needed someone to talk to. Was it nuts, how flattered she was that he'd picked her?

That he trusted her enough to do that.

"She cheated on you?"

Another dry laugh shoved from his throat. "No. Although in a way it would've been easier if she had. At least that would've been cut-and-dried. But she wasn't upfront about how she really felt about my work. Not the work itself, exactly, but the fact that it kept us apart so much."

"And I take it she didn't want to go with you?"

"Nope. Not that I blamed her. I'm often in not exactly the safest places in the world. But what hurt the most was…" He glanced away, then back at Emily, his forehead crunched. "She never really understood why what I do was—is—so important to me."

"Did you ever tell her?"

"More times than I could count."

Emily shifted to relieve her numb butt. "And maybe," she said gently, "it's about telling the right person."

Colin watched her for a moment with those searing eyes before shoving himself to his feet and going over to an old desk wedged into a corner of the room. He seemed to hesitate, though, before grabbing a compact two-in-one computer/tablet combo and returning, lowering himself to the floor again and flipping the tablet open so the screen faced her. His gaze glanced off hers again before, slowly, he began scrolling through dozens of photos of children, some smiling, some crying, many whose faces radiated such fear and uncertainty Emily's eyes filled.

"Where…?" she finally said through a throat so tight she was surprised any sound came out at all.

"Various places." His voice was so low she could barely hear him. "Greece. Turkey. Jordan." He paused at one picture, a stunning black-and-white photo of a laughing little boy, the sun shimmering in his dark, straight hair. Emily stared for several moments at the photo, transfixed, before realizing how still Colin had gone beside her. She lifted her eyes to the side of his face—

Without thinking, she rested her hand on that strong, muscled arm, resisting the urge to stroke away the chill she felt there. "Who is he?"

"What? Oh." He seemed to shake himself free, then

shook his head. "Just one of the kids in the refugee camp. But this pic...it gets me, every time."

"I can see why," Emily said, removing her hand. And, for that moment, her trust. Because she seriously doubted the child had been *just* some kid in the camp. Then again, it wasn't as if Colin was under any obligation to rip open his soul to her. Especially if that soul, like hers, had been recently wounded.

A second later he shut the tiny laptop and stood to set it back on the desk, his hunched shoulders twisting Emily up inside.

"Are those going into your book?" she asked after what felt like an appropriate lapse.

"Some of them." Colin turned, looking very much like a man asking for understanding. Although—again—why from her, she had no idea. And for what, exactly, she had even less. "The publisher's going to donate a portion of the profits to The Little Ones' Rescue Fund."

"Put me down for ten copies," she said, and his grin at least somewhat unwound the tension.

"So..." She brought the tea to her lips again, only to make a face because it'd already gone cold. "How long ago was..." Her head tilted. "What was her name?"

"Oh," he said, as though surprised by her question. "Sarah. A year."

Emily got to her feet, shaking out her achy legs as she went to the kitchen to nuke her tea. "And you're still not over her, are you?"

Colin imagined she could probably feel him staring a hole between her shoulder blades as she set the mug inside a very early-generation microwave, punched in thirty seconds. When he didn't answer her, though, she turned, the microwave whirring behind her. "Sorry. Didn't mean to overstep—"

"No, it's not that, it's…"

Uh-huh. Answer that one, big shot.

Frowning, he cupped the back of his head for a moment, then shifted to lean back against the edge of the coffee table, one wrist propped on his raised knee as he let himself sink into those sweet, kind eyes. But he sensed a steeliness behind the sweetness a smart man would heed. Although how smart he actually was, was open to interpretation.

Colin looked down at the pup, passed out by his hip, curled up so tight he looked like a little potato. "I think…" He lifted his gaze to hers again—bracing himself against that damned tug of longing. "I think it's more that I wanted to believe she'd eventually see things my way. That somehow we'd work it out. My mistake was…" He stroked the dog, who groaned in his sleep. "In not realizing she was thinking exactly the same thing. So basically we wasted a couple years of our lives hoping the other person would change." A breath left his lungs. "Dumb."

The microwave dinged, after a fashion. Emily retrieved her tea and returned to the living room, then kicked off her flats to settle into Dad's old beat-up recliner, her feet underneath her, her hair rippling over her shoulders. Across her breasts. "Because you believed she was worth waiting for."

Not what he'd expected. Although what that might have been, he had no clue. Still, he pushed out a short laugh. "Sarah was—is—a great person. Funny, smart, gracious— all the boxes ticked. Except the biggie. Well, two biggies."

"And what's the second?"

Colin went very still for a moment, a little surprised to realize how weird it felt to talk about the woman who'd once taken up so much space in his head. His world.

"Kids," he said on a breath. "As in, she wanted them. After everything I'd seen… I wasn't so sure." He paused, waiting out the wave. "I'm still not."

It'd taken him a long time to fully admit that to himself. Let alone anyone else. Especially considering how genuinely crazy he was about children. But that was the problem, wasn't it?

"For way too long," he said, "I'd let feelings blind me to logic. To the truth, of who we both were. What we both wanted. Or didn't. A huge mistake I'm only grateful we realized before things got worse."

And wasn't that a careful expression on Emily's face? Then again, she'd hardly be the first woman to be repelled by a man saying he didn't want to be a father. But then she said, with a shrug, "Not everyone's cut out to be a parent. Different strokes and all that."

Of course, his reasons for not wanting children were more complicated than he was about to share with someone who was still more or less a stranger. Sure, he'd learned the hard way that without honesty, no relationship had a snowball's chance in hell of succeeding. But this wasn't a relationship. Nor would it become one, for many reasons. In which case he was under no obligation to give this woman total access to what lurked inside his skull.

Never mind that he'd already given her more of a glimpse than he'd intended.

So Colin picked up his own tea again and lobbed the conversation back to her.

"What about you? You want kids?"

On a half laugh, Emily cupped the mug to her chest, frowning into it. "Yes, but…" On a gusty sigh, she met his gaze again. "That was part of the fantasy, you know?"

"The fantasy?"

Emily nodded, then set the mug on the table beside

the chair before somehow rearranging her limbs to prop
one elbow on her knee and rest her chin in her palm, a
frown pinching her forehead. "Between the engagement
and the wedding planning and everything…looking back,
I have to wonder how much of that, really, was me playing *my* part in what my parents wanted for me." Another
dry laugh preceded, "Okay, what I'd convinced myself I
wanted, too. Because nobody forced me into this engagement, believe me. But…"

Shifting again, Emily set the mug on the side table to sit
cross-legged, then leaned forward with her hands clasped
in front of her. "I used to pore over my parents' wedding
album for hours, absolutely fascinated with the whole…
spectacle. *Lavish* doesn't even begin to cover it. The flowers, the crystal, the doves…the Carolina Herrera wedding
gown. Which looked like sparkling whipped cream. Cannot tell you how much I drooled over that thing. Although
my taste changed—blessedly—my jonesing for the dream
wedding did not. The dream…life. You wanna talk *dumb*."
Straightening, she jerked both thumbs toward her chest.
"This girl, right here."

"Daddy's princess?"

Another snort preceded, "The definition of, believe me.
Which is why…" Her mouth twisted to one side. "Even
aside from the obvious, it's probably a blessing, the way
things worked out. Or didn't. Because I obviously wasn't
going into it with my eyes wide open. Or as a complete
person, who knew what she needed. Wanted. *Deserved.*
And I'm not talking about doves and a ten-thousand-dollar
wedding gown."

Colin's brows slammed together. "Your gown really
cost that much?"

"It really did. However…over the past few weeks I've
realized I really, really missed the point. If not the boat.

Yes, I want kids. And to be a wife. But I wasn't as *ready* to be a wife and mother as I'd wanted to believe. Because I had gotten caught up in the fantasy. In everyone's expectations. Which in turn blinded me to the simple, if highly embarrassing, fact that I still had some growing up to do."

He hesitated, then said, "How old are you, anyway?"

She smirked. "Twenty-seven in two months. So not a child. Even if—" She stretched her arms up, arching her back, before letting them drop again. "Even if I often still feel like one."

Colin averted his gaze from her breasts. "Because you ran away from home."

Her eyes crinkled. "Says the man who did the same thing *how* many years ago? And hadn't been back in years?"

Touché.

Colin scooped up the dog and got to his feet, depositing the pup in Emily's lap before taking his empty cup to the kitchen to rinse it out. "You hungry? I've got popcorn—"

"No, thanks. I'm good. So you know why I escaped. Your turn."

"And there's such a thing as taking this forthrightness thing too far."

"It's not exactly a secret, Colin. That you left, I mean. Why, however—"

"And my brother didn't fill you in?"

"Actually, I don't think he really knows. Or if he does, he's not saying. Fraternal honor, or something."

Of course, Josh had been a teenager when Colin bolted from the nest like his tail feathers were on fire. And it wasn't as if Colin had talked things over with any of his brothers, not even Zach. Still, speaking of things not exactly being secret...

"I felt like I was about to suffocate here," he said, shoving a popcorn packet into the microwave and hoping for the best. "What you said, about expectations?" He turned back to see she'd twisted around in the chair to watch him, the puppy nestled in that sweet spot between the tops of her breasts and her chin. Hell. He almost had to literally shake his head loose from his ass. "The family's been here for generations, working cattle and horses on the Vista. We are all on horses by three or four, rounding up cattle by six. So it was assumed that Zach and I, especially, would follow family tradition in one way or another. And when Zach announced he wanted to become a vet, Dad naturally assumed the ranch foreman mantle would fall to me."

Emily frowned. "Without bothering to find out if that's what you wanted to do?"

"There was never even a question in his mind. Only around the time I hit puberty, I realized I felt like I was choking. And not only from the dust kicked up by a hundred head of cattle deciding they didn't want to go where you wanted 'em to. The funny thing is, we traveled a lot when my brothers and I were kids—there were enough hands to fill in so we could do that—because my folks insisted we see there was a world beyond this little corner of New Mexico. What they didn't realize, however, was that those road trips only whetted my appetite for more. I may not have known what that *more* was, at that point, but I sure as heck knew I'd never find it if I didn't leave. And Dad and I didn't exactly see eye to eye on that."

"Because this *was* his world."

"Exactly. And he couldn't, or wouldn't, see my side of things. Said I'd never be happy looking for something 'out there' if I didn't find it right where I was first."

Emily looked down at the puppy for a moment. "Not an unreasonable point."

"On the surface? No. Even if at the time I thought he

was off his nut. Because all I could think was that I'd die if I had to live out the rest of my life within twenty miles of where I'd been born."

"And I take it you still feel that way," Emily said behind him when he turned to get the scorched popcorn out of the microwave, dumping the mess in the garbage.

Colin shoved open the window over the sink to air out the place—not to mention his head—before facing her again, his arms crossed over his chest. Gal had enough of her own crap to sort through without him dragging up his own conflicts. "I wanted to make a difference," he said at last, deciding keeping things in the past tense was safer, for the moment at least, than messing around in the present. "In the world, I mean. And I couldn't do that here. Not like I wanted to, anyway." Then he pushed a short laugh through his nose. "Although all these years later, it's not like I'm a doctor or anything. I'm not exactly saving lives—"

"And don't you dare sell yourself short," Emily said, almost vehemently. "There's a lot to be said for simply bearing witness to what's going on in the world, shining a light on all the stuff a lot of people don't know about. Or don't *want* to know about. Maybe you're not healing bodies, but…but if your work shakes some people out of their complacency, heals a few souls in the process…" Her cheeks flushed as her mouth clamped shut. Then she shoved out a breath. "We all have our place in the world. If that's yours, just own it, dude." Then she pushed out a tired laugh. "Listen to me, sounding like some expert."

One side of Colin's mouth pushed up. "You ask me, most of those *experts* spend way too much time talking out of their butts. And you look like you're about to topple over."

A short laugh collided with her yawn. "I guess I am.

Well, puppydoodle," she said, pushing herself upright with the pup still nestled under her chin, "guess I better turn you over to Uncle Colin." Naturally the dog swung around to gnaw on the ends of her hair, making her laugh… And her scent, and that damned laugh, drifted up to Colin, surrounding him like a hug.

He didn't want her to leave. Meaning he desperately needed her to do exactly that.

Especially when they got to his door and she looked up at him, a half smile teasing that full mouth, and said, "Sometimes, all you can do is trust that things will work out exactly the way they're supposed to."

Colin crossed his arms, in no small part to keep from touching her. "Meaning?"

"That's where the trust part of that comes in," she said softly, then left, taking her scent and her laughter and a good chunk of Colin's good sense with her. He watched her until she disappeared, then shut the door and set the pup back down on the rug. With a shudder of pure joy, the tiny thing belly-crawled over to the rope toy Emily had bought for him and started to gnaw on it, blissfully unaware of the storm raging inside Colin's head. Because *damn it*—who the hell's bright idea was it, anyway, plopping this woman in front of him? It was downright cruel, the way the light shined from inside her as steady as a little lighthouse grounded on solid rock, impervious to the crashing waves determined to take it under.

Granted, maybe her situation didn't even begin to compare with the horrors he'd witnessed. And by her own admission, she'd fled from "real" life to give herself space to heal. Kinda hard to fault her for that, though, since wasn't he doing the same thing? Even so, what he'd seen in her eyes when she looked at those photos—even without knowing the whole story—punched Colin in the gut almost as bad as the subjects had to begin with. However much her own heart might still be shredded, it still overflowed with compassion for others…the hallmark of somebody made of far sterner stuff than she probably even realized. And damned if that hadn't put *his* heart in danger.

In other words, Emily wasn't the only one being assaulted by some big-ass waves.

Colin could only pray for the strength to withstand the ones crashing over him half as well as the woman who'd just caused the tsunami.

Chapter Seven

"I think you've got customers," Emily whispered to Dee, who was helping Jesse Aragon, a young Native artist she was promoting, hang one of his in-your-face paintings of the nearby mountains on the deliberately neutral wall. Dee had decided the smartest thing was to set up the gallery as a co-op for now, the artists themselves pitching in with their labor and time to help run the place until it was in the black.

Although judging from the pair of tourists currently peering and pointing through the large plate glass window, that wasn't going to take long.

In a floaty-print top and dusty capris, Dee crossed to the door to let them in, even though the official opening wasn't for another week yet. And in they swooped, along with the lilac-scented May breeze.

"Are you even open?" a middle-aged, much-too-tan man asked, his eyes hungrily darting around the gallery, and Emily smiled. Ninety percent of them were looky-loos, more curious than serious. But this one—and his wife, her wrists and chest choked with heavy silver-and-turquoise Navajo jewelry—were so obviously collectors it was almost amusing.

"Close enough," Dee said with a big grin, shoving a hand through her freshly cropped hair. "As long as you don't mind a little dirt." From the portacrib set up apart from the chaos, baby Katie let out a squawk. Dee laughed. "Or kids."

"Oh…" The woman made a beeline for the baby, who gave her new admirer her brightest, most adorable grin. "Isn't she precious! Is she yours?"

Chuckling, Dee joined the woman to haul Katie up into her arms, while her husband and the artist immediately slipped into a deep conversation about the painting…which the guy had apparently fallen immediately in love with. Dee glanced over at Emily, her eyes sparkling even more than the tiny diamond in her nose. Her cousin had reverted to the edgy look from her DC gallery days—a costume, yes, but at least one Dee knew she was wearing. And why.

A thought that led Emily to thinking about Colin. Again. In fact, she'd come into town with Dee today partly to distract herself from exactly that, even though she hadn't seen Josh's brother in the week or so since he'd taken the puppy. Because something told her Colin was also wearing a costume, of sorts, even if his was entirely mental. Granted, after Michael, her Spidey senses were probably on overdrive, but…

And did she need such folderol in her life? She did not. Bad enough she'd already fallen in love with a *dog* that would never be hers.

Especially since she knew—*knew*—that objectivity probably wasn't her strong suit right now. Maybe her wounds weren't open and raw and bleeding, but even she knew she was still too bruised and tender to think straight. Because who was in classic rebound mode right now, yearning for affirmation that she was desirable? Uh-huh. Meaning the way Colin looked at her that night had gotten all sorts of juices going, as one would expect when said juices had been neglected—if not outright ignored—for more than a year.

Her cell phone chirped at her. Not her mother, at least, whom she'd finally talked to a few days ago. Because a pleaser doesn't simply flip a switch and become *that* daughter. Alas. But it had been a strained—and strange—conversation, one that God willing wouldn't be reprised anytime soon.

Although seeing her father's number on the display didn't exactly fill Emily with glee, either, since Stewart Weber and she had never really had much to say to each other. Her father had been perfectly content to stay out of his wife's way, letting Margaret steer the family ship as she saw fit. Emily supposed her father loved her, in his own detached way. Even if he'd often looked at her as though not quite sure how he'd come to have a daughter. So his calling her now...

She braced herself.

"That you, Emily?"

Figuring she probably didn't want witnesses for this conversation, she stepped out of the gallery to sit on a wrought iron bench in front, where the warm sun convinced her to unbutton her cardigan. "Nobody else is going to be answering my phone, Dad."

"Oh. Of course." She imagined him blinking behind his steel-rimmed glasses, tugging on the bow tie he was never without, even when he was hermited in his study, researching or writing. Hiding out from his wife, most likely. Although he'd had other "outlets," too, hadn't he? Outlets Emily hadn't known about until she was in high school. "So. How are you?"

"I'm fine. Which I'm sure Mom told you."

"And maybe I wanted to hear it for myself and not through your mother's filter."

Whoa. Had he actually snapped at her? She'd never known her father to lose his cool with anyone. Not even with her mother, who, heaven knew, provided the man with ample opportunity for losing it. Not to mention an excuse, she supposed, for his behavior.

"What's going on, Dad?"

"You need to come home, that's what's going on."

Home. Yes, she'd told Colin she'd probably go back. Because that was logical. Practical. Because she had no reason, really, to stay here. Except what was *there* for her now? Really?

"Why?"

"Your mother's about to drive me crazy. She's in here every five minutes, either in tears or yelling or both. I can't get a damn thing done for all the interrupting. The…emotions exploding all over everything…" No, he'd never liked those very much, had he? "I know she's worried about you, but she's taking it out on me. And that's not right."

Anger—which wasn't exactly in short supply these days—surged through Emily's chest, heat racing up her neck, across her cheeks. "And you know what? *I'm* the one who had the rug yanked out from under her, the one who was humiliated. The one who was *cheated on.*" Okay, so she might've put the screws in a bit with that one. "So I'm sorry if Mother's taking her frustration out on you that *her* plans got screwed up, but right now, I need to take care of myself. Figure out what *I* need to do. To *be.* Meaning it's up to you guys to figure out how to deal with each other.

Or not. Go complain to one of your mistresses, Dad. Or is that not part of their job description?"

Her father's silence actually rang in her ear.

"What did you say?"

She pushed out a harsh laugh. "You honestly think I didn't know? That I haven't been playing the same game the two of you were, pretending everything was fine when it wasn't? Being the good, obedient daughter because it kept peace in the house. Or maybe that's only what I wanted to believe, that if I somehow tried a little harder I could fix whatever was broken between you. That I could…" She swatted at a tear that had escaped out of the corner of her eye. "That I could somehow make us into something that at least *looked* like a real family."

In the wake of her father's silence, she scrubbed the space between her brows. "Which I suppose made me exactly like Mother, didn't it? Who's only ever cared about appearances. Which is why she's got her panties in such a twist now, because *her* dream wedding for her daughter went up in smoke. Yes, I'll own my role in going along with it all, which is part of what I'm dealing with now. I wasn't a totally innocent bystander. Still. Whatever your issues are with Mother, I can't be your buffer anymore. Because you know what? If I'm here trying to figure out how to handle my own life, I think it's way past time the two of you figured out yours. Stay together or don't, I don't care. But for heaven's sake, be freaking *honest* with each other. Not to mention with yourselves."

Another long spate of silence preceded, "That's no way for a child to speak to her parent."

"Yeah, well, maybe that's because I'm not a child anymore."

Shaking, she cut off the call…

…only to look up to see Colin standing a few feet away, his expression unreadable behind his sunglasses.

Guessing by the deep blush that blazed across her cheeks, Emily really hadn't known he was there. Not that Colin had tried to sneak up on her or anything—as big as he was, that would've been impossible, anyway—but apparently she'd been too engrossed in her conversation to notice much of anything.

And by the time he realized exactly how personal the call was, it was too late for any kind of a graceful exit. Meaning he couldn't decide whether to feel like a jerk… or proud as hell of her.

"Sorry," he said, grateful they were alone, at least. Things would get busier later on, once school let out and the summer tourists descended, but this time of year what passed for downtown Whispering Pines vacillated between slow and dead.

"It's okay," Emily said, her eyes closing as she let her head drop back against the adobe wall behind the bench. Although the frown etched into her forehead said otherwise. "How much did you hear?"

"Probably more than you want to know." Eyes still closed, she grunted. "That can't have been easy."

After a moment, she opened her eyes, then patted the space beside her on the bench. Colin hesitated, then sat. And of course a breeze picked that exact moment to blow her scent in his direction. Whatever it was, it should be illegal. Especially since, even after a week, he could still smell her in his house. Although he'd be willing to bet that was the power of suggestion.

She forked her fingers through her ponytail, which cascaded over one breast like a caramel-colored waterfall, and

Colin had to look away. "At least you had the courage to leave before things got toxic," she said.

Feeling his own face warm, Colin leaned forward, his hands linked between his spread knees. "I don't know that I would've put it that way back then, but…maybe." His mouth pushed to one side. "Levi was the one who seemed to actually get off on getting up in Dad's face about stuff. Whereas I…"

"Escaped?"

"Pretty much." He hauled in a breath. "It's hard to stand up for yourself when you haven't figured out yet who you are."

Emily released a soft laugh. "Tell me about it."

His gaze swung to the side of her face. "So I take it you just did?"

That got another, stronger laugh. "I wish. I mean…" Her brow pleated, she faced him again. "I think I'm finally getting a feel for what I *need* to do. To *be*." She looked away again. "But right now, it's like…a glimmer. A promise. I've got a ways to go before I get any real handle on who I am, you're right. That conversation…it was a first tiny step on the beginning of a long, very overdue journey. One I have to take by myself."

In other words, she was right where Colin had been all those years ago, when everything was so new and shiny, if a little scary. In some ways he almost envied her.

He also hadn't missed the "by myself" part of all of that.

She was absolutely right, of course. Trying to figure out all the stuff she clearly needed to figure out would be nearly impossible with another person tossed into the equation. And her *recognizing* that was admirable as hell. Never mind the small, selfish, extraordinarily stupid part of him that actually had the nerve to feel disappointed. What the hell?

Half smiling, Colin leaned back again, his arms folded high on his chest. "No, I'd say the *first* step was you coming out here. Breaking away. But what I just heard… I'd say that was a much bigger step than you're giving yourself credit for."

"Thanks," she said after a moment. "Although I can't hide forever. Much as I might like to. A little space to get my head on straight is all well and good, but even I know I need to face my issues with my parents head-on. Otherwise I'm simply doing what I've always done." Her mouth pulled flat. "And sooner rather than later, before I totally wear out my welcome. But not until after the wedding, I imagine."

Colin watched as a young couple he didn't recognize walked hand in hand across the street, window-shopping. "That's next week." A realization that hit him way harder than it should've, that she'd be leaving soon. After all, wouldn't that make his own decision easier?

"Ten days. And I know. My parents don't, though. That I'm staying until then."

"Rebel," he said, and she laughed. A nice laugh, low and rich. One he wouldn't mind hearing closer to his ear…

"So what're you doing in town, anyway?" she asked.

"Needed to get out for a minute," Colin said, jerking his thoughts back in line. "Get away. Like I said before. And Josh'd said something about Deanna being almost ready to open the gallery, so I thought I'd kill a couple birds with one stone and come see." He twisted around to look inside through the plate glass window. "She's already got customers?"

Emily chuckled, then got to her feet. "Heck, she's already sold three pieces, and arranged a commission on a fourth. Not that I'm surprised," she said, facing the wide window with a grin stretched across her face. "I never doubted for a minute Dee could make a go of this. She's got an eye like none other. Not to mention business smarts that'd put most CEOs to shame."

And damned if her obvious pride in her cousin didn't provoke an ache so sharp it actually hurt. Ignoring it—sorta—Colin stood as well, his hands jammed in his front pockets. "Deanna's real lucky to have a friend like you."

Emily twisted around, her smile somehow reaching inside Colin to twist him up even harder. "Dee's been a good friend to me, too. Even when I didn't deserve it. Well." She nodded toward the door. "Shall we?"

"Sure," Colin said, when all he really wanted to do was take his butt somewhere, anywhere, where Emily wasn't. Where he couldn't see the sun teasing those silky golden strands tangling with her eyelashes or hear that laugh or *smell* her, God help him.

Someplace where that combination of bone-deep goodness and rebelliousness couldn't slap him around until he didn't know which end was up…even as it reminded him of someone else who'd had that exact same effect on him.

And look how that had worked out. Or hadn't.

However, he supposed he could tough it out for another couple of weeks, if he had to, until she left, went back to her real life. Another couple of weeks to ignore the ache and the pull and all the rest of it.

He could do that, sure. Piece of cake.

The next morning, Emily came out to the kitchen to see her cousin seated at the table rocking a wailing, red-cheeked Katie, Mama looking pretty much like she was an inch away from tears herself. On his knees in a chair beside her and fisting spoonfuls of Cocoa Puffs into his mouth like there was no tomorrow, Austin kept giving his baby stepsister the side-eye, as though wishing she'd shut up already.

"Another tooth coming in," Dee said over the cater-wauling. She was still in her pajamas, her hair porcupined around her slightly gray face. "I'm supposed to take Austin into school this morning, but…"

Already dressed in jeans and a lightweight cardigan over her sleeveless shirt, Emily drew a cup of coffee from the pot on the counter and sat across from Dee, her heart turning over in her chest at the miserable duo in front of her. She knew how grateful Josh and Dee both were for the part-time preschool the town's sole elementary school had set up for kids headed for kindergarten the following year, not only to get Austin used to the classroom setting but to give all of them a little breathing room while baby Kate was being so fussy. And normally Josh would have taken the boy to school, since clearly Dee wasn't going to make it this morning. But he'd gone with Zach into Taos to check out a potential addition to his stable and wouldn't be back until later that morning.

"So I'll take him," Emily said with a grin for the little boy, who grinned back around a mouthful of mashed cereal. "And then when I return—" she turned her smile on her exhausted cousin "—I'm taking over the wee banshee so her mommy can get some sleep."

"Oh, I couldn't—"

"Dee? Shut. Up." She glanced over at a wide-eyed Austin. "And don't you dare repeat me or your mother may not ever let me talk to you again."

Deanna pushed out a tired laugh. "You kidding? At this rate I may never let you leave."

A thought that provoked all manner of ambivalence inside Emily's already overwrought brain. Especially since, truth be told, she hadn't been getting a whole lot of sleep, either, these past few nights. Add to that her conversation yesterday with the reason behind her sleepless nights and…uh, boy. Although even she knew the chat itself had far less to do with her insomnia than what hadn't been said. And most likely wouldn't be. But man, oh, man—being around Colin was like walking under a power line in a thunderstorm. *Zzzzt!*

Because everything she'd said, about needing space to figure out who she was and what she wanted, was true. She didn't dare let herself get sucked into another relationship. Certainly not anytime soon. And *especially* not with someone who sent those Spidey senses off the charts, man. But the way he looked at her…

"What time's school start?" Emily said, carrying her empty mug to the sink, as if she could walk away from all the stuff going on inside her head. Stuff that could oh-so-easily lead to wrapping the man up in her arms and…

Yeah. *And.*

Such an innocent little word, so rife with the potential for disaster.

Emily rinsed out the mug, thinking it wouldn't hurt to give the kitchen another once-over. Not to mention get on her cousin's case about finally letting a cleaning service come in every once in a while. Especially now that the gallery was about to open for real.

"Nine," Dee said behind her. "And take my car, since the booster seat's already in it. I can go into town later."

Emily turned, glaring at her cousin as she swiped a towel inside the mug. "After you've had a nap."

Dee's mouth twisted. "Yes, Mother."

"You ready, munchkin?" she said to Austin, who gave a vigorous nod and more or less fell out of his chair, rolling his eyes when Dee reminded him to go pee before he got in the car. A moment later, he roared to the back door, emitting something like a battle cry. Although you could barely hear it over the baby's screams.

The volume stayed full blast as they wended through sun-drenched ranchland and peaceful forest on their way to town, Austin singing gustily behind her. The weird thing was, even though she'd been an only child in a house that redefined *hushed*, the noise and general craziness of her cousin's house didn't bother her. Because at least that was *real*.

Children of all ages swarmed the entrance to the small brick school building, predominantely black-haired heads gleaming in the sun, the local population being more Native or Hispanic than gringo. Austin's teacher, too, wore a long, dark braid that trailed between her widely set shoulder blades, her wrists and fingers adorned with turquoise-and-silver jewelry Emily was guessing had been in her family for a while.

"This is Emily!" Austin announced, his little chest puffed out, which in turn sparked something lovely and warm inside Emily's.

"Deanna's cousin," she said, shaking the teacher's hand. The young woman's smile was almost blindingly bright against skin not dissimilar in tone to the reddish-brown tones so prevalent in the landscape…as befitted the Natives' spiritual ties to Mother Earth.

"Susana Ortiz," she said, smiling, then cupped Austin's curls. "Go on inside, cutie. Have a seat in the reading circle."

Glancing inside the classroom, chock full of little kids, Emily frowned. "I thought Dee said there were only ten kids in his class."

Susana sighed. "Normally, yes. But our pregnant kindergarten teacher is now on bed rest until she delivers. So we're down one until we get a sub. Which isn't that easy out here in the sticks, as I'm sure you can imagine. I hope we find some-one soon, though. Twenty-five little kids is a lot to handle, even with a teacher's aide. At least, to handle well. Give them the individual attention they deserve. And *need*, especially when they're on such different tracks. At least it's only for a few weeks, until school lets out. I only hope they find some-one for next year while she's on maternity leave... What?"

Emily had had no idea what seeing all those little kids together would do to her head, not to mention her heart. But surely she couldn't...

Could she?

And what's stopping you, missy?

She met the teacher's curious gaze again. "I'm accred-ited in Maryland and Virginia, to teach kindergarten and early childhood. I'd be happy to help out, if you need it—"

"Are you kidding?" Susana's dark eyes glittered. "If you're already certified... We'd have to rush through a background check, but...oh, my goodness. Are you sure? I mean, that would be such a blessing, I can't tell you!"

"Then whatever you need, I'm good." Emily looked back into the classroom, where Susana's assistant was doing a passable job of corralling enough energy to light up a small city.

A small girl-person attached herself to her teacher, tug-ging her back into the classroom. "Stop by the office," Su-sana said before the horde swallowed her up, "talk to the principal. We'll take it from there..."

Forty-five minutes later, Emily rushed back inside her cousin's house, apologizing profusely before she'd even found Dee calmly nursing little Katie in a pool of sun-shine in the great room.

"It's okay," the brunette whispered, smiling down at her daughter, then back at Emily. "She calmed down right after you left, and it's been totally copacetic since. We both even passed out for a while. So what's going on?"

Emily had texted her, of course, to tell her she'd be a little late, so she wouldn't worry. But she hadn't said why, hadn't wanted to until she knew it was a done deal. Now she sat on the chair across from Dee, her heart pounding a mile a minute as Smoky jumped up on her lap, *mwwrowing* for attention.

"I think I just talked my way into a job," she said, laughing, and her cousin's eyes went wide as dinner plates.

Chapter Eight

The midday sun beating down on his shoulders and uncovered head, Colin snapped photo after photo of his soon-to-be sister-in-law seated in her special saddle as she calmly instructed the young boy on the palomino a few feet away on the other side of the corral fence. Even though he couldn't use the pics without the boy's parents' permission, it felt good, getting back into the swing of things. Shoot, before this morning he hadn't even taken any landscape shots, and that was a crying shame.

But something—maybe seeing the artwork up in Deanna's gallery the day before, maybe simply being here—had prodded his muse awake at the crack of dawn to catch the sunrise drenching the mountains in shades of violet and rose, gilding the pastures and barns, even the horses his brother had already let out to graze. He wouldn't publish those, either—hell, everybody and his cousin took sunrise pictures, for God's sake—but he hadn't realized until today exactly how much he'd missed this crucial part of who he was.

Off in another paddock, Josh worked a young horse, training him to cut cattle from a small, young herd here on a short-term arrangement for that very purpose. The place was definitely quieter now than when he'd been a kid, on those early mornings when cutting calves from their mamas for branding and deworming had resulted in a whole lot of mournful lowing, human as well as bovine. Add to that a bunch of cowboys yelling and dogs barking, the whoops of victory when a particularly ornery calf finally cooperated…the enormous breakfasts his mother and Gus, the Vista's old housekeeper, had provided when the morning's work was done…

Colin lowered the camera, his forehead puckered. No, maybe he'd wanted more than that life. But thinking back on it now, even the parts he'd been so sure he hated hadn't been all bad, had they? In fact, watching Josh working that horse, the animal's beauty and grace and intelligence as it darted and danced in the dust at his rider's cues, cutting calf after calf from the fidgety clot on one side of the corral, brought to mind a whole lot of pleasant memories.

As did watching Mallory calmly encouraging the boy on the sweet, patient horse—

Footsteps in the dirt behind him made him turn, his heart knocking as he watched Emily striding toward him, looking far more like a country gal in her jeans and sleeveless shirt than she had any right to. Especially with her hair pulled off her face into a single braid trailing down her back. She was even wearing cowboy boots. Deanna's, he was guessing, by how beat-up they were.

Wordlessly, she came up beside him, her hands shoved in the back pockets of a pair of jeans that might as well have been painted on her. He'd seen her pull up to the main house in Dee's truck a little bit ago, had wondered where she'd gone. Now he noticed she was practically crackling with energy, wearing a grin that was doing very bad things to his head. Among other things.

"Whatcha doing?"

He held up the camera. "Getting back in the groove. You?"

"Actually…" The grin flashed again. "I might have a job."

A weird little *ping* went off in his midsection. "A job? Here?"

"Yes, *here*. Although it's not definite yet." She tilted her head, probably in response to his horrified expression. "Is this a problem?"

Colin turned away. "No, of course not." He took another shot. "Doing what?"

"Herding small children, aka teaching. They're short a teacher at Austin's school, so I might fill in for the rest of the year. If I pass the background check, that is."

"Any reason why you wouldn't?"

Her laugh brought his gaze back to hers. "I might've thought nefarious things about my ex, but since I didn't carry any of them out…" She shrugged. "I think I'm good." Damn. She was positively glowing, no other word for it. "But seriously, it's as if an angel dropped the perfect thing right into my lap, you know? And right here in itty-bitty Whispering Pines. Crazy."

"Although it's temporary, you said?"

"Well, there's a possibility of it becoming full-time next year, but… I don't know. I can't really think that far into the future at this point. For now, though, it's perfect. Because *kids*," she said, releasing a blissful sigh. "Since getting to teach is the next best thing to being a mama myself one day. Although…" She made a face. "Heaven knows when that might happen. I suppose I could adopt as a single mom, though. Right? Which might be a more viable alternative than waiting for the—" she made air quotes "—*right guy* to come along. For me, anyway. Since my judgment clearly sucks."

Colin fiddled with the aperture on the lens to get another shot of the kid. In other words, her life was every bit as unsettled as his. If not more. At least he had something to go back to, something he was good at, that defined him. Clearly Emily didn't have a clue. Nor should she right now, not after what she'd just been through.

"And maybe you shouldn't be so hard on yourself."

She shrugged again, unconcerned. "At least it's an excuse to pig out on junk food, so there's that. Although since I'm like a brownie away from not being able to button my jeans anymore, that particular indulgence is about to come to a screeching halt."

He had to smile. "You think your folks will be okay with this new development?"

"Since it's my life, what can they say? God, it's a gorgeous day," she said, twisting around to rest her elbows on the fence's top rail, lifting her makeup-free face to the sun. The way the light angled across her nose, her lips…he itched to take her photo so badly he practically hummed with it, but he had no idea how to do that without coming across as weird. Or lame. Or both.

"Hope you're wearing sunscreen," he said, looking away.

That got another throaty laugh before she heaved herself up onto the top rail, hooking the heels of her boots on top of the one below. "Not my first time out here, remember? I know all about the high altitude." Her hands clamped on to the rail on either side of her hips, she twisted to watch Mallory with the boy. "You know about the kid?"

"Not really, no."

"He's the son of some friends of Mallory's from back in LA. They're staying up at the resort, ran into her and Zach in town. Josh said the kid's got some sort of developmental issues, although he's not sure what they are. But Mallory apparently told them about her facility—with the idea that when she was fully up and running, they might consider sending the boy there. Only they immediately asked if she'd work with him a little while they were here. And being Mallory, she said yes. That's her son's horse," she said, nodding toward the beautiful animal, his coat glistening in the sun. Then she humphed a short laugh. "Waffles."

"Pardon?"

"The horse's name. Waffles."

Colin smiled. "There were some crazy names when I was a kid, too. For years, I rode one named Ebenezer."

"As in Scrooge?"

"Yep. Have no idea who named him that. Or why. I took to calling him Jack, though. He didn't seem to care."

Emily crossed her arms. Wobbled. Colin instinctively clamped a hand on her thigh to steady her, heat shooting through him when she covered his hand with hers, her other one grabbing the edge of the fence rail again.

"Got it, thanks, I'm good," she said, and he removed his hand. Could still feel her, though. As in, his palm downright tingled. Among other things. "Was he your buddy?"

"He was. And not only mine. Every so often Deanna's folks would invite groups of kids from as far away as Albuquerque to come to the ranch, to ride and learn how to work cattle, stuff like that." He felt another smile push at his mouth. "Jack was such a ham bone, I swear. He totally ate up the attention. And some of that attention was pretty intense, believe me. There were other kids, though…" A huge breath left his lungs as the memories came roaring back. "A lot of the kids came from not-so-great situations. Some were foster kids, removed from their homes because they'd been neglected. Or worse. Those kids…"

He met Emily's gaze again, his heart fisting at the look in her eyes. "The resentment, the fear and anger, just poured off 'em. Some wouldn't even talk. But Jack was so patient with them, like he knew they needed him to be more than a horse. And the kids…they knew Jack wouldn't judge them, or ask questions they couldn't answer, or even expect them to say anything. And by the end of those days, you'd be surprised how many of 'em…" He shook his head, then looked back out toward Mallory and the boy. "I'd like to think by the time they left, they felt a little better about life than they had when they got here."

"I'm sure," Emily said softly, and for a good two or three seconds his face warmed under her intense scrutiny. Then she glanced away. "Sounds like Jack was a good listener."

"He was. Especially for me, back when I needed to figure out a few things, too."

"Hmm." Emily was quiet for another several seconds before she said, "The other day when Mallory was here for lunch, she said something about how she could have never imagined five years ago—when the doctors told her she'd probably never walk again—how any good could have possibly come out of that. And yet her accident set off a series of events which led her back here, where she met Zach, who got her riding again when she'd convinced herself that would never happen. And now she's starting up this facility that maybe will help other people see beyond what the world sees as limitations."

Colin felt the muscles alongside his spine tense. "And your point is?"

"How differently people see things, I suppose. Places."
Her forehead pinched. "How Mallory saw promise and
potential and new beginnings in this little corner of the
world after seemingly losing everything—her career, her
first marriage. And I guess it's sort of the same for me, although heaven knows what I've been through doesn't even
begin to compare with her experience. Even so, I look at
all of this—" she waved one arm out to the sky "—and I
feel freer than I can ever remember. Like the possibilities
are as endless as the sky. And yet you…"

She lowered her arm to clutch the top of the rail again.
"You don't see it that way at all, do you?"

And damned if her question didn't arrow straight to the
very knot he was trying to unravel. "Life here felt very…
small." He hmmphed a short, dry laugh. "Which I suppose proves your point. That where you see all this endless possibility, I felt like I couldn't breathe."

"Almost exactly what Dee said, when she came to live
with us after Aunt Kathryn died. Huh."

"What?"

"I wonder…if it's not so much the where, or even the
what, but more of a need to break away from what we
know, what we're used to. That some people simply need
different in order to… I don't know. Feel complete, maybe?
As though they've explored *all* the possibilities. Others—
like Zach and Josh, your dad—don't. It's all about finding
our own place in the world, isn't it? Our purpose."

"Have you always been this philosophical?"

Her laugh warmed him. "Not hardly. Kinda hard to see
the bigger picture when you're busy trying to keep the
smaller one neatly framed. But it's true, isn't it? How we
go along, assuming we're on the right path, doing what
we're supposed to be doing, and then something happens
that forces us to rethink everything we thought was real…"

Another laugh burped from her chest. "I'm sorry, the thinner air is clearly wreaking havoc with my head. Feel free to ignore my ramblings. So…" She lowered herself to the ground again, dusting off her butt. "I guess next up is your brother's wedding?"

What she'd said about the air and her head? True. "Guess so."

For one crazy moment, he considered asking her to go with him. Because clearly she wasn't the only one dealing with the effects of the high altitude.

Except it was more than that, wasn't it? Because Emily Weber made him feel good. Made him *feel*, period. Not to mention, she listened. *Got* him, even, he thought. Hell, it was almost like being around old Jack again. Well, except for the fact he'd never been attracted to his horse.

And if he had a lick of sense he'd squelch his attraction to the woman standing beside him now. Just…swallow it down, bat it away, pretend he wasn't feeling what he was feeling.

"Any idea what's next?" she asked. "After the book's done?"

Perfectly logical question, considering what she knew about him. What he'd let her know, anyway.

"There's a couple of options." Which was true enough. "Haven't decided which one to go for, though." Also true. But honest to God—how was it he'd been a hundred times more sure at eighteen of what he at least *thought* he wanted than he was now?

She gave him one of those looks, like she could see straight through his BS. As unnerving as that was, it was also strangely comforting. Or might have been, if he hadn't been so thoroughly screwed up. "Options are good."

"They are. Absolutely."

Sympathy softened her gaze, made him want to lean in, see if—

"Guess you'll be glad to get away from here again."

"It hasn't been entirely horrible," he said quietly, by now nearly trembling with the urge to touch her. To somehow infect himself with her warmth and humor and resilience. Except how selfish, how unfair would that be? To both of them, but especially to her? She'd been through enough without his foisting Jerk 2.0 on her.

"Good to know," Emily said, smiling. "Well." She tapped the top of the fence rail, then started to back away. "If we don't run into each other before, guess I'll see you at the wedding. Give the pup a pat for me, okay?"

Then he watched her return to the house, the braid swishing against her back, thinking sometimes it was hell, being the good guy.

The wedding was a small affair, mostly family. Although, Emily mused as she tried to get Zach's toddler Liam to sit still long enough to clip on his bow tie, once you got all the family members together, *small* took on a whole other definition. And it had been tempting, too, to feel like an outsider, except for everyone's insistence that as Dee's cousin she was family by default.

Definitely light years apart from her own childhood, she thought as another toddler—a girl this time—raced through the bedroom in Mallory and Zach's house set aside for the children's prep space. Emily caught the dark-haired cutie, a bundle of giggles and tulle, and plopped her on the bed to put her shoes back on, her heart turning over when little Risa launched herself into Emily's arms to plant a great big squishy kiss on her cheek.

Her eyes stinging for reasons Emily didn't want to examine too hard, she hugged the little girl back, breathing in her sweet innocence and unfeigned optimism. She'd still been an infant, Emily knew, when her father had been killed while serving overseas…when Josh's brother Levi returned from his own service to make good on a promise he'd made to his best friend to look out for his wife and two young daughters. A promise that turned into nothing short of a blessing for all concerned.

Naturally, thinking about one Talbot brother led to thoughts of another she couldn't keep out of her mind, no matter what she did. Honestly, it'd taken everything she had in her, when he told her about his horse Jack and how he'd helped all those kids, not to point out it hadn't only been the *horse* who'd enjoyed the encounters so much. That for all Colin swore he'd felt hamstrung by life in the boonies, the way his face practically glowed when he shared those memories proved to Emily that clearly there'd at least been times where he'd felt a sense of purpose and fulfillment right here.

Of course, those experiences could've also been the seeds of what eventually pushed him out of the nest, to do more, *be* more…to be who he had to be.

Well. Once he left, he'd be out of her life for good, and that would be that.

This was nothing more than two people who happened to be in the same place for five minutes. And one of those people—as in, herself—was still smarting from some seriously raw battle scars. Even so, when Colin looked at her as though he wanted to suck God-knew-what out of her, somehow those scars didn't feel so prominent. Ugly.

Permanent…

In a simple, floral-print sheath that emphasized her long, pretty neck, Deanna stuck her head into the bedroom, managing to look elegant and harried at the same time as she struggled to keep a wriggling infant in her arms. "Need help?" she said over the shrieks of several excited children.

Since corralling squirts was her forte, Emily had volunteered for short people duty so the family could get ready in relative peace...only to quickly realize there was a huge difference between handling kindergartners confined to a single room and a half dozen hyper kids already amped up on the many and varied goodies spread out on the picnic table on the deck out back.

The little girl disengaged from her neck, Emily swept a hank of loose hair off her cheek, only to relieve her cousin of baby Katie, kicking up a storm in her mother's arms. Squealing with delight, the baby settled onto Emily's lap to immediately grab her long necklace and stuff it into a very slobbery mouth. "You might want to check on the older boys, make sure shirttails are still tucked in, faces are clean, that sort of thing."

Her cousin laughed. "Since none of them are actually in the wedding party, Nanny Em, I'm gonna make an executive decision and say it's not worth the bother." Then she frowned. "You okay?"

"I just said—"

"Not talking about the kids," Dee said gently, coming into the room to sit beside Emily on the edge of the bed. "I mean the wedding."

Ironically, her own wedding to Michael would have been today, as well. Which only Dee knew, since she was supposed to have been Emily's maid of honor. Certainly Mallory and Zach hadn't when they finally settled on a date a few weeks ago.

"Don't be silly," Emily said, twisting Katie around to bounce her on her knee. "Of course I'm okay."

"Really?"

Her gaze swung to her cousin's. "Jeebus, Dee—are you *trying* to bum me out?"

"No. But I know you. Meaning I'm very acquainted with this annoying little habit you have of pretending you're all happy-happy when you're not."

Emily looked back at the baby to make a funny face at her, smiling when Katie giggled. "Which is better—" she buried her forehead in the baby's tummy, only to have to pry her hair out of a slimy fist "—than bringing everyone down with my own troubles. Right?"

"Except this is me, Em. And I'd hate to think I invited you out here to recover from what happened only to—"

"Only to what?" Emily said, swinging the baby back around on her lap to rest her cheek in her downy hair. "Unwittingly provide me with an opportunity to face a demon or six? To prove to myself I'm well and truly over Michael?"

Deanna rested her hand on Emily's back. "Are you?"

Emily huffed a breath. "Guess I'm about to find out, huh?"

"Oh, Em…"

"Okay, fine—watching you and Josh, and Levi with Val… Has it been hard, seeing you guys living the life I want? The life I thought I was going to *have*, up to a few weeks ago? Sometimes. Shoot, sometimes it's been hard to breathe, no lie. Envy can be a real bear. However…" Smiling, she shifted the chunky monkey on her lap to lay a hand on her cousin's wrist. "For one thing, I'm well aware of what you all went through before you got to this point. That your happy-ever-afters didn't simply fall in your laps. And knowing that makes me far more thrilled for you guys than sorry for myself. And for another…" She squeezed her cousin's wrist. "I refuse to let other people's joy make me miserable." At the tears welling in Dee's eyes, Emily tried a smile. "Seriously, how dumb is that? If anything it gives me hope. And anyway, since the job came through, you guys are stuck with me now, right?"

Pushing out a short laugh, Dee reached for her daughter, then leaned over to give Emily a one-armed hug. "That part, I'm not sorry about. And I guess we better get out there…"

"You go on. I probably need to fix my hair."

Her cousin glanced up and burbled another laugh. "You might want to, at that," she said, then left the room.

Sighing, Emily dug out a comb from her purse, then stood in front of the mirrored closet to undo her mangled 'do. A quick comb-through, a couple of twists and she was back in business, jabbing hairpins into it hard enough to scrape her scalp. The partially open bedroom window faced the back; she could hear voices, laughter. Joy. Tears threatened again. She blinked them back. Because she was happy. Thrilled, even, that at least one area of her life was falling into place.

Then her phone rang.

She was tempted to let her mother's call go to voice mail again, only to realize two things: one, of necessity this would be a short conversation, which worked to her advantage; and two, that she couldn't avoid the woman forever. Especially after the text she'd left her the day before about the job.

"Honestly, it's about time you answered the phone—"

"I know, Mother, I'm sorry. And unfortunately I can't stay on long now, either. Zach's wedding's about to start. You remember Zach? The oldest Talbot brother? Your niece's brother-in-law?"

She could practically hear the bristling. Meaning either the significance of the day hadn't occurred to her mother or she was being diplomatic enough not to mention it. Although Emily's bringing up Deanna hadn't exactly been diplomatic of her, she supposed. For reasons harking back to Dee's mother "marrying that damn cowboy" so many years before. And now...

"You can't be serious about staying out there."

"Why not?" The noise outside increased. "This is perfect for me, Mother. And I feel at home—"

"Your home is here, Emily Rose—"

"Sorry, I've got to go. Say hi to Dad for me."

If you two are talking, that is.

And yes, she heard the squawk as she disconnected the call. But honestly—all her life she'd done her mother's bidding. Gone to the schools her mother chose, took music lessons because her mother wanted her to, only hung out with friends her mother approved of. Nearly married her mother's choice for her.

"Well, no more," Emily muttered, checking her reflection in the mirror one last time before leaving the room. Because she was done being the good girl, doing what was expected of her in order to please someone *else*.

Meaning from now on, it was about her life, her choices. Her mistakes, if it came to that.

And she didn't think it was insignificant that the first person she saw when she got outside was Colin, his eyes finding hers like a pair of magnets.

Colin, who'd be leaving town sooner rather than later. Yep.

Now or never, a little voice whispered, and she shuddered all the way down to her freshly painted toenails.

"Throw it to me, Uncle Colin!"

"No, me!"

Chuckling, Colin lobbed the battered Frisbee toward Jeremy, Zach's oldest boy, laughing harder when somebody's hound dog intercepted the plastic disk and bounded off with it. Because, yes, this family brought dogs to their weddings. All pumping limbs and shrill yells, a small herd of kids raced after the coonhound as he led them on a merry chase around Zach and Mallory's park-like backyard, currently suffused with enough grill smoke to probably reach the Colorado border. Man, there were a lot of kids, between Zach's two and Austin, his brother Levi's two stepdaughters and Mallory's middle schooler, Landon. Chaos, in other words. Much like his own childhood, he thought as the tricolor hound brought back the Frisbee, the children hot on his heels.

Amazing, how quickly the family had grown in the past year. How much it would in all likelihood continue to expand, he thought, his gaze snagging on his sister-in-law Val's huge belly. Three weddings, there'd been in that short amount of time. None of them big, fancy affairs— Josh and Deanna, in fact, had gone the justice-of-the-peace route. But it was kind of hard to ignore the fact that Colin was now officially the only unmarried son.

And even harder to ignore how much that bothered him. Even though contemplating the alternative didn't exactly sit well, either.

He tugged the disk out of the dog's jaws, motioning for the kids to get back so he could toss it again. One of the older girls caught it before the dog did, doing a little victory dance before tossing it to Austin. But at the poke at his knee, Colin looked down to see a little redheaded elf grinning up at him. Liam, Zach's youngest. Without a moment's hesitation he hauled the preschooler up into his arms, even though he nearly choked on the bittersweetness that holding his youngest nephew close provoked. The memories, of another little boy, on the other side of the world—

The puppy—still with him, still nameless—waddled back to attack Colin's sneaker. Laughing, Liam wriggled out of Colin's arms to plop on the grass by the little mutt-sky, laughing even harder when he suddenly had a face full of excited doggy, trying to lick everywhere at once. Colin lowered himself to the ground, his heart lurching when Liam immediately snuggled into his lap as if he'd known his "new" uncle all his life, and Colin felt like he'd just won the lottery.

From the other side of the yard, he heard Emily's laugh as she chatted easily with his parents. More easily than he did, probably. When she'd come out of the house before the ceremony, and their gazes had caught…well, for a moment there he could have sworn there was something between them. Something real, that was. The kind of something you grabbed with everything you had in you and hung on to for dear life.

And clearly all that smoke was getting to him. Although, the way she was glowing…what was that all about? Not her job, he didn't think, since that wasn't exactly news anymore. And anyway, she'd said it was probably only temporary. Interesting, how they both got off on kids—

Colin closed his eyes against the stab, which he'd hoped would have dulled by now. And he supposed it had, a little. Not enough, though. Not nearly enough.

"Liam!" Jeremy called to his little brother, his hands cupped around his mouth. "Wanna play tag?"

"Yeah!" the kid yelled back, pushing up from Colin's lap and taking off toward his cousins, who'd commandeered a flattish patch of grass bordering a small orchard, the later bloomers still in full flower. The property, though still suffering some from more than twenty years of abandonment and neglect, was one of the prettiest he'd ever seen, edging closer to the forest than most in the area. Colin smiled—he somehow doubted that when Mallory bought the property in the fall she'd had any idea she'd be married right here less than a year later.

Colin heaved himself to his feet and returned to a weather-beaten picnic table set apart from the deck, underneath a lazily shivering cottonwood, whistling for the pup to follow. Zach had told him earlier he might've found a home for the mutt; Colin in turn told himself the news hadn't poked at a sore spot he hadn't even known was there. Yes, despite logically knowing he couldn't keep the dog, not with the kind of life he led. He parked himself on top of the table to watch the goings-on from a relatively— as it were—safe distance. Not that he'd be alone for long, he imagined, since it was inevitable that a brother or parent or kid would sidle over sooner or later to engage him in conversation. But for right now, this worked. For him, anyway.

Because all this copaceticness was a bit hard to take. Especially concentrated like this, all in one spot.

His own grumpiness irritating the hell out of him, Colin lifted his previously abandoned can of beer to his lips as the pup rustled around in the sparse grass underneath the table, hunting bugs or something. Josh's twin, Levi, was manning the grill, one arm draped around Val's shoulders, her hands cupped over her huge belly—another girl, his mother had said, due any minute. Over near the house Zach and his new bride were laughing at something Dad was saying. The setting sun seemed to envelop the couple, sizzling in Mallory's wild red hair, glinting off the rims of her wheelchair. Zach stood slightly behind her, one hand underneath all that hair, resting on her shoulder, protective and *there*. And despite his own bad mood, Colin had to smile at his brother's loopy grin when Mallory's hand reached up to rest on his…only to feel his gut torque when Zach leaned over to brush a kiss over his wife's mouth. And how stupid was that, being envious of his brother for finding a second shot at heaven after the hell he'd been through?

Soundly chiding himself, Colin looked away…only to feel his gut fist all over again when he noticed Emily coming toward him, a can of diet soda dangling from her long fingers, her lips curved in that Mona Lisa smile that drove him crazy. She was wearing a sleeveless, pale yellow dress that rippled around her calves as she walked, so plain it should have been boring. How she somehow made it anything but was a mystery.

How she'd somehow fused herself to his psyche in a few short weeks was even more of one. The absurdity, not to mention the impracticality, of that fusing aside.

"Hey," she said, then bent to let the puppy chew her fingers for a minute before picking him up to cuddle underneath her chin. She'd twisted her hair into some sort of sloppy bun, leaving a bunch of strands dangling over her shoulders like Spanish moss. The whole look was crazy sexy, although he doubted that'd been her intention.

Colin nodded, telling himself it was this whole lovey-dovey atmosphere making him want to tug her close, feel her softness. Her warmth. Hear that chuckle in his ear. Not loneliness. No, certainly not that. "Congratulations," he said, and she gave him a puzzled little grin.

"For what?"

"Surviving a Talbot family do."

She laughed. "Thanks. Although your congrats might be a bit premature. Since it's not over yet." Grinning, she waved the can at the table. "Mind if I join you?"

Oh, hell, yes. "Not at all."

Shifting the dog into the arm holding the soda, she

clutched a fistful of dress to hike it up to her knees, then climbed onto the table's seat and plopped beside him, and he suddenly felt like he was fourteen again and trying to figure out how to get Chelsey Diaz to talk to him without sounding like a complete idiot.

Apparently unaware of his sudden awkwardness, Emily took a sip of her soda as she gazed out over the crowd. "I hope you realize how awesome your family is."

He felt his face warm. "I do. I always have."

"But…?"

"I'm just wired differently. That's all."

"I can understand that," she said. "*Boy*, can I understand that." Then she laughed when the dog twisted to nibble at her chin. "Yes, I know, it's been a while since I've seen you." The puppy yipped and she tilted her head toward Colin. "Have you named him yet?"

He jerked. "No. Since I'm not keeping him. Since I *can't* keep him," he said to her pursed lips. "Can't exactly haul a dog around the world with me. And having to board him all the time…no. You could take him, though."

"Actually…that might be possible now. As soon as I find my own place, that is."

Colin frowned at her. "What?"

She smiled at him, clearly delighted. "The permanent job came through. I'll be working at the gallery during the summer before that, but…" The grin got bigger. "You're looking at Whispering Pines's newest kindergarten teacher."

"Oh. Wow. That's great."

"Thanks. Cannot tell you what a relief that is, since returning to DC would feel like going backward, frankly. And anyway, after what I said to Dad, not to mention my mother…" She pulled a face. "I'm just burning bridges right and left here."

"You don't sound too torn up about that."

"Probably because I'm trying not to think about it too hard. Frankly I pretty much suck at this cutting-the-cord stuff."

He took a sip of his beer. "Got news for you—everyone does."

"Still. I probably could've finessed things with both of them a little better, maybe. However. What's done is done. No place to go from here but up, I suppose." She toyed with the puppy's ears for a moment, then chuckled. "What do you think of *Spud*?"

"Excuse me?"

"As a name." She lifted the dog to face her, chuckling at his rapid-fire darting tongue. "Because you look like a little potato."

Despite the roiling in his head, Colin pushed out a laugh. "You do realize he's not gonna stay that size, right?"

"Which will make the name even funnier. But only if you approve."

"Me?"

"Sure. Since he's your dog, too."

"*Spud's* fine," he said, not looking at her. Then she released a huge sigh. "What was that for?"

"Now that I'm going to be a doggy mama again, it's made me think even more about my own parents. Our strange relationship. I mean, I know they want the best for me. But that's not necessarily what *is* best for me, if you know what I mean."

"I do, actually. Although I'm not sure which is scarier—how your brain works, or that I *get* how your brain works."

Emily laughed, then took a sip of her soda. "Love is such a strange thing, isn't it? I thought I loved my parents, because that's what you do, isn't it? And it's not as if they were ever actually mean to me or beat me or anything. So why wouldn't I love them? Like I thought I loved Michael."

"So you're really over him?"

Cuddling the dog, she shrugged, a gesture that came across a lot sadder than she probably thought it did. "I've accepted that what I thought we had wasn't real. Is that the same as being over him? I'm not entirely sure."

And he knew all about that, didn't he? How rarely logic and emotions saw eye to eye? Suddenly fury roared through Colin, that this sweet, crazy-good person hadn't been loved the way she deserved to be loved. And he wished...

No. You don't.

Because let's listen to the logical side, shall we? That the woman who'd just admitted she wasn't entirely sure she was over her ex didn't need...complications.

As in, him.

"For what it's worth?" he said softly. "I have complete faith in you, that you'll figure it all out."

She turned to him, and what he saw in those pretty blue eyes, that smile, knotted him up inside so badly he could barely breathe. "Oh, yeah?"

"Yeah."

Nodding, she turned away, nuzzling the pup again. "I'd love to see the book. If you're good with that, I mean."

And wasn't it strange that, despite the fact that a whole bunch of people would see it eventually, the thought of *her* seeing it gave him the willies? Because none of those people—editors and marketing people and the like—knew him. None of those people, he didn't think, would read between the lines like he strongly suspected Emily would.

Would see through the thin veneer that separated his public persona from his soul. What passed for his soul, anyway.

"Not sure how much there is to see. That makes sense, anyway. It's mostly a bunch of essays to go with the pics on my computer. The production team will make it all pretty."

"So that's a no?" she said, humor shimmering through her words.

There. She'd offered him the perfect out. All he had to do was accept it—

"It's a… Don't expect a finished product."

"I won't." She awkwardly lowered the pup to the ground, where he raised his nose to the fragrant breeze… and promptly piddled. Chuckling, Emily lifted her gaze, tilting her can toward Zach and Mallory. "Those two are so cute together it almost hurts to watch."

"Truth," he said, and she laughed again, then sobered.

"This was supposed to be my wedding day, too."

His head snapped around to her, although she wasn't looking at him. "Oh, hell…"

"No, it's okay, I'm fine. Especially when I remind myself how horrible it would've been to have found out the truth after we'd gotten married. Maybe after we'd had a kid or two. So no regrets here," she said, lifting the can in a toast to no one in particular. "Believe me."

"And why am I tempted to sniff that can to see what's really in it?"

Emily snorted another little laugh. But again, he heard the sadness. Regret? Perhaps not. Not for him to say, at least. But something he recognized all too well. Then she set the can on the table before leaning back to rest her palms behind her, a move that stretched the lightweight material across her breasts, her thighs, a belly that was all the more enticing for not being completely flat, and he thought at this rate his libido was going to have a stroke. In spite—or maybe because—of the way her expression mellowed.

"You're really at peace here, aren't you?" he asked.

The kindness, the genuineness in her expression when her eyes met his made him ache. More. "I really am. Or at least I'm pretty sure here is where I'll find it." She arched her neck to look up at the sky, and every drop of spit in his mouth evaporated. Especially when a strand of hair toyed with her throat. "But let me guess…" Sitting up again, she linked her hands around her knees. "You're absolutely itching to get away again."

Perhaps *itch* wasn't the best word to bring up right now, when at the moment it applied equally to two entirely conflicting needs. Once more he angled away from that trenchant gaze. "Something like that."

But not for the reasons she thought. Although at least he could be grateful that nobody knew what he'd been considering. Now, however, with Emily staying…

"It must be nice, to be able to go with the flow like that," she said. A gentle laugh washed over him. "I actually envy your sense of adventure."

"Don't," he said, startling himself. "It's not always that great."

He could feel her gaze on the side of his face before she reached for her drink again and took a long swallow. "You mean, because of what you've seen?"

He paused. "Yes."

She jiggled the soda, making the fizzing carbonation ping against the inside of the can. "Thank you."

His brows crashed together as he faced her again. "For what?"

"For trusting me enough to admit that." The space between her own brows creased before her gaze caressed his, a blush sweeping across her cheeks. "I'm just putting this out there, okay? Since I know how hard it can be to talk to the people who know you *too* well. Or think they do, anyway. Because that opens the door to all this advice. Or judgment. Whatever. However…"

Her fingers on his wrist were smooth. Warm. "I also know how crappy it is keeping stuff inside. How it sits there, festering, becoming worse and worse the more you think about it. So if you need someone to talk to…"

"I don't."

She removed her hand, and Colin had to force himself not to grab it back. "Fine. But if you change your mind, I can promise you, no advice. And certainly no judgment."

A frown biting into his forehead, Colin let his gaze swing back to her profile. "Why?"

"Because…because in the past few weeks you've let me *be* me more than anyone else ever has. Except Dee, maybe. But that's different. You didn't have to. Seems only fair to return the favor. And the best part?" Smiling, she met his eyes again, and he could have sworn he saw something in them that had nothing to do with what she was actually saying. Although that could have been wishful thinking on his part. "Once we go back to our lives, we'll probably never see each other again. So there's that. But even, um, a momentary connection is better than nothing."

That last sentence had been spoken so softly, so gently, Colin almost wondered if he'd imagined it. He looked back out over the yard, at the kids running around, the smoke curling up from the giant grill, the normalcy blanketing a moment that he had a strong suspicion had just zoomed so far past normal it wasn't even recognizable anymore.

Except it was. If you knew what you were looking for.

"Are we still talking about…talking?"

Another laugh slapped his libido clear into the next week. Then Emily slid off the table, the move shifting her hem so he got a good long glimpse of gorgeous long leg before she faced him again.

"This is me going with the flow." Her breasts rose with her deep breath. "Seizing a moment."

"Being reckless."

"That, too. But the great thing about knowing what the possibilities are—or aren't—from the get-go, is that there are no expectations. So you can relax and enjoy that moment."

By this point Colin's blood was pumping so hard he could barely hear her. Then he frowned. "Were you... Did you have this in mind when you came out here?"

Her mouth twitched. "Maybe."

He punched out a breath. "Emily... I can't take advantage of you."

"Not asking you to. But, hey, if you don't want to—"

"*Want* has nothing to do with it."

She glanced away, then back at him. "Actually, it has everything to do with it. With...whatever's in your eyes. The stuff you're not telling me. That I'm not asking you to." A half smile curved her mouth. "I can keep your secrets, Colin," she said, her gaze hooked in his. "But I'm good with you keeping them, too."

Then she walked away, that stupid, shapeless dress leaving everything to his imagination.

Which had taken flight like nobody's business.

Chapter Nine

Emily could feel Colin's gaze on her back, five times hotter than the setting sun slicing across the vast yard. And almost hotter than the blush searing her cheeks at what'd just happened.

That she'd come on to a man. With reasonable grace, even.

Although knowing there was no future for them actually made it easier to consider the one thing she'd never before considered in her life—sex simply for fun. For *now*. Because for so many months the implication had been that it'd be some sort of prize for after the wedding, which she'd gone along with because she'd thought the *real* prize was worth the wait.

How wrong she'd been. How very, very wrong.

Oddly—or maybe not—Colin stayed out of her way for the rest of the evening. Although whether because he didn't want his family playing any guessing games, or because he'd found her suggestion utterly abhorrent, she had no idea. Since he hadn't exactly leaped at the opportunity, had he? Still. Nothing ventured, nothing gained and all that. She was hardly going to get her panties in a wad over something that had been a huge gamble to begin with.

Which did not mean her heart didn't whomp up against her ribs like a boss when she got a text from him the next evening, as she sat outside on the Vista's veranda, cocooned against the evening chill in some old shawl of Dee's.

Okay.

Man of few words, that one. Although she might feel a teensy bit more confident with a little expansion. Especially since it had been more than twenty-four hours since she'd tossed down the gauntlet.

Okay, what?

To your suggestion.

Her heart thudded again. She took a deep, deep breath in some lame attempt to steady it, then texted.

You sure?

Roughly a million years later, her phone dinged.

Are you?

And, a second after that:

And yes, I'm giving you an out.

Holy hell. Never, ever in her life had she done anything

like this. Or wanted to. Then again, she'd never been in a situation like this before, had she?

I'll be over in a minute, she texted, then slipped her phone into her jeans pocket before he could respond.

She found Dee and Josh in the great room, cuddled together on one of the couches watching TV. Both kids had zonked out some time ago, their parents' relief obvious on their faces.

"Colin just texted. He says the pup's acting weird. He wants me to come take a look."

Amazing, how easily the lie slid right off her tongue.

Josh glanced up, the light from the screen flickering across his face. "Maybe I should come, too," he said, starting to rise. "Make sure it's nothing serious—"

"And Em can let you know if it is," Dee said, clamping one hand around her husband's forearm and giving Emily a knowing look. Because she was no good whatsoever at this clandestine stuff.

Although Josh, bless his heart, was clearly clueless. "Okay. But I'm here if you need me."

"Thanks." Then she boot-scooted out of there before anyone could see her burning face.

Wrapped more tightly in the shawl, she clomped across the wooden porch, the sound then muffled in the dirt as she made her way past the paddock to the foreman's cabin. The clear, starry night was silent and still, save for the thrum of crickets' chirping, the distant howl of a coyote. The cabin's front door swung open before she reached Colin's porch, a spear of light guiding her way. And with that, the full ramification of what she was doing—or about to do, anyway—slammed into her.

But she had no idea what it might mean to Colin, she thought as his broad-shouldered silhouette filled the doorway, fragmenting the light. Maybe nothing, really—oh, hell, her heart was about to pound right out of her chest, since men were much more adept at these things than women. Weren't they?

Spudsy scampered out onto the porch from behind Colin's feet, wriggling up a storm when he saw her, and Emily's heart stopped its whomping long enough to squeeze at the sight of the bundle of furry joy she'd come to love.

At least she'd be able to keep the dog, she thought as she scooped up the little dog to bury her face in his ruff, trying to ignore Colin's piercing gaze.

Oh, hell. That whole sex-as-fun thing? Who was she kidding? That wasn't her. Never had been. What on earth had made her think a single event would change *her*?

Although this one just might.

"I made a fire," Colin said quietly. Carefully. As though afraid she might spook. Never mind this had been her idea.

"That's nice."

Ergh.

Something like a smile ghosted around his mouth. "We can always just talk. No expectations. Isn't that what you said?" He shoved his hands in his pockets. "You're safe, honey. With me." His lips curved. "*From* me."

Still cuddling the puppy, she came up onto the porch. Closer. Too close. But not so close that she couldn't, if she were so inclined, still grab common sense by the hand and run like hell.

"And from myself?"

"That, I can't help you with."

Another step closer. Then another, each one a little farther away from common sense, whimpering in the dust behind her. "Kiss me," she whispered.

There was so much ambivalence in his smile she almost withdrew her request.

Almost.

* * *

Her mouth was soft and sweet and giving under his, as Colin threaded his fingers through all that shiny, slippery hair to still her trembling. Or maybe to still his—right now he couldn't tell. Her lips parted, trusting; he cautiously accepted her invitation, not wanting to lose that trust. He still wasn't sure of her motivation, but he damn well knew she was still hurting. If he could, even in some small way, ease that ache, even if only a little...

Even if for only a little while...

The dog yipped between them, making them laugh, breaking the tension.

"That was nice," he said, and she smiled.

"Very," she said, that twinkle he'd come to like so much reappearing in her eyes, almost but not quite banishing her obvious uncertainty.

He brushed a kiss across her temple, her sigh making his shudder. "What do you want? Really?"

She angled her head to meet his gaze, her pale neck tempting. "You," she said. "This. Now."

"You sure?"

"Yes."

But he caught the momentary hesitation before her response.

Colin slid a hand to her waist, led her through the open door. Even though he wasn't a total slob—he couldn't work in a pigsty—he'd made even more of an effort to straighten up. Because this mattered. *She* mattered.

Emily lowered the puppy to the floor; he immediately toddled into his crate, curled up like a little bean and passed out.

Good dog.

Hugging herself, Emily released a strained laugh. "I

told Dee and Josh you said the dog was acting funny, that I should come check on him."

"And did they buy that?"

"Your brother, maybe. Dee? Not so much."

"Yeah, I'm thinking you probably suck at poker," he said, and another shaky chuckle pushed from her throat. "Look, Emily—"

Then her hands were on his chest, those guileless eyes hooked in his. "And the longer we chitchat, the more nervous I'm going to get. So can we get on with it, already?"

"And aren't you the sweet-talker?"

"I'm sorry—"

"No." He took her hands, folding them both over his pounding heart. "But I'm not entirely sure why you want to do this."

"Do I need a reason?"

"If any other woman had asked me that, I'd say no. Only you're not any other woman. Yes, I know what you said, about this being for the moment and all. And while *I'm* good with that, I'm not entirely sure you are. Not as much as you might think—"

"Colin—"

"No, let me finish, so there's no room for misinterpretation, on either side. I won't hurt you, not if I can help it. But I have no control over what might happen inside your head."

Or mine, he thought, immediately adding, *Oh, hell, no.*

A sly, if none too steady, grin spread across her face. "Because you're just that irresistible, you mean?"

Again, the tension eased. "It has been said," he said, and she laughed, full out. And linked her hands around the back of his neck, bringing their pelvises together, and things stirred, eager as hell...and he picked her up and carried her to the bedroom, leaving regrets scattered behind him like confetti after a parade. Then she murmured, "Und-dress me. Please," and his heart knocked against his ribs at the slight stumble, like he might decline for some reason.

Because clearly someone else had.

"So is this revenge sex?"

Her gaze darkened. "No. Never."

He believed her. "Then…with pleasure," he whispered back, taking his time, bending to remove her boots before letting his fingers deliberately tease silk-slick skin as he removed her sweater, both of them chuckling when her hair went all staticky. Her bra was plainer than he'd expected, but sheer, her nipples trapped beneath the shimmery nude fabric. With a single flick of the front clasp he could free them, if he wanted. Give them air, give him one of many ways to make her moan. Make both of them very, very happy.

But not yet.

Torture is what this was, what he was doing to himself, to her, going so slowly. Holding back. And yet with each touch, each glance, each hitch of her breath as he unzipped her jeans, tugging them down to carefully kiss first one hip bone, then the other, he ached more, *wanted* more.

But more than anything he wanted to give her everything she'd given up for some schmuck who'd never deserved her.

Not that he did, either. But at least he could give her this.

"Step out," he murmured, guiding her out of the jeans and tossing them aside before pressing his lips to the top of her panties, the same sheer fabric as her bra. Then lower, making her gasp.

And laugh. With delight, he thought. Anticipation. Good.

He stood to claim her mouth again, the kiss so deep and tender and full of promise he nearly wept, and he picked

her up again, her legs tightly wrapped around his waist—
speaking of promise—and carried her to the bed before
lowering her onto the mattress. Then he finally unclasped
the bra, sighing at her beauty, pale rose against flawless
ivory, only to feel his throat close up when he caught her
gaze in his, that mixture of hesitation and bravado that
would be his undoing.

"Now you," she whispered.

He toed off his sneakers, shrugged out of his shirt, his
jeans—

"Commando?" she said, that smile playing around her
lips. "I'm impressed." Her gaze lowered. "Very impressed."

"Careful. You'll give me a swelled..." He grinned.
"Head."

"Oh, jeez," she said, rolling her eyes, then got to her
knees on the mattress to link her hands behind his neck
again, and the feel of all that softness, skin to skin...that
mouth—oh, merciful heavens, that *mouth*, on his neck,
his chest...

"A year, you said?"

Chuckling, she raised herself up again, skimming her
fingers through his hair. "Longer, now. But some things,
you don't forget. Although..." Her eyes melted into his,
and he was a goner. "You inspire me."

He gripped her waist. Tugged her closer. She was still
wearing her panties, an oversight he needed to remedy
ASAP. "To do what?" he teased.

Something more serious flickered in her eyes. "Give
more," she whispered, running the tip of her tongue along
his jaw. "Do more." She pulled back again, her lips barely
curved. "*Be* more."

"And if you were any *more*," Colin said, lowering her
to the bed again, "my head might explode."

Her eyes glittered again. "I thought that was the idea."

Chuckling, he positioned her beneath him to finally pay some attention to those lovely breasts, as rapidly mounting need trampled regrets underfoot. Even though he knew how resilient those suckers could be. He hooked his fingers around the panties, eased them off. "And maybe I should stop talking now."

"Works for me," she said, and then there was nothing between them except touches and sighs, the occasional gasp…kisses finding their way to secret places, lingering and hot…quiet *yeses* leading to the guttural sounds of pure, perfect pleasure as he held her hands over her head and plunged inside her, her tightness more than making up for the condom's barrier between them.

Colin watched her expression morph from anticipation to wonder, then complete submission to the moment as her cries rang out in the small room, until she wrapped herself tightly around him and pulled him close, closer, taking him inside her in far more ways than one, as *This, I can give you*, whispered through his brain.

Only, when they were done, as he tugged her close to lay his cheek in her hair, feeling his heart pound against hers, he realized what an idiot he'd been, thinking he could give her this and not give her…

Himself.

Except that wasn't possible, was it?

Emily knew, even before the tremors died down, that everything she'd suspected—okay, had already known—about her not being one of those people who could use sex as simply a recreational activity was absolutely true. And not because of the whole swapping-bodily-fluids thing that supposedly bonded a woman to her man, or whatever, because Colin had insisted on using a condom. Even though she'd told him that wasn't necessary.

Which made her wonder how much more bonded she'd be feeling right now if they *hadn't* used one. Scary thought.

Of course, she thought as he tugged her closer, his fingers making slow, sweet circles on her shoulder as they lay snuggled together like a pair of baby rabbits, what she might be *feeling* had nothing to do with what was actually going to happen. That much she'd known going in. No changing the ground rules after the fact. Although—her practical side weighed in—why should she be surprised, really? She'd only recently been jilted/dumped/betrayed/ done wrong, for one thing. Add to that the fact that it'd been a while…and add to *that* the fact that Colin was quite possibly the world's most attentive lover and…

Right.

Seriously, this was the confluence of events to beat all confluences. She wasn't in love with the man, she was just…mellow. That's all.

Incredibly, wonderfully, out-of-body-experience mellow.

Except she needed to pee. Bummer.

"Where you going?" Colin asked as she shimmied out from under his arm, grabbing his shirt off the floor before shrugging into it.

"Bathroom."

"Hey."

She turned back, holding the shirt closed over her breasts.

"You okay?"

Her cheeks ached with her forced smile. "You really have to ask?"

Frowning, he stretched his arms to fold his hands behind his head, the sheet barely covering the good bits. What was behind that frown, she didn't want to know.

Didn't need to. So she'd reassure him...as soon as she got back.

When she returned, however, he'd gone into the living room, his jeans back on and zipped but not buttoned as he stood in front of the desk, his laptop opened.

"You said you wanted to see the book," he said, not looking at her, and she felt as though a storm had come up suddenly, sucking all the air out of the space.

"Um...sure."

He turned then, his smile sad. But his eyes... Oh, dear God. *Tortured* was the only word for what she saw in them. He gestured toward the chair in front of the computer.

"Sit. Although like I said," he said when she did, "it's only a rough draft."

She laughed, although the sound was hollow. "You expect me to read the whole thing tonight?"

"I can send you the file, if you'd like. But this chapter..." He leaned close enough for her to smell herself on him, which naturally awakened the barely quenched ache all over again. "You should probably read this now."

The chapter focused on one particular group of refugees he'd apparently spent some time with, enough to get to know them fairly well. The pictures, especially, kept coming back to one little boy—the kid she'd seen before. Then she read on, about a virus of some kind that swept through the makeshift camp, claiming mostly children—malnourished, exhausted children whose immune systems simply couldn't fight off the microbes' relentless assault.

Tears welled in her eyes, even as her stomach knotted, knowing what was coming. "The boy—"

"An orphan," Colin said from behind her, seated on the sofa. She turned, her soul weeping at his ravaged expression. The pup had awakened and was sitting on Colin's lap, offering whatever comfort he could. Colin heaved out a breath. "Tarik's parents had been murdered by militants. Friends had somehow smuggled him out of the country, even though they had no idea where they might even end up." He paused, toying with the puppy's ears before meeting her gaze again, the corners of his mouth pushed into something like a smile. "For reasons I never fully understood, the kid glommed on to me. He'd follow me around, asking questions about the camera. In makeshift sign language, of course, since we didn't exactly speak each other's language. But…"

"But you fell in love with him."

"Head over heels."

"How old was he?"

"Six." He hauled in a shaky breath. "The UN workers at the camp knew me. One of them called me the day he died."

On a soft moan, Emily went to him, curling up on the sofa to wrap her arm around his waist. To his credit, Colin accepted her meager, and futile, attempt to comfort him, lifting his arm to pull her close, kiss her hair.

"That's the real reason you came home, isn't it?" she said after a long moment. "The book…that was simply an excuse."

"A convenient excuse, but…yeah."

The weird thing was, she understood why he'd chosen to seek sanctuary in the very place he'd refused to come back to for so long—because for all Colin's noise about how much he'd felt restricted here, he'd also felt the same peace that now made her want to call Whispering Pines home, too. Maybe he wouldn't—or couldn't—admit that, but when you need to heal you don't run someplace you *don't* like. In a way, she realized, he'd become like one of the kids he—and his horse, Jack—had helped all those years ago.

But there was more, wasn't there?

"And what happened…that's why you don't want children? Now, I mean."

A long moment of silence preceded, "I felt like I broke a promise to him. And I know that's illogical, especially since I didn't actually make a promise, not in so many words. I couldn't adopt him myself…how on earth would I take care of a kid on my own? Still, the way he'd wrapped himself around my heart, I would've done whatever I could to…"

"Colin," Emily said gently, twisting to rest a hand on his cheek, her insides more twisted up than his expression. "You can't blame yourself for something that was totally out of your control—"

"Except I *knew* not to let it get personal, that the moment I lost my objectivity, I was screwed. Even if I had no idea how much." Sensing that wasn't all, Emily kept quiet, waiting for him to gather his thoughts. His words. "It was hard for me to even admit to myself, let alone anyone else, how much his death shattered me. With all the crap I've seen, I'm not exactly a wuss. But that…it threw me. Bad."

Emily nuzzled her cheek against his chest, inhaling his scent. His warmth. Wishing she could somehow absorb some of his anguish. "And your breakup…?"

Her face lifted with his breath. "Happened a few months before. I hadn't realized how hard I'd fallen for her, either. That, though, I could get over. And had, mostly. But watching so many people go through hell… I thought I'd become inured to it. I was wrong."

"And yet…" She sat up to meet his eyes. "You want to go back."

A sad smile preceded, "I have to. To honor Tarik, if nothing else."

Emily thought for a moment, frowning. "Even though

you don't want to open yourself up to that kind of pain again. I don't mean just witness it. I mean let yourself experience it."

What felt like an eternity passed before he said, "I don't think I can. Not if I want to keep doing my job."

"Which you'd die if you couldn't do."

In answer, he tugged her close again. *Yes. That.*

Even so, Emily strongly suspected—especially in the light of what had just happened between them—that *detachment* wasn't even remotely part of this man's skill set, no matter how much he might wish it to be. If it were, he wouldn't be able to do what he loved.

"And all of that was my long-winded way of saying—"

"You can't be the person I need."

Another sigh preceded, "And you have no idea how much I wish I could be. How much I wish…"

For a brief moment, she saw tears gather in his eyes before he pulled her close again, the gesture again saying what he couldn't. That what he wanted, whether he could admit it or not, was in direct conflict with what he needed to do, even after everything he'd seen. And he had no earthly idea how to reconcile the two.

And neither did, *could*, she—a thought that shredded her inside. Because they'd crossed a boundary that should've never been crossed.

That *she* should've never crossed.

"It's okay," Emily said, fighting to keep her voice steady. "I already knew that coming in, remember? Our goals, our plans, our *needs* don't mesh. This was…" She cleared her throat. "This was never meant to be anything more than what it was."

"I'm sorry—"

"For *what*, for heaven's sake?" Twisting around to straddle his lap, she cupped his jaw in her hands. "For making me feel more *cared* about tonight than anyone else ever has?"

That got another gut-shredding smile. "That was the idea."

"And a damn fine one it was, too. So thank you," Emily whispered, brushing her lips across his, her skin sweetly sighing when his hands skimmed her bare waist underneath his shirt. She shoved her hair back over her shoulder and smiled into his eyes. "Because if nothing else, you have seriously raised my standards—"

From several feet away, she heard her phone ding.

"You should probably see to that," Colin said. Even though his thumbs were stroking the undersides of her breasts.

"Why?"

"Because if it's your cousin and you don't answer, she's likely to jump to conclusions."

"And I think that falls under the category of 'too late, buster.'" But she crawled off the man's lap—reluctantly—and took her grumbling hormones over to the other side of the room and picked up her phone, frowning at the text from her cousin.

You should probably get back.

Accompanied by a pic of her mother standing in the ranch's great room.

And looking very, very pissed.

Chapter Ten

"What is it?" Colin said behind her, his murmured words jarring her enough out of her shock to think, *Oh, hell.*

"My mother just showed up," she said, heading back to the bedroom to yank on her own clothes, tossing Colin's shirt on top of the rumpled bedclothes. She caught a glance of herself in the mirror over his dresser and grimaced. Between the rat's-nest hair and the beard burn...

Yeah. *Screwed* was definitely the word of the moment. See, this is why she'd always been the good girl, because she could never get away with a damn thing—

Colin came up behind her to quickly squeeze her shoulders before grabbing the shirt off the bed and punching his arms into the sleeves. "I'm coming with you."

Her fingers tangled in the mop, Emily wheeled around. "Oh, no, you're not—"

"Yes, I am," he said calmly, sitting on the bed to tie his shoelaces. "Because I doubt your mother is either blind or stupid. And the minute you walk through the door at this time of night, looking like that, she's gonna know." He frowned. "You really think I'd let you deal with the fallout by yourself? And before you pull your hair out of your scalp, there's a comb in the bathroom. If you don't mind my cooties."

"I think our cooties are definitely BFFs by now," Emily muttered, then hurried into the tiny en suite and grabbed the comb off the sink. And if she artfully arranged the waves, maybe the red patches wouldn't be so noticeable? No?

Then she glowered at her reflection. *Wait a goshdarn minute…*

Colin was tucking in his shirt when she roared back out of the bathroom, the man's expression remarkably calm for someone who'd been as good as caught with her in a very compromising position. And thank God for that, since *calm* was one thing Emily definitely was not right now.

"What the hell is she doing here anyway?"

"I assume that's a rhetorical question? Although that fury you're feeling right now?" He buckled his belt, then snagged her shawl off the chair and tossed it to her. "Hold on to that. 'Cause something tells me you're gonna need it."

That stopped her. And forced a tight little laugh from her throat. "And it's a lot easier to be angry with someone from two thousand miles away than when they're right in front of you, isn't it?"

"Yep," he said, then reached for her hand. "I have no doubt whatsoever you've got this, baby. But I've also got your back."

She turned to him, fighting the burning sensation in her eyes. "And I repeat, you don't have to do this. Play the white knight or whatever. Especially since…this isn't— wasn't—real."

Something like anger shunted across his features. "You don't think what happened here tonight was *real*?"

For a moment, she was confused. "After everything we just said—"

His grip on her shoulders almost hurt. Although not nearly as much as the regret in those pale green eyes. "This is about *now*, Emily. This moment." She saw the muscles in his throat work. "True, maybe I can't be what you need for the long haul, but sure as hell I'm not pretending like tonight never happened. That it wasn't important. Because believe me, honey...it was. More than you have any idea."

Except, in a blinding, breath-stealing flash...she did. Even, somehow, over all the other crap crashing around underneath her skull.

The turkey was every bit as much in love with her as she was with him.

And compared with the frustrating futility of *that* little situation, dealing with her crazy mother was child's play.

"Should we bring Spud?"

"Why not?" Colin said, whistling for the pup. And as they walked in silence to the main house, the pup tumbling over his big feet, the twinkling stars in the blue-black sky seemed to chuckle at them.

With good reason.

"A little warning would've been nice, Mother," Emily said a few minutes later, after her mother had clearly put two and two together and arrived at *suitably appalled*.

"Clearly," she said, seated across from Emily in the great room, the light from the wrought iron chandelier overhead gleaming in her artfully highlighted auburn hair. The others had retreated to the kitchen, although Colin had refused to leave until Emily promised to let him know if she needed him. Even though she knew that *he* knew she needed to handle this on her own. Because "having your back" came in many different flavors.

"And why are you here, anyway?"

"We'll get to that in a minute." Her mother blew out a breath between lips rimmed with what was left of her signature bright red lipstick. And for a moment Emily felt a twinge of sympathy, that the woman had endured a long travel day, with layovers and the drive here from the airport stretching the trip to nearly twelve hours. Still, no one had asked her to make the trek out here. Least of all Emily. "But for God's sake, Emily—I can't believe you hooked up with someone this soon after your own wedding day."

She supposed, from her mother's point of view, that's exactly what she'd done. And what the hell, she might as well own it. "Except, in case you missed it, I did not, in fact, get married."

Her mother's expression went from *frosty* to *arctic*. "And whose fault was that?"

"You know, I believe we'll have to cede that one to Michael."

"Oh, for heaven's sake, Emily...that's what men *do*. And it's not as if you were married yet."

"And thank God for that. Except, really? That's what men *do*? Or only men you happen to be married to?"

Her mother's face went as red as the lipstick she'd probably chewed off by Dallas. "Your father's always been a good provider. And loyal, in his own way. So I learned to look the other way."

"Oh, jeez, Mother—"

"Your father's and my relationship is none of your business."

"And neither is mine with...well, whoever, actually. Because it's *my* life? Where I get to make my choices?"

That got a hard stare, one that even a few months ago would have made Emily's stomach go wobbly. Now? Nope.

"So, what? This—" her mother waved at the beard burn "—was about, what? Getting even?"

"Actually, it was about being with someone who actually cares about my feelings."

Her mother scoffed. "Oh, please, Emily…you can't be that naive."

"You mean, the way you and Dad raised me?"

"Don't be ridiculous. We didn't—"

"Careful, Mother. Considering a second ago you took me to task for walking away from someone who cheated on me because… What was that you said? Oh, right… 'That's what men do.' So, two things." She crossed her arms. "One, no, they don't. At least not all of them. And two, that naïveté thing? Done."

"I hardly think a fling with a cowboy is a way to prove your maturity. Do you?"

Somehow, Emily steadied her breathing. Somehow, she didn't give in to the impulse to storm out of the room and leave her mother to stew in her own juices. Because that would be playing right into her hand, wouldn't it? Giving her all the ammunition she needed to verify her accusation, her assumption, that Emily was still a child who couldn't be trusted to make her own decisions.

That she was a stupid little girl who needed guidance. Direction.

By the same token, neither was she about to let herself get sucked into an argument, which would give her mother another kind of satisfaction. Funny, how she could almost feel Colin's go-get-'em-tiger from down the hall. The sort of support she'd never felt, not once, the entire time she and Michael had been together.

"Believe it or not," she said quietly, "I wasn't trying to

prove anything. To anybody. All I was doing was living my life, on my terms. Not anyone else's—"

"You can't stay, Emily. And I'm not leaving until you come to your senses."

Her laugh clearly startled her mother. "You seriously came out here to bring me home?"

"Since talking to you over the phone wasn't working... yes."

"And what on earth made you think you'd get a different result in person? Mother... I have a *job*, a commitment I fully intend to honor. I'm not about to leave these people in a lurch simply because you have issues with it. Issues which for the life of me I don't understand—"

"Then let me make it simple for you. You don't belong here. This life...it isn't *your* life. Oh, I know, it might seem like some sort of big adventure right now, but you'll tire of it soon enough, believe me." Her mother tried to soften her voice. It didn't entirely work. "Look, I understand, the whole thing with the wedding getting called off...that's enough to shake anybody up. To make you do... Well, to make you not think straight. Do things you wouldn't do if you were. But if you believe being out here is going to somehow magically fix everything..." Her voice hardened again. But not before Emily caught an unmistakable flash of fear that made her frown. "Don't be a fool, Emily—"

"And I'd stop right there if I were you," Colin quietly said from the doorway. Emily's mother whipped around.

"This is a private conversation, if you don't mind."

"Which was edging a mite too close to abusive for my taste."

Her mother's jaw dropped. "*Abusive?* Are you serious?"

"Colin, it's okay—"

"Not sure what else you'd call it—"

"Both of you! Cut it out!" Emily struggled to her feet,

feeling as though her brain had been stuffed in a blender. "Jeebus. Colin…" She crossed to him to fit her hand in his. Because it wasn't as if this couldn't get any worse, so what the hell? "I appreciate your coming to my defense, but seriously—I don't need it." She turned. "Although, actually, Mother—he's right. All my life you've tried to manipulate me into being who you want me to be, *what* you want me to me, as a reflection of you. It stops now."

"Why, you little ingrate—"

Still hanging on to Colin's hand—Colin's warm, strong hand—Emily held up her free one. "I'm not ungrateful for the things I should be grateful for. Really. I know I had a charmed childhood, that you and Dad gave me everything I ever wanted. But that doesn't mean…" She took a deep breath. "That doesn't mean you own me. Or that I owe you anything *besides* my gratitude…"

But her mother clearly wasn't listening, her gaze instead zeroing in on Colin's hand linked with hers. When she lifted her eyes, Emily saw the fear again, more intensified. "So are you two actually together?"

"No," they said at the same time, and confusion *almost* cramped her mother's Botoxed forehead. Must be time for a tune-up. Emily slid her hand out of Colin's.

"But what we are, or aren't, is frankly none of your business. I tried it your way, Mother," she said before the woman could interrupt. "And it was an unmitigated disaster."

Her mother's gaze zeroed in on Colin before returning to Emily. "And this won't be?" she said quietly, then brushed past Emily on her way out of the room.

After Deanna's filling Colin in on a few things over the past fifteen minutes, neither Margaret Weber's dismissal nor her lobbing the last word as she swept from the room surprised him.

Neither had Emily's standing up to her mother. For herself. Because from that first conversation all those weeks ago he'd glimpsed an inner strength he doubted she'd even been aware of at that point.

A *woman's* strength. That indefatigable resilience that held families together, protected children…stood up to tyranny with no regard for personal safety.

But what had surprised him—as in, rattled him to the core—was his reaction to her courage. Hell, her outright defiance of her mother's domineering attitude. Emily Weber was one tough cookie.

A tough cookie Colin was falling in love with so hard it almost hurt to breathe. And what exactly was he supposed to do with that, for God's sake?

"You were supposed to stay away," Emily said, standing in front of the open French door with her back to him, her arms folded across her ribs. A stiff breeze whisked across the large room, stirring the drapes, rattling papers on the coffee table.

"I couldn't."

"I told you, I didn't need rescuing."

"That wasn't why I couldn't stay away."

Her forehead knotted, she turned. Then, shaking her head, she released a sad little laugh. "Did you feel like this, when you stood up to your father?"

Colin frowned as he rammed his fingers into his back pockets. "Not sure what you mean by 'like this'—"

"Loyalty knocking heads with needing to find yourself. *Be* yourself." Tears glistened in her eyes. "Did it… did it tear you up inside?"

For the first time, he saw what her rebellion was costing her. A realization that only made it even clearer that she didn't need any *more* obstacles tossed in her path to self-discovery.

Never mind that for a moment there, when they were still at the cabin, he'd been tempted to backpedal, to take another stab at something he knew from experience would never work. Because it hadn't before. Because *feelings*, no matter how strong, never trumped logic. Practicality.

Inevitability.

"Some, sure." Then he blew out his own laugh. "Who am I kidding? Of course it did. I love my folks, I think the world of them, and I knew Dad didn't understand what I was doing. What I had to do. But—"

Too late, he caught himself.

"But the family dynamic isn't exactly the same," Emily said. "I know." Heaving a huge sigh, she walked back over to the sofa and dropped onto the edge, her arms tightly crossed over her stomach. "My mother isn't an easy person to love. But I do love her. And she's got her good points. Like taking in Dee after Aunt Kathryn died. Maybe her reasons weren't entirely altruistic, but we were raised like sisters. If anything, Mother might've overcompensated a bit with Dee to—in her mind—make up for what had happened. But..." She blew out another breath. "She never got over her only sister moving so far away, embracing a life she couldn't understand. So I know it's killing her to think I might do the same thing."

Again, Deanna had filled him in a little bit ago, about her aunt's issues with Whispering Pines. Even though Colin's reasons for not wanting to stay were entirely different from Margaret Weber's old fears about her sister, he still had to sympathize with her, at least to some extent.

"This really feels like home?"

Emily's gaze met his. "It really does. Yes, I love your family, and the landscape—the obvious things. But it goes beyond that. It simply...feels right. Feels like me." A small smile touched her still-swollen lips. "It always did, even when I was a kid."

Then she got to her feet and slowly walked over to him to wrap her arms around his waist, and he felt his heart crack. "I know, to you, this probably seems like I'm settling. That I've chosen something small and quiet and safe. Except..." She sighed. "When I look into those children's eyes in the classroom, or when I see the love all these people have for each other, how they show it, every minute of every day... to me, that feels pretty darn big."

Colin tugged her close, his own eyes burning as he pressed his cheek against her hair. "Reminds me of what my dad said to me," he whispered, "when I told him I was leaving. But I can't—"

"I know," she murmured into his chest, then leaned back to look up at him, tears brimming on her lower lashes. "And I totally understand. Believe me. Different purposes, different paths..." She shrugged. "That's how it goes sometimes. Nobody's fault." Then she snuggled close again. "Doesn't mean my heart's not breaking right now."

"I know what you mean," he pushed out, holding on to her as tightly as he dared before saying, praying his voice held, "I'll take the pup back for tonight, but Josh said I could leave him here tomorrow morning."

Then, with another kiss to her soft, soft hair, he let her go.

Holding on to her shaking self as though she'd fly into a million pieces if she didn't, Emily watched Colin walk away, wondering if she'd even ever see him again. A thought she let play through a dozen times, simply to torture herself. Because she didn't need to hear the words to know he'd be gone by tomorrow, if not before. Why else would he be bringing Spud here in the morning? After all, there was no reason for him to stick around, now that the book was done. And even though she'd laid bare her soul just now—because he deserved to know the truth about how she felt—not only was that not a reason for him to stay, if anything she'd given him that final little push to leave sooner rather than later. Would she ever willingly hurt him? Of course not. But he didn't know that, did he?

How it was even possible that she'd fallen in love, and so hard, in such a short time she had no idea. Especially after what she'd just been through. But she had. And now, standing in the vast room by herself, she blew out a dry laugh, that her mother had been right. Not that whatever had happened between her and Colin even remotely compared with the ignominious end to a three-year relationship with someone she'd expected to spend the rest of her life with. This one at least had come with a built-in end date, one they'd both been fully aware of from the beginning. So humiliation wasn't even an issue.

Pain, however…

Emily sat back on the sofa, her legs tucked up underneath her, realizing the only person she wanted to talk to about her feelings was the only person she couldn't. That if nothing else, she'd found a friend in Colin, a *good* friend, someone she knew she could trust with her life.

And had, whether she wanted to admit that or not.

"Oh, sweetie…"

She hadn't heard Dee come in. Or realized she was crying until a box of tissues plopped on the sofa beside her a moment before her cousin followed suit—the only other true friend she'd ever had. The only other person she knew she could trust with her life, her sorrows, her secrets.

Dee wrapped Emily up in her arms and tugged her close, much the same way Emily had for her only a few months before when her cousin's world had shattered, as well.

"You slept with him, didn't you?"

There wasn't the slightest trace of judgment in her cousin's gently spoken words. And not only because considering Dee's history she had no room to talk, but because that had never been part of their relationship, anyway. Not with each other. Although remembering their conversation that first night, Emily pushed out a puny little laugh.

"Hey," she said, a soggy tissue clutched in her fist. "It was your idea."

"Yeah, well, that was on a par with 'Why *not* eat the whole cheesecake?' Fun to think about, major regrets after you've actually done it."

"Speak for yourself," Emily grumbled, and Dee chuckled. Then Emily pushed herself upright, partly to grab another tissue, partly to get hold of herself. "I did know what I was getting into. Except I never thought…"

"You'd fall for this insanely good, and good-looking, man who's the diametric opposite of the schmuck who screwed you over? No, I bet you never saw that coming." At Emily's pathetic little laugh, Dee said, "So what do you want to do?"

"Besides eat that cheesecake, you mean? What *can* I do? Colin doesn't feel… He doesn't want what I do, Dee. Family, home." Her mouth pulled flat. "A quiet life. And he especially doesn't want any of that here."

"And you're sure about that?"

"I can only go by what the man said."

Except…deep down, she suspected he did want those things. Even if he hadn't figured out how to make the pieces fit.

Or how to handle whatever the fear was that made him believe he didn't.

Letting her head drop back onto the buttery, cushioned leather, Emily blew a breath toward the beamed ceiling.

"It's crazy, how up until a few weeks ago I hadn't fully realized how much I was living someone else's life. Being who other people wanted me to be. Other than my teaching, I mean. Aside from that…" Her head rolled sideways, her gaze meeting her cousin's. "It was almost as if I'd made a bargain of sorts, with my parents—'Let me do this, and I'll give you everything else. Give you myself.' Then, with Michael, I even gave up teaching. In exchange for the family I thought I was going to have. But it was all a crock, wasn't it? An illusion."

A tight smile pushed at her mouth when she felt Dee's hand fold around hers. "So I came out here to figure out who I really was. What I really wanted. Instead I found…" She almost laughed. "The real version of everything I thought I already had. Who I *already* was. So here I am, finally living what feels like a truly genuine life, *my* life, someplace that finally feels like home…"

Emily pushed herself off the couch to close the French doors before they froze to death, only to stand facing outside, still grasping the door handles. "Not gonna lie, right now it's tempting—*so* tempting—to revert to that obedient little girl who'd do whatever it took to make someone like me. Accept me." She faced her cousin again, sitting backward on the sofa, sympathy shining in her eyes. "To suck it up, to *give* up what I've only just found in order to be whoever Colin might need me to be. Even though I know that's not even possible. But giving *him* up…it hurts, Dee. Oh, God, it hurts."

"More than Michael?"

"God, yes," she said on an ugly laugh. "As crazy as that sounds. But for one thing, I know Colin wouldn't let me do that. Any more than I'd expect him to change who he is, or not follow his path, for me. Because…" Her eyes stinging, she shook her head. "Finding the right person doesn't mean losing yourself. Or shouldn't, anyway. Something that's taken me twenty-seven years to figure out. Damned if I'm going to throw all that away now. But honestly—to finally find someone who actually gives a damn about what I think, how *I* feel, what *I* need to be, only to realize…" Emily pressed a hand to her mouth, then dropped it again. "Only to realize we want different things…man, that sucks."

Her own eyes brimming, Dee got up to pull Emily into her arms, the second time that evening someone Emily loved with all her heart had hugged her.

But whoever said hugs were always comforting was talking out of their butt.

"The thing is, dog… I know I'm doing the right thing."

The puppy sat in front of him on the floor, head cocked. Damn, he was gonna miss the little turkey. But—

"Because the sooner I leave, the faster Emily'll get over me and get on with her new life." A life, from the sound of things, she'd chosen for herself for once. "Right?"

The pup yipped, then bounced over to crawl into his lap and start gnawing on his fingers. And of course Colin immediately thought of the dog's doing the same thing to Emily, of her grins and giggles when he did, of how she didn't care one whit about puppy slobber on her face.

And he was here in the living room instead of in the bedroom, packing, because it still smelled of her in there. Felt like her. And, yes, he went ahead and tormented himself with thinking about how a couple hours ago he'd been inside her, feeling her pulse around him, hearing her soft cries in his ears, then that damned laughter when it was over, so fricking pleased with herself.

With him.

About how perfect sex wasn't about crazy-ass contortions that only left you with pulled muscles, anyway—it was about being with the right person.

No matter how wrong she was. You know, from a logical perspective.

The pup yipped again, then squirmed around to flip upside down in Colin's lap, showing off his spotted tummy.

"You're right, I'm an idiot—"

At the tentative knock on his door, his stomach lurched. Not his brother's knock, that was for sure, since Josh was more of a pounder than a rapper. But if it was Emily...

He'd deal. Somehow.

Shoving himself to his feet, he crossed the room, taking care not to step on the dancing dog who clearly thought he was playing. He hauled in a breath, plastered on a neutral expression and opened the door.

"We need to talk," Emily's mother said, then pushed her way inside.

Chapter Eleven

Because his psyche hadn't been battered enough. Got it.

"About—?" Colin said, slugging his hands in his pockets and slapping on a neutral expression. He hoped.

"Is there somewhere you can put the dog?" Margaret asked, scowling down at the pup. Who was bowing before her, butt in the air, tail a blur.

"You allergic?"

"No, but…" Eyes nearly the same color as Emily's, but colder, harder, met his. "But he's—"

"A dog. Who'll probably pass out in a minute, not to worry."

Her gaze still fixed on the pup, Emily's mother pushed her chin-length hair behind her ear. And smiled. Not a warm, boundless grin, like her daughter would give. But the corners of her mouth definitely turned up. "A little undisciplined for my taste," she said, more to herself than him, Colin suspected. "But cute. I don't suppose you have any tea?"

"Yes. Which I have no compunction about holding hostage until you tell me why you're here."

That actually got a laugh. "You drive a hard bargain," she said, which was when Colin realized a Southern accent soft-edged her words. The pup attacked the toe of what was probably a very expensive flat shoe. In a single move, the woman bent over to gather him into her arms, where he promptly snuggled in and went to sleep. Huh. "My daughter doesn't know I'm here."

"Didn't figure she did."

"And you're going to make this difficult, aren't you?"

Colin crossed his arms. "Out of deference to not only my parents, but your daughter, I'll try not to be rude. But my loyalty is to Emily. And you still haven't answered my question."

A long, harsh intake of breath preceded, "That girl's already had her heart broken once this year. The thought of it happening again, especially so soon after the first time, breaks mine. In spite of whatever it is you might think about me, and/or my relationship with my daughter."

The woman had been in his space less than five minutes and had already surprised him three times. Not that he was about to let her know that.

"And your point is?"

"Oh, for God's sake, young man—please do not play the fool with me. Emily's obviously in love with you. Only she seems convinced the two of you can't work it out."

A long moment passed before, deciding she'd earned her tea, Colin yanked his gaze from hers and went into the kitchen to pull out assorted boxes of tea bags. Placing them on the counter between the two rooms, he indicated for Emily's mother to make her choice. A moment passed before she pointed to what she apparently deemed the least offensive, then set down the puppy before hiking herself onto a stool on the living room side to watch Colin as he poured water into a mug, set it in the microwave.

"So what I've gathered thus far," he said as the microwave whirred behind him, "is that you're worried I'll break your daughter's heart. Although whether because you're afraid I'll stay or leave I haven't quite worked out yet. Let alone what you'd like me to do to remedy the situation."

"Can you even do that?"

He felt his mouth tuck up on one side. "Assuage your guilt about what happened before, you mean?"

"You sure don't pull any punches, do you?"

"Not if I can help it." The microwave dinged; he pulled out the steaming mug, dunking the bag into it before setting it in front of the woman, along with a sugar bowl. She looked at it like he'd offered her arsenic.

"To tell you the truth, I'm not entirely sure why I'm here. Let alone what I expect, or want, the outcome to be. All I know is there's been far too little truth telling in this family over the last thirty years. And when I overheard Emily talking to her cousin a little while ago… I guess I didn't fully realize how much damage her father and I had done. Not that we meant to—we both love her, I swear— but sometimes when parents are so focused on what *they* think is best for their child, they totally miss what the child really wants. And needs. Especially when…" Staring at her tea, Margaret huffed a sigh. "When the parents have royally screwed up their own lives. Of course the irony is, the more things go wrong, the more you think you can fix them by repeating the same mistakes."

She finally lifted the mug, only to set it down again without tasting the tea. "I want to think Emily's *fascination* with being out here stems from her being unhappy with, well, all sorts of things, I suppose. Things I don't think she even knew she was unhappy with until this craziness with Michael. But now it occurs to me, she was living a lie, wasn't she? A lie her father and I perpetuated, all in the name of appearances. So what I'm saying is…she's vulnerable. A lot more vulnerable than I realized. And I should've done more, to protect her, to keep her from…"

Her mouth clamped shut, Margaret lifted her tea again. Although more to hide behind the mug than to take a drink, Colin suspected.

"To keep her from making the same mistake you believe your sister did."

The woman's eyes shot to his. "What do you know about that?"

"Only what Deanna told me. About how upset you were when Deanna's mother married her father, made her home out here—"

"Away from her real life, yes. It killed her, you know. Or maybe you don't."

He knew enough, although Deanna hadn't been specific. But what it boiled down to was that Deanna's mother had made a choice her sister couldn't reconcile herself to. Emily's mother had then subsequently woven her own story about her sister's death to suit her own prejudices.

"From what little I know, I think it's safe to say your daughter's not your sister."

"Be that as it may, she's not thinking clearly. Obviously. Whether Michael—" She took a deep breath. "Whether he was right for her or not, three years is a big chunk of your life when you're that young. His cheating on her…" To his surprise, the older woman's eyes watered. "Emily's not like me. She has different…expectations. And she's still so young, as I said—"

"She's not a *child*, Mrs. Weber. And pardon me for saying this, but I find it very strange that you want so much to protect her when you threw her into that situation to begin with. How does that work, exactly?"

Her face colored, but give the woman props for standing her ground. "I'm not saying her father and I didn't make mistakes. Which is why I'm trying to head this one off at the pass now—"

"There's nothing to head off. There never was. While I'm hardly going to get specific about…things between Emily and me, we both knew going in exactly what the expectations were. Or weren't. Trust me, I didn't seduce her. Or make promises I had no intention of keeping. I was at least honest. And I'd put out my own eye before treating her like the man you picked for her did. *My* mistake…" Colin sucked in a breath. "My mistake was in not realizing how vulnerable we *both* were. And I cannot tell you how sorry I am for that. Especially since…since I care very deeply for your daughter. *About* her. And because I care, I wouldn't dream of quashing her dreams. Or putting her in a situation that would only make her unhappy down the road."

"Exactly what she said you'd say," Margaret said.

And hell, yeah, that hurt, for a whole mess of reasons. Not the least of which was how well Emily knew him, even after such a short time. "The point is, whether you came over here to warn me off, or somehow fix things between me and Emily…" His head wagged. "The first is moot, and the second isn't up to you. And never would be. Because nobody can make things work for someone else simply because they want them to. No matter what the motive. The fact is, Emily and I want different things. *Need* different things. And we're both mature enough to see that. Right now. Before we make any more mistakes than have already been made."

Margaret's eyes narrowed slightly. "One question—do you love her?"

Speaking of not pulling punches. "If I didn't," he said quietly, "I wouldn't be leaving tomorrow."

"Does she know that?"

"I'm going to say yes." Then he crossed his arms. "But my question to you is…what do you really want for her? Not for yourself. For *her*?"

Emily's mother slid off the stool, leaving her tea mostly undrunk. Her eyes welled again. "Happiness. That's all. Just…happiness."

"Then we're on the same page," Colin said, even as it felt like a knife was twisting in his gut. "Obviously you know your daughter a helluva lot better than I do, long-term. But you haven't been around her in the last few weeks, haven't seen…" He swallowed. "The way she smiles now…it's nothing like when she first got here. Like…like she's *whole*, finally. And finally herself. You really want her to be happy? Then trust that she'll figure out whatever she needs to figure out, in her own good time. Even if that's in some dinky little Southwest town."

"Which my niece hated. Which I gather you were pretty keen to leave, too—"

"Oh, I don't know. Deanna seems pretty content here these days, don't you think? And my reasons for leaving back then…" His mouth pushed up at the corners. "Oddly, they were—are—not unlike your daughter's for wanting to stay. Home's a funny thing, you know? Some of us find it right where we were born, others…maybe not so much. Maybe I don't feel Whispering Pines gives me the opportunity to do what I feel I need to do, but that doesn't make it a bad town." His voice softened. "And my family…they're good people, all of 'em. They'll keep an eye on Emily. Make sure she's never lonely. Make sure she's…safe."

This last part he said through a throat so thick he wasn't sure how he he'd gotten the words out.

Emily's mother was quiet for a long moment before she said, "Guess you've given me a lot to think about." She started for the door, then twisted back, her brow furrowed. "I can tell you're a good man, Colin. From my experience, those are pretty rare these days." A tiny smile flicked across her mouth. "And I wish you well. I really do."

Took a good five minutes after she left for Colin's heart to stop hammering in his chest.

Emily didn't see her mother again until the following morning, when she'd gone into the kitchen to make herself coffee and the older woman sat at the kitchen table, dressed and perfectly coiffed, lying in wait. Or sitting, in this case. In an ideal world, she would have acted as though everything was perfectly fine, that her mother's presence was neither here nor there, that whatever the woman had to say—and Emily had no doubt she had plenty—would simply bounce off her as harmlessly as Nerf bullets.

In reality, however, she hadn't slept worth spit, her heart was in tatters, and the anticipation alone of whatever was about to fall from her mother's freshly reddened lips made her feel about five again.

Except she wasn't. And even though Emily still wouldn't call herself fierce, she was a survivor, wasn't she? Hell, she'd lived through not only the mortification of having to let several hundred people know that, nope, sorry, there wouldn't be a wedding—not to mention the extra-added-value mortification of everyone knowing *why*—but the indignity of a broken heart brought on by nothing other than her own foolishness. Not that loving Colin was wrong, but letting things get as far as they had…

Just hand over the dumbass medal and be done with it.

So not really in the mood to chat with dear old mom right now.

"Everyone else is gone," Mother said, patting the space at the table next to her. "Although on Josh's recommendation I went into town early to pick up some breakfast things at that diner. Annie's. Since we all know I do not cook. Although I nearly killed myself in that truck—it's been a million years since I drove stick."

Her mug clutched to her chest, Emily stood frozen to the spot in front of the coffeemaker, letting the steam open her pores. Her brain cells. She wasn't sure who this woman was, but sure as shootin' it wasn't the one who'd given birth to her. By C-section after a twenty-eight-hour labor, she'd been told more times than she could remember. However…she was hungry, and Annie's churros and breakfast burritos were the stuff of magic. So she sat— her mother had already set a plate—and took a burrito, not sure what to say. Or do. Or think.

"You were already asleep when I got back from Colin's last night," her mother began, and Emily's head whipped around.

"What?"

"I peeked into your room, but you were out like a light—"

"No, the Colin bit." Although she hadn't been asleep, she'd been playing possum. The burrito forgotten, Emily's brows crashed. "You went to see him? Why on earth—?"

"Because I'm a meddling old biddy who's absolutely no good at keeping her nose out of everyone's business. Most notably yours. Eat up, honey, those things are disgusting when they're cold. Anyway, you'll be relieved to know he set me straight. About your relationship. About more than that, actually," she said, her mouth turning down at the corners. "But that's… Never mind." Her mother's eyes met hers. "What a remarkable young man. Youngish, anyway. He loves you, you know. Maybe even more than you love him. How on earth that happened in a few weeks is beyond me. But apparently it did."

As if there was any way in hell she'd be able to eat now. Although whether Colin had admitted his feelings or her mother had leaped to her own conclusions, who knew? But since she'd done her own leaping not that long ago, this didn't come as a surprise. What had, however, shocked her expensive, bought-for-the-honeymoon-that-never-happened designer panties right off her butt was her mother's calm acceptance of all of it.

Although since it was all a moot point, that might account for the calm. However…

"None of which changes the fact that I'm staying."

Her mother lifted her own mug to her lips. "Oh, I know."

"And…you're okay with that?"

"I will be. Once I unstick my head from my butt." As Emily sat there, more or less in shock, her mother said, "Colin made me realize a few things, not the least of which is that you have to live your own life. *Deserve* to live your own life. And that I can't fix what's wrong with my life by trying to manipulate yours. Or use you as some sort of shield between me and your father. But more than that…" Her eyes watered. "Keeping you close won't bring my sister back. And Deanna swears Kathryn was happy here. Most of the time, anyway."

Although Emily hadn't been around her aunt enough to be all that aware of the mental illness that robbed her of a good chunk of her adulthood, she, too, had heard enough to believe that the good outweighed the bad, even near the end. "It definitely seems that way. But I don't—"

Her generally undemonstrative mother wrapped a cool hand around Emily's wrist. "I've let fear color things for much too long, honey. Fear for you, especially, that history might repeat itself. So I've promised myself I won't do that anymore. And now I'm promising you."

Finally, Emily pinched off a chunk of the burrito and stuffed it into her mouth. "And I'm supposed to believe that?"

Her mother sighed. "It won't be easy—old dogs and all that—but I'm going to try. Although…" Her head tilted. "Maybe you should try to make Colin stay? Or go with him…?"

"Mother. Really?"

She sniffed. "Dignity is overrated, you know."

"Reality, however, isn't. All done with the fairy tale, Mom. Not really cut out for this dream-chasing business."

Another breath left her mother's lungs, but she nodded. "Well. I'm going back today. To face the mess that is my own life and leave you to live yours in peace."

Her throat closed around the bite in her mouth, Emily could only nod. Although fortunately her mother waited for her to swallow before saying, "That doesn't mean, however, that I'm not hoping either you or Colin change your mind."

A harsh laugh tumbled from Emily's mouth, and her mother shrugged. "I might be able to change how I act, but that doesn't mean I can change who I am. I'm so sorry, honey," she whispered, her eyes filling again. "Really and truly. For letting my own will blind me to how perfect you are, just as you are. When I think how I almost lost you…" Her face paled. "Or am I jumping the gun about that, too? Have I totally screwed this up?"

"Well, you might've come really close," Emily said with a small smile, "but…" Instead of finishing her sentence, she stood to wrap her startled mother in the first hug they'd shared since Emily was a little girl. What was more startling, however, was that her mother returned it.

And, *yanno*, that left her feeling pretty darn fierce.

Despite an ache in the center of her chest she doubted would ever completely go away. Because Michael—a dime a dozen, those types. Colin, however…

He was a Talbot. And those guys were priceless.

"When's your flight?" she said, sitting back down.

"At three. Josh said he'd take me into Albuquerque. Since I might've lucked out in finding an Uber driver to schlep me all the way out here, getting one to take me back—"

"Forget it, I'll drive you."

Her mother smiled, her eyes twinkling. "Making sure I actually leave?" she asked, and Emily laughed, only to then feel a lump rise in her throat.

"No," she said, surprised to find herself fighting tears. "Because the ride will give us another couple of hours together." And her mother smiled, her own eyes just as glittery.

Colin pulled up in front of his parents' house, not sure whether he was more relieved or sorry that his dad's truck wasn't in the driveway. His mother, however, greeted him at the door…along with the sounds of several high-pitched voices winnowing through the house from the small backyard. Zach and Mallory's kids, he remembered—his parents were babysitting while his brother and his new wife enjoyed a short honeymoon.

"Your father had to go into Taos for a doctor's appointment," she said, standing aside so he could come in. "A standard follow-up, that's all. Nothing to worry about. He'll be back soon, I imagine. So. To what do I owe the pleasure?"

A simple question, one that shouldn't have made the back of his throat clog, his eyes burn. But between his father not being there and the sounds of his nephews…

Not to mention other things…

"Catching a plane in a few," he said. "Figured I'd come by before I left."

His mother went immediately into Mom Alert—narrowed eyes, set mouth, that slight shake of her head that said she knew damn well there was more to it than that.

"Kind of sudden, isn't it?" she said, heading toward the kitchen and clearly expecting him to follow.

"You knew I was leaving after the wedding," he said, which earned him an even sharper glance.

"Not right after, I didn't. I mean, I figured we'd have a little warning. That you'd at least come over for dinner or something, say goodbye properly."

The barely masked hurt in her eyes killed him nearly as much as what he'd seen in Emily's the night before, when they both realized—and admitted—what they were really feeling. And that it didn't make a lick of difference.

"I know, I'm sorry. But a new assignment came up suddenly. Since the wedding was over, I figured I might as well jump on it before somebody else does."

Not entirely a lie. Another editor had dangled something different in front of him, wondering if he'd consider doing a human interest piece on how changing energy options were affecting residents of one area of the country. Not his usual focus, but something that'd been tickling the back of his brain for a while, anyway. And if nothing else it provided him with a viable, and reasonable, excuse to leave. And one nobody would question.

His mother crossed her arms. "So what're you running from this time? As if I couldn't guess."

Nobody but Mom, that was. "Excuse me?"

"Josh has a big mouth, God love him. Not to mention he's worried about you."

"Why on earth—?" Mom gave him a don't-talk-stupid look that halfway made Colin regret stopping here on the way to the airport. She glanced out the kitchen window to check on the boys, then turned back to him, her gaze managing to be both sharp and soft at the same time. A particular talent of hers, as it happened.

"Whatever's going on with you and Emily—or not— that's between you and her. And I've got no issues with your devotion to your work. I know how it feels, finding something that feeds something deep inside you. A lot of people never do, so you've got a leg up there, at least. However…"

She closed the space between them to clamp her hands around his arms, her expression twisting him inside out. "What worries me," she said gently, "is that I'm guessing you haven't been entirely honest with yourself, about why you came back. Because you and I both know you could've worked on that book anywhere. You didn't have to do it here. Especially considering how you and your daddy left things all those years ago. But it's not that easy to turn our backs on our roots, is it? Especially if we haven't set down new ones somewhere else."

Now he was really regretting stopping by. "And again— where is this coming from?"

"The look on your face, for one thing. Which is not the look of somebody excited about getting back to his chosen life."

When he didn't answer—couldn't—Mom returned to the window, chuckling at something the kids were doing, her sleeveless blouse showing off arms as toned as those of a much younger woman. "You know, one of the hardest things we all have to learn is that it's okay to change our minds." She looked back at him. "That there's no shame in admitting we were wrong."

And how terrible a son would he be for blowing off his own mother? Although, come to think of it, probably no worse than he'd already been. Except the thing was, he wasn't that kid anymore. Besides which, being back here had not only shoved his face into everything he'd given up, but everything he'd refused for so long to admit he wanted. His mother was right—he'd wanted to return to his roots, to reground himself. Badly.

Except unfortunately this wasn't only about him. Not anymore.

"You're way too smart for your own good, you know that?"

Mom snorted. "You're not telling me anything I don't know," she said, and Colin smiled. Then cupped the back of his head.

"You're right, I'm not happy about this. But…" He pushed out a dry laugh. "I'm not running away. I swear. It's more that… I'm deliberately getting out of someone else's way."

"Oh, sweetie…" Tears gleamed in his mother's eyes. "You're in love with the girl, aren't you?"

From out front, he heard his father's truck door slam shut. Clearing his throat, Colin dug the rental's keys out of his pocket. Tried a smile. "Close enough. The thing is, though, I know what would happen if I stayed. What we'd both want to happen. Except Emily's right where I was ten years ago, just beginning to find her own footing, to figure out who she is, what she wants. She needs the space to figure that out.

But if I stick around—" He shrugged. "*Space* isn't something you get much of in a small town."

"And maybe you're not giving either of you enough credit—"

"For what? *Listening* to her? Paying attention to what she needs? You and Dad…you showed us by example that selfishness has no place in a working relationship. And I can't…*won't*…" He swallowed painfully past the knot in his throat, then glanced up at the kitchen clock. "Sorry, I need to get going or I'm gonna miss my plane—"

"You're leaving? Already?"

At his father's voice, Colin turned. And man, seeing the look in his father's eyes…at that moment he hated himself, hated the situation, hated life, pretty much.

"Something came up, I…"

"It's okay, son," Dad said, even though he was clearly fighting off disappointment. "It's not like we expected you to hang around. As it is…well." Grinning, he clapped Colin's shoulder, then hauled him against his still-broad chest. "We're grateful you hung around as long as you did."

"So am I, Dad," Colin said quietly. "Really."

"I know." His father let go, managing a piss-poor smile that tore Colin up inside. "You have a good trip, you hear?"

Then his mother also yanked him into a hard hug and kissed his cheek before holding him at arm's length, her mouth twisted to one side. "I swear, every one of you boys has a head harder than granite. Can't imagine where you get that from."

"I'm gonna say both of you," Colin said, and she harmlessly swatted his chest before they both followed him out to the front door. When he got there, though, he turned, his hand on the knob. "I will be back, though. I promise."

Dad crossed his arms. "Sooner rather than later, I hope."

"Sure thing," he said, then got out of there before somebody called him on his lie.

The ride down to Albuquerque had given Emily and her mother an opportunity to talk to—rather than at—each other in a way they never had before. So much so that their hug before Margaret went through security left Emily far more torn up than she would have expected even a week ago. Not that they'd magically become BFFs or anything, but at least they'd arrived at some sort of understanding of where they were each coming from. As though they were equals, even, she thought as she got on the escalator to go down to the lower level and out to the parking garage. Not to mention that, for the first time in years, she really *felt* her mother loved her. That was something—

At the bottom of the escalator, she lost her breath. Because, yep, that was Colin striding across the vast, tiled expanse toward her, his camera bag draped over his shoulder as he stared at his phone, gracefully dodging the smattering of passengers this time of day. Meaning he probably wouldn't even see her, if she kept going—

His head snapped up as if she'd called to him, a frown giving way to a dozen other emotions as he changed course and headed toward her, his mouth curved in a slight smile. He hadn't shaved, she could now see. Or slept, she was guessing.

"Hey," he said softly when he reached her, and Emily nearly melted from how badly she wanted to touch him. "What are you…?"

"Just dropped off my mother."

"Really?" He glanced around, as though expecting to see her. "She left already?"

"Yeah. She…" Emily gave her head a sharp little shake, then shrugged. "Yeah. She, um, told me she went to see you."

She couldn't read his expression. "Really."

"But not what you two discussed. And I didn't ask. Although she did leave, so…thanks?"

His gaze met hers again, and everything inside her trembled, glowed, with the memory of his touch, rough and tender and almost hesitant…those eyes locked on hers, anything *but* hesitant. His smile incrementally grew. "I'm surprised you let her live."

Emily almost laughed. "Things were definitely a little dicey there for a minute. But you know what? She's always gonna be who she is, nothing I can do about that. What I can control is whether or not she gets to me. And those days are over."

Colin's smile broadened. "So she couldn't talk you into going back to DC?"

The obvious pride in his voice, his eyes… Oh, dear *God*, just kill her now. "As if," she said, and he laughed, but it didn't sound normal. Or maybe that was her hearing.

"When's your flight?" she asked.

"Not for a couple of hours yet. I like to get to airports early. Although I forget it's not that big a deal here."

"Not really, no." Yeesh, could this conversation be any more inane? Could her heart be hammering any harder? Or splintering into any more pieces?

"Where are you headed?"

"Coal country. Or what used to be. Kentucky, West Virginia. A piece on how things have changed there."

"A new direction for you, isn't it?"

"Maybe. Or not." He shifted the camera bag. "It's still about the people." A smile ghosted around his mouth. "It's always about the people."

Don't get sucked in, she wanted to say. But she knew

that wasn't possible, not for this man. Any more than it would be for her.

"Take care," she whispered, and he nodded.

"I will. Promise."

"Well. I guess…"

"Sure. It was—"

"I know." Crap. She was going to cry. "Um…" She swallowed so hard she nearly choked. "Have a good trip."

"Thanks."

She nodded, then walked quickly away, her eyes burning so badly she could barely see—

"Em?"

Muttering an obscenity under her breath, she turned, helpless to do anything save watch Colin march toward her again, even more helpless to resist when he somehow shifted everything aside to take her face in his hands and lower his mouth to hers for a kiss that was a desperate, mournful meeting of mouths and tongues and souls and hearts…until he broke the kiss to press his lips against her forehead before taking off again, his long legs eating up the tiled floor as he strode to the escalators.

And didn't look back as he ascended.

Emily, however, watched until he was out of sight, although whether from a false sense of hope or a hitherto unknown masochistic streak, she had no idea. And she wondered, gripping her purse's shoulder strap like a lifeline, how a life decision that only the day before had made her feel empowered and independent and all grown-up now made her feel like a horse stall that hadn't been mucked out since the dawn of time.

Have a fling, they said. *It'll be fun*, they said.

You can handle it, they said.

Except if "they" were here in front of her right now?

She'd slap those bitches silly.

Chapter Twelve

Twisting off the beer's cap, Colin shoved aside the patio door to the bland Midwestern condo he'd used as little more than a mailing address for the past ten years, letting the humid June air—not to mention a swarm of gnats—grab at his face before he dropped into some sorry old webbed chair he'd picked up for a couple bucks when the old lady downstairs died and her kids sold off all her stuff. The apartment wasn't horrible by any means, the kind of place he knew he could leave for long periods without worrying overmuch about break-ins. Not to mention maintenance. The rent was reasonable, the neighbors as oblivious to his comings and goings as he was to theirs, the location almost ideal for getting anywhere else with a minimum of connecting flights. It was also fairly quiet, especially since the college kids had moved out. And if it didn't exactly feel like home... Again—not here that often. It was...enough.

Or had been, anyway.

Because for the first time, when he'd gotten back from his assignment late yesterday afternoon, instead of he and the condo greeting each other with bored indifference, Colin had felt a definite pang of annoyance. Like when you suddenly realized the girlfriend you'd stayed with out of habit more than anything wasn't who you really wanted to be with anymore. That, suddenly, you wanted more. *Needed* more. Even if you didn't know what, exactly, that *more* was.

Only—he glanced across the reasonably green, reasonably kept courtyard toward the bank of balconies that looked exactly like his, save for slight variations in grills and doodads—who was he kidding? He knew exactly what he wanted. Who he wanted.

And he'd known it long before he'd gotten on that plane a few weeks ago.

Before he'd gotten naked with a woman who'd stripped him bare long before that night.

Before his mother sent him that text, a few days after he left—

His phone buzzed, startling him. Colin picked it up off the also-crappy glass table by the chair, frowning at Levi's number. He doubted whether any of his brothers had the slightest clue why he'd left. Although if he'd bothered to tell them why he'd really returned to his hometown to begin with, they might have.

"Figured I should let you know your newest niece is here," his younger brother said, the obvious grin in his voice making Colin smile even over the fresh stab to his heart.

"She is? That's terrific."

"A relief, is what it is. Kid took her sweet time making her appearance. The due date was nearly two weeks ago.

Then after all that she came flying out like a greased pig. Although don't tell Val I said that." He laughed. "Mom barely had a chance to catch her. A little blondie. Like her mama."

Trying to ignore the tug, Colin said, "What's her name?"

He heard Levi clear his throat. "Hope," he said quietly. "Val's suggestion. Like I was gonna say no, right?"

His own throat tightening, Colin glanced back out into the green space between the buildings, right when a young family walked by with a toddler streaking toward the complex's little playground, and an infant in a stroller, black eyes wide in a gleaming brown face. Newish residents, he guessed, since he'd never seen them before. The dad apparently said something to get a rise out of his wife…and succeeded, judging from her squawk, followed by a gentle smack on his muscled arm, their blended laughter. They caught Colin looking at them. He grinned and waved; they waved back, and a thousand thoughts seemed to take flight inside Colin's head, a swarm of locusts intent on devouring everything in their path.

Like all those good intentions that seemed to make less sense with every passing day.

Aka the masks for his fears.

"I'd like to… I want to come see her," he said into the phone, clearly startling his brother. "If it's not too soon. I don't want to mess things up if you're still trying to get settled—"

"No! I mean, not at all, anytime's good. That'd be great." Levi paused. "But I figured you'd be busy, you know. With your work and stuff. Like always."

"Like I was when Zach's boys were born, you mean."

A moment of silence preceded, "I wasn't here, either, being in the service—"

"You had an excuse, Lev. Me? Not so much. And I know Zach never understood, not really." He pushed out a dry laugh. "Hell, I didn't fully understand myself, so why would anybody else? Anyway…not sure when I'll get there—"

"No hurry, bro." His brother chuckled. "Kid's not going anywhere. Although, even setting aside whatever it is you do…that's not the only reason I'm surprised you're coming home."

Yeah, Colin wondered how long it'd take Levi to get around to that.

"Not that I'm about to get into the middle of that mess," his brother continued. "Or whatever you want to call it. But let me say this, and then I'm done, I swear—I can tell you from experience that sometimes the one thing that seems to make the least sense is exactly what you need to do. You got that?" At Colin's snort, his brother added, "So you want me to give Emily a heads-up, or no?"

"I'm only coming to see the kid, I…" He shoved out a breath. Like anybody would believe that. "Do whatever you think best, okay?"

Then, on another breath, Colin disconnected the call. Hell, at this point he was way past worrying about anything making sense. Right now—especially when faced with the prospect of seeing the woman he hadn't been able to stop thinking about from the minute he walked away from her in the airport—all he wanted was to know, and do, whatever was right. For both of them.

He only hoped to hell he figured that out before he balled things up even worse. Although he wasn't counting on it. Not at all. Because it was still too soon, for Emily. Wasn't it? Really, had anything changed? It wasn't as if they were somehow different people now than when he'd left…

Except without trying, what was the point of living?

Something he had the definite feeling nobody would agree with more than the woman who'd made him realize that *more* had been right under his nose all along. Because everything he wanted, and could be, was right in that dinky little New Mexico town.

Because making a difference had nothing to do with where you were, but what you did.

And who you did it for.

Still watching the little family, Colin tapped his phone against his chin, then brought up his mother's text again. One of her favorite Bible verses, he remembered.

For where your treasure is, there your heart will be also.

A promise, he realized. For everyone.

Even him.

Colin could practically hear God's sigh of relief, that *finally* he'd caught on.

Carefully rocking the prettiest little baby girl in the whole world, Emily barely heard the doorbell ring over toddler Risa's clattering her mama's pie tins against the kitchen's tiled floor. Of course, then Levi and Val's hound dog, Radar, started baying his head off, so it's not as if she could've missed that "somebody's at the door, woman, *fer* God's sake!"

So much for poor Val trying to get a nap, Emily thought as she shoved aside the dog to open the door, a task made far more difficult by the toddler's clinging to her legs.

"Hey," Colin said, and every bit of spit in Emily's mouth evaporated and every one of the pep talks she'd given herself since she last saw him, about how this was for the best and she was strong and happy and good on her own, *blahblahblahbityblah*, flew right out the window. Then he frowned at what must have been her gobsmacked expression. "I'm guessing Levi didn't tell you I was coming."

At least she thought that's what he said. Hard to tell over the pounding in her ears and Risa's shrieks of joy as she launched herself at her uncle's knees and Radar's *roo-rooing*. Because the dog was high on life, basically.

"Who's that?" Val said behind her, in jeans and a floppy, sloppy shirt but otherwise giving no indication whatsoever she'd popped out a kid two days ago. "Colin!" The blonde zoomed across the room to throw her arms around her brother-in-law, her long ponytail swinging against her back as she laughed. "Oh, my god! I certainly didn't expect you to show up!"

"Surprise," Colin said quietly, his gaze hooking Emily's as he said, "I heard there's a new Talbot in town."

Val pivoted, took one look at Emily's still-gobsmacked expression, pivoted back to Colin and said, "Who you can see later. First things first." Then she pried her new daughter out of Emily's arms, called the dog and her little girl and steered the whole lot out back.

A moment before Colin stepped inside, cupped Emily's face in his hands and kissed her as though his life depended on it. Or hers, maybe.

"Where's Spud?" he asked when they came up for air, and Emily sputtered a laugh.

"At the cabin," she said. "Where we live now. He's gotten so big, you won't even recognize him—"

"We need to hash out a few things," Colin said, his hands still cradling her face, all warm and firm and goose bumps–inducing…his mouth still right there, much too close for rational thought. Somehow, she squeaked out a little "Okay" before he laughed—oh, Lord, did she love that laugh!—and took her hand to lead her to his brother's living room, where he shoved aside a layer of little girl toys from the scarred sofa and pulled her down onto his lap. And Emily had no idea what was going on, and frankly she didn't care, because she'd never been as happy as she was right at that moment. Since, you know, she doubted he was going to say "So here's the thing…" and get up and leave.

And if none of that made any sense from a practical standpoint…

Screw it.

Colin tucked her against his chest, his cheek on the top of her head, and said, "Okay, so here's the thing… What's so funny?"

"Nothing," she said, swallowing her laughter and snuggling closer. "So what's the thing?"

He was quiet for a moment, stroking her back, chuckling when Val's little gray tiger cat jumped up beside him and promptly settled in, purring. He stroked the blissful beast for another couple of seconds, then said, "I have no idea how—or even if—this could work between us. Or even if it should. But this pansy-ass pussyfooting deal is for the birds."

Frowning, Emily sat up to look into those pretty, tortured green eyes. "Oh, yeah?"

Matching her frown, Colin sighed, then linked their hands on her lap. "I told myself I'd left to give you space. That the timing sucked, I didn't want to crowd you…you name it, I trotted it out."

"Not to mention," she carefully ventured, "I want to stay here and you don't."

One side of his mouth pushed up. "Except…" He lifted her hand, brought it to his mouth, then tucked it against his chest. "I do. Want to stay. At least, to make Whispering Pines my home base." A sad smile curved his lips. "My *home*. Again. See, the plan *had* been to shove my pride aside enough to finally admit that I've wanted to come home for a while. That when all was said and done, this was the only place I ever felt as though I belonged. Only..." His eyes moist, he lifted a hand to brush her hair away from her face. "Only then you happened."

"And I totally messed up your plan?"

That got a soft laugh. "Sort of. But not the way I'd convinced myself you had. I really was thinking of you, I swear. That you were on the rebound, that you didn't need complications. Which means that's something we still have to work out. If you want. *But...*"

He paused, his gaze fixed for several moments on the space in front of him before he pushed out a breath. "But even before I left, I had to admit that your issues were a convenient excuse."

"For?"

His eyes locked in hers. "For me avoiding mine."

Emily went very still, half honored that Colin was about to really open up to her, half petrified of what that might mean. Except she once again reminded herself...he was *here*. And that the way he'd kissed her...

Breathe, she told herself. *Just...breathe.*

"I was so sure it'd be safe here," he said. "That *I'd* be safe, from anything even remotely like temptation. That this...that it'd be not only a safe haven for when I need a break from my work, but—" He pressed their entwined hands to his chest. "But that my heart would be safe here, too," he said quietly, and Emily's cracked. "That I could enjoy my brothers' families without having to..."

He swallowed.

"Be afraid for your own," Emily said gently.

Tears shimmered in his eyes when he let their gazes meet. "It's not that I don't want a family or children, Em.

It's that, after everything I've seen, the idea of losing them…"

"I know," she whispered. "I do."

"*But* I'm far, far more afraid of losing the best thing that's ever happened to me." He let go of her hand to cup her jaw, his fingers forked through her hair. "Which would be you."

Emily kept her gaze hooked in his for several seconds before she pushed up from his lap, earning a pissed *chirrup?* from the cat.

"Em…?"

"So what happened to logic?" she said, not facing him, and Colin laughed.

"Don't know," he said. "Don't care. And if it's still too soon, I'll understand. But…" He got to his feet and closed the gap between them to wrap her up from behind and whisper in her hair, "How could I not love the woman who made me face everything I've ignored for years? Who's made me figure out who I am? What I *truly* want?"

Emily shut her eyes, by now sure they could hear her heart thundering as far north as Wyoming. Then she turned in his arms, all that hope in his eyes knocking clean out of her what little breath she had left. "Same here," she somehow got out. "But I haven't changed my mind about wanting children, Colin. If you still don't—"

"You know what I finally realized? That there's probably not a single parent alive who doesn't worry about something happening to their kids. At least sometimes." His gaze softened. "That's not the same as not wanting them. Even if I'd told myself that for so long I almost—almost—believed it. And to have them with you… I get almost dizzy just thinking about it," he said, and she laughed, only to suck in a deep breath.

"And your work? Your calling? You know no way in hell would I ever interfere with that, right?"

A good two, three seconds passed before Colin said, "I do. But I promise you, even if I can't always be around, I'd always be here for you. Be in your camp. Because you're my treasure," he said, and she absolutely melted.

"Crap," Emily muttered, then snagged a tissue out of the box on the end table to loudly blow her nose. "You're my treasure, too, you big g-goofball..." Then, apparently no longer capable of coherent speech, she made some strange, strangled little sound, and Colin pulled her close again, his heartbeat steady against her ear...and then their mouths met, and... *Oh, my, yes.*

Yes.

Then, after what seemed like an eternity of some very satisfying spit swapping, they simply stood wrapped in each other's arms, listening to Val and the kids outside, an overloud dove cooing outside the living room window. Until at last Colin said, "From the moment I saw you standing on the porch with the damned dog, I was a goner. By the time we left Zach's after getting Spud fixed up...it—you—felt right. I mean, crazy, earth-shatteringly right. And that pull, that rightness..."

"I know," she whispered. "Me, too."

"But—"

"I know," she repeated, snuggling closer.

Chuckling, he kissed her head. "Forgive me?"

"I'll think about it."

He paused, then whispered, "Marry me?"

Her head jerked back so hard her neck snapped. "Are you serious?"

"Hey. If the universe went to this much trouble to throw the two of us together..."

Had to admit, the man had a point. Because actually, the timing couldn't have been any more perfect—

"But only if you want to," he said.

And Val yelled, "Oh, for heaven's sake!" from the kitchen, making them both jump. "Put the poor man out of his misery! Not to mention me!"

Laughing, Emily linked her hands around Colin's neck. "Oh, I want to, all right," she said, and he blew out a very relieved breath. Then she grinned. "Although my poor mother will have kittens."

Colin's smile melted her heart. "And we'll find homes for them all," he said, after which Emily discovered exactly how hard it was to kiss somebody when you couldn't stop smiling.

Epilogue

"You nervous, son?"

Colin smiled over at his father, feeling such warmth toward the older man it nearly took his breath. He looked away, into the cloudless fall sky stretching above the Vista's front acreage, where a couple dozen folding chairs had been set up for the simple ceremony to follow. Just family and a few friends. Emily's parents, in from DC. They'd separated, although to hear Emily tell it this was not only not a bad thing, but long overdue. Sounded to him like his almost mother-in-law had finally grown a pair, frankly. In no small part due to her daughter's example. His smile broadening, he met Sam's gaze again.

"Not at all."

Dressed almost exactly like Colin in a Western-style shirt, tucked into "good" jeans, and a silver bolo tie, Dad clapped Colin's shoulder, muttered, "Oh, what the hell?" then pulled him into a brief, hard hug. They'd probably talked more in the past few months than in the whole eighteen years prior to Colin's leaving for college. Funny, the way adulthood had of smoothing out the edges. Especially when those edges had been far more on one side than Colin might've wanted to admit. His father was a good man. Hardheaded, maybe, but good. But the most important thing was that he adored Emily. Both his parents did. As did she, them. Hell, even her snooty mother had warmed up to Billie. Although this was not a surprise, knowing his mother.

What had been a surprise—or maybe not, come to think of it—was how easily Colin had settled back into life in Whispering Pines, with his family, the community. How between assignments he'd found a renewed sense of purpose in working alongside Mallory in her therapy facility, helping both kids and adults with various challenges find theirs. Seeing those smiles…

Because there was no *small* way to make a difference, was there?

Then people were taking seats, trying to corral children long enough for the minister to do what they were paying him for. And a minute after that his bride was coming down the aisle, her estranged parents on either side, looking resigned to the inevitable if nothing else. Emily, though…

Colin's throat clogged. Emily had adamantly refused to let Margaret Weber anywhere near the wedding preparations, such as they'd been. In fact, most of the decorations bore the distinct hallmarks of a pair of nine-year-olds with more love and enthusiasm than skill. Emily's dress, though, had been a secret from everyone—she hadn't even let Deanna go into Albuquerque with her to get it. And now he couldn't catch his breath at how freaking gorgeous she was in the simple, shimmery ivory dress, her long hair loosely wound around a few little flowers. The woman simply couldn't not do classy, that was all there was to it.

Even in the midst of a woefully outdated foreman's cabin, or mucking out a horse stall…or traipsing through a mud-bogged Central American village with a batch of chattering children clinging to her hands.

Still, Colin was barely aware of what she was wearing for her radiant smile, the same one she'd given to all those children, and anyone else who crossed her path—brighter than the late September sun flashing through the yellowing cottonwoods. Then their hands and eyes were joined, along with their hearts, and the minister pronounced them husband and wife…

And his bride laughed into his eyes, and he was finally, forever, home.

* * * * *

Find the other Talbot brothers' love stories in previous books in Karen Templeton's
WED IN THE WEST *series:*

THE RANCHER'S EXPECTANT CHRISTMAS *(Josh)*
BACK IN THE SADDLE *(Zach)*
A SOLDIER'S PROMISE *(Levi)*

Available now from Mills & Boon Cherish!

MILLS & BOON®

Cherish™

EXPERIENCE THE ULTIMATE RUSH OF FALLING IN LOVE

A sneak peek at next month's titles...

In stores from 9th February 2017:

- **Proposal for the Wedding Planner** – Sophie Pembroke
  and **Fortune's Second-Chance Cowboy** –
  Marie Ferrarella
- **Return of Her Italian Duke** – Rebecca Winters *and*
  The Marine Makes His Match – Victoria Pade

In stores from 23rd February 2017:

- **The Millionaire's Royal Rescue** – Jennifer Faye *and*
  Just a Little Bit Married – Teresa Southwick
- **A Bride for the Brooding Boss** – Bella Bucannon
  and **Kiss Me, Sheriff!** – Wendy Warren

Just can't wait?
Buy our books online before they hit the shops!
www.millsandboon.co.uk

Also available as eBooks.

MILLS & BOON®

EXCLUSIVE EXTRACT

Pastry chef Gemma Rizzo never expected
to see Vincenzo Gagliardi again. And now
he's not just the duke who left her
broken-hearted… he's her boss!

Read on for a sneak preview of
RETURN OF HER ITALIAN DUKE

Since he'd returned to Italy, thoughts of Gemma had
come back full force. At times he'd been so preoccupied,
the guys were probably ready to give up on him. To
think that after all this time and searching for her, she
was right here. Bracing himself, he took the few steps
necessary to reach Takis's office.

With the door ajar he could see a polished-looking
woman in a blue-and-white suit with dark honey-blond
hair falling to her shoulders. She stood near the desk
with her head bowed, so he couldn't yet see her profile.

Vincenzo swallowed hard to realize Gemma was no
longer the teenager with short hair he used to spot when
she came bounding up the stone steps of the *castello*
from school wearing her uniform. She'd grown into a
curvaceous woman.

"Gemma." He said her name, but it came out gravelly.

A sharp intake of breath reverberated in the office.
She wheeled around. Those unforgettable brilliant green
eyes with the darker green rims fastened on him. A

stillness seemed to surround her. She grabbed hold of the desk.

"Vincenzo—I—I think I must be hallucinating."

"I'm in the same condition." His gaze fell on the lips he'd kissed that unforgettable night. Their shape hadn't changed, nor the lovely mold of her facial features.

She appeared to have trouble catching her breath. "What's going on? I don't understand."

"Please sit down and I'll tell you."

He could see she was trembling. When she didn't do his bidding, he said, "I have a better idea. Let's go for a ride in my car. It's parked out front. We'll drive to the lake at the back of the estate, where no one will bother us. Maybe by the time we reach it, your shock will have worn off enough to talk to me."

Hectic color spilled into her cheeks. "Surely you're joking. After ten years of silence, you suddenly show up here this morning, honestly thinking I would go anywhere with you?"

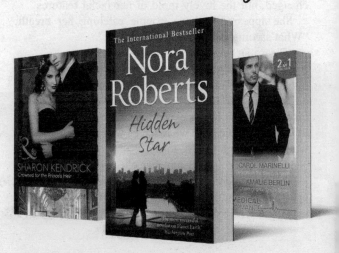